MODERN MAGICK

Book One of the Omnichron Chronicles

R.J. Johnson

RJ Johnson Publishing

Writing a book is hard. It's a lot easier when you have an amazing team of friends, mentors and editors who can help make your book become the very best version it can be. Special thanks to my fellow Red Sneaker writers, Kenneth Andrus and Rick Ludwig who provided me a wealth of invaluable notes. Thank you to Lara Bernhardt for all your edits, patience and kindness! And last, but certainly not least, William Bernhardt whose advice and leadership has allowed me to embrace my passion for writing.

For everyone who creates a little magic in their world...

If you enjoyed this book and have a moment, I'd like to request that you please leave a review on Amazon.com and Goodreads.com! Independent authors like me live and die by the number of four- and five-star reviews we get. So, help a struggling artist eat and pay rent by leaving a positive review if you liked the book!
Thanks!!

May 17th, 2022

CHAPTER ONE

Daniel Armstrong stood atop the tallest skyscraper in down-town Los Angeles, legs apart, staring at the sprawling city beneath him. Only one thought was running through his mind as he looked out at the view: Money made the world go round. Everything else was bullshit.

As he eyed the towering pillars of concrete and steel humanity had built in the middle of an arid desert, he didn't see bricks, mortar, and glass—he saw stacks of cash piled high on one another, reaching into the sky. To him, these buildings represented a quality of life and access to power that only belonged to other, more well-connected people.

Tonight would change all that.

He stepped closer to the edge of the building and looked down. The view from seventy stories above the streets of L.A. was not enough to give him second thoughts about his mission. As a former soldier who had spent more than his fair share of time conducting clandestine operations overseas, tonight would be a relative cakewalk.

He glanced over at his partner, Letty Montez, and watched her use a drill to secure three bolts into the side of the concrete walls. He checked his Rolex and saw they were getting close to the appointed time of their operation.

"How long?" he asked.

"Don't rush me." Her tone was hostile at his perceived interference. "If you don't wanna end up as a red smear on the sidewalk below, it'll take me as long as it needs."

He grunted, then turned to the other member of their party, his little brother, Cody—who no one would confuse as little. His brother loomed over him at an impressive six foot nine inches tall and boasted a physique that would make most professional wrestlers jealous.

"You ready for this?" he asked, jumping down from the ledge.

"I'm ready to get paid," Cody grunted as he concentrated on laying out the ropes they would use for their descent.

He slapped his brother on the back and chuckled. "That's the spirit."

His phone buzzed, and he removed it from his pocket. The text message contained two words.

It's time.

He smiled and put his phone away, turning back to his crew.

"The old man has left the apartment. We have thirty minutes. If we do our job right, tomorrow morning will see us with enough money to buy a little slice of heaven anywhere on earth."

"Preferably one with a beach," Letty added.

Daniel nodded and stepped forward, his team matching his motions as he clipped the ropes and attachments to his harness. He watched his team gear up with a critical eye. Nothing could go wrong tonight.

He was the brains. Cody was their muscle. Letty was the jack-of-all-trades who could hack any network and drive anything with an engine. All three had extensive marksmanship training and wouldn't blink an eye before killing anyone who got in the way of completing their mission.

Daniel had dubbed their little ring of thieves The Triumvirate, a name he thought was fitting for their skills. They had been working together over the last ten years on a variety of jobs that included breaking into bank vaults and large estates, while stealing anything that caught their eye.

For tonight's job, the Triumvirate were hired by a mysterious employer through an intermediary who contacted them through the dark web—not unusual in their business. Their employer provided all the information they needed to break into the penthouse owned by the real-estate billionaire Alan Knickerbocker.

Tonight's mission was for Daniel and his team to steal a priceless amulet currently locked in the billionaire's safe. Everything else in the apartment was off-limits according to their employer, but Daniel didn't care about that. If they were successful, their employer had promised to pay the three of them thirty million dollars for one night's work.

The challenge was getting to it. Their objective securely locked inside a safe on the 33rd floor in the massive skyscraper they were currently standing on. The building was part of Knickerbocker's empire of real estate he owned across the Western United States and was famous for its richly appointed penthouses and unique look against the Los Angeles skyline. The seventy-story building wasn't the tallest in the city (that record currently belonged to the Wilshire Grand Center), but it was a must-see for anyone who enjoyed architecture.

Thanks to Letty's extensive hacking skills, the Triumvirate already had access to the building's internal security system, which Letty had used to disable the security cameras and motion detectors.

The three of them stepped up to the building's ledge, pausing for a moment before lowering themselves over the edge, then rapidly rappelling down the side of the building.

Mere moments later, his team paused on the thirty-third floor, dropping silently onto the balcony where the billionaire's suite was located. They discarded the rope, unclipping the line from their belts, and Daniel pointed to the door that led inside. He and Cody stepped forward to the door to enter the luxury apartment while Letty remained behind as their lookout and to prepare their escape route.

Cody finished picking the lock and nodded, indicating he was ready. Daniel tried to keep the tension out of his face—this was the moment of truth. If this were a setup, the alarm would go off and they would have to flee the scene, tails between their legs, with no amulet, no money, and no sunny beaches to look forward to.

But to his relief, the door swung open without a sound. He nodded to Letty who stood guard as he and Cody entered the living room of Knickerbocker's suite.

The apartment was spotless, decorated in a modern design, with dozens of priceless works of art hanging on the walls. He raised an eyebrow and grimaced. He knew Knickerbocker's vast wealth meant these paintings weren't reproductions or fakes. He noted the value of each piece of art with a bit of consternation. If he'd known these pieces were here, he might have taken them instead. One or two were worth just as much as what they were getting for the amulet tonight.

He noticed Cody eying the paintings as well. His brother knew their value too.

"Those aren't the mission," he whispered.

Cody grunted, sounding disappointed, but returned his attention to their objective.

Checking the map their source had given him, Daniel and Cody made their way to the other side of the penthouse where Knickerbocker's study was located.

When they reached the study door, he tried the doorknob, but found it locked. This was not an unexpected development and Letty had provided them a way to get inside. He removed a small plastic box about three inches across from a pocket in his vest and pressed a button located on the top. There was the sound of a slight whirring behind the door, until there was another louder clunk of the lock releasing. He opened the door and waved for his brother to follow him.

"This is too easy." Cody scowled as he stood at the entrance to the study.

"Don't jinx this." Daniel didn't have time to assuage his younger brother's fears—no matter how well-founded they might be. If he were being honest with himself, a similar thought had occurred to him as well. But they were too deep to turn back now.

They entered the billionaire's study, the large office stuffed with memorabilia, knick-knacks, and bookshelves filled with books from around the world. A variety of items in Knickerbocker's office sparkled as the gold and silver jewelry inlaid with diamonds and sapphires played with the low light.

"Holy shit," Cody blurted out looking around the room.

"Holy shit is right," he agreed.

He again ignored the greed whispering in his ear, begging for a chance to scoop up a few of the priceless jewels on display, and remained focused on the mission. He spotted the small safe that the source said contained the amulet and stepped behind the massive mahogany desk, crouching down next to it. He removed a second small plastic box from another one of his vest pockets and flipped it open. Inside, a small thumb-sized piece of rubber rested on a non-stick gel.

He removed the counterfeit thumbprint Letty had made for them after she lifted Knickerbocker's fingerprints from a glass the billionaire used at a fine-dining restaurant where she had posed as a server. He placed it against the safe's fingerprint scanner.

Daniel was elated when he heard a soft beep and the sound of the lock releasing. He opened the safe, moving the stacks of cash and gold bars aside until he discovered what they had come for.

He withdrew the amulet, staring at it for a moment and wondering what in the hell made this thing so special. It was about four inches in diameter and one inch thick and made of electrum—a gold and silver alloy. It was heavier than he expected, but, beyond an interesting and intricate scribble that lined the side of the amulet, the jewelry looked inconsequential. It certainly didn't look like it was worth thirty million dollars.

He brought the amulet closer to his face for a better look when he discovered small, scratchy writing lining the edge of the artifact. The words were legible, but they didn't resemble any language he'd seen before.

"Did you find it?" his brother asked from the doorway.

He held up their prize, grinning, and his brother whooped in excitement. Daniel scowled at him, but his brother was still too excited.

"That's the easiest thirty million we'll ever make," Cody said, still a little too loud for his brother's liking.

"Don't spend that money yet," he cautioned. "Time to go."

Cody rolled his eyes and grunted. Daniel closed the safe door, leaving the gold and cash behind. As they made his way back down the hallway to their escape, he allowed himself a moment to privately celebrate their imminent victory.

Those thoughts disappeared when they exited the hallway and entered the living room—and saw a teenage boy standing there, holding a glass of chocolate milk.

"Oh shit," Armstrong muttered. He held up his hands, the amulet in one hand. "Easy kid . . ."

The boy looked at them both and began shaking so much he dropped the milk, a brown splotch spilling all over the pristine cream-colored carpet.

Before the teenager could run and alert anyone to their presence, Daniel took two giant steps across the room and grabbed the young man, yanking an iPhone out of the boy's hand and throwing it against the wall, where the screen smashed into pieces.

He grabbed the boy's neck and tossed him across the room into the living room wall, where the boy landed, crying out in pain.

Cody looked around the room, his frantic energy alarming Daniel.

"Where the hell did he come from?" Cody demanded.

He glanced over at the boy, who was still shaking and crying, when the phone in his pocket buzzed. He took it out and felt his heart drop when he saw the message on the screen.

KNICKERBOCKER COMING BACK. GET OUT NOW.

"We gotta go," he said, turning to their exit. "Leave him."

But before he could take another step, the door to the apartment opened and Knickerbocker entered, holding two large bags of takeout. He stood there for a second, as if trying to absorb the sight of the two intruders in his home.

At first, Knickerbocker looked as if he were about to flee when he spotted the boy cowering next to Cody. His face changed from one of anger and confusion to one of deep concern.

The billionaire's voice was soft and pleading. "Whatever you want, I will offer you no resistance. Please, let my grandson go."

Knickerbocker's eyes fluttered to Cody and then over at Daniel, clutching the amulet. The billionaire's face changed again, this time his eyes went wide in shock and terror.

"You can't . . ." Knickerbocker stuttered. "Whoever you are, take whatever you want, but the amulet must not leave this place. It's far too dangerous, more than you can comprehend."

Daniel didn't take his eyes off the billionaire in front of him and for a moment, he considered Knickerbocker's request. From what he had seen of the apartment, there was far more money hanging on the walls than what he held in his hand.

Then, his phone buzzed again, and Daniel glanced at the screen. It was another text from their mysterious benefactor.

READ THE INSCRIPTION.

Daniel returned his attention to the amulet in his hand, briefly wondering about the motives of his source and what the hell was going on.

"Take anything else," Knickerbocker said, pleading with them. "I'll pay you double whatever you've been promised for this job. Triple. You surely know who I am. I have the money."

Knickerbocker dropped the plastic bags filled with food and fumbled in his pockets for his wallet. He pulled it out and threw it at Daniel's feet. "I'll put you on a private jet tonight and help you and your friends disappear to any country you wish. But you must not take the amulet. I beg you. You have no idea what it would mean for the world. For its future."

Despite the billionaire's escalating and hysterical pleas, Daniel couldn't take his eyes off the amulet. Whatever this thing was, if it meant this much to a man worth more than eleven billion dollars, he believed he might be able to renegotiate his deal with the person who hired him.

"I work one job at a time," Daniel said. He gazed at the amulet, weighing his options, and then attempted to pronounce the words written on the edge.

"Onliesende . . ."

"No!" Knickerbocker cried out. The elderly billionaire raced toward Daniel, much faster than he expected a man his age could move.

Cody withdrew his pistol and aimed it at Knickerbocker, pulling the trigger on his weapon and shooting the billionaire three times in the chest, the gunfire echoing in the expansive living room. The teenager shrieked in shock, covering his face with his hands.

Daniel ignored the chaos around him. He focused on the words on the amulet. Something was forcing, no, enticing him to say the inscription, as though nothing else on the planet mattered except reading the full inscription.

"Balocræft . . ." he continued, sounding out the word.

Knickerbocker stretched out a hand toward the amulet, blood running down his chest. His grandson wailed in pain as if he had been the one who was shot and rushed to Knickerbocker's side, holding his grandfather as he bled out on the luxurious cream-colored carpet.

"You don't understand," Knickerbocker said, his voice weak. "The world isn't ready . . ."

But Daniel was too far gone, hypnotized by the words written on the amulet's edge as he finished reading the inscription.

"Synbysige ġefeoht," he said, finishing the incantation.

A bright burst of purple light filled the room, blinding him momentarily. Wincing in pain, he opened his eyes to see Letty entering the living room, her sidearm at the ready.

"What the hell was that?" she demanded.

She glanced around the room, taking stock of the situation and noticed the wailing teenager crying over his grandfather's body. Letty approached the boy, grabbing him by his arm, yanking him to his feet. She dragged him to the sofa and pushed him down, looming over the crying young man.

She leaned in close to the boy's tear-streaked face, her eyes narrow, voice low and threatening. "Listen, you little shit," she leaned in closer, mere inches away from the teenager's tear-streaked face. "You don't know who we are. You never saw us. All you know is you found your grandfather dying on the floor."

The boy whimpered, the tears still flowing from his eyes as he cowered under Letty's intense gaze.

"If you tell anyone what we've done here tonight," she said with a furious intensity, "I will carve you up and sew your skin together over and over again—a thousand times—until you bleed to death."

A bright flash of orange light filled the room. The boy shrieked. Letty stepped back, her eyes wide as she watched the boy's skin split open, blood pouring from the wound before it sealed.

"What did you do?" Daniel demanded. He crossed the room and grabbed Letty's shoulders, trying to pull her around to face him.

But the moment he touched her, another bright flash of energy exploded from her fingertips, propelling him back across the room where he collided with the wall, a dull thud echoing in the space.

He gasped and struggled to his feet, looking for the threat that had sent him flying. Letty was staring down at her glowing fingers in shock.

"What . . . is . . . happening to me?" she whispered.

He looked down at his own fists and saw they were glowing as well. The amulet had grown hot in his hand, and he dropped it to the ground as if it were radioactive. Whatever that thing had done, he wanted no part of it any longer. Thanks to the boy's screams, the gunshots, and the light show put on by the amulet, it would only be a matter of moments before the authorities would arrive. This mission was over.

The boy shrieked again, drawing his attention in time to see another six-inch-long cut split open on the teenager's forearm. Blood spilled out of the boy's body until the wound sealed itself shut. The boy writhed in pain and confusion, fear in his wide eyes.

"What did you do?" he asked Letty again.

Letty gawked at the boy, looking as shocked as he felt. "Nothing . . . I don't know . . ."

Daniel swore. This was not how he imagined this night was going to go.

"We need to get the hell out of here," Cody said from the back of the room.

Daniel didn't reply. He was still staring at the boy writhing in pain as he tried to make sense of what he had seen tonight.

"You hear me?" Cody said, moving to the window, looking for any police lights. "We gotta move."

Something in Cody's voice snapped Daniel back to reality. "Time to go. Find me at the rendezvous in twelve hours. If you're late, you better be dead."

Letty and Cody acknowledged him with a nod, understanding the instructions. They moved outside to the balcony where they'd come in and helped each other onto the ledge. Daniel watched as Cody and Letty strapped themselves into their parachutes they brought, and stepped off the side of the building, opening their parachutes and sailing off in opposite directions into the twinkling lights of downtown Los Angeles.

He took one last glance back at Knickerbocker's suite and stepped off the ledge, into the night, releasing his parachute as he left the amulet and their promised payday behind.

CHAPTER TWO

THE OPENING THEME SONG for his podcast sounded in his headphones as John Jupiter waited for his cue. He took one last glance at the stack of notes sitting in front of him as the soft, pleasant tones changed into an ominous score. He cleared his throat before tapping the button that would open his mic.

"Good afternoon, good evening, and hello to everyone listening five years from now. This is your host, John Jupiter, and you're listening to the Jupiter Mission, where we demystify the mysterious, debunk the bunk and bring you all the strangest, most fascinating stories from history you never learned about in school."

He paused, taking a sip of his water as his show's theme song trailed off. He picked up his notes, looking for his opening statement.

"Today we're talking about a fascinating bit of lore concerning the Knights Templar," he said. "The history of the organization is already well-known to many historians, and Dan Brown fans, as the church's 'enforcers' during the Crusades throughout the eleventh and twelfth centuries. However . . ."

John paused, smiling as he waited for maximum effect. His audience always paid attention more when he allowed a little dead air.

"Our guest says he has discovered proof of a little-known sect of the Knights Templar known as The Guardians, a group of zealots who charged with a mission to seek out anyone found to be practicing magic or witchcraft. It's not totally inaccurate to compare these Guardians to those who ran the infamous Salem Witch trials a few hundred years later. But one key difference according to our guest, is that these so-called Guardians, were said to have used magic themselves whilst in pursuit of their enemies."

John hit a button on his computer and a dramatic sounder echoed through his headphones. He smiled. It was cheap theatrics, but that's what the audience liked. And who was he to question the taste of the five hundred thousand people who downloaded his show every month?

"He's a professor of medieval history at Hoover University here in Los Angeles, with a specialty in the occult."

He squinted at his notes and sighed, remembering the conversation he had recorded with this guest last week. He really needed to speak with his producer about finding better guests for the show.

"Please welcome Professor Desmond McKaig to the Jupiter Mission."

He tapped a button to mute his mic as the pre-recorded interview automatically played back for his listeners. It had been an interesting, if occasionally dry, slog. As the host of the show, he always did whatever he could to liven up a dull conversation. Some guests just didn't have the charisma. Often that was because of nerves, but sometime the interview was doomed from the start.

Fortunately, the professor livened up once they began talking about the Guardians and John found himself becoming caught up in the man's stories about humanity's legends of magic.

He could have simply inserted the interview using the software on his computer without listening back to the recording, but he wanted to review what the man said before he finished the rest of his show. Producing his show from home was a cinch these days thanks to advances in broadcasting technology, but he was still a radio reporter by heart and found that if he used too many shortcuts, it corrupted his appreciation of the work.

His guest was in the middle of a long answer, and John felt his mind beginning to wander—never a good sign when the host can't be bothered to listen. He wrote the time down on a slip of paper, intending to go back later and tighten up the interview with a few edits.

"The fascinating thing about the Guardians," the professor was saying, "is that historians have not found records of their existence outside a rare historical document that has not been vetted. In fact, the only historical reference with any providence is on loan at the Hoover library."

"Is that common professor?" John heard himself ask on the recording.

"Oh, very much so, yes. Documents thousands of years old like that take time to authenticate. Besides, some of the claims made in this volume are so grotesque and fantastic, many will be difficult to prove."

"Such as?"

"Well, one story I translated just last week involves the Guardians coming together to defeat a powerful demon that had the potential to end the world as we know it. According to the tale, a warlock summoned an exceptionally powerful demon, a henchman of the devil himself."

"And the Guardians defeated this devil?"

"The Agamoth, yes," the professor said. "The stories describe the demon as a nightmarish creature that absorbed and grew with every person it consumed. Others weren't so lucky. The ones who weren't absorbed by the demon were allegedly enthralled by the beast."

"I'm sorry," John said. "Enthralled? Like mind-controlled zombies?"

"If that helps your audience, yes," the professor replied. "The story describes the Agamoth as an ever-consuming force of nature that feasted on human souls, using them as raw material for its form. The victims who weren't consumed, the demon would take control of their minds, using them as an extension of its will to accomplish tasks it couldn't on its own."

John had become so caught up in the professor's story that he nearly missed seeing his phone flashing as multiple text messages popped up on the screen. He lowered the volume on the interview and read the number on his phone's screen, groaning. The expletive-filled texts were from his boss, Percy Washington, who was threatening him with unemployment if he didn't call back on the double.

He sighed. Finishing the latest episode of his podcast would have to wait. He paused the recording of the professor's interview and picked up his phone, dialing a number and bracing himself for his boss's grating tone.

"John?" A voice raised on whisky and cigars answered the line.

"Yeah, boss? You texted?" He pretended as if he had no idea why his managing editor was calling him this late at night. In truth, there could be only one reason—there was a juicy story brewing.

"Your story from earlier today was shit." Percy didn't sound happy with him.

"That's because the story you assigned me was shit," John shot back. The assignment desk had sent him down to the annual Auto Show to work on a puff piece the station would use to court advertisers. "I'm not here to make the station money, I'm here to report the news."

"Please." Percy snorted. "You know better than that. That auto show story was worth an enormous chunk of change to sales, and you blew their chance at a million-dollar deal thanks to your questions about his production facilities."

"Dude is hiding something from his investors," John said. "That's the story. If he wants to brag about his electric trucks on Twitter all day to pump up his stock prices, he ought to sell one occasionally."

"Sales is pissed."

"Why? 'Cause they'll have to work for a living now? Like I said, the story you assigned was shit. My story on the other hand, was picked up by the AP and is currently making its way across the wires. I've been turning down interviews about the piece all day, and I'm tired. It's nearly midnight, Percy. You call me for any other reason than to berate me for doing my job?"

Despite their back and forth, he knew Percy respected his journalistic integrity and doggedness in pursuing the facts. If his boss was calling this late, that meant something big was cooking.

"I dunno if you deserve it now," Percy said. "Hanson filed something earlier today that got us a nice hundred-thousand-dollar commit from a client."

He grunted derisively. "Colby Hanson is a hack who thinks owning a Mr. Microphone makes him a reporter."

"Yeah, well, he's here and you're not, so . . ."

"You wouldn't be calling if you didn't want me on whatever it is you're so excited about," John was tired of the games. "So, why don't you just tell me what's up?"

There was a pause.

"Percy?" John asked. There was a moment where he was briefly worried his boss might give the story to someone else.

"There's been a murder," Percy began.

"Okay," John said. "That's been known to happen in a city like L.A."

"The victim is Alan Knickerbocker."

John stood up in shock, hitting his head on the bookshelf he had installed next to his desk. Knickerbocker was one of the richest, most powerful real estate investors in the state of California—which put him fairly high on that list for the rest of the world. A story like this might lead to book deals or even a Netflix documentary—depending on what he discovered of course.

"How'd he die?" John asked, his mind racing with possibilities.

"Police aren't saying," Percy said. "But if it was something normal like a heart attack or stroke . . ."

"Then we'd have heard about the death by now through a carefully worded press release from the Knickerbocker Foundation," John agreed. "Wow. You aren't kidding. This *is* big."

"How far are you from downtown L.A.?" Percy asked. "I assume you're still at home. Knickerbocker has an apartment there. That's where his body was discovered."

"I'm ten minutes away," he said. "Have the assignment desk text me the address of his place."

"They've already sent it to you," Percy said. "And John?"

"Yeah, boss?"

"This is one of those stories we handle with kid gloves. Don't you go in there making a big scene. All we need right now is coverage for the station. None of your investigative bullshit, you hear me?"

"Why, Percy," John said, trying to sound as innocent as possible. "Would you expect anything less from me?"

His boss grunted an acknowledgement, and the line went dead.

John opened the Twitter app on his phone and searched through the trending topics while he gathered his equipment and go bag that contained an extra change of clothing and a bathroom kit. You never knew how long a story would keep you away from home and he liked to be prepared.

His quick scroll through the trending topics on Twitter showed him that no one else had picked up the news of Knickerbocker's death yet, which made it a race against the clock to get something filed ahead of his competition. When word of the billionaire's murder got out, it would kick up a shitstorm he wasn't sure the city was ready for.

He put his London Fog jacket on and his hat, his adrenaline pumping in anticipation as it always did before a juicy story. He grinned as he exited his apartment, heading out into the night where the mystery was just getting started.

CHAPTER THREE

THE HOSPITAL WAS QUIET this time of night, something Dr. Apsara Choi was always grateful for. The quieter moments allowed her extra time to catch up on paperwork, review case histories for her patients, and scan any interesting articles about her field to keep abreast of the latest research.

One of the sadder facts of the U.S. medical system was that many doctors only had about fifteen minutes to work with and diagnose their patients. She had always hated that reality and vowed early on in her career to be the kind of doctor who cared—even on her longest days.

But, because time is the one resource no one had found a way to make more of, she sacrificed other parts of her life for her work. Her usual routine had her day begin at four thirty in the morning with a five-mile run. By six a.m., she was already at the hospital where she attended to her patients until about four p.m. After a sensible dinner and an hour with her favorite book or TV show, she was in bed by nine p.m. ready to do it all over again.

Unfortunately, her precisely regimented schedule had been rudely disrupted after one of the attending physicians broke his leg while skiing at Lake Tahoe last week. The hospital asked her to cover the night shift, and she had reluctantly agreed. It had not been an easy transition so far, but that's what the caffeine was for.

She yawned and checked her watch. She still had a few hours left on shift, and it was shaping up to be a quiet night, but her stomach was rumbling. Time for another shot of coffee and a snack.

She entered the cafeteria that served as a breakroom of sorts for the staff and turned on the lights. She approached the coffee machine and made her selection, opting for a double caffeinated shot. She wasn't a surgeon and didn't have to worry about jitters.

There was a light knock at the door of the breakroom. She turned to see the hospital's Chief of Staff enter with a serious expression on his face. She blinked, surprised to see him at the hospital so late.

"Good evening, Dr. Choi," he said.

"Dr. Moreno," Apsara said. "You're here late."

His gentle smile tightened. "It's nothing good, I'm afraid. May I have a few moments of your time?"

"Of course." She removed the coffee the machine had just dispensed for her and nodded. "Would you like me to make you a cup? Best coffee in the city."

"Another time perhaps," he said. "I wanted to alert you about a VIP who will be joining us tonight."

"All patients are equal," she said, a slight smile tugging at her lips. Dr. Moreno was known around the hospital as a fair and equitable boss, but he had risen to his current position in no small part due to his political machinations behind the scenes with the hospital's board of directors.

Moreno paused, searching for the right words. "This patient is far more than an average Hollywood celebrity. This is someone the hospital cares very much about."

"I care about all my patients," she replied.

"Of course," Dr. Moreno said, looking startled. "I don't mean—"

"I apologize," she replied. "Please, tell me about the patient."

"Subject is a white male, fourteen years old, presenting with a novel and potentially deadly skin infection."

She tilted her head in surprise. "Wouldn't Dr. Hochel be a better consult for something like this? I haven't covered dermatology since med school."

"This . . . isn't a routine skin infection," Dr. Moreno said, his face grim. "Take a look at this."

He moved closer to her, took out his phone, and selected a video. He hit play and held it out for her to watch.

The video showed two paramedics trying to restrain a teenage boy who was screaming and writhing in so much pain it sounded as if he were being tortured. Just listening was agonizing. The person shooting the video zoomed in to get a closer look at the boy's skin and wounds, and she immediately understood why Dr. Moreno had come to her.

Dozens of cuts, ranging from a few inches to a foot, gaped all over the boy's chest, arms, and legs, blood pouring out of the body where the skin split open like an over-boiled hotdog.

As she watched, her eyes went wide, and her hand shot up to her mouth.

"My God," she whispered.

Even more bizarre, moments after the wounds broke out all over the boy's body, the skin would knit itself back together with no evidence of the previous wounds.

Apsara had functioned as the primary physician on dozens of cases that would turn anyone's stomach, but this was unlike anything she'd seen before. The boy's screams as each wound split open were haunting, and she turned the audio down. She knew pain when she saw it. She didn't need to hear the poor boy being tortured at the same time.

She watched as the cuts opened and noticed that they were precise and not something you'd expect if the dermis had been torn or fallen apart.

"It almost looks like he's being sliced open by a knife," she said, thinking back to her time spent doing shifts in the Emergency Room. She knew what a knife wound looked like.

Dr. Moreno nodded.

"How is this possible? It's generating too fast for it to be an infection. Chemical burn?"

"Unlikely," Dr. Moreno said, shaking his head. "The symptoms don't match. Our best guess is a rare topical infection that hasn't been documented before."

She took the phone from Dr. Moreno and replayed the scene, looking for clues. Dr. Moreno watched her, allowing Apsara to go through her process of elimination in trying to diagnose the disease.

"Fascinating," she said, pausing the video on a close-up of the boy's wound. "I'd have said this was a fake video if you hadn't been the one to hand it to me."

"Now you understand why I'm here," Dr. Moreno said grimly, taking his phone back. "The patient is on the way, and you're our physician on duty. We need you to scrub up and get into a hazmat suit."

"How long until he gets here?" she asked looking up at him.

"Seven minutes," he replied.

"That's not much time."

"They took him to another hospital first, but they weren't equipped to deal with whatever this" — he waved his hand at the screen — "is."

"I'm assuming you already hit the panic button?" she asked.

"Before I came down here," he nodded. "They're setting up the fourth floor. The entire area will be yours."

"I'll need staff," she said.

"You shall have whatever resources you require," he agreed.

She raised an eyebrow. "That was easy."

"Like I said, this is no ordinary patient," Dr. Moreno said. "The patient's family likes to keep their affairs private, but you'll find out eventually anyway. This is Alan Knickerbocker's grandson."

The lightbulb went off. Just last year, she'd met the billionaire at a humanitarian award banquet held in his honor after he pledged a ten-million-dollar donation to the hospital's trust fund.

She nodded. Now it all made sense. If they saved the life of Alan Knickerbocker's grandson, the hospital would never need to worry about money ever again.

"I'll meet you downstairs in a few minutes," she said. "I want some time to look through case histories and see if anyone else has documented something like this."

"Five minutes," he said. "Don't be late."

He retrieved his phone from her and turned to exit the breakroom. Apsara unlocked her smartphone and opened an app that allowed her access to a database that might help her find similar cases to the Knickerbocker boy's strange skin infection.

Even as she felt the excitement of a new challenge flowing through her, the anxiety was also present—did she have the skills to save the young man? She had a stellar reputation at the hospital and was well-known as one of the smartest people there. But nothing in her extensive career had prepared her for what she had just witnessed in the video.

She took a sip of her coffee. Whatever caused that poor boy's wounds, she would need to be laser focused over the next few hours and the caffeine would help. She turned her attention to the search results playing across her screen hoping she could think of something that would help that poor child.

CHAPTER FOUR

JOHN JUPITER STOOD AT the base of the Bank of America Tower in Downtown Los Angeles and gazed up at the skyscraper in front of him. For years, the building had stood out on the skyline of one of the largest metropolises in the United States.

That is, until Alan Knickerbocker's company constructed a monument to the billionaire's ego directly across the street. The newly constructed, futuristic-looking building was all anyone could talk about when it came to the city's skyline these days. Enormous LED panels installed on the surface of every window on the building gave it the ability to display whatever image or message Knickerbocker wanted to program.

John admired what the billionaire had been able to accomplish with his fortune, and knew if the man had been murdered, the news would rock the city harder than the Big One.

The night was still young enough that people were stumbling home from bars, and the various characters that inhabited the night downtown were still out and about. John nodded politely to one person wearing a bright pink bra and lowcut jeans, who was shouting at no one in particular in a language he didn't recognize. They didn't pay any attention to John and continued down the block, still arguing with persons unknown and unseen.

He waited until his new friend had walked out of sight to cross the street. As he approached Knickerbocker's building, he pulled his collar up, trying to hide his face from any of the security cameras that might see him.

The scene was quiet, except for one black and white patrol car that spotted him and rolled up on him, the light bar blazing. John leaned down, recognizing the officer inside. It was Sgt. Bill Pepper, a good man whom he had grown close to during his time at the station when he was on the city hall and police beat.

"John," Bill said, his voice deep and measured. The greeting was conditional, as if he already knew why his friend was there.

"Heya, Bill, what's the good word?"

Bill grunted. "If you're here, then you know why I'm here."

"You know me better than anyone else," John didn't bother hiding his smirk. He leaned in closer to his friend's patrol car to get a better look.

His friend eyed him with a quizzical expression. "I should be surprised you got here before the brass did, but I'm not."

"It's a curse. My finger is on the heartbeat of the city," John said, smiling for his friend. He dropped his voice. "So come on, off the record, did the old man get murdered?"

Bill was stone-faced. The seasoned officer wasn't about to give anything away, but then finally relented. "Off the record, I'll put it this way. He died of lead poisoning."

"What they did to the kid was worse," Bill's partner chimed in. John craned his head to get a better look at Bill's partner, Skye Holsen, a two-year veteran on the force.

Bill sighed and rubbed his face. "Yeah, that's a whole other thing."

John could feel the excitement building in his stomach. There was a real story here all right—something even bigger than Percy could have known.

"Alan Knickerbocker's son?" John asked. "What happened?"

"His grandson, and you know better than to ask. I can't tell you that," Bill's voice had a nervous edge to it that John had never heard before. But his voice softened, and he continued. "Then again, after what we saw, I 'spect no one would believe you anyway."

Skye's face had gone grey, and John was more curious than ever. He understood why a gory scene might have upset the rookie, but for a man like Bill Pepper, bloody crime scenes were just another day at the office. If he were this unnerved by what he had seen in Knickerbocker's apartment, then things had to be bad.

"Bill," John said, his voice low and urgent. "When have I ever burned a source?"

Bill looked up at him, then appeared to make a decision. "The kid had these—"

"Boils?" Skye chimed in. "Burns?"

"No," Bill said. "Cuts. They started like boils, or a bad burn, but then the skin would split open, and I swear it looked like someone took a Bowie knife to the poor kid."

"That's not the damndest thing," Skye said, sounding miserable.

"Yeah?" John asked. "What else?"

Skye swallowed and shook his head, refusing to answer. Bill turned his attention back to John; his face pained at the memory.

"These wounds would reseal themselves after the kid would bleed a bit. They appeared on his chest, his arms, his legs, face, hands . . . everywhere," the rookie said. "They'd grow and grow until they'd burst."

"Then they'd heal and start all over again," Bill said. "John, I shit you not."

John raised an eyebrow. Bill wasn't the type to exaggerate, but this sounded too fantastic to be real.

"Sounds awful," John said. "What do you figure it was? Some kind of disease?"

"They don't know," Bill said. "That's why they're keeping everything low-key for now. The thirty-third floor is shut down. They're not letting anyone in or out of the building."

"They think it's a biological weapon?" John was incredulous. "Why wouldn't they evacuate the area?"

"They still might," Bill said, his face looking grave. "Personally, if I were you, I'd file this story from home."

John chuckled. "Come on, Bill, you know that's not my style."

"Yeah, well, you may not have a choice when someone with a lot more decision-making power gets here," the police officer retorted. "But they're not here yet."

"Until then, we were instructed to keep the scene locked down," Skye added.

"Kid's been taken to the hospital?" John asked.

"Hoover Medical Center," Bill said.

"Can I get a look at the scene?"

"Now I know you're not that stupid," Bill rolled his eyes at him, and John felt appropriately chided. It was worth a shot.

"Sorry, I had to try," John said. He turned and looked up at Knickerbocker Tower.

"I gotta be honest, John," Bill called from the car. "I know you like to be the big, bad investigative reporter, but there's something about this case that makes me want to run far, far away. In fact, soon as I get back to the station, I'm requesting a few days off so I can get away to Big Bear and do some fishing."

"That bad huh?" John asked, not looking back.

"John," Bill's voice was ominous, prompting John to turn around and look at his friend in the patrol car. "That boy wasn't just hurt. He was . . ."

"Cursed," Skye finished for him.

Bill nodded. "It's a weird thing to say, but I got no other word for it. The cuts appeared and disappeared like they weren't even there."

"But there was blood?" John asked.

The two officers glanced at each other and then back at him.

"Like you wouldn't believe," Bill's face said it all. Whatever he had seen happen to that poor kid, it was clear it would stay with the veteran officer for years to come.

The sound of sirens began echoing down the street. John looked up to see what appeared to be the entire Los Angeles Police Department heading toward them. Bill handed him a sketch of the boy's wounds.

"That's my best recollection," Bill said. "Keep that off your station's goddamn website. I see that on there, you and I are done."

"Bill, if I say off the record, I mean it," John said firmly. He tapped the top of the patrol car's roof. "Stay safe out there tonight. Keep yourselves far away from that bad juju."

"You know it," Bill said. "And John?"

"Yeah?"

"I wasn't kidding about ditching town over this case. There's something bad in the air. I can smell it. And you know I don't scare easy."

The man looked more serious than he'd ever been in his life. He nodded, then waved. Bill nodded back, rolled up his window, and put the patrol car in gear to go meet the rest of the officers who were beginning to set up barricades down the block.

John turned back to the building. Bill was right. If things were as bad as they said, then there was no point in him hanging around here at Knickerbocker's offices. Officers responding to the scene were working to secure the site and set up an area where a spokesperson would give a press conference that would tell him nothing.

He could have his producer back at the station monitor the presser, which would allow him more time to investigate a bit more. Perhaps his time and energy were better spent at the hospital learning whatever he could about the boy's mysterious injuries.

He returned to his car, still thinking about his friend's frightened face. What the hell would scare someone like him that much?

CHAPTER FIVE

ELLIE SARKISSIAN HOISTED THE stacks of books contained in her bag and felt her stomach churn at the amount of material she had to get through over the next seventy-two hours as she entered the Hoover Research Library for a planned marathon study session. She was no stranger to working hard—after all, you didn't become a gold-medal Olympic-champion archer without dedicating yourself to a little hard work.

As she made her way into the library, weighed down with the collective knowledge of some of the world's finest minds, she paused when she spotted a large glass enclosure that displayed an incredibly special bow and quiver filled with arrows. The University had set up this display dedicated to the dozens of Olympic athletes who had attended the university over the years—including her. She looked at the nameplate, reading the names displayed there until she reached her own and thought back to the pivotal shot that won her the gold.

It had been the best moment of her life.

Her favorite memory of all time was standing on the podium and leaning forward while a small blonde Frenchwoman bestowed the gold medal around her neck. The national anthem played in the background, but she had no memory of that. All she could remember was the cheers of the crowd and feeling a tinge of satisfaction as the silver medal winner scowled in her direction.

When she returned to the U.S., she donated her favorite bow and quiver set to the university for them to add to the Olympian display. With that part of her life over, she felt it was an appropriate and symbolic gesture—a moment that represented her turn from sports to the pursuit of knowledge—more specifically a PhD in chemical engineering. Still, as she looked at the bow and quiver contained within the case, her fingers itched, and she found herself wishing she could get back out on the range one more time.

But after achieving her life's goal at the 2024 Olympics, she was left feeling a little lost after a lifetime spent working toward one objective. For the first few months after coming home from France, interviews, and appearances on the talk show circuit about her Olympic glory kept her busy, but those only lasted as long as the public's attention span.

Besides, she'd never seen archery as the key to long-term success. It had been a challenging sport she enjoyed and happened to be exceptionally good at. She relished the precision and concentration needed for her arrow to strike a target no bigger than a dime. Plus, the feeling of nailing a target under near-impossible conditions was better than sex. But now that she had nothing left to prove in that arena, it was time for her to take on another challenge.

That's why she was weighed down by a stack of books she needed to get through before her finals on Monday. Attempting a PhD in chemical engineering seemed liked a promising idea at the time, but as she immersed herself in the material, she was struck by an overwhelming sense of dread.

What had she gotten herself into?

Putting aside the existential and mental health crises, she knew it didn't matter how hard the material was. She was a smart woman who had already learned so much about the material in front of her. It was just a matter of understanding the rest. She had her mind set on a highly sought-after internship at a local aerospace company and would need decent grades if she had any chance of scoring the job.

Thanks to the nonstop demands of college life, these were the last few hours available to study before the exams on Monday. Thankfully, Thursday nights didn't see many students clamoring for space in the library, which meant she would have all the peace and quiet she would need to concentrate on her studies.

She finished setting up her study cubby hole and looked it over one last time with a satisfied glance. She had her snacks (hummus and carrots), her hydroflask was filled to the brim, and her laptop was warmed up and ready to go. She stretched and glanced around, seeing the light in Professor McKaig's office illuminated. He was the only other person on the floor—a blessing she would take.

She reached for the top book on the pile to revisit what she knew and didn't know about statistics and put in her earbuds, the sounds of her classical music playlist scoring her studies as she got to work.

CHAPTER SIX

THERE WASN'T A BETTER smell in the world than the research library at Hoover University.

Professor Desmond McKaig considered the library, where he had spent much of his professional life, as his sanctuary or temple. He was awestruck by the enormous repository of knowledge contained within the building's walls. He saw books as the ultimate tale of humanity told in thousands of ways across hundreds of languages.

Of course, he didn't mean to romanticize his career—it was work and it felt like it at times. His specialty was medieval research and there wasn't exactly a big demand for new professors in that area of study. Consequently, the only thing keeping him employed was his tenure and occasional usefulness as a fundraiser among alumni.

Lately, he had been spending all his free time in the library researching a curious sect of Knights Templar. His interest in the subject had been part of his entire career, but the newly discovered "Guardians" had excited him in a way that he hadn't felt since grad school.

No one had written about the Guardians before, which meant he could be the first to publish a paper about these mysterious, magic-wielding vigilantes. And after years of working among his fellow ivory-tower elite, he knew provoking a little controversy was an effective way to goose fund-raising from alumni.

He opened the library's app on his smartphone and began a search for any relevant documents that might contain information on the so-called "Guardians."

As the computer ran its search, he began outlining the paper in his mind. He would raise the audience's expectations about a previously unknown secret sect of the Knights Templar and dangle the idea of a conspiracy and secret sect, then dash all those weighty expectations with the final few paragraphs of the paper. It would play well with the conspiracy-minded folk who loved stuff like this while publishing an interesting paper for his field.

The app chimed and displayed a list of relevant books and contemporary accounts with which he could start. He was surprised by the amount of material available to him and decided to start with the rare items. You never knew what you could dig up while poking around the library.

He grabbed a nearby cart and hauled it around the library, pulling the relevant volumes from the bookshelves. By the time he was done, he had collected twenty-four books, all of which claimed to have information about the Knights Templar.

Wheeling the cart back to his office, he unpacked the books, looking at each one critically. Many of the volumes hadn't been touched since they were donated to the library, but one volume caught his attention immediately.

According to the notes in the app, the large, leather-bound book was on loan from the Knickerbocker Collection and dated to the eleventh century. It was currently untranslated, but the description of the volume called it a grimoire that contained information about spells and potions. He had been working with the book for the past several weeks now after discovering it languishing in the rare books vault.

Every time he examined the book, he was surprised it was listed as being more than nine centuries old. He was impressed with how sturdy the volume was, and the preservation was far beyond anything he had seen before. It looked as if it had just come off the shelf.

He opened the book and paged through it, admiring the illustrations inside. The book was written in Old English, but, as he paged through, he discovered Cyrillic script, as well as ancient Egyptian hieroglyphs. He had even discovered several pages filled with archaic Chinese lettering that he had not yet translated.

He had a working knowledge of Old English and was able to translate most of the book. Unfortunately, it read more like a recipe book than anything informative. The more he read, the more the professor became convinced he had found the eleventh-century version of a recipe box. There were all sorts of fantastical claims about the potions and spells contained within, but it wasn't anything more outlandish than claims he saw people making on Facebook.

He chuckled. *I've discovered a peasant's recipe for essential oils from the eleventh century.*

He sighed and returned the book to the shelf, disappointed. While the volume had been remarkably well-preserved, it was nothing more than a collection of an unknown author living in the Middle Ages writing down their thoughts and theories about the natural world. He doubted there was anything to gain by reading the volume.

The professor turned his attention to the next book in the pile and examined the title: *A Modern History of the Knights Templar*. This was a modern title, written in the thirties by a prominent historian with solid credentials.

The professor placed the book on his desk and went to the small kitchenette in his office where he turned on the electric kettle.

After all, one couldn't research history without a cup of Earl Gray.

CHAPTER SEVEN

Dr. Apsara Choi tapped her thumb to the tip of each of her fingers as she awaited the arrival of her new patient while trying to ignore the discomfort brought on by the Level A hazmat suit. The self-soothing technique helped ease her anxiety for what her team was about to face. After seeing the video, she had decided to take maximum precautions until they could be certain of the transmission vector. They would treat the boy's disease as a potential endemic threat until they could prove it was not.

She and the rest of her staff looked like they were about to land on the moon. The janitorial staff had cleaned the entire fourth floor top to bottom with the strongest disinfectants the hospital had on hand and cleared of patients. Apsara felt guilty for inconveniencing them, but they had plenty of beds at the hospital, and the staff was filled with professionals who had been able to complete the transfers in record time.

The elevator chimed and she felt her heart race, anticipating the patient's arrival. Even before the doors to the elevator opened, she winced, hearing the poor boy's screams as the cuts on his body opened and closed.

"Get him into the room," Apsara snapped. Her staff moved to take over for the exhausted ambulance crew as they wheeled the boy's bed down into a medical unit where they could contain any potential biological specimens. Apsara turned to the two medics who looked tired, but ready to help.

"Go get decontaminated and then head for my office. I'll need detailed notes about what you saw when you arrived on scene," Apsara instructed. "I'll be down here, so it may be a few hours before I get to you."

"Take your time doctor," one of the ambulance workers said. She could see the pain in his eyes. The boy's condition had clearly affected him. "We'll wait as long as you need."

"Did you give him anything?" she asked. "Any pain medication?"

"We considered it, but after seeing the way those cuts appeared . . ." The ambulance worker shook his head. "We thought it better to get him here as quick as we could and try to stem the bleeding instead."

She looked them over and could see they were debating telling her something.

"What is it?" she asked.

One of the techs extended a hand, holding out a chain with a large amulet attached to it. "He was hanging onto this thing. Didn't want to give it up. Seemed to get even louder every time we tried to take it away from him."

His partner nodded. "He was in so much pain, his hand had clenched around it to the point we needed forceps to pry it free."

Apsara took the necklace and held it up to the light. The heavy amulet looked old. Other than that, she found it unremarkable and doubted it had anything to do with her patient.

"Log it and put it in isolation with the rest of his things," she said. "Perhaps there was an infectious agent on it."

"We'll take care of it," the first medic said, taking the amulet back from Apsara.

She nodded her thanks to them, then turned and walked briskly to the quarantine unit where they'd taken her patient, the sound of her footsteps echoing in the hallway.

When she arrived, the boy was still screaming in pain as the wounds continued to appear and heal all over his body. The green hospital sheets were soaked with the boy's blood even as her staff struggled to keep the boy restrained. The slickness of the blood made it difficult for the staff to get a solid grip on the wiry fourteen-year-old.

"Get a line in him now," Apsara ordered. "Type O negative blood for now, cross-match his blood and get him what he needs."

"Blood pressure's dropping," one of the nurses called out.

Apsara felt herself slip into the flow of diagnosing and working on a patient, going through all the options and potential problems the boy had to be suffering from. Right now, the best she could do was treat his symptoms and stabilize him, so that's what they would do.

"What have you given him?" Apsara asked her staff, alarmed that the boy was still contorting in pain. They were shoving a lot of meds into his system, which should have knocked him out already.

"Two milligrams of IV morphine," one of the nurses said, sounding alarmed. "I don't dare give him another one."

"No, don't," Apsara agreed. "We could lose him."

Another nurse announced she had managed to get a blood line in the boy and Apsara felt her anxiety begin to ebb. They wouldn't be able to do this for long, so whatever they were going to do, they needed to do it before the boy's body gave up.

Her mind raced with possibilities. Was it bacterial? Should she give the teenager broad spectrum antibiotics? What if it were viral? She could try anti-viral drugs, but there were too many unknowns. With so much blood loss, there was little time for a debate.

Time became a blur as her team raced to care for the boy. They worked together as a well-oiled machine, the bright lights of the room shining down on them, the smell and taste of the blood clashing with the antiseptic smell in the air.

"He's delirious," the resident said, holding the boy down, his gloves covered in the young man's blood.

The boy had stopped screaming and was now muttering incomprehensible nonsense under his breath.

"Get those samples to the lab," Apsara ordered. "Code them STAT. I want to know what we're dealing with."

She looked down at the boy in front of her, fascinated by the sight of a cut splitting open the boy's skin on his arm. Blood pouring out of the three-inch slice spurted onto her helmet. She snapped her head back in reflex before remembering she was protected by the suit.

The boy was finally unconscious as the medication took effect. Apsara felt her heart rate return to normal as the boy stabilized.

"What did he say?" she asked. "I couldn't hear him."

One of the nurses leaned closer to the boy and listened as he repeated the whispered words to her. The nurse looked up at Apsara, a confused expression on her face.

The nurse shrugged. "All I could make out was, 'It's back.'"

Apsara cocked her head in confusion. The boy had become delusional. If she couldn't find anything that might give her a clue as to what he was suffering from, she had little hope of helping him.

"Let me know as soon as the results come back from the lab," she said. "Try and keep him as comfortable as possible. I'm gonna go speak with the paramedics who brought him in."

"Understood doctor," the nurse answered, and she disappeared from the room.

Apsara turned and walked down the hallway to the decontamination unit where she could change back into her street clothes and begin her research to try and figure out what was wrong with that boy. By the amount of blood, she didn't think the patient had much longer than twenty-four to forty-eight hours left—even with their intervention.

The door to the decontamination area opened and she entered, waiting for her suit to be cleaned. It was going to be a long night.

CHAPTER EIGHT

Twelve hours after they fled Knickerbocker Tower, Daniel waited for the rest of his crew at the designated meeting point they'd agreed upon before splitting up in downtown Los Angeles.

He was the first to arrive at their rally point at the Griffith Observatory. It was already a busy morning at the popular tourist hotspot located in the hills above Los Angeles. Early morning hikers were out in force, giving him and the rest of his group cover as they discussed what went wrong with the mission.

For his part, he had spent the waning hours of the night furious at himself and the rest of his crew. They'd failed in their mission in retrieving the amulet and would now miss their multi-million-dollar payday. Their employer had already gone silent—his many texts to their mysterious source that had hired them going unanswered.

He spotted Letty approaching him from the east and re-moved the cigarette from his mouth, tossing it to the ground before stubbing it out with his boot. She looked about as pissed as he felt.

"Where the hell is Cody?" he asked without preamble.

She scoffed. "I'm not his babysitter."

His eyes narrowed and he was about to bite back with a cutting remark when he saw his younger brother exit a small sedan that arrived at the observatory. The relief he felt quickly turned into fury as he watched Cody casually chomp into a breakfast sandwich after exiting the Uber.

Cody sauntered over, a bag boasting the name of a local fast-food restaurant in his hand.

"You stopped for breakfast?" he spluttered at his little brother. Not a word to let them know he was okay, but he had time for drive-through?

"I need to eat or I'm useless," the man complained. Cody pushed his sunglasses up as he took another bite of the sand-wich. "You mad I didn't get you anything?"

Daniel sighed and decided to get to business. "First, the bad news. We failed to retrieve the amulet and our employer is radio silent. No payday."

Letty looked as if she expected this news, but Cody was more shocked.

"We're not getting paid?" his little brother moaned.

That was the only thing the little whiner could think about? He slapped the fast-food bag out of his brother's hands and pushed him back, holding him by the throat.

"That is the least of our concerns right now, you moron," he said through clenched teeth. Cody had a good six inches in height on him, but being the older brother had its advantages.

"Let. Me. Go." Cody gasped, trying to push his older brother off.

He felt the fury build inside him—it was Cody's fault they lost everything. If he hadn't panicked and killed Knickerbocker, they wouldn't have half the city looking for them. And after he'd vouched for the little shit too. Letty never would have botched a job like that.

He watched his little brother's face go red as he choked the life out of him. It wasn't until Letty touched him on the shoulder that he eased the pressure on Cody's windpipe, letting him go.

Cody crumpled to the ground, choking, spitting up pieces of his breakfast sandwich.

"What the hell?" he said, gasping for air. "It wasn't my fault we—"

"Yes, it was!" Letty snapped at him. "You didn't have to kill the old man."

Cody looked over at Letty and narrowed his eyes. "Yeah, well, at least I didn't curse anyone."

A silence fell over the group, and he knew it was time to talk about the elephant in the room. He turned to Letty who was still silently fuming at Cody's sullen attitude about their failure.

"How did you do that?" he asked her. "Tell me exactly what happened."

Letty glanced over at him, looking chagrined. "I told the little shit that if he even thought about telling the cops about us, I'd come back and slice him up into little pieces."

"And then cuts began appearing on his skin," Daniel finished. "But . . . they healed."

"I also said I'd stitch him back up, over and over."

"I saw it," Cody said, standing up, still rubbing his neck. "It was like the kid got cut by some knife."

Daniel thought back to the amulet and the mysterious words their employer had instructed him to read from it. It was becoming clear they were dealing with something beyond anything modern science could explain.

That was when he remembered a story his grandmother used to tell them when they were children.

"Cody is right. You cursed the boy," he said.

"What?" Letty asked.

"Like the witches Nan use to tell us about." He nodded to his brother. "They were in the old country when she grew up. She told us stories about how the witches cursed anyone who went against them. One of the curses was a blood curse that killed its victim. It was magic."

"Superstition," Letty corrected, but Daniel shook his head.

"You saw it yourself. How superstitious do you feel?"

"I didn't . . ." Letty trailed off, then nodded. "It was like something inside me had to get out, and I couldn't stop it. I knew what I wanted, I imagined it, and it happened."

But Daniel was no longer listening to her. He was thinking back to the amulet and the power he had felt as he held it in his hands.

"I felt it too," Cody added. His face had flushed over the last few minutes. "Power."

A surge of adrenaline coursed through Daniel as his brother described what he had felt inside the apartment. He was beginning to believe the amulet had been far more than just some trinket. It had given them all a gift. If what they were all thinking, but not saying, were true, it was no wonder the amulet had been worth so much to their employer.

His hands were glowing orange again, just like they had back at Knickerbocker Tower while he was holding the amulet. Daniel spotted a nearby tree and extended his hand.

Something inside him released. A powerful burst of energy exploded from his hands and hurtled toward the tree he was aiming at, which exploded into a thousand pieces. Letty and Cody shouted in surprise, throwing up their hands in shock.

"What the hell was that?" Letty shouted. The explosion had attracted the attention of the early morning hikers. Some had already raised their phones, recording the scene, while others were calling the police.

"Something wonderful," Daniel said, noting the other people in the park were coming closer to see what the ruckus had been all about.

"Come on, let's get some real food. I'm beginning to believe we might have gotten something out of last night's heist after all."

CHAPTER NINE

JOHN JUPITER ENTERED HOOVER Medical Center holding a bouquet of flowers, trying to fix his face into a look that mixed concern and confidence. He had spent the night waiting in the parking lot after a not-so-friendly guard informed him "visiting hours wasn't until morning."

So, he waited and worked on a plan to get close to the Knickerbocker boy and see these strange wounds for himself. He had been debating whether he should take video as proof, but there were limits to his scumbagginess when pursuing a story. He was a reporter, not an asshole. There were other ways to verify a story.

When visiting hours began, he entered the hospital and tried to blend in with the crowd. He figured if he showed up holding flowers and didn't bring any attention to himself, he should be able to find out where they were keeping the kid. If anyone tried to stop him, he would rely on some good old-fashioned charisma and playing dumb—an act that had proven more than convincing in the past.

Besides, the worst thing they could do was kick him out. A once-in-a-lifetime story like this meant he needed to do whatever it took to stay ahead of the competition. He didn't have faith the LAPD would be able to keep Knickerbocker's murder secret for much longer.

He walked by the nurse's station and grabbed a clipboard. Between that and the bouquet of flowers, he felt confident he could walk into the hospital's CEO's office if he wanted.

There was a tense, strange mood around the hospital, but he didn't think it had anything to do with the patients on this floor. The nurses and staff clustered together, whispering amongst themselves even as they went about their normal business.

He eased his way down the hallway trying to look busy by absent-mindedly making notes using the clipboard he was holding. He kept his ears open as he paused near a group of nurses whispering.

"They've got the fourth floor quarantined," he heard a young blonde woman tell her colleague. "They wouldn't do that unless it was a serious threat."

"They do it for other reasons," the older heavyset woman said in a voice filled with the wisdom of a world-weary veteran of the hospital. "There's no reason to jump to Ebola every time the suits upstairs want to run a drill or give some young starlet privacy while she recovers from an OD."

"If it was a drill, we'd have known about it a week ago," the younger woman shot back. "And if it were some star, we'd have seen it on TMZ by now. I'm telling ya, we're getting quarantined by the end of the day. I bet you good money."

"I'll take that bet," the older nurse looked amused. "I've seen it a thousand times. Today's nothing special, hun."

The pair continued to argue as he set his clipboard down on the desk and tried to look busy on his phone. The two women were now arguing over the terms of their bet, and he used the opportunity to lift the older woman's hospital ID badge she had left on the nurse's station.

John edged his way back down the hallway, unlocking his smartphone, and searched for a map of the hospital online. He wanted to see if there was a way for him to get to the fourth floor without being noticed.

Scrolling through the search results, he found what he was looking for and examined the map for several minutes, formulating a plan.

His footfalls echoed as followed the painted lines on the hospital's walls to a service elevator. He had a hunch that unlike the main elevators—which would have been programmed to bypass any floor that was quarantined—the service elevator might still be able to access the floor. In places like this, service elevators were on a different system, and it was possible that using a little light hacking he could make his way onto the floor and get a closer look at what was happening.

"Hey," he heard a voice call out. "Excuse me, sir?"

John ignored the voice, knowing it was for him and that he needed to keep moving if he wanted to make it to the fourth floor.

He turned the corner and began jogging, hoping to put some distance between him and the security guard who was gaining on him.

He spotted a nearby office that was still dark, with no one inside. He waved the nurse's badge over a keypad near the handle, hoping the senior nurse had access to everything.

Thankfully, the lock clicked, and he was able to push open the door without any trouble. He entered the office and eased the door closed. Placing his back against the door, he breathed in and out, trying to control his heartbeat and the anxiety he was feeling.

He heard squeaking footfalls and a deep voice echoing through the hallway, giving a description of John to everyone else in the hospital.

The guard's footfalls faded away, and John released the breath he was holding. He took a moment to get his bearings and after appraising his surroundings, realized he hadn't ducked into an office—in fact, he was in a storage room of some kind filled with a random assortment of items in plastic bags.

He pawed through the plastic bags for a few moments until he realized his dumb luck. The hospital used this storage closet to hold patients' personal items while they stayed at the hospital.

He moved through the rows of shelves, searching for the 'K' section, and flipped through the envelopes. Several of them were large and heavy, while others were smaller. They all contained a variety of personal items such as money clips, cell phones, and purses.

After a few moments, he gave up his search. There was nothing here that had the Knickerbocker boy's name on it. He figured they must be keeping the boy's possessions upstairs—which brought him back to his original mission of getting on the fourth floor.

He searched the closet and discovered a janitor's uniform hanging off a hook in the back of the room. He fluffed out the uniform a bit, then put it on, cinching the jumpsuit across his broad frame.

He stepped out of the closet, looking both ways down the hallway for anyone who might still be looking for him. He didn't spot anyone lurking nearby and sauntered into the hallway, tugging his brown hat low over his eyes to further conceal his look.

He made his way down the hallway holding a mop—another item he had "liberated" from the maintenance closet—and continued to walk with purpose as if this was just another day.

Security was surely still looking for him, but so far, his disguise was holding up.

John made his way down to the service elevator and pressed the button, calling it to the third floor. He kept his eyes low and tried to blend in, holding his mop while the elevator made its way toward him, each second he was out in the open passing excruciatingly slow.

Finally, the elevator arrived, and he sighed in relief. He stepped inside and held a breath, waiting for the doors to close. He hit the fourth-floor button, which did not light up.

John removed his penknife from his pocket and pried open the service panel, pulling it aside to reveal the wires behind the plate. He pulled at the multi-colored wires, trying to find what he was looking for.

He located and traced the wire he needed back to its source and grunted in triumph. He used his penknife to cut it open and then used a power wire that fed the LED display to activate the elevator.

The service elevator dinged and began moving. He grinned, satisfied with his work.

When the doors opened, a blast of wind blew in his face. He grimaced as he stepped out of the elevator, a thick antiseptic odor burning his sinuses. Hospitals always smelled stringent, but this was on another level.

He stepped into the deserted hospital corridor, more than a bit creeped out by the eerie silence that surrounded him. A hospital this size was usually filled with doctors and staff attending to patients. Those administrators wouldn't give up a full floor unless there was a serious threat to the hospital.

He peeked into offices as he crept down the hall, trying to find a room that resembled the storage closet he had stumbled upon earlier. The Knickerbocker boy's personal possessions might contain a clue about the murder.

He headed for the same spot where he found the previous storage closet on the third floor. Architects would often mirror floor plans to save on costs and make each floor familiar for the patients and staff. After gathering his bearings, he spotted the door he was looking for and again used the stolen keycard to access the closet and step inside.

This storage closet was bare, save for one manilla envelope sitting on the shelf near the door. John figured the staff must have cleared out the storage after they shut down the fourth floor for their special patient.

He reached for the manilla envelope. The ink used to print the boy's name on it was still fresh. He turned it over and untied the back, pouring the contents out onto a nearby desk. He found a pencil in the desk drawer and used it to poke through the items.

There wasn't much—some clothing, gum, cash, and a wallet. When he pushed a shirt aside, he spotted a gold chain attached to an amulet.

He raised an eyebrow and used the pencil to pull the amulet up out of the clothing. He grimaced when he saw the ornate gold and silver jewelry, still covered in the boy's blood. He angled the pencil, trying to get a better look at the other side of the jewelry.

He squinted and spotted intricate lettering written all around the edge. It wasn't any language he knew, but his best guess was it was an older, dead language. He eyed it and tried to sound it out.

"Onlíesende Balocræft Synbysige ġefeoht."

A bright orange flash emanated from the amulet. He cried out, startled, shutting his eyes against the blinding light, and dropped the amulet to the ground.

The door to the storage closet flew open and what appeared to be a monster made of plastic shouted at him in an incomprehensible language.

Only after his eyes cleared from the flash of light did he realize the plastic monster was just a woman yelling at him from the inside of a Hazmat suit.

The reality of the situation crashed down on his head. This wasn't just a stabbing like the cops back at Knickerbocker Tower said—the hospital believed they were dealing with a potential outbreak of disease.

"Wrong floor?" he asked, his voice squeaking as he shrugged.

The woman shouted something at him, which he couldn't understand through her suit.

"Say again?"

"I said you may have just killed yourself." The disgust on the woman's face was evident through the protective suit that covered her head to toe. "If you have any interest in living through the next forty-eight hours, you'd better come with me."

He followed the commanding woman into the hospital corridor, hoping they were being overly cautious.

Did he just sign his own death warrant?

CHAPTER TEN

DR. APSARA CHOI COULDN'T remember a time when she had been this angry. Her one request had been that the fourth floor remain inaccessible to all visitors and staff until they had been able to discount any potential biohazard that might lead to an outbreak of this terrible disease.

She glowered at the man who had snuck on the floor, wondering for the first time in her career if she could ignore her Hippocratic oath while treating a patient. He had been stripped down out of his clothes and a team of her nurses in decontamination suits were scrubbing the interloper with soap and hot, scalding water. It was an unpleasant process, and she felt some satisfaction the man was supremely uncomfortable after violating her quarantine order.

Her boss, Dr. Moreno, was standing next to her, watching the intruder get decontaminated.

"You know who that is, right?" he asked, sounding miserable.

"No, should I?" The impatience in Apsara's voice revealed the fury she was feeling. She had better things to do but her boss had insisted she be here to personally debrief the man who had managed to infiltrate their unit.

"That is John Jupiter," he said. "Investigative reporter at KTLK. He made his career breaking the kind of news stories like the one we have in the ICU right now. Odds are good that if he's here, he knows about the boy."

"So what?" she scoffed. "What could he possibly do?"

"If he's here, it's enough to bring a media circus down on us," Dr. Moreno's expression was grim. "That is something we wished to avoid."

"So, what would you have me do?" Apsara waved her arm at the reporter. "Babysit him?"

Dr. Moreno didn't answer.

"You have got to be kidding me!"

"Babysitting is not how I view this opportunity," Dr. Moreno said, turning to her. "I want you to bring him in on the case with you, help him understand this disease so we can avoid triggering an outright panic. I have no desire to go through the kind of media firestorm that would be brought down upon us if the public believes we are hiding a deadly viral outbreak."

"You want someone to play PR?" she said, rolling her eyes. "You do it."

"You know as well as anyone what happens when the public thinks a virus is on the loose. This man can help us bridge the gap," Dr. Moreno said. "He has connections, and he is not the type to give up. We can control the story through him, and we can control the narrative. That will save lives, Dr. Choi."

"How very *1984* of you," she replied.

"Oh, grow up," he reproached her. "If you haven't gathered the severity of the position we're in, allow me to enlighten you. The very moment the federal government becomes involved, we lose all control. Media from all over the world descend on our hospital. Panic sets in. People across the country inundate hospitals with their own imagined maladies. The situation would devolve into chaos, and you know it."

"We lose the donation from the Knickerbocker family you mean." She was not here to mince words. Not while her patient was busy dying in a room a few yards away.

She saw her dig left a mark on Dr. Moreno and she almost felt bad for a moment. Still, he knew she was right, he just didn't want to say the quiet part aloud.

He ignored the accusation and continued berating her.

"Regardless of your personal feelings, Dr. Choi, if we can convince Mr. Jupiter to hold the story while you investigate, we will buy time to help that poor boy without having to answer to the media or anyone else with an agenda. Are you really so anxious to end up on cable news?"

She tried to push back the sinking feeling in her gut, but she knew he was right. She turned her attention back to the man, who was still being scrubbed down by the two nurses and grunted. Wisely, Dr. Moreno didn't press the issue and took her silence to mean she was onboard with his idea.

Besides, the reporter's decontamination shower was ending, and it wasn't as if she had anything else to do. She had sent every test she could think of off to the labs, and she had a few hours before she knew more about what was happening to her poor patient.

One of the nurses handed the reporter a pair of blue scrubs to put on, and he accepted them with thanks.

He exited the room and rubbed a hand through his thick black hair ruefully as he approached her.

"That was one hell of a shower. I feel like they scrubbed off dirt from five years ago," he said. "You all have my things? I'm pretty partial to that jacket. Gift from my aunt."

"Mr. Jupiter?" Her icy glare and tone with him could have frozen the room solid. "I'm Dr. Apsara Choi. I'm the lead physician on the case."

"John, please," he said extending his hand.

She stared at him, and he dropped his hand after several awkward moments. He rubbed his palm on the side of his new scrubs, moved over to where his belongings had been set aside and took out a notepad and pen.

"So, what do we have in there?" he asked. "I understand they're some kind of slash wounds that continually open and heal themselves, keeping the boy in incredible pain?"

She was surprised at his description. He wasn't far off—for a man with limited medical knowledge.

"That's correct," she said. "But—"

"Have you ever seen anything like this before, Doctor?"

She cocked her head and narrowed her eyes. "Understand something, Mr. Jupiter—"

"John, please."

"Mister Jupiter," she emphasized, ignoring his interruption, "you are only here because my boss believes you can help us prevent a panic, which in turn, will allow me the time I need to differentially diagnose what is wrong with that poor boy. I am not here to be your personal Physicians' Desk Reference. I am a practicing medical professional, and I don't appreciate you cutting me off when I have something to say."

The reporter nodded, putting down his notebook. "Dr. Choi, I understand the higher ups have foisted me off on you to help with the politics of the situation, and I know that can't feel good. But, in case you don't know anything about me, I made my career on bringing the truth to the people, and I take that job seriously. I don't care about awards, accolades, or the assholes who try to stop me. My awards are the careers of corrupt politicians I've exposed. My accolades come when a mother looks me in the eye and says my reporting helped her family get back on their feet.

"I'm here because one of the most powerful men in America was murdered and his son is currently in the ICU battling a previously unseen disease. That tells me there is a deeper mystery behind both incidents and I intend to discover the truth. Because the world deserves, no, demands nothing less.

Despite what you might think about my peers, I'm an honest reporter who tells honest stories."

When she didn't respond, he cocked his head. "I'm here to observe what I can and ask questions I believe are relevant. I swear to you, I won't get in your way or prevent you from doing your job. I won't bullshit you if you don't bullshit me."

She eyed him, searching his face for any hidden motivations as he looked back at her earnestly. To her chagrin, she felt her resolve weaken and decided to take him at his word—for now.

"All right," she said after a moment. "Let's get to work, shall we?"

"Great!" he said, picking up his notebook. "What's first?"

"We talk to the drivers who brought the boy in and then we'll take a look at the results from the labs," she said. "Let's get moving. They've been waiting for quite a while thanks to you and your shenanigans."

"Lead the way," John leapt to his feet, and put on his brown felt fedora.

Apsara stood and walked out the door to her office with John following closely behind.

CHAPTER ELEVEN

THE ALARM NEVER WOKE Mike Madsen up the first time. His daughter had always been his best alarm clock and today was no different. When he opened his eyes, he found himself being studied by his daughter, who had planted herself squarely on his chest.

"Good morning," he said, rubbing the sleep out of his eyes. He looked up at the young girl peering curiously down at him. "Something I can do for you?"

"You're ugly in the morning," his daughter Shayla told him. She pursed her lips and scowled at him in disapproval. "You have beard face."

"Beard face?" He chuckled and wiped the sleep away from his eyes. He grabbed his daughter and began rubbing his scruff against the arm of her T-shirt, lest he accidentally scratch his little girl. "This doesn't feel like beard face to me."

"Stop!" she squealed, trying to get away and laughing at the same time.

"What are you doing up anyway?" he said, looking over at the alarm clock. It was six a.m. Early, but nearly time for him to get up and get ready anyway. Owning your own business meant long hours, and he was no exception to that rule. Today was his first day off in two weeks, and he intended on spending it with Shayla.

"I want pancakes," she said, hugging her body as she rocked back and forth on the bed. She looked up at him with an expression that said she already knew he wouldn't say "no."

"Good thing you got me up then," he said with a smile. "'Cause now I've got time make 'em blueberry style."

"Chocolate chip!" she countered, narrowing her eyes.

He laughed and grabbed her by the waist and lifted her as he got off the bed. "You'll have blueberry pancakes and like it, young lady."

She shrieked, laughing as he hauled her to the kitchen. He forgot his aching back for a moment and the long week he had spent at work behind him. Her smile made everything worth it. She was his entire universe, and he didn't need anything more out of life than time with his daughter.

They reached the kitchen, and he set her down then shifted his attention to gathering what he would need for the promised pancakes.

In the distance, he heard his phone ring and glanced over at his daughter who had already buried her nose in her tablet. She had started up a cartoon while she waited for breakfast.

His eyes flitted back to the bedroom, and he thought about who might be on the other end of the line. Shayla had already settled in front of the screen, which meant he had a few minutes to himself before she began wondering where her pancakes were.

He made his way back to the bedroom and picked up his phone. He read the name on the display and raised an eyebrow.

"Heya, Cy, whatcha got?" he asked his assistant on the other end of the line.

"Nothing but good news." Cy Tolliver's youthful voice was filled with energy. "It's why I thought I could get away with calling you this early."

"Hit me with it," Mike said, bracing for the worst. Cy said it was good news, but you never knew with the guy.

"Gus officially decided to sell his business," Cy replied. "You'll be getting the tab from our dinner last night that helped me make that happen, by the way."

Mike pumped his fist. "You sure?"

"I got the confirmation email just now. Dude's hanging it up to live that Miami life."

"What about his routes?" Mike asked, holding his breath. This was just the kind of thing his company could use right now. He had seen his business through the recession with only a few hiccups, but things hadn't quite gotten back to normal just yet.

"That's why I'm calling," Cy said, sounding proud of himself. "All I need is your signature, and we can take them over today if we want."

"Really?" Mike said, becoming excited. "What's the catch?"

"There's no catch," Cy said. "The guy always liked you, so I think he wants his customers to go to someone he trusts. All I need is to email you some documents for you to sign. We've got the inventory on hand already so we should be able to slide right in without any trouble."

"Cy," Mike said. "Gus had government contracts. Are you saying those are all ours now?"

"That's what I'm saying, sir," Cy said. "This is a big effing deal."

Mike covered the receiver and shouted in glee. This kind of contract meant he could take his business to the next level. He could hire more people to take care of things for him, giving him more time at home with his daughter.

"Send it over," Mike said. "I'll sign it now. Shit, sign it yourself."

"Only thing, there is a bit of bad news," Cy said apologetically. "Because we're taking over his routes today, we don't have anyone extra who can go out. Which means . . ."

"Which means I've gotta come in and work on my day off," Mike said. "You really know how to mix the sweet and sour, kid."

"What can I say? You're an inspiration, boss," Cy said.

"Send me the information on the routes and get the warehouse folks prepping the packages for delivery. I'll cover things for the next few days," Mike said. "We'll talk next week about hiring someone permanently for the route."

"Great!" Cy said. "Deliveries start at eight a.m. sharp, so you'll have to get a move on."

"Yeah, Cy, I hear ya," Mike said, sounding far less enthused than his young assistant. He hung up the phone and saw Shayla looking at him, holding a spatula with a look of disappointment on her face.

"Pancakes for another day?" she asked, sounding sad and hopeful all at the same time.

Mike felt his insides implode and hoped one day she might understand.

"Yeah, princess," he said. "Pancakes on another day."

He stood, forcing a smile. "Until then, what do you think about getting French toast fingers on our way in?"

Shayla's face brightened, and she nodded.

"Good," Mike said, still feeling embarrassed for having ruined their breakfast plans. "Go get dressed and get your schoolwork together. You'll be spending the morning with Stacey."

"Stacey?" she wrinkled her nose. "The lady at your work with too much perfume?"

Mike held back a laugh as he thought about the layers of perfume Stacey put on to impress Cy at the office every day.

"Yes, honey, she'll take you to school later on," he said. "Now go get dressed."

"Roger that, Daddy-o," Shayla said. She offered him a mock salute and then turned to race out of the kitchen to her room upstairs.

Mike watched her go, a smile on his face. Once she was gone, the smile faded and he rubbed his face, trying to ignore the feeling that he was failing his little one every day.

She deserved so much better than the life he was giving her. But today's news would go a long way toward helping him create a better life for them both—the life she deserved.

He sighed, pushed the thoughts about being a failure of a father out of his head, and headed for the bathroom to get ready for the day.

It wasn't as if there was anything he could do about it.

CHAPTER TWELVE

JOHN LOOMED BEHIND APSARA as she peered into the microscope at tissue samples taken from the now-sedated fourteen-year-old. She glanced back at him, annoyed with how close he was getting.

Realizing his faux pas, he stepped back, clearing his throat. "See anything good?" he asked, trying to sound normal.

Apsara raised an eyebrow, looking at him as if she were trying to decide if he was a creep or someone who lacked social skills. He awaited her assessment, keeping his eyes locked on hers, the question still hanging in the air.

She turned back to the tissue sample in front of her and began narrating what she had discovered so far.

"I've never seen anything like this before," she said. "We've ruled out the most common poisons, venoms, and chemical agents. But there are millions of possibilities and nothing to go on. There is nothing in any of the journals on record that describes something as horrific as these slashing wounds."

John cocked his head, motioning to the microscope in front of them. "May I?"

She nodded and he leaned down to look, but to him, there wasn't anything remarkable about the tissue sample.

"I'm not seeing anything special," he said, looking up from the microscope and back at Apsara. "Can you describe what I'm supposed to look for?"

She appraised him, as if trying to gauge the level of intelligence behind his eyes.

"All right," she said, studying his eager expression. "I'll start with the obvious. Slash wounds that heal within moments, then reappear on the body again are unheard of in the medical community. Occasionally, as we age, our skin can become incredibly thin and is easier to tear, but this isn't that."

"I get the feeling there's a 'But wait, there's more!' coming," John said.

"Oh, you better believe there's more," Apsara said, motioning to the microscope. "A fourteen-year-old boy shouldn't have the skin of an eighty-five-year-old, yet that's what we're seeing in the microscope. Human cells don't change overnight like this unless there's an outside force working on them. Generally, that takes the form of a virus or radiation."

"Radiation?" John said, looking worried. "As in . . ."

"Yes, like mutations that lead to uncontrolled cell growth," Apsara said. "But even then, we don't see anything approaching this rate of tissue generation."

"How long does he have?" John asked, not really wanting to know the answer.

"It's hard to say," she said after a moment. "His blood pressure is what worries me. The transfusions we started should help, but there's no way to know when, or if, we can stop the bleeding. If we can't, it won't matter how much blood we pump into him. He'll bleed to death in our care and there won't be a thing we can do about it."

"You're just full of happy answers, Doc," he said, looking back at the display. "So where do we start looking?"

"Case histories," she said. "I have my staff scouring every medical journal ever published for anything that resembles fast-growing slash wounds like these."

"And then?"

She shrugged. "And then we go from there."

"Sounds exhausting," he said.

"No one said it would be easy," she said. "Now, if you don't have any other questions, I have work to do. I imagine you have a story to file."

"Not yet," he said. "I've already sent my audio on Knicker-bocker's death, so the station is happy with me for now. I'm all yours."

She stared at him, and he felt uncomfortable, waiting for her to say something first. But after a few moments, he couldn't stand the silence.

"It's getting awkward now, you just looking at me like this and not saying anything," he said.

She continued to stare at him until a soft knock at the door announced one of her staff members holding a clipboard at the door. Finally, she broke off that uncomfortable stare. She went to the door, and the two doctors exchanged some hurried words that he couldn't hear. He saw Apsara take a clipboard and flip through the pages, her face grim. Whatever the printouts said, it didn't look like good news.

Apsara dismissed her assistant and moved back to the desk where he waited patiently. He watched as she read the results and cursed, which prompted him to chuckle.

She glanced up at him, a quizzical expression on her face. "What?"

"You don't strike me as the cursing type," he said shrugging.

"By the look of the boy's chart, I think cursing is the appropriate response," she said.

"What does it say?"

She sighed and rubbed her eyes. "Nothing. Everything is normal."

He raised an eyebrow, confused. "Isn't that . . . good?"

She shrugged. "If there were something noticeably wrong with the patient's body chemistry, it might lead me to an answer or treatment. You can read the report for yourself if you like, but I doubt things like ADL levels mean anything to you."

He chuckled again and shook his head. "A lifetime of reporting has taught me to listen to the experts."

"Except this expert doesn't have the slightest idea what the boy's problem is," she frowned, shaking her head. "Nothing about this case makes sense."

John watched her place her hands on her head and face the wall. He got the feeling she was not used to failing like this.

He thought back on the photos he'd seen of the patient's body. "You know, back when I was in college, I had a roommate who majored in computer science."

"So?" she asked, sounding miserable. "What's that got to do with anything?"

"Well," he moved closer to her and sat down in a chair opposite her desk. "Whenever he'd get a bug in his programming, he'd talk it out to a little cartoon robot that he had sitting on his desk. Inevitably, he would figure out what the problem was."

"And?"

He waved his hands out with a flourish and bowed. "I volunteer to be your inanimate object."

She considered his proposal.

"Okay . . ." she said, drawing out the word. She got up out of her chair and began narrating as she paced the small room. "Patient is a fourteen-year-old white male, approximately one hundred forty-five pounds, five feet, eight inches tall.

He presented with recurring slash wounds that heal within thirty seconds of first forming on the boy's skin. The wounds resemble those you'd find from someone involved in a knife fight."

He waited for her to work it out all on her own. But he couldn't help but feel like there was something in the back of his head that was related to this case.

"The wounds do not appear to have any variation in size or in the amount of blood lost. Standard medical response to infections has failed. No infection presents on biological markers. The boy complains of pain at the most extreme levels and his screaming is testament enough to that."

John shuddered, thinking back to the sounds he had heard when he first opened the quarantined floor. The boy might be young, but he had a set of lungs on him.

"Doctors induced a coma about two hours ago, but we have not observed any change in the boy's condition," she continued, her voice almost monotone. "The wounds continue to appear and reseal themselves. Our attempts at intervention have so far been unsuccessful."

John listened to her, but there was something about her voice that reminded him of the interview he conducted for his podcast with the professor. Something about curses and—

"What?" she asked, looking down at him. John snapped back to attention, realizing his thoughts had drifted away. "You've got something."

"I've got nothing." Then after a moment, "I've got . . . an odd coincidence."

She shook her head and looked up at him. "Whatever it is, I'm all ears. My patient will die in less than thirty-six hours without any major intervention. What is it?"

"I host a podcast," John began.

"You and everyone else in Los Angeles," she retorted. He grimaced, and she held up a hand. "I apologize, please continue."

"Anyway," he eyed her for another sarcastic response, "A guest on my show described something like what you're seeing with the boy."

"How similar?" she leaned forward and from her tone he could tell her interest was piqued.

"It was something you said about the slash wounds all being the same shape," he confessed, running a hand through his hair. "It's exactly what my guest said about a hex that swept through a town in the Middle Ages."

She snorted and rolled her eyes. "I should have known."

"Hey, what do you expect from someone who lived that long ago?" he asked, indignant. "They all used whatever knowledge and language they had available to explain the natural world around them. It's not surprising that they would call something like cancer a 'curse.'"

Apsara shrugged and then nodded. "All right, fair enough. You got me there. So, what else did Professor Crazy Pants say?"

John hesitated. If he hadn't lost her with the hex talk, he would certainly lose her now.

"He said people who found themselves cursed like that sought out the help of a powerful witch who could brew a potion that would reverse the curse and allow them to recover."

He watched her face as he described what the professor had told him. She was staring off into space, not responding to his story.

"I get it," he said, shrugging. "It's a lot to believe. People tell all kinds of crazy stories to explain the natural world."

She stared at him again in that unsettling way she had, and he wondered what was going through her mind. It was probably something about how crazy he was coming off as. After all, what did she really know about him?

"Where could we learn more about this . . . 'hex'?" she asked after a moment.

"Wow," he was unable to hide the shock in his voice. "You really are desperate."

She got up out of her chair, took off her lab coat, grabbed a black jacket, and shrugged into it. "All the fancy equipment and tests I've got here have failed me so far. I'm humble enough to know when desperate hope starts to make sense. Maybe it's an old virus that disappeared and recently resurfaced."

"That's a leap," he admitted. "But then again, why am I arguing against my side? Let's go. I know where we can learn more."

"Where's that?" she asked.

"Our local library," he answered. "Shall we?"

She nodded and moved out the door. He followed, the excitement building with every step.

He really loved working on a story.

CHAPTER THIRTEEN

PROFESSOR DESMOND MCKAIG WAS slumbering peacefully when he was startled awake by a knock on his office door. A piece of paper, one of his notes from earlier, stuck to his forehead. Disoriented, he pulled the piece of paper then stood, crossed the small office space, and opened the door.

"Professor McKaig?"

He ogled the motley couple standing in front of him. One was a larger, scruffy white man, about six foot two, wearing jeans, a flannel shirt, and a long London Fog overcoat. The other was an Asian woman wearing a tasteful blouse and flowing skirt that reached down to her knee-high black boots.

The man's voice sounded familiar, but the professor was having trouble placing where he knew the young man. He was too old to be a student. Perhaps a lecture somewhere?

"You found me," he said, extending his hand and stepping back to allow the two people into his office. "Can I help you?"

He stepped back to his desk and organized the papers scattered on the desk. He moved a stack of files off the two chairs that were set up in front of his desk and moved them to the side. "Please, take a seat,"

He couldn't help staring at the couple as they made themselves comfortable. Why did the man seem familiar somehow?

"I'm sorry," he said when neither of them spoke. "I wasn't aware I had any appointments this morning. I was in the middle of my research last night and—"

"My apologies, Professor," the woman said in a pleasant voice. "My name is Dr. Apsara Choi. This is John Jupiter."

That's when it clicked. Of course, this was the gentleman who had interviewed him on that podcast about the occult and other such mysteries.

"Oh of course, Mr. Jupiter, how are you doing, sir?" the professor said, relieved that the connection clicked into place. "I did enjoy our interview. I am curious, do you know when our episode is coming out? I've been bragging to all my friends about my appearance on your show and I must say, they are extremely excited to hear my thoughts on—"

"Actually, Professor," John interrupted, an apologetic smile on his face, "Dr. Choi and I are here to discuss something we touched on in our episode."

"Please," the professor said. He stood and began busying himself with making another cup of tea. "Whatever I can do to assist."

"In our episode, you described a curse—"

"Hex," he corrected over his shoulder. "There is a difference, my dear boy."

"Of course," John agreed, nodding. "This hex you described sounds an awful lot like what a patient of Dr. Apsara is currently going through."

The professor looked back at the two of them, feeling a shock of pity and dismay. "It was like one of the hexes we discussed? Which one?"

"I recall you mentioning a hex that involved slashing wounds that repeatedly appeared on a person's body only to heal and reform again moments later."

"You're talking about the 'Death by a Thousand Cuts,'" the professor said, twisting the tea bag on a spoon over the hot water. "Yes, I'm almost certain that's what you must be referring to."

"What can you tell us?" the woman said, her lilting voice eager.

"Not much more than the name I'm afraid. As I've gotten older, I've found my brain can only store so much information," he said, tapping the side of his temple. "A better answer awaits us in the stacks."

He set down his fresh cup of tea and edged past his two visitors, retreating into the library, lost in thought as he accessed that part of the brain that allowed him to pinpoint exactly where the information was.

His guests followed him through the stacks until he stopped at a door at the rear of the building. He lifted the cover to a security pin pad and typed in a four-digit code.

The LED light over the lock turned green and an audible *click* sounded through the library.

"Follow me," he said. He handed them each a pair of white gloves he had retrieved from inside the clean room. "If you wouldn't mind putting these on?"

They complied and followed him into the cleanroom where some of the oldest and most valuable books in the world were stored. The university library boasted a wide variety of texts both old and new, but he had always loved this section a little more than the rest. He couldn't help thinking about all the history contained in the walls around him. Some of the books stored here had a longer history than many countries. These volumes were written by humans who lived generations ago, but their legacy lived on inside a climate-controlled vault in Southern California.

He walked to the end of the cleanroom where he began rotating a large dial sitting on the side of the wall. As he moved the dial, the wall opposite them separated into large stacks of books on shelves, a small fissure appearing between each bookcase. Once the gap was large enough for the professor to enter, he did, pulling a short stepstool behind him.

He moved through the stacks, searching for the book he was seeking. There were so many, but this one was special. When he had checked it out earlier that day, the library records indicated it hadn't been touched since the Knickerbocker estate donated the item more than thirty years ago.

Finally, he spotted the spine of the ancient book he was looking for and took it off the shelf gingerly.

"Ahh, here we are," the professor said, presenting the book to the pair in front of him. *"The Omnichron."*

The professor gently placed the book on the display table, opening it carefully.

Dr. Choi leaned down and began examining the pages. "Annotated and written by authors unknown."

John looked at him in surprise. "Is that common?"

The professor shrugged. "It's not as if authors had agents in ancient times."

He began paging through the notes he'd taken about the book, searching for the section that described hexes.

"Describe the hex to me again?" he said absentmindedly as he paged through the book in front of him.

Apsara began reciting everything she's seen on her patient. He absorbed her words while remaining focused on the manuscript in front of him.

"Ah hah," he said, pausing at a page with an illustration. "Does this look familiar?"

He showed them the illustration, and they gasped. By their reaction, the picture had nailed it.

"So that's your curse, huh?" he asked, reading the text. "If what I'm seeing here is correct, it is certainly a nasty one."

"What's it say?" John asked.

"According to the text, the Death of a Thousand Cuts was cast by warlocks who desired to make their enemy suffer a long, painful death," the professor said.

"Anything about a cure?" Dr. Choi asked, her voice sounding hopeful.

"In fact, there is," he said, perusing the manuscript. "It's ingredients common to the day. I don't believe you would have any trouble finding what you need, so I believe it's more than possible to make a modern equivalent."

He translated the ingredients, writing them down on a piece of notebook paper John gave him.

"I hope this is something you can use," he said, looking at them both. "Even if it's not, it's always nice to have an excuse to get out of my office."

"Thank you, Professor," John said, clasping his hand. "I'll have to get you on the show again soon to talk about your work here. This was a fascinating trip into the past."

The professor smiled and drew inward for a moment, accepting the compliment with a bright red face. "I did enjoy my time on the radio."

"Podcast," John corrected.

The professor nodded as Dr. Choi stepped forward to give him a hug. He was surprised by the gesture but went along with it anyway.

"Thank you," she said.

"Of course, my dear lady," he replied. "If you are set on doing some chemistry work with that list, I do hope you'll let me know how it all turns out."

"We will," John said.

Apsara nodded politely in his direction, and they turned to leave. He watched them go and set his gaze back on *The Omnichron*, wondering exactly what it was he had just given them.

CHAPTER FOURTEEN

JOHN AND APSARA DROVE back toward the hospital while Apsara sat there re-reading the list of ingredients.

"He wasn't kidding about these ingredients," she said looking down at the list.

"Eye of newt and all that stuff?"

"You know, I think you could find most of this at a decent grocery store," she said looking at the list. "It's mostly basic roots, spices, and other odds and ends."

She examined the rest of the note and raised an eyebrow. "This part, however, is a bit more surprising."

"What is it?" John asked.

"An incantation," she said. She began feeling out the words, trying to see if she could master what it was supposed to say. The language was strange, awkward to her tongue, and unlike anything she had seen before. It wasn't Latin, or any other language she recognized. It was almost alien in its pronunciations. The professor had provided a translation of the words, but she felt silly after she read them.

"Why don't I drop you off at the hospital while I go on a grocery run?" John offered.

"Agreed."

When they reached the hospital, she got out of the vehicle while John went to pick up their ingredients. As she looked around the hospital grounds, she was relieved to see her new reporter friend had kept his word. The story about Knickerbocker's grandson hadn't made it to the local news channels yet.

The hospital was busy enough that she was able to slip in without being noticed or accosted by a nurse needing a signature or consult. She always loved to help whenever or wherever she could, but her patient needed her, and she needed to concentrate.

Arriving in her lab, she looked over the instructions and set up a variety of beakers she would need to create her concoction. According to the translated recipe the professor had given them, once they combined the ingredients, she would be left with a poultice that was supposed to heal the wounds and prevent them from reforming.

Around forty-five minutes later John arrived at her office, slightly out of breath and loaded down with bags.

"The only thing I didn't find was virgin soil," he said as he organized the groceries. "But I got us some potting soil, which I'm hoping will do the trick."

"I think that's about as virgin as it gets in the middle of L.A.," she said, looking at the bags he'd set on her desk.

"What else do you need?" John was rolling his sleeves up.

"To get to work," she said.

He chuckled. "I get it. Lone wolf and all that. But going by that slip of paper the professor gave us, I bet you need a lab assistant."

"I have an entire staff of fully trained doctors and nurses at my disposal," she said, bemused. "If I needed help, don't you think I would have called one of them in here?"

John cleared his throat, looking abashed.

"Still," she said. "Your inanimate object story helped us out once. Maybe I can yell at you while I'm working to help me get this thing right."

He perked up and zipped his lips, mimicking throwing away the key. "You won't even know I'm here."

She sighed. "You just spoke. I know you're here."

"Right, sorry." He sat down on the couch and took out his phone.

She turned back to the ingredients in front of her and got to work.

CHAPTER FIFTEEN

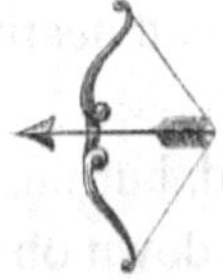

ELLIE CLOSED THE BOOK in front of her and leaned back, stretching her arms out and trying to shake off the aches and pains that accompanied a marathon study session. Her stomach rumbled. She grimaced. It was already midafternoon and all she'd eaten so far today was a stale bagel while on her way to the library earlier this morning.

She opened her backpack and removed the lunch she'd prepped and packed, looking at the Tupperware container with trepidation. She'd prepped the chicken and rice dish three days ago to rid her life of all distractions for the study marathon, but the meat was looking grey and the rice unappetizing.

Still, she needed to eat. She stood and made her way back to Professor McKaig's office where he kept a microwave and small refrigerator. Food and drink were discouraged in the library, but the staff ignored offenders so long as you cleaned up after yourself and weren't obnoxious.

She opened the microwave door and placed her meal inside. She didn't think the professor would mind if she used it, but ideally, she wanted to get in and out of his office before he even knew she was there to avoid any potential embarrassment.

She closed her eyes and began to meditate, trying to bring some balance back so she could better focus on the material she still had to study. She always found organizing her thoughts like this made her a better archer and the skill had translated nicely to studying.

The microwave signaled it had finished heating up her food, and she opened her eyes, feeling refreshed and hungry. As she closed the microwave door after retrieving the food, she turned to leave the office and nearly ran into a man who had appeared at the door.

She recovered her food, burning her hand on the heated glass container, and set it down on the professor's desk. She looked up at the man now standing at the doorway, looking chagrined.

"Sorry about that," he said, motioning to the small cart filled with snacks and goodies. "I didn't mean to startle you. I'm just here to restock the professor's fridge."

"Sorry?" she managed after a moment, her stomach rumbling at the sight of the snacks and sandwiches on the cart. Her unappetizing lunch hadn't been improved by the microwave. She'd kill for a banana nut muffin right about now.

"The professor pays to keep his office stocked with goodies," he said, wheeling a cart into the office. He moved past her and opened the small refrigerator the professor kept on the counter of his office. "And meal-preppers like you are gonna put me out of business."

"That's a lot of snacks for one guy," she said, eyeing the cart in front of them.

He chuckled and closed the door, turning back to her.

"I've got a few other customers," he said. "I'm supposed to stock the office kitchens and vending machines around campus, but the professor is a special case according to my notes here."

"Must be nice," she said. "All I've got today is chicken and rice."

"Hey, it smells great," he said. "Besides, I get the feeling that the professor doesn't have anyone to make him a home-cooked meal which is why he has to rely on guys like me."

"Ellie," she said, extending her hand.

"Mike," he said, taking her hand. His smile was warm, and she felt herself slightly flush. "Are you a professor? What do you—"

"Oh no," she said, interrupting. "I'm a student. I've been studying up on things before finals next week."

"Tough material?" he asked.

She shrugged. "It wouldn't be worth it if it was easy."

"Nothing ever is," he said. He got behind his cart and began wheeling it out of the office. "Looks like the good professor is all stocked up now. Maybe I'll see you around next time he needs a refill?"

"Maybe," she replied, feeling her stomach churn. She didn't have the heart to tell him that by then, exams would be finished, and she wouldn't need a reason to come up to the library.

Or would she?

He squeezed by her, pulling the cart along with him. His body came within inches of her own, so close she felt the warmth of his skin. There was an undeniable attraction there. But, if she was honest with herself, between exams, work, and her personal life at home, she didn't have time to start anything new—even if he was incredibly cute and had a nice body.

She exhaled softly after he left and picked up the cooling chicken from the professor's desk. She examined it and sighed, taking it back to the desk where she'd left her things, feeling a lot less enthusiastic about her rubber chicken and stale rice.

CHAPTER SIXTEEN

Daniel Armstrong and the rest of the Triumvirate pulled up to a dilapidated pawn shop located in the notorious Skid Row section of downtown Los Angeles. He wanted answers about their mysterious employer and the only person who might have any was located behind three inches of bulletproof glass.

"Watch the car," he said to Cody. "Letty, you're with me."

They approached the pawn shop, and he pressed a button. A muffled buzz sounded behind the closed door. Daniel looked up at the camera installed in the corner of the doorway.

"Open the door, Larry," Daniel said.

A loud click sounded, and he opened the steel door, allowing Letty to step inside first. He took one last look at the street where Cody was standing guard and entered the dank, stuffy room.

The smell of dust and stale air greeted him as they approached the counter where an enormous four-hundred-pound man was sitting on a stool, eyeing them up and down.

"Larry," Daniel said in a cheerful tone. "You fucked us over."

He took two steps forward and slammed a glowing orange fist through the bulletproof glass, shattering the barrier between him and the obese man, who cried out in shock.

Daniel hopped through the new hole he'd created and pushed Larry to the ground, grinding his foot on the man's neck.

"You have some explaining to do," he said. "You need to tell me who the hell hired my team."

Larry gurgled, and he couldn't understand the man through his sobs. Daniel removed his boot from the man's neck and crouched down.

"You need to tell me what I want to know, unless you want to find yourself in a lot of pain," he said. His eyes flashed orange. "Who hired us?"

"They . . . They came through the dark web," Larry sputtered. "I have no idea. No connection. You weren't supposed to know who hired you."

"How do we find him?" Daniel stood, threatening to mash the man's throat again.

"You don't," Larry sobbed. "You have to wait for him to come to you."

"The problem there," Daniel said in a soothing tone, "is that I am not a very patient man. Ask Letty."

He stood and nodded to her. She hopped over the counter and smiled maliciously at the crying man.

She waved a hand. The man flew up from the ground, thrown clear across the room where he slammed into the opposite wall with a dull thud that rocked the old building. A blue-green wave of energy flowed between her hand and the pawnbroker's chest, holding the four-hundred-pound man in midair.

"Larry, tell me what I want to know," Daniel said, sounding bored. "Otherwise, I'm going to let her play with your sword collection there."

The proprietor screamed. Daniel sighed. He turned and headed into the back office where a surprisingly modern computer sat on the desk.

"Larry, what's the password?" he called out. No answer. Then another thud.

"Strawberry123, tilde," Letty called out.

"A what?" Daniel looked up, confused. "Tilty?"

"A tilde. Tilde. You know, that squiggly looking thing next to the one button on the keyboard."

"Thank you." He typed the password into the man's computer. The screen dimmed for a moment as it brought up the desktop. He began going through the man's files, unsurprised by what he found. Larry wasn't just hiring out mercenaries for heists, he also had his fingers in various other pies, including a sex-trafficking operation, laundering money, and drugs.

"Larry, you are a very, very bad boy," Daniel called out.

After a few minutes of searching through the man's computer, he found what he was looking for. He wrote a message to their so-called employer and sat back, tapping his fingers.

In the distance, he could hear Letty having fun with Larry, torturing the man for his transgressions against their team.

A chime sounded, and he was pleased to see their employer had immediately gotten back to them. He read the message, his eyes narrowing as he finished.

He got up from the computer and focused his will on the machine. A burst of energy flew from his fist, setting the machine on fire.

He emerged from the back office to see a desiccated body where Larry had been only a few moments before. The once four-hundred-pound man was shrunken down, his mummified corpse a dry, dehydrated husk. He raised an eyebrow at Letty who shrugged.

"Let's go," he said. "I found our employer and he agreed to meet with us. But only if we recover something else for him."

"Another job?" she asked. "Are we going to get paid for this one?"

He held up his smartphone, which displayed their offshore bank account balance. Thirty million dollars—the price of the amulet.

"He paid us our fee, and says he'll double it for another item," he said. "Something called the 'Omnichron.' And we won't even have to work that hard to get it."

"I don't like it," she replied. "Might be a trap?"

"Could be," Daniel shrugged. "But then again, the man paid us in advance, and we have a major advantage against anyone who might try to stop us."

He held up his fist, which glowed orange. Letty grinned. They exited the shop as the fire Daniel set in the back office spread, burning the evidence of their presence there.

CHAPTER SEVENTEEN

SEVERAL HOURS PASSED AS Apsara meticulously prepared the poultice from the recipe they had copied from *The Omnichron*. After following the directions to the letter, she had ended up with a fine grey paste that she suspected functioned as a coagulating agent.

The only problem was the voice. That voice in the back of her head screaming about how unethical this all was and how it went against every ounce of training and schooling she had ever received.

But her brain could not overcome the gut feeling she had that everything she was doing was going to work. There was no scientific explanation for it. But all the anxiety and worry she had felt about this case melted away once she began working on this poultice. There was a strange sense of satisfaction and rightness to what she was doing.

It was only a gut feeling. There was no evidence this treatment would work, but she had thrown everything modern medicine knew about wounds like these at the case, and they had all failed. Every treatment, every medication, salve, and anti-viral, all of it had been useless. Her patient's wounds continued to reappear and heal, slowly bleeding him to death faster than they could replace his blood. And unless they found something that worked, the patient was going to die in a matter of hours.

Which explained why she was going along with this insane scheme. It didn't matter if it was a longshot—this poultice she had created represented hope. And sometimes, that's all a person needed.

She re-examined the bowl filled with the fine grey paste in front of her, then glanced one more time over the notes she had taken.

She looked back at the potion and shook her head. Some of her staff were advocating some incredibly risky treatments. All she was doing was pouring what amounted to a little turmeric mixed with beet root onto the patient. What harm could that do?

John entered the room. She glanced over at the reporter and back down at the dish in front of her.

"First batch is ready," she held the glass filled with the potion. She had done everything the note had told her to do, except the last step.

John tilted his head. "Did you recite the incantation?"

"It's bad enough you have me trying this homeopathic bullshit, you think me muttering a few words will help?" she snapped, glaring at him.

He shrugged. "We did get the recipe from something called *The Omnichron* after all."

She sighed, put on her white coat, and picked up the bowl. "We don't have time for this."

John followed her down the hallway and to the elevator where she pressed a button to summon the lift. She stood there, staring straight forward, not speaking while John eyed her.

"Stop it," she said.

"I didn't say a word," he protested. "It's just that the recipe specifically said—"

"Uh huh," she interrupted. The door to the elevator opened with a chime, and they stepped on. She pressed the button for the fourth floor and the doors shut.

"Are we putting on the biohazard suits?" he asked.

"Transmission is unlikely through touch or air," she said. She handed him a pair of latex gloves and an N95 mask. "Of course, that doesn't mean we aren't wearing some protection. Don't touch him. Leave that to me and my staff."

The elevator chimed, announcing their arrival. She stepped out, nodding to the nurse who handed her a chart.

Apsara read the chart and grimaced. By the looks of the boy's vitals, they didn't have much time left. They were continually transfusing new units of blood to replace the blood he was losing, but the constant stress his body was under was taking a toll. The wounds now appeared to grow after they healed, and his rate of blood loss was increasing.

She shuddered, trying not to think about it and entered her patient's room. John stood behind her, watching from the doorway, holding his hand to his mouth.

She stared at the mixture in the bowl in front of her and stepped forward, reaching for a cotton swab. She dipped the swab into the poultice and began spreading it across her patient's body.

The boy didn't move, the slashing wounds still forming on his skin, bleeding, and healing. She examined the wound, feeling like a fool that she had wasted the last few hours on this idiotic idea.

The machine monitoring the fourteen-year-old issued several alarming beeps as the boy's heart rate dropped.

"Code Blue!" she called. "He's crashing!"

Members of her staff rushed in and began working on the patient, trying to save his life. She stepped aside, watching them work their magic, while she stood there stupidly holding the bowl with the poultice. She turned, looking at John, feeling the failure well up inside.

He held out the notes she'd taken from the library. "You have to say the incantation. It's the only way."

She refused to acknowledge him for a moment, then reached for the note he offered. He released it and she unfolded the paper, shaking her head at the strange language scrawled out in front of her.

"I feel like an idiot," she muttered.

"We either believe *The Omnichron* knew what it was talking about and maybe the boy dies, or maybe he survives because you said a few silly words." John watched with an earnest expression on his face. "The alternative is allowing your patient to die while we stand here, never knowing if that potion works."

She sighed and gazed at the notes the professor had provided them.

"It's a poultice," she corrected. She cleared her throat and began waving her hand over the bowl as instructed by the professor's notes.

"Be gone now and hear my verse, the time is now to break this curse. May it be gone, and this hex undone." Apsara felt like a fool, but John was right, she'd come this far, what was a little more humiliation?

She closed her eyes and repeated the words seven times as instructed. All her life, she had trained to be a scientist. It had been a long time since she'd taken something on faith.

John tapped her arm. She slowly opened her eyes, looking down at the concoction she had whipped up in her lab.

It was glowing.

"Bioluminescence?" John whispered, looking down at the poultice. "Some kind of bacteria activated?"

"No," she said, as she struggled to come up with scientific explanation for what they were seeing. "There's nothing in here that would do anything like that."

"Then I'd say it's worth trying again, don't you?" John asked, a smile tugging at the edge of his lips.

She looked over at the dying boy, and stepped forward, elbowing her way between two nurses who were still working to stabilize the young man in front of them.

Apsara withdrew the cotton swab again and rubbed it over one wound that had erupted across the boy's neck.

To her amazement, the moment she touched the wound with the swab, the bleeding stopped and the skin sealed shut.

Her eyes widened. Eagerly, she spread the rest of the poultice around the boy's face, arms, and hands. Her staff noticed what she was doing and moved aside, seeing the immediate results.

"What the hell is that?" one of the nurses demanded.

"An experimental drug," Apsara said. "Keep him stable until I can treat his whole body with this stuff."

The nurse paused, as if she couldn't quite believe what she was seeing in front of her. Apsara turned, glaring at the nurse. "*Now*, if you don't mind."

"Yes, Doctor," she answered.

Finally, after a half hour of swabbing every nook and cranny on her poor patient, the wounds ceased appearing and the boy rested comfortably for the first time all day.

"Congratulations, Doctor," the nurse said quietly. "It will be some time before he fully recovers, but his vitals are stable and improving by the minute."

She looked up to see John watching her, a smile on his face. She smiled back, and despite her success, she felt unsettled by what she had just done—and not due to any scientific or ethical principles. Something about the words she'd uttered had activated the poultice's magical properties.

And she was determined to find out what that meant.

CHAPTER EIGHTEEN

JOHN WATCHED THE DOCTORS, nurses, and staff celebrate the fact they had just saved a young man's life. Even if they didn't quite understand how it had happened, the boy was going to be okay.

The phone in his pocket buzzed. A message from his boss. He was out of time. Another station had the story about the Knickerbocker boy and was working to confirm the details.

John slipped out through a side door and headed for the exit, intending to go to his car and file the story he had promised his boss twelve hours ago. Now that the Knickerbocker's grandson was safe and was likely to fully recover, he considered his end of the bargain with the hospital complete.

Apsara spotted him and followed him into the hallway, calling after him. "Hey! You can't just bail after what we did here tonight."

He turned, holding out his phone, pointing at it.

"I've got a story to file," he said. "Now that we know your patient is gonna be all right, I've got work to do, presuming I still have a job at this point."

"You're not going to report the . . ." Apsara struggled, and he could tell she was trying to avoid the word "magic."

"The magic potion that cured the Little Prince of Los Angeles?" he asked, a wry grin on his face. He shook his head. "That's a story I only intend to tell when I learn more about what we saw and why those specific words managed to turn that spice rack of ours into a miracle cure."

"You can't tell anyone what we did here tonight," she insisted. "It would ruin my career."

"You don't have to worry about that," he said. "I'm fairly sure me trying to tell that story would ruin my career too. I'll protect your information in my report the best I can."

"The best you can?" Apsara's face reddened, and he could tell she was about to lay into him. He didn't have time for that.

Instead, John walked away leaving her spluttering incomprehensible threats at him. On one level, he felt bad, but this wasn't personal. This was going to be his big moment and he intended to make it count.

Retreating to his car, he set up his laptop inside the SUV workspace he had cultivated over the years and began working on his story. It would include everything he knew about Knickerbocker's murder, which, admittedly, wasn't much and everything he knew about the boy's injuries. He made Apsara and the hospital look like geniuses, referring to the poultice only as an unconventional treatment that saved the boy's life.

He then grabbed his phone where he spoke with a few sources trying to reconstruct Alan Knickerbocker's final twenty-four hours. The stories were secondhand, but for a powerful man like Knickerbocker, his movements, meetings, and interactions with other people were well-documented by multiple sources. After spending hours on the phone, he felt confident that the story he was about to file would be the most accurate and compelling thing out there on the murder.

From what he had put together so far, he believed that Alan Knickerbocker had returned home with his grandson after picking him up from lacrosse practice. Their house cleaner finished for the day at around five p.m. and returned home to her apartment located on the fortieth floor. Surveillance cameras and security logs didn't show anyone else had entered Knickerbocker's penthouse suite until the boy pressed the panic button, summoning police.

What he hadn't been able to confirm was any mention of magic or otherwise strange occurrences. Knickerbocker was known to be an extensive collector of antiquities and old-world artifacts, but the billionaire's friends chalked it up to an eccentric man's yearning to collect something just because he could afford it and others couldn't.

He thought about the amulet he had taken from the boy's possessions and withdrew it from his jacket pocket. He had forgotten all about it in the excitement of developing a cure for the boy. Now as he held it, he thought of Knickerbocker's penchant for collecting antiques, and the strange orange flash that occurred when he had discovered the item in the hospital's storage closet.

He eyed the amulet, holding it in front of his face, frowning. What if the amulet was imbued with a mystical power that allowed its owner to cast magic spells? Apsara had been near him when he said the incantation from *The Omnichron*. Perhaps that's how it worked? But if that were true then—

A tapping at the window startled him. He looked up to see Apsara standing there, waiting patiently. He grimaced and rolled down the window.

"You know it's really bad for the environment running your engine like this," she said. "And near a hospital of all places."

"I told you I had work to do," he said.

"Take a break." She moved around to the passenger's side of the car and opened the door, hopping in. "You and I aren't done yet."

"Where exactly are we going?" he asked, bemused.

"I've decided I will not allow you to discredit my career and everything I've worked for after we saved my patient's life." Her dark eyes bored into his. "We're going back to the library to meet with the professor. He has some explaining to do."

He considered her proposal and shrugged. She was right. If anyone knew what the hell was going on, the egghead would. He put the car in gear and angled it out of the parking garage. The sun was setting. If they had any hopes of catching Professor McKaig before he left for the day, they needed to get on the road.

CHAPTER NINETEEN

HIS FIRST DAY OF stocking the various vending machines and cafeterias scattered around the Hoover University campus had Mike Madsen feeling good. His business earned a percentage of every item sold and so far, this looked like it would be an incredibly profitable route for him. He suspected that had to do with all the stressed-out college kids needing a large amount of comfort food during finals.

Despite the long day, he found himself loitering in the parking lot outside the research library. His daughter was already asleep. He'd Facetimed her during his last few hours at work while his mother got her ready for bed. He knew she wouldn't mind watching her for the night.

He wanted to do something but was still working up the courage to go through with it. The woman he'd met at the library earlier today had stirred something inside him he hadn't felt since his wife died.

Ellie was far more than just a pretty face—he had noticed the books she was holding during their conversation and figured she had to be a smart cookie to tackle that kind of material.

Still, he wasn't sure if he was ready to ask anyone out. After all, it was fair to say he was an emotional mess after his wife was killed in action five years ago. He and his daughter had been regularly attending therapy sessions—which had been a tremendous help—but, raising a daughter on his own didn't allow him time for dating and he was terribly out of practice.

Plus, if he was being honest with himself, the idea of asking anyone out terrified him. Strange for a man who once led a squad against enemy combatants in Afghanistan.

But despite his best efforts, he hadn't been able to get her face out of his head all day. That had to mean something. And if he was ever going to move forward with his life, then he needed to take the first steps—as his therapist often reminded him.

For a moment, he fantasized how their conversation would go—he'd go back upstairs where he'd met her, make an excuse about forgetting a special treat the professor liked. She would see right through him of course. They'd exchange numbers and text at all hours of the night. They'd date, fall in love. He would introduce her to his daughter, and they would be crazy about each other—

He snapped himself out of the reverie. His therapist had also warned him about putting too much stock in fantasies. Thinking like that and planning out an entire future before he even knew her last name wasn't healthy.

He sighed and made his decision. Tonight, was not the night, but he made a deal with the universe that if he ever ran into her again, he'd shoot his shot.

Mike put the keys back in the ignition and was about to start the car when he spotted three shadowy figures race across the lawn and into the library.

Something seemed ominous about their behavior. He shook his head, wondering if the long day and exhaustion were finally catching up to him. It was probably nothing. Drunken frat boys at the end of the semester playing dumb tricks that would get them arrested if campus police spotted them.

He squinted and watched the three figures pause briefly underneath a lamp located outside the library's exterior. Two men and one woman, all dressed in black. They quietly conferred a few dozen feet away from the entrance. This seemed less and less like a frat-boy prank.

His heart dropped when he saw the larger man pull out a handgun and check the chamber and clip. Whoever these three were, they were up to no good.

He scrambled for his phone and dialed 911, waiting anxiously as the line connected.

"Nine one one, what's your emergency?" an authoritative voice asked.

"Hi, I'm outside the Hoover research library, and I just saw three people with guns loitering outside the entrance," he felt the old instincts kick in as he described the scene to the operator. "It looks like most everyone is gone, but I don't like the looks of these three."

"Okay, can you describe them for me, sir?" the voice on the line asked.

"Two men, one woman, all dressed in black," he said. "One man is about six foot seven, large scar on his face. Big, big guy."

"Are they white? Black?" she asked.

"I can't tell from here," he said. "Maybe white or Hispanic?"

He saw the three turn to enter the library, with the shorter man pausing and surveying the parking lot before he also disappeared inside.

"They just went into the library," he said, feeling the panic rise. "You gotta get someone here quick."

"We're working on it, sir," the operator said, her voice trying to soothe him. "Remain calm and wait for police. Campus security should be there within moments."

"But what if they open fire before the cops get here?" Mike asked. His gut was telling him something unbelievably bad was about to happen. He wouldn't be able to forgive himself if anyone were hurt. Including Ellie.

"I'm gonna try to get a better look at what they're doing," he told the operator. "Standby."

"Sir!" the operator cried out. "Please don't—"

He ignored the voice squeaking from the receiver and lowered the volume. He got out of his car and kept a low profile as he ran across the grass to the library's entrance.

Lights flashed in the parking lot, and he saw an SUV enter. He glanced back at the entrance and kept moving, entering the building.

He stepped inside the cavernous, brightly lit lobby looking for the trio that had entered only moments before. He heard footsteps running upstairs. He headed for the stairwell on the opposite end of the lobby.

He opened the door cautiously, not wanting to give away his position to the trio, who were still making their way up to the top floor. He steeled himself and jogged up the stairs, trying to do so as quietly as possible. It had been a long time since he had been in the field, and he wasn't exactly in the best shape. By the time he reached the top of the stairs, he was out of breath and needed a moment to recover.

Still breathing heavily, he opened the door to the library's top floor and entered. That's when he realized what section they were in and his eyes widened, immediately thinking of Ellie. If she were still in the library's annex, those three would be heading right for her.

He peered around the library cart and saw the trio making their way through the stacks of books. Seeing them provoked a deep, visceral sense of dread that he didn't quite understand.

He didn't feel like this very often, but when he did, he had learned to trust his gut.

He tailed the trio through the bookshelves, making sure to keep his distance. He reached the edge of a balcony that looked down on the interior of the library. Below, he heard the library's doors open and two people enter, their footsteps echoing across the lobby. Mike paused, looking over the edge to see if it was the police.

Instead, it was a man and a woman he didn't recognize—and they weren't cops. One of them, a woman in her mid-thirties, was wearing a sensible blouse and form fitting leather jacket, while the man, who appeared to be in his mid-forties, was wearing a long London Fog jacket, and a brown felt fedora.

He debated whether to wait for them and warn the couple that tonight was an inconvenient time to study for finals or stay on course. He needed to get to Ellie in time to warn her about the armed men and woman who had entered the library. There wasn't time do both.

Weaving his way through the stacks, he made it back to where she had been set up earlier in the day. She was curled up in the corner, the desk light shining on her face while she dozed. He looked at her, unsure now if he had been paranoid and those three were a product of his imagination.

The doors to the floor opened. Three people entered and he could hear them quietly talking amongst themselves. It was hard to make out what they were saying, but his gut told him he didn't want to be around the library much longer.

He shook Ellie gently by the shoulder, trying to wake her. "Ellie? Hey, it's Mike."

She came around and looked up at him in sleepy confusion. "Mike?"

She drew back from him, pulling her sweater around her body and looking at him with a curious smile. "I was hoping you'd come back."

She was hoping he'd come back? He'd hardly dared hope. But more pressing issues needed to be resolved before he could pursue that further.

"Yeah, say, listen," he fumbled, unsure how to tell her a trio of armed people were skulking around the library, possibly plotting to kill them. "How about we get out of here and get something to eat?"

"I'm starving." She grinned and sat up, closing the book in front of her. "There's a great taco shop not too far—"

Two sets of footsteps came toward them. Mike turned, holding an arm out as if to protect Ellie from the threat he had seen coming up the stairs.

Instead, it was the couple he'd spotted coming into the library. The tall gentleman wearing a brown fedora grinned at them and threw a quick wave.

"Howdy, folks. We're looking for Professor McKaig. He still around?" The goofy smile on his face widened when he spotted Ellie sitting behind Mike. "Sorry to interrupt."

"You're not interrupting," Ellie said, standing and extending a hand to him. "I'm Ellie, this is Mike."

"John," he said, shaking their hand. He indicated the woman standing next to him. "This is Dr. Apsara Choi."

Mike reluctantly took the man's hand, who gave him a strong handshake. He turned to the woman next to John and nodded his hello, which she returned with a tilt of her head.

"Long night of studying ahead of you two?" John asked, looking at them both.

"Finals on Monday," Ellie said, pointing to the books on the desk. "But we were about to step out for a bite to eat."

"Ah, well, don't let us keep you," John said. "But if you could point us in the direction of the professor? We already checked his office."

"If he's not there and hasn't gone home, then he's in the vault," Ellie said, pointing to the rear of the library.

"That's where he kept it," Dr. Choi said, turning to John.

Mike watched John's face light up with interest and wondered what that was all about.

"Let me see . . . Was the vault . . .If you wouldn't mind pointing us in the direction of the vault, we'll try there next." John's cheer was beginning to wear on Mike's nerves for some reason.

"It's just past the medieval history section and against the other corner," Ellie said. She got up and stood closer to John than Mike thought was necessary. "Go down to the right and you can't miss it. There are signs."

"Thanks," John said, returning her smile with one of his own. "I recognize you, right? You were at the 2024 Olympics in France. Archery if I'm not mistaken."

"Gold medalist," she said, her face turning a bright red. "Decided to go back to school after it was all said and done."

"Glad to meet you," he said, shaking her hand once again. "Dr. Choi, I think we'd better get to the vault if we want to catch McKaig and ask him just what the hell—"

Suddenly, there was a crash, and the four of them glanced toward the other side of the room. Mike stepped forward, his body tense, ready for anything.

"What was that?" Dr. Choi asked, her voice a whisper.

"Nothing good," Mike answered, feeling his body tense. He turned back to the group, feeling his battle confidence return. "I think there's—"

Dr. Choi screamed. He whirled around to see the three people he'd spotted in the parking lot approach the four of them. The trio loomed over them, the two men holding their weapons casually pointed at the group. The woman watched them, her eyes constantly flicking back and forth between John and himself.

"Lost?" Ellie asked. She sounded more fascinated than scared.

"This is a public library, pal," John said. "Guns aren't allowed."

The shorter man smiled, held up a hand, then put away his gun. That only served to make Mike even more nervous.

"What do you want?" he asked.

"We're here to check out a book," the man in black replied, a sinister smile plastered across his face.

"Funny, you all don't strike me as the reading type," John snorted. Mike found himself trying to stifle a laugh.

"Have you heard of *The Omnichron*?" the man continued, ignoring John's insult.

Mike saw John flinch at the name and knew something was up.

"Nope," John said. "Never heard of it."

The shorter man stepped forward, his eyes narrowing. "A lie. So easily told."

John winced but didn't back down from the man trying to intimidate him. Mike found himself beginning to respect the man standing next to him.

"Sorry, bud," John said, his voice gaining steam. "I'm more of a Stephen King kind of guy. I'm just here to pick up my friends. So, if you'll excuse us . . ."

It was the expression on the man's face that made Mike even more nervous. He'd seen it before on dozens of men just like him. He was suddenly very certain that they wouldn't leave the library alive unless they were able to escape these three.

Mike examined the shorter man's two companions. The one on the right was an attractive olive-skinned woman whose thick, jet-black hair and trim body belied the danger behind her cool grey eyes. He'd seen that brand of crazy before and wanted no part of it. In addition to the .45 in her hand, a short dagger attached to her belt.

The man on the left stood a foot taller than everyone else in the room. Up close, Mike could tell his initial estimate of the man's height at six foot seven was woefully inadequate. The man was closer to seven feet tall and looked like he ate barbells for breakfast. The man's juiced-up muscles were comically large—so large they threatened to rip through his massive black T-shirt. Mike knew that if it came to a physical fight, they would be hopelessly outclassed.

"You three make quite the cast of characters," Mike said, looking the three of them over. "Is this a live-action roleplay kind of thing? Or do you seriously dress like this all the time?"

"They look like Rambo went Goth," John said, glancing at Mike, who had to hold in another laugh.

The leader of the three stepped forward. Mike readied himself to launch at the leader when he heard the woman behind him speak.

"You won't find what you're looking for here," Dr. Choi said. "The campus bookstore should have any book you might need for your class, but you should have bought one earlier in the semester. They might be out."

The leader grunted in frustration. "Enough! Where is the rare books vault?"

Mike felt his body tense. He recognized that tone of voice. He'd heard it from men who believed they held the advantage and considering that the three people in front of them were packing some serious hardware, he didn't think the man was wrong.

"How should we know?" Dr. Choi asked.

"You do know. You lie!" the man pressed.

"We're not lying," Dr. Choi said, her voice remaining even. "We're just meeting our friends and going to dinner. What would we possibly know about a rare book vault?"

Mike glanced at the good doctor standing next to John. Her voice communicated a cool detachment from the situation, one he imagined she had learned over years of stressful situations at the hospital.

"You asked us a question, and we answered," Ellie piped up from behind Mike. "Don't get mad at us just 'cause you don't like what we have to say."

Mike suppressed a grin at her voice. He was beginning to take a real liking to this group of folks. They had all shown a remarkable amount of confidence against a mysterious enemy and that took guts.

The leader eyed them all for a moment and then nodded. "If you're sure then."

The woman standing next to him withdrew a dagger, a crystal embedded at the top, while the giant standing next to her took out a large hammer strapped to his back. Mike's eyes went wide, and the four of them backed away from the armed threat currently menacing them.

"Hey, come on now," Mike said, his throat going dry. His body tensed, and he waited for the first blow to fall. "We don't need to get violent."

"Oh, you won't get violent," the woman standing behind the leader said. "But we will."

Everything seemed to move in slow-motion, much like his previous experiences with combat. The trio attacked. Mike pushed Ellie under the desk while John and Dr. Choi dashed to the side, trying to run away.

The woman standing in front of them flipped her dagger and aimed the crystal at Mike's chest. He heard her utter a word he couldn't quite make out, and a bright flash of energy emitted from the crystal.

The charge flew through the air and struck him in the center of his chest. He fell back, crashing into the library stacks behind him, momentarily stunned and believing he was dead.

He heard Ellie shout as he tried to regain his footing, but he couldn't focus on where she had ended up. All he could see was the woman slowly walking toward him, still holding the dagger in her hand. The orange crystal attached to it glowed.

She raised it and was about to swing her weapon down on his head when one of the large shelves she was next to toppled over. His attacker cried out in protest, falling to the ground as the heavy shelving fell on her.

He looked up gratefully to see John and Dr. Choi grasp at his arms, trying to get him to stand up.

"Is he hurt?" John asked, a worried expression on his face.

Dr. Choi felt his chest where a large burn wound spread across his chest. He sucked in air through his teeth as her soft brown hand began running through his chest hair, looking for the burn. His chest felt like it was on fire and whatever the good doctor found there was not encouraging based on the look she gave John.

At the same time, he spotted Ellie dart out from underneath the desk where he had shoved her and grab the bow that had fallen out of the glass case that knocked over after the shelving fell.

In one practiced motion, Ellie grabbed one of the arrows, nocked it in her bow, and aimed it at the massive man advancing on them. The arrow flew through the stacks and struck the giant in the chest, knocking the giant to his knees. She nocked another arrow and let it loose, nearly taking the smaller man's head off.

Ellie grabbed the quiver that had fallen along with the bow and stepped back, covering their position as John picked Mike up from the ground.

"We need to move." John pointed to the rear of the library. "The vault. We'll be safe there."

Behind them, they could hear the shelves thrown aside as the leader of the trio advanced on their position.

"Move!" Dr. Choi cried out and they did—at least as quickly as they could while carrying a wounded man. Barely able to stay ahead of the rampaging man behind them, they dodged several books that rocketed through the air, with no indication of what was propelling them.

One of the books hit John in the head. He stumbled but picked himself back up with Dr. Choi's help. Mike was beginning to lose consciousness and felt himself fall to his knees, only to raised back to his feet by Ellie and Dr. Choi.

Finally, they reached the rear of the library where the vault was located. John stepped up to the keypad and looked desperately at Dr. Choi and Ellie.

"Either one of you know the code to get in here?" he asked, looking worn out.

"Just go in!" Ellie shouted. "The professor doesn't lock it when he's inside."

Dr. Choi tried the latch. The door opened. Dragging Mike inside, they dropped him once they crossed the threshold and closed the door.

That's when he finally lost consciousness.

CHAPTER TWENTY

ONE OF THE THINGS Professor McKaig enjoyed the most about his work was the fact he had the ability to do much of it while listening to music on his headphones. Over the years, he'd accumulated quite a collection of MP3 players.

His current phone was the latest model that he exclusively used to stream his tunes. With no family and more work than friends, he often wondered why he even paid for the phone service. After all, the Wi-Fi was more than enough for him to answer emails and keep up to date on world events.

Tonight, he had brought his headphones and music inside the vault where he intended to learn more about the Guardians and that strange book he'd discovered. Despite his earlier examination of the book, he felt drawn back to the volume. Any book that purported to teach magic was worth a second glance—especially considering the subject of his research. If the Guardians were charged with rooting out magic in the world, a book called *The Omnichron* should be able shed light or at least provide context about the so-called "magic" they were practicing.

The Omnichron had turned out to be a fascinating read. Not only did it offer dozens of recipes for "potions" that could cure all kinds of illnesses, but it also included a large list of magic spells, runes, and types of magical weapons. There were incantations in languages long dead and beyond the scope of his expertise and strange drawings of mythical beasts that no one had ever seen in modern times.

But it was the section on the Guardians that had him at the library this late. Normally, he'd already be home with a glass of wine watching the unreality of reality TV, but what he had discovered was far more fascinating than his guilty pleasure.

According to *The Omnichron*, the Guardians had existed for decades, defeating magical creatures, killing evil warlocks, and protecting the world. In fact, the book claimed it had been the Guardians themselves who had used an amulet to remove all magic.

It wasn't until he reached the last paragraph of the section describing the amulet that he understood the implications. The Guardians intentionally drained the world of magic in a last-ditch effort to defeat a demon that had been well on its way to taking over the world.

But before he could digest the meaning of the words he was reading; he heard a crash over the music that scored his research.

Removing his earbuds, Professor McKaig made his way to the front of the vault where he found Ellie, the reporter, and the doctor he had met earlier today, dragging a man's body inside.

"Is that . . ." The professor gawked at the bleeding and panting group in shock. "Are you all right? What on earth is going on here? Is that Mr. Madsen? Is he . . .?"

"He's hurt," Dr. Choi said in a businesslike tone.

The group gently lowered Mike to the ground as the doctor opened his shirt to check on the wound that was now bleeding profusely.

"What are you people doing in here?" he was aghast. Then, he saw John was leaning against the door, trying to close it against someone determined to get inside.

"Help me," John shouted.

Professor McKaig was frozen for only a moment, but something in John's voice prompted him to step forward and throw his weight into the steel door to close it against the intruders on the other side.

Finally, the door shut, and the professor spun the lock, securing them inside the vault. He turned his attention back to the doctor, who was taking Mike's shirt off, exposing a large burn the size of a bowling ball on his chest.

"My God." Professor McKaig was still in shock at the disruption of his quiet evening. "What happened? Is there an active shooter?"

"Worse," Ellie said.

That's when he noticed that Ellie was carrying, of all things, the bow and quiver set that was supposed to be safely locked up in a display case. He looked down at his student in shock. "Young lady, you cannot carry weapons on campus, even if you did manage to win a gold medal with one of them."

"She didn't have much of a choice, Professor," John said, pacing in front of the door. "Thanks to our uninvited guests out there."

"Did anyone call the police?" the professor.

"I'm not sure the police can handle what we just saw," Dr. Choi said.

A primal scream sounded from the other side of the vault door. Professor McKaig felt his stomach drop.

"Some kind of escaped animal?" he asked.

"Professor, you know that book you showed us earlier today?" John panted, still out of breath. "Turns out, it's filled with all sorts of magic that actually works, and we think those psychopaths outside are here to claim it for themselves."

"What?" He tried to absorb what this young man was saying. "No, no, it makes no sense. No one kills for a book!"

"Hate to say it, but they've already tried killing us for this one," John said. "And I believe this amulet has something to do with all this."

John reached into his pocket and removed the amulet he'd taken from the Knickerbocker boy's things. Dr. Choi gasped, then her cheeks flamed in anger.

"You son of a bitch," she said. "You stole that from the hospital."

"I borrowed it," he shot back, yanking his hand back from her. John turned back to the professor. "This isn't just any normal jewelry. Is it, Professor?"

The professor reached out for the amulet, his hands shaking. John let the older man take it from him. He examined it carefully, hands trembling. It was just as *The Omnichron* had described it. If everything the book said about it were true, they had a huge problem on their hands.

"It exists," he said in wonder, his voice cracking.

"Professor, that potion recipe you gave us didn't work until Apsara said the magic words," John said. "I think it's because that book of yours is filled with all sorts of magical tips and tricks, and it looks like some very bad people have figured that out too."

The pounding on the door grew louder, sounding as if the monster man had recovered from Ellie's arrow.

"The way I figure it, this amulet is the key and that book of yours is the lock on some very dangerous information," John continued. "And there are three incredibly determined people on the other side of this door looking to get their hands on both. I doubt it's for anything good."

The entire floor shook as the trio outside the vault continued their assault on the door.

The professor looked back at the desk where the book still lay open. He glanced back at the group in front of him, still uncertain about what he was hearing.

"Professor, the people trying to get inside this room shot Mike with some kind of fiery energy blast," Ellie said. "It may not make any sense, but we're not lying to you."

The door to the vault shimmered with a bright orange glow and John cried out, leaping away from the door.

"Hot!" John cried out, shaking his hands.

"Where's the book?" Dr. Choi asked, looking at the professor.

"There, but I can't imagine—"

She didn't even let him finish. Dr. Choi pushed past him and to the desk where he had left the book open. She ran her finger down the text as if looking for something.

"What are you doing?" John cried out. The door in front of them was beginning to glow, heat pouring off it.

"Finding a spell we can use to defend ourselves with," she answered. "If what I did at the hospital means I can manipulate magic, then it's time to get off the bench."

She inhaled deeply and waved her hands in a circle, aiming them at the door as she muttered under her breath.

Professor McKaig had seen a lot of things over the course of his long life. Some had been impressive, others mysterious, and a small number had been world-changing events like the assassination of John F. Kennedy or the 9/11 tragedy.

But he had never witnessed anything like what he saw over the next thirty seconds of his long and storied life.

A blue wave of energy emanated from the palm of the doctor's hand and rapidly expanded, extending all around the melting vault door.

"What the hell is that?" Professor McKaig exclaimed. He noted that, thankfully, the room's temperature dropped significantly after the doctor cast her spell.

"A shield," John said in wonder.

The blue energy emanating from the doctor's hand surrounded the vault door as it began melting. The professor looked over at her, seeing large beads of sweat forming on her forehead.

"John," she cried out. "I need help with this."

He nodded and pointed to Ellie, who was still tending to the wounded Mike. "You and you," he pointed to the professor. "Copy everything she did."

Ellie stood, looking bewildered at the energy flowing out of the doctor's hands. "You cannot be serious."

"As a heart attack," John responded. He grabbed them both by the arms, bringing them over to The Omnichron. The professor looked down to see the instructions laid out on the paid, an easy spell according to his quick translations.

"Professor," John looked at him. "Can you read this?"

"Of course," the professor was still flummoxed by the show the doctor was putting on. "But you can't expect me to do what she's doing?"

"Believe you can, and you will," John said. "Watch me."

He scanned the pages from the ancient volume and began to wave his arms in the same way the doctor had earlier. A blue wave of energy flowed out of his palms and surrounded the shield, John's energy reinforcing the barrier.

Ellie and the professor stared at them both in wonder. John turned to them and nodded. "Quickly now."

Ellie stepped up to the pages and mimicked what they had done, but nothing happened.

"It's not working," she cried out in frustration.

"Let go," Dr. Choi said through gritted teeth. "Let go and believe you can perform the magic."

Ellie tried again, but, again, nothing happened.

"Professor," John called out. "You give it a try."

He looked at John and Dr. Choi, stunned at how rapidly his life was being turned upside down. Nothing had ever prepared him for what he was witnessing. And now they were saying he could perform magic as well? It was a preposterous notion.

The vault doors creaked, the building moaning under the strain of whatever those three outside were doing. The metal door was glowing bright red, and the shield was beginning to fail.

"What have I got to lose?" the professor muttered. He stepped up to the diagram and performed the same ritual he had seen Dr. Choi and John perform before they had cast their shield. But as it was with Ellie, he was also unable to conjure a shield.

"It's not working my boy," the professor tried performing the ritual again, and nothing happened. "We just don't have your magic."

"The magic," John became excited. "That's it. The amulet, Professor. Read the amulet's inscription."

Professor McKaig looked at the amulet in his hand as there was an enormous crash and the screeching sounds of steel being torn apart. Their attackers would be inside within moments.

He held the amulet out in front of him and adjusted his glasses to read the tiny inscription that lined the edge.

"Onlíesende Balocræft Synbysige ġefeoht!" the professor called out, reading from the amulet.

A bright flash of orange light lit up the entire vault, extending across the entire room. Ellie, Mike, and the professor cried out in unison, as magic reentered their bodies.

"What the hell was that?" Ellie shouted.

"Try the spell now!" John shouted.

Ellie and the professor performed the ritual and this time, a wall of blue energy shot out from both their hands and covered the now open entrance to the vault door. Three figures approached the shimmering wall of energy. The giant lunged toward the shield they cast and was repelled back by a brilliant flash of energy discharging through the room the second he touched the field.

"It's real," Professor McKaig whispered, looking down at his hands that were projecting an otherworldly energy. "It's real!" he repeated, shouting in delight.

Their combined strength had created an impenetrable energy field preventing the three shadowy figures on the other side from reaching them.

"How are we doing this?" he asked the group.

But John and Dr. Choi were in no mood to answer, still concentrating on the shield barrier to keep their attackers out.

"Is there another way out?" John called over his shoulder.

"No," he said, feeling terrible about the answer. The only exit to the vault was blocked by their energy field.

"John," Dr. Choi said through tight breaths, "start looking up some offensive spells we can use."

John released his spell and dashed to the book, frantically flipping through pages as he searched for anything that might help them fight back.

"This ought to be interesting," John said, a smile touching the edge of his lips. "Apsara, when I say, drop the field."

She nodded, the sweat pouring off her body and her hands shaking.

John breathed in deep and readied himself, closing his eyes.

"Now," John said, eyes opening and focused on the three strangers beyond the shield.

They relaxed, releasing the blue energy field. John waved his hands in a cross motion across his chest and shouted, "Profusa."

A blinding white ball of energy flew from his hands and split into three smaller balls, which struck the three mysterious strangers. They grunted in pain as their bodies were thrown back into the library where they had come from.

Professor McKaig looked down at his hands in awe. What the hell was going on?

Dr. Choi turned to him, a fierce expression on her face. "Grab the book! This is our chance."

All he could do was nod in agreement. He wasn't afraid exactly. Whatever was happening to them right now was far too strange to be frightening. Instead, he felt himself overcome with a curious excitement that he knew would never be extinguished unless he followed this group wherever they were going.

"We can get out through the emergency exit," he said, pointing to the other side of the library. "Follow me."

Dr. Choi pointed to Mike, who still wheezed in pain. "Help him. We've got to move."

Ellie didn't hesitate. She lifted the man who was lying on the floor and brought him to his feet. He could tell he was still alive thanks to the groaning coming from him. The wound on his chest looked nasty, but bigger problems awaited them.

"John, you and I hold off those three while everyone else escapes through the emergency exit," Dr. Choi announced.

John nodded, cautiously moving into the library to see where their attackers had gone after his energy blast. Dr. Choi extended another shield that went from the floor to the ceiling and covered their retreat.

The professor draped one of Mike's arms around his shoulders and helped Ellie steer him through the stacks of books, dozens of which were scattered haphazardly around the library following the attack. They ducked and weaved as books flew off shelves and rocketed for their head. He clutched *The Omnichron* like a precious family heirloom, trying to avoid damaging it as they fled.

John and Dr. Choi returned fire against their attackers. The professor and Ellie continued to drag Mike through the library. Bright flashes of energy thrown by John and Dr. Choi lit their way.

He felt himself running out of breath and promised that he would immediately quit smoking his pipe and start going to the gym if he survived tonight's insanity.

A bright flash hit one of the library shelves, knocking it over and blocking their path. Professor McKaig glared at John, who shrugged, an embarrassed look on his face.

The professor struggled to keep the younger man on his feet and get him out of the building. After what felt like an eternity—but was only ten to fifteen seconds—the group reached the emergency stairwell.

"Keep going," John told him. "Apsara and I will cover your retreat."

Professor McKaig nodded. "Good luck, boy."

"Just get Mike out," John replied. "Leave those three to me."

Ellie opened the door, and they moved down the stairs as fast as they dared. Mike was still unconscious, and carrying his dead weight made negotiating the stairwell difficult.

After what felt like a thousand steps, they exited to the parking lot. The professor gulped in the cool night air, recovering from their efforts.

"You okay?" Ellie asked, her bright blue eyes wide with concern.

"I'm old, not dead," he said, waving her off. "Did John and Dr. Choi make it out?"

She shrugged. "I didn't hear anyone following us down the stairs, did you?"

He shook his head, hoping her younger ears might've noticed something his didn't.

A bright flash burst from the top floor of the library. They threw their hands up, shielded their faces from the blast.

"Get down!" he shouted.

They ducked behind a nearby SUV, pulling Mike's body after them. He could feel the flames as the library exploded and shrapnel rained down around them.

Once the echo faded and the dull heat of the explosion waned, the professor peered over the hood to see the top floor of his precious research library going up in flames.

His heart sank, wondering if there were anyone still inside when the explosion occurred and prayed no one else had been in the building.

He looked up to see Dr. Choi and John flying through the air in a blue bubble that tumbled end over end. The bubble fell victim to gravity, hit the ground, and bounced several times, sending the passengers inside rolling around wildly.

The bubble popped, and the pair fell to the ground in an unceremonious heap.

John snapped his head up, his eyes wide, watching the explosion in a daze.

"Are you all right, Mr. Jupiter?" the professor asked as he and Ellie rushed forward to assist the pair.

"Holy hell, I can't believe I just survived that." John stared at the building, his eyes wide.

"Was that you?" Professor McKaig asked, looking up at the fire in awe. "Did you do that?"

"No," Dr. Choi said. She got up and dusted off the front of her skirt. "It was that man who spoke to us. I was able to cast a shield in time to protect the both of us."

John took her hand as she helped him to his feet. He nodded gratefully to her.

"We'd better go," he said. "Those three don't look like the type to give up easily."

"Guys," Ellie said, looking worried. "Mike is hurt pretty bad."

"Let's get him to the hospital," Dr. Choi said. "My car is right over there."

The group picked Mike up and drag him over to the doctor's vehicle. He looked back at the library now fully in flames as sirens echoed in the distance. He clutched the book, knowing that an ancient volume like this was not supposed to be managed like this.

Still, he figured this was not the time to worry about the finer points of ancient book care and climbed in the SUV, joining the party to figure out what the hell they had just witnessed.

CHAPTER TWENTY-ONE

IN LOS ANGELES, TRAFFIC was a twenty-four-hour problem, but tonight was the rare exception to that rule, a small stroke of luck John was thankful for. The confrontation at the library and his newfound powers had left him feeling a peculiar mix of both fright and excitement.

He found himself thinking about the energy bolts he had lobbed at the trio trying to stop their attackers and the shield spell Apsara had cast without any effort. It had all come so naturally.

"As if we knew how to do it all along," he whispered to himself.

Apsara glanced over at him after hearing John muttering under his breath.

"You're talking about the magic," she said in an equally quiet tone.

He glanced back at the rest of their group, who were still busying themselves over Mike and his wound. John figured Apsara wanted to keep their conversation private for now because they had been the only ones who had manifested their magical abilities so far.

"Yeah," he nodded. "That . . . pulse of energy I threw. It came out of nowhere."

"Not nowhere," she said. "It came from within us."

"That's not how the universe works," he said. "Rule number one: Energy cannot be created or destroyed. It had to come from somewhere."

"That's what I mean," she said, watching the road for a moment. "Mana, Ka, your spirit, soul . . . Whatever you want to call it, I think we may have tapped into something humanity hasn't even agreed exists."

"This amulet activates these powers in people," John said. "You and I were exposed back at the hospital and our new friends in the vault. How do you think those three interlopers were able to do what they did back there?"

"You believe they got their hands on the amulet first?" Apsara said.

"I have no solid proof, but it stands to reason they're the ones who killed Knickerbocker and were responsible for his grandson's nearly-fatal skin condition," he replied. "They may not have known what they were doing at the time—"

"That's why the boy had it on him," she said, finishing his thought.

"The kid knew what they were trying to steal," he said. "He was trying to protect it."

"The drivers who brought him in said they had to pry it out of his hands," she replied thoughtfully. She activated the signal to get off the freeway and catch the exit for the hospital.

"You really believe we were tapping into our souls to blast those three?" he asked.

"I don't know if it's our souls exactly," she said. "I don't know about you, but I was exhausted by the end of that fight. Didn't you feel something similar?"

In fact, he had. However, he had chalked his fatigue up to the stressful situation they had just gone through. He had guns pointed at him before and that always got the blood pumping. He originally believed the way he felt was the inevitable comedown after their confrontation. But now, he was having second thoughts.

"I felt it," he admitted. "I feel fine now though."

"So do I," she confided. "In fact, I feel—"

"Stronger," he finished.

She nodded.

"It's as if whatever we tapped into allowed us to expand our ability to use that magic," she said, tapping her chin and beginning to sound excited. "I'm betting the next time we need to cast a spell; we'll be a lot better at it."

He chuckled. "We leveled up."

"Pardon?" she asked.

"It's an RPG, role-playing game, thing," he said. "The more experience characters get while fighting or by using their magic, the more they're able to use or manage. That's when you, 'level-up' and can take on stronger spells and . . ."

He realized the implication. He turned back to the professor who was hovering over the still-unconscious Mike.

"Professor, can you give me that book for a second?"

The professor's white beard dropped as the man frowned. It was clear he didn't like the idea of allowing him to get his grubby hands on it.

"Come on," he said. "I promise to take loving care of it."

The professor withdrew a pair of white gloves from his jacket pocket and threw them over to him.

"Put those on," he said. "Then we can talk about me teaching you all on how to properly care for a book like this."

John didn't see any other choice and pulled on the white gloves. The professor handed him the book.

"Take your time," the professor instructed.

John nodded. He felt the heft in his hands and was impressed by how solid the ancient volume was, despite the professor's protests. The hardbound leather book was similar in size to a hardcover novel found in any given bookstore. The outside was decorated with an intricate pattern that surrounded the spine and covered the entirety of the protective cover.

He carefully lifted the vellum pages one by one, marveling at the brightly colored illustrations and cramped script that filled the volume. Finally, he found the page that contained the "Profusa" spell he'd used back at the library. It had been the first one he saw when pawing through the book, but he had the feeling it wasn't the only one in there.

He read down the page, but it was impossible for him to translate what the text said. The script was in a language he didn't recognize and unfamiliar to him. The illustrations on the other hand, gave him context to the various offensive and defensive spells and how they worked. Most spells required a small wave of one's hand in a certain motion and a specific word.

"What'd you find?" Apsara asked him.

"Nothing specific, but I can see why those folks back at the library were so interested in this thing," he held it up, showing it to her as she glanced away from the road.

"What is it?" she asked. "I can't exactly take a study break here."

"It's . . . it's all the most terrible things you can imagine a person doing to someone," John said. He spotted a familiar spell and grunted. "Including that nasty curse."

He saw her shudder. "The less said about that the better. What else?"

"Oh good," he said, looking over the illustration on the next page. "They have a spell for raising the dead."

She eyed him then rolled her eyes. "Forget zombies. What's our plan?"

"First and foremost is getting our friend to the hospital. While you're helping him out, I plan on heading over to Knickerbocker's apartment to try and discover what that man really knew about magic and this amulet. He must have known what it could do, but my question is, why didn't he try to use it for himself?"

"Who's to say he didn't use it?" Apsara asked. "He was a billionaire after all."

John darted his eyes over to her and then back to the road in front of them. "If the old man had magical powers, why didn't he use them to defend himself or his grandson?"

Apsara frowned, then nodded, acceding his point.

"Professor," John called from the front seat. "Can you to translate the information in this book for us? If what we saw back at the library was any indication of what we're up against, I have a feeling we're going to need as many spells as we can master."

The professor leaned forward and took *The Omnichron* back from John. "My boy, there is enough reading material here to keep a team of researchers busy for months to decipher it all."

"We don't have months," Apsara said as they pulled up to the hospital. "So, I suggest you start studying."

She exited the vehicle and rushed for the entrance, going to retrieve someone who could help them get Mike inside safely.

The professor sighed as he watched Apsara dash off then acknowledged John with a nod. "I'll . . . do what I can."

John looked back at Mike, who was still unconscious, which he knew wasn't a great sign. "I think that's about all we can ask of anyone right now."

He got out of Apsara's vehicle and headed for the parking lot where he'd left his SUV, his stomach feeling empty. The excitement he'd felt at the beginning of this story had been replaced with a gnawing fear that this wasn't just a story anymore—this was the beginning of a new era for humanity.

CHAPTER TWENTY-TWO

ELLIE HAD BEEN QUIETLY watching her new friends all night and had been feeling useless. So, when several orderlies arrived with a gurney for Mike, she jumped at the chance to do something useful. She assisted the team as they worked to gently transfer Mike from the vehicle. But Mike didn't look like he was feeling much—he was still unconscious from the nasty wound he had suffered during their battle back at the library.

"Ma'am," one of the orderlies said. "You can't bring that in here with you."

He pointed to the bow that she was still hanging onto, and she snapped back to reality, forgetting she had hung on to it after the fight. It had felt so natural.

"Oh, right, of course. Sorry about that," she stammered. "Let me just go put this back in the car. Where are you taking him?"

"They'll let you know at reception," the orderly replied, calling over his shoulder as he and a team of doctors rushed Mike into the hospital.

She turned on her heel and made her way back to the SUV where Professor McKaig cleaned his glasses, his hands still shaking. The moment he spotted her, he stood up straight and cleared his throat.

"What a night," he offered.

She returned his smile with one of her own. "That's the biggest understatement I've heard in my life."

The professor nodded, withdrawing a small handkerchief that he wiped his forehead with. Ellie glanced around the parking lot, noticing John was missing.

"Where'd John go?"

"Ahh," the professor put the handkerchief back in his jacket pocket. "Our reporter friend said he was off to go investigate Mr. Knickerbocker's collection. He hopes to uncover information about the magic we seem to have stumbled into."

She exhaled a breath that she hadn't realized she had been holding and relaxed next to the professor, leaning back on Apsara's SUV.

"Magic is real," she said after a moment. "That's gonna take some getting used to."

The professor grunted as he replaced his glasses on his face. "You can't get more unscientific than that. I think we're all having a reckoning with how we view the world."

"Yeah, well, we all have to do that at some point," she said. She placed the bow carefully on the seat of the SUV, taking a moment to admire the weapon. It had served her well for many years in competition and it had been nice to feel the weight of it in her hands once again. She hadn't realized how much she missed archery.

"You were pretty handy with that thing," he said, his voice filled with admiration for her. "I knew about your accomplishments of course and what you did. And what you had to deal with . . ."

She paused, knowing exactly what he was talking about. She shrugged. The less she thought about that time in her life, the better. It was odd how a person could go from the best moment in their lives to the absolute worst in mere moments.

Ellie turned back to the professor who was eyeing her thoughtfully.

"You stood up against the system," he said. "That takes a kind of courage that you don't see very often."

"I'll never see the Olympics again," she replied, casting her eyes to the ground.

"It's amazing to me that they could get away with what they did to you, a gold medal winner," he said. "It's not like you did anything wrong or called your abilities into question."

"When you cause an international incident by assaulting a judge from another country, they don't really want to let you back in," she said with a wry grin. "I'm not officially banned of course. At least nothing in writing that would lead back to someone. They ban me in other ways, penalizing me at qualifying tournaments, finding whatever violations they can in the 'spirit of fair games.'"

"You were blackballed for calling out an abusive system," he said. "It's unconscionable."

"I was blackballed for my temper," she said after a moment. "And honestly, how you're perceived has a lot more to do with how you get to the next Olympics than you'd think."

She shut the door. "Besides, it was time for me to move on. I accepted what happened and knew I had to get a life outside competition. School was my way to do that."

"You're not wrong," he said. "After all, look at what you learned tonight."

She chuckled for the first time all night. It felt good.

He nodded toward the hospital's entrance. "Shall we go inside to see how our new friend is fairing?"

"Better than standing out here waiting for the creepy crawlies to come after us again," she said.

He nodded and they walked toward the hospital, unlikely partners in a strange and new magical world.

CHAPTER TWENTY-THREE

DANIEL, LETTY, AND CODY were busy licking their wounds in the library's parking lot, watching the emergency responders scurry about, trying to put out the flames that had erupted inside the most prestigious collection of knowledge in the Western Hemisphere outside of the Library of Congress.

"That was unexpected," Daniel said, watching firefighters hook up their equipment so they could fight the raging fires. "Do we know where they went?"

"No," Letty said. "They got away with *The Omnichron*."

"Does it matter?" Cody asked. "We already got paid. What do we care about some book?"

Daniel whirled around and shook a finger in his brother's face. "You have no idea the power we possess, do you?"

Cody shook his head. "No."

He sighed. "You still don't get it yet, do you? Money is irrelevant to us now. With these powers, we can take whatever we want. Do whatever we want! We weren't coming here to get *The Omnichron* for our employer. We were coming here so we could use it for ourselves."

Letty tilted her head in surprise, her face turning dark. "What do you mean?"

"Thirty million, a hundred million, those numbers are meaningless to us now," he said with a dismissive wave of his hand. "The only thing of value to us now is that book. Our employer wanted it and the amulet. That means they know what those two things are capable of."

He made a fist and shot an energy bolt to a nearby building, which exploded into flames. People cried out as the emergency rescue crews began shifting resources to take on the second fire Daniel had just started.

"*The Omnichron* belongs to us by right," he said. "That book contains everything we need to learn about magic and how to use it to our advantage."

Letty grinned. "You mean, more ways to mess shit up?"

"You think too small," Daniel scoffed with a wave of his hand. "If what I think is in that book is true, we could use it to take over the world."

"How?" Cody asked. "The world is big."

"And with that book, we are bigger," Daniel answered his little brother.

Letty clapped her hands, a sly grin plastered on her face. "I'm in, so long as I get the western half of the U.S."

His younger brother shrugged after a moment. "Let's see how far we can take this."

"Excellent," Daniel said, looking at his team with pride. "Our first order of business is learning who those people were and where they took *The Omnichron*."

Daniel allowed his gaze to wander the parking lot, ignoring the flashing emergency lights and puzzled onlookers. He found his attention drawn to a box truck with a cartoon ice cream bar on the side giving a thumbs up.

"That looks familiar," he said, pointing to the van.

Letty turned her head to see the van and the cartoon ice cream bar and laughed, nodding along with him.

"What?" Cody asked, sounding confused. "What am I missing?"

"It's like I always tell you little brother, you have to pay attention to your surroundings," Daniel chided. "The man who tried to stand against us wore a jumpsuit with that exact cartoon figure on it."

"That truck will lead us right to him," Letty finished. "The registration will tell us more."

Daniel clasped Letty's shoulders, beaming with pride.

"This is why I always say I have the best team in the world." He stepped off the sidewalk and began walking for the truck. "Come along, we don't want to waste any time."

Cody and Letty nodded. They followed him to the truck where Cody broke the window and reached in to unlock the door.

Letty hopped up into the cab and searched through the glove box while Daniel kept watch. It didn't take long before she popped her head back out of the truck, triumphantly waving a small piece of paper in the air.

"Say hello to Mr. Mike Madsen," Letty announced. "A resident of Sylmar."

"Excellent," Daniel beckoned Letty and Cody to follow him. "Let's go. We don't have much time."

CHAPTER TWENTY-FOUR

ABOUT AN HOUR AFTER they arrived at the hospital, Apsara finally collapsed in the chair in her office as she waited for an update on Mike's condition.

Mike was under the care of one of the best doctors she knew at the hospital, but the prognosis for their new friend wasn't good. He was still unconscious after taking the full force of the spell cast by the woman in black back at the library. His vitals weren't looking great, and Apsara was beginning to suspect they would need *The Omnichron's* help once again to cure him.

Magic was real. There was no denying it. After treating the Knickerbocker boy with the poultice and what she had not only witnessed but accomplished with her own two hands back at the library, the voice that had been screaming at her about science all day had fallen silent.

She had cast a shield. She had protected her friends. She had watched John use his hands to cast bolts of energy at their attackers.

The world had changed dramatically over the last hour and her brain needed a moment to catch up with their new reality.

But there was no time for that. There were people out there counting on her to deliver soman explanation of what they were going through. And she had nothing to offer.

Professor McKaig and the young woman she had also met at the library entered her office. She sat down behind her desk and took a breath, trying to compose herself. They looked up, waiting for her to begin.

"I know you're all wondering about Mike," she said, surprised at how steady her voice sounded. "There's good and bad news."

"Good news?" Ellie asked, a hopeful expression on her face.

"He's in stable condition," she said, trying to remain clinical and not give her new friends any unrealistic expectations. "His heartbeat is strong, and the chest wound he suffered appears to be a second-degree burn. That will be painful, but it's not anything we can't deal with."

"And the bad news?" the professor asked.

"He's still unconscious," she said, her voice faltering. "And I don't know why. As far as I can tell, he should have regained consciousness by now. The injury wasn't that serious. That leads me to believe we're dealing with more—"

"Magic," Ellie finished.

Apsara nodded. "Indeed. We all saw what I was able to do out there. What John was able to do."

"What we were able to do," Ellie finished.

The group fell silent, and she decided this was as good a time as any to try to get scientific answers out of this.

"I'd like to run a series of tests on us all," Apsara said. "Serology, MRIs, CAT scans, anything and everything I can think of. I want to compare our biological markers to see if this magic has altered our bodies' internal chemistry in any way."

"I've got plenty of blood," Ellie offered both her arms out. "But we barely escaped those three back at the library. Do we really have time for something like that?"

Ellie began pacing the room. "I think we can agree local law enforcement isn't exactly equipped to deal with someone who can throw fireballs out of their hands."

"Or cast curses on teenagers," the professor added.

Apsara glanced at the older man, who had, until now, remained quiet in the corner of the room. "Professor?"

"I agree with Ms. Sarkissian," he said. "But I am intrigued by your idea of trying to understand the potential mechanics behind the magic. Especially before we go off using it again. We don't know the risks."

"I think our biggest risk comes from those three back at the library, Professor," Ellie shot back. "I don't think they're gonna give us a time-out to let us finish the debate."

The professor tilted his head, acknowledging Ellie had made a good point. The young woman stopped pacing the room and turned her attention to the book in the professor's hand.

"They wanted the book, right?" Ellie asked. "What do you think they needed it for?"

The professor hesitated then glanced over at the box of gloves sitting on the shelf. When she nodded, they each grabbed a pair and donned them. He stood and approached the desk, removing *The Omnichron* from its protective sheath, placing it carefully on the desk. Apsara opened it and began paging through the ancient grimoire.

"What I'd like to know is how those three we met in the library managed to learn magic without *The Omnichron's* spells," Apsara said.

"Is that why John went back to Knickerbocker's apartment?" the professor asked.

She nodded. Ellie looked at them both, confused.

"I don't follow," Ellie said.

"I had a patient come in the other day dying of a strange disease. Large lacerations would repeatedly appear on his body and then seal themselves shut. In a desperate attempt to cure him, I took John's suggestion to visit the professor at the library where we found instructions on how to remove the curse from the boy in *The Omnichron*."

"And it worked?" Ellie looked skeptical.

Apsara nodded. "The boy was carrying the amulet when he arrived at the hospital. John believes reading the inscription causes it to release a type of energy that grants magical abilities to anyone nearby."

"So, what I did back at the library. . .?" Ellie's eyes were wide, "these powers are permanent?"

"It appears so. We all have powers at this point," Apsara glanced at the professor who looked troubled at the news he now possessed magical powers. "Professor, is there another copy of *The Omnichron* out there?"

The older man didn't respond and was staring off into space. Apsara leaned down and waved at the man, catching his attention.

"I'm sorry, my dear," the professor removed his glasses and cleaned them with a small cloth. "You were saying?"

"Is there another copy of that book out there?"

He tilted his head and then shook it. "I don't believe so. It was on loan to our institution. I personally had never heard of it before, but there's no telling how many copies are out there. It would not surprise me if we were to learn that this was the only copy available."

"Then what do we do?" Ellie asked.

Apsara stood. "First, the professor helps me decipher *The Omnichron* so I can find something that will help Mike."

"What about me?" Ellie asked.

"You're gonna make copies of the book for all of us," she replied. "Use your phone's camera and take multiple photos of every single page. Even if we lose that book, I don't want to lose the information contained within it."

The professor made a small noise.

"Please, no flash photography," he said.

Ellie flashed him a thumbs up. "I'll be careful."

"What do you say to ordering some takeout?" Apsara asked, reaching into a desk drawer, withdrawing a menu. "We've got a long night ahead of us."

CHAPTER TWENTY-FIVE

JOHN PULLED UP TO Knickerbocker Tower in downtown Los Angeles, flashing his press pass to the assembled police and crime scene technicians. They were directing all media to the other side of the street where the department had appropriated a garage. John felt a bit ashamed of himself—he hadn't filed anything resembling an update on the Knickerbocker case for hours. Percy, his boss, would be pissed—if he were even still employed.

Then again, a story about the reappearance of magic and all the implications of that would be the biggest news story in human history, so it wasn't as if he would have to be choosy when this was all over with.

He stepped out of the SUV and ran his fingers through his hair before putting his brown felt fedora hat on. There hadn't been much time for changing clothes or even taking a shower, so he was looking more rumpled than usual. The hat would go a long way in taming (or hiding) his wild hairstyle.

John searched through the crowd of rescue workers, looking for any friendly faces who might be able to help him get closer to the scene. The crowded street was filled with police and federal agents from all kinds of different agencies. He even saw a few people in FBI jackets loading boxes of evidence into trucks and grimaced.

If the feds were already here, that was a huge complication for him getting inside. He relied on local sources and had no contacts of his own in federal government. He was on his own.

He watched the crowd for a few minutes until he was struck by an idea. He took out his phone and typed a quick message to Apsara. Two minutes later, a chime sounded from his phone.

Ellie had texted him photos of *The Omnichron's* pages. One note said: *Here's a good one to help you sneak past the cops.*

He read the instructions on the screen. He re-read them and shrugged. He waved his arms in a serpentine pattern and began muttering the phrase *The Omnichron* said would turn him invisible.

As he finished the spell, he was stunned to see the world around him suddenly lose its color. He gasped in shock, then waved his hand in front of his face, but it had completely disappeared.

John glanced around and then placed himself in front of a nearby pedestrian. The man ran into his invisible body, stumbled, then whirled left to right looking wildly for whatever it was he had just run into.

But John was long gone before the pedestrian could catch up with him. The spell worked, but he was still solid matter. He'd have to keep that in mind as he navigated through the various forensics and police officers who were milling about the scene.

He didn't waste another moment and moved across the street trying to stay out of everyone's way. The world around John had been thrown into sharp relief, looking very much like a detailed black and white movie.

After making his way through the crowd of police, FBI agents, and other emergency responders present at Knickerbocker Tower, he followed a crime scene technician into the elevator, hitching a ride up to John Knickerbocker's apartment on the thirty-third floor.

John was beginning to feel woozy and wondered how long he might be able to keep the spell going. His experience with magic so far had shown him that casting a spell took a lot of energy. But he was beginning to wonder what might happen if he pushed it too far. If they didn't arrive soon, he would suddenly appear inside the elevator with two police officers and no explanation for how he got there. John held his breath and gritted his teeth, concentrating his remaining willpower on maintaining the spell.

Finally, they arrived at their floor and the tech exited, John following behind.

The elevator doors shut, and the tech continued with his case down the hall to Knickerbocker's apartment. John exhaled and released the spell. The world shimmered for a moment and then everything lost its fifty's-movie quality. He leaned against the wall, feeling dizzy, weak, and incredibly hungry.

After taking a moment to recover, he made his way closer to Knickerbocker's apartment where he spotted a police officer standing guard. The crime scene tech approached him and flashed his badge. They talked briefly and both chuckled.

The tech entered the room with the uniformed officer close behind. The apartment door was still open—this was his chance. He felt weak from casting the invisibility spell but was confident he could do it one more time to get inside Knickerbocker's home.

He waved his arms in the serpentine motion again and muttered the phrases associated with the cloaking spell.

The world faded to black and white once again, and he moved down the hallway, cautiously lifting his feet at every step to make sure he wasn't heard by the police officer and the tech.

Reaching the door, he glanced inside. The tech and the police officer had retreated to the living room where the body had been found.

John felt the world fade back into reality as he released the cloaking spell. Exhausted, he panted as if he had just run up ten flights of stairs. He thought again of his 'level-up' analogy from earlier and hoped there was something to it. After all, the more a person worked out, the better their muscles learned how to lift more weight. It would make sense that one's ability to use magic might follow the same rules.

He looked around Knickerbocker's apartment, where a phalanx of crime scene technicians and agents from the various responding agencies had gone over everything with a fine-tooth comb. There didn't seem to be anything left for him to find, but then again, the agents were trying to solve a murder, not find evidence of magic.

His first thought was Knickerbocker's computer. He proceeded to the man's study, hoping he wasn't on a wild goose chase.

CHAPTER TWENTY-SIX

Dr. Apsara Choi paged through *The Omnichron* until she finally found the potion she was looking for. The description of the spell included a passage that claimed it could help a warrior recover from any wound—even those that had the patient on the brink of death.

The potion also came with a warning that it was not intended for use on anyone who had died. The warning explicitly stated that those souls would not return to their bodies, and the rotting bodies would be cursed to wander the earth forever.

"Zombies," she grunted. That was the last thing they needed. Fortunately, Mike was very much alive, despite remaining in a coma that had so far defied her knowledge of modern-day medicine. The professor had gone off in search of food and coffee and would be returning soon, but for now, Ellie had proven to be an adept assistant with a quick and curious mind for the work they were doing.

Apsara stood next to Ellie, who was busy reading her scans of *The Omnichron* for something that might help.

"Find anything good?" she asked. "I found one spell that claims to bring anyone back from the brink of death, but it also warns about zombies, which I'm not thrilled about."

Ellie looked up at Apsara in alarm. "We can create zombies?"

Apsara shook her head. "The book says that only happens when you cast the spell on someone who's already dead, but I'm not ignoring a warning like that. I imagine there's a better treatment available. Have you seen anything meant to alleviate burns?"

Ellie shook her head.

"I'm not really sure what I'm seeing to be honest," Ellie paged through her photos of *The Omnichron's* pages, looking at each one. "The book makes it easy to understand what each spell does. But the words, pronouncing them? I'm not sure anyone really knows how to do that besides the professor."

Apsara pursed her lips, thinking it over. "I managed to cast a shield spell back at the library without knowing any Old English. I was also able to get my potion to work on the Knickerbocker boy."

Ellie shrugged, and then returned to the photos on her phone. Apsara turned to check on Mike's vital signs, the medical monitors beeping in the background. Mike's status hadn't changed since they had arrived at the hospital.

Apsara turned back to the healing potion, which was beginning to bubble over onto the Bunsen burner. "Can you bring the book over? I want to make sure I get the incantations right."

"You really think this will work?" Ellie asked as she lugged the ancient volume over to Apsara.

She shrugged, "The professor seemed confident that this basic healing potion would go a long way in curing Mike. It can't hurt."

Ellie glanced at Mike, who remained unconscious, and opened the book to the page Apsara had marked with the revival potion.

"Double bubble, toil and trouble," Ellie joked. Apsara shot her a glance. The young student cast her eyes down to the floor, embarrassed.

Apsara turned her attention to the book in front of her and re-read the incantation. She closed her eyes, memorizing the phrases in her head and feeling the power of the words wash over her.

When she opened her eyes, she could see the beaker's flame had turned a bright green and the small potion she had prepared earlier was now roiling to a full boil. Smoke began to flow off the top.

Ellie stepped back. "Are you sure that isn't going to explode all over us?"

Apsara wasn't sure of anything, but that wasn't how a little cinnamon and sugar were supposed to act when brought to a boil. She reached for a syringe to withdraw ten CCs of the sweet-smelling brew, then brought the syringe over to Mike's IV line and pushed the plunger down.

The reaction was almost immediate. A bright blue glow surrounded the young man and Mike coughed once, then again. Then he sat up, looking around in panic.

"Where are they?" he shouted, thrashing about the bed. "Where'd they—"

Apsara and Ellie lunged forward to get control of Mike before he fell or hurt himself.

"Easy now," Apsara soothed. "You're okay, we're okay. You took a nasty hit back there and we had to bring you to the hospital."

Apsara watched Mike's panic ebb as he took stock of his surroundings and figured out he was no longer being threatened by a trio of mercenaries. He patted his chest, looking for the wound. It was slowing fading away.

"Did everyone get out all right?" Mike's eyes darted back and forth.

"We're fine," Apsara said, smiling. She turned back to the potion on her desk and wondered how long it would take her to make enough to help all the patients in the hospital.

"What happened to those . . . thugs?" Mike asked.

"We don't know," Ellie said, answering for her. "Near as we can figure that spell John cast blew them into next week."

Mike nodded, then his face fell. He kicked off the sheets and jumped out of bed, bare-chested and dressed only in his skivvies. The two women averted their eyes as Mike searched through his clothes that were folded neatly in the chair opposite him. "My phone. Where's my phone? Shayla, my daughter, I have to check on her to make sure she's okay."

Mike found his pants, put them on, and grabbed his cell phone. He turned on the display.

"Oh my God," he whispered.

Apsara turned. "What is it?"

Mike showed them the display to his phone. On it was a photo of a young woman being held hostage by the same three they had encountered at the library.

A three-word message was attached to the photo.

Bring the book.

Mike turned to them, his face pale. "What book?"

"Oh my God," Ellie brought a hand to her face, her eyes filling with tears. "They wouldn't..."

Apsara sat next to Mike and placed a hand on his shoulder. "How much do you remember from the library?"

Mike's eyes were wide. "What is going on?"

Apsara and Ellie nodded at each other and then recounted everything that happened after he had been knocked unconscious by the trio. The explosion, *The Omnichron*, the fact they all had magical powers. That the amulet that had granted them these powers had belonged to a murdered real estate billionaire.

Mike stared at them blankly as they recounted everything he needed to know, his, mouth open in stunned silence.

"Mike?" Ellie offered.

"We . . . we need to call the police," he said dumbly. "The FBI, hell the whole goddamn army. What you just told me is—"

"Impossible and unbelievable." Apsara reached out to touch the man's arm. "Which is exactly how anyone would react if we tried to tell them what and who we're up against. I understand how difficult it is to believe what I'm saying. If you don't believe me, you could try a magic spell for yourself. You were charged with magic along with the rest of us."

She pointed to the glowing syringe that still held a bit of the healing potion. "Everything I know about science, medicine, and the universe tells me that potion over there should not have been able to bring you back and heal your extensive wounds. And yet, a mere ten CCs of that liquid repaired the burn on your chest and brought you back within moments. Do you think anything other than magic could explain that?"

Mike laughed, but the sound was hollow, empty of any humor. "My daughter has been kidnapped. There's no debating this. We're calling the cops."

"And tell them what? What do you think they'll say?" Ellie challenged. "They'd call us crazy and be right to do so."

"Show them the magic," Mike said. "This can't possibly fall on us."

"We've all seen what those three are capable of," Ellie piped up. "There's no way the LAPD is prepared for someone who throws fireballs from their hand."

Mike shook his head, then turned back to Apsara, looking at her for answers. She had no idea what the man was going through, but she knew it must be pure torture. The man's child was being held hostage over a book they possessed. But bringing authorities into this would only get more innocent people killed.

"We are the only ones who can stop these three," Apsara said. "If you truly believe the police will just happily accept our tale about magic blowing up the library, then by all means, here's my phone." She withdrew her phone from her pocket and extended it out to Mike. "I believe you know the number. Nine one one."

Mike didn't say anything. He only looked down at the phone in her hand. "If what you say is true, and we can't call the police, then what?"

"Let's go get 'em," Ellie said.

"I'm sorry, what?" Apsara said, looking over at the young woman, alarmed.

"We've got the book of spells, we've got the magic," Ellie said, her voice gaining confidence with every word. "We know those three back at the library don't know much about the magic they do have, which just might give us the edge we need. They have no idea who they're up against."

She finished her sentence with a grin and Apsara chuckled at the young woman's enthusiasm.

"Even so, they had magic too," Mike said. "What do we have?"

"All the spells they don't have," Ellie said, pointing to the book. "I say we study up and go get your daughter."

"What about John?" Apsara asked.

"Call him and have him join us once he finishes his investigation," Ellie said.

Apsara wasn't sure she liked the idea, but Ellie was right. They held all the cards, and Mike's girl was in danger because of them.

"Do it," Apsara said, making the decision. "Call John and tell him we're gonna go get Mike's little girl."

CHAPTER TWENTY-SEVEN

JOHN RUMMAGED THROUGH KNICKERBOCKER'S desk, looking for something, anything, that might indicate what the billionaire knew about the amulet and how it had somehow brought magic back into the world.

But despite his initial excitement, the billionaire's suite was enormous, and the man had been something of a hoarder. He was better off looking for a needle in a haystack.

He sighed. There was little chance of him getting through everything in the man's apartment tonight. He just didn't have the time.

Frustrated, he slammed his hands down on the desk—and was rewarded by the sound of a click. The wall across from him slid open.

The billionaire had constructed a secret room that contained what looked like hundreds of little trinkets, all glowing with the same orange-blue energy he saw when casting spells.

His eyes went wide as his brain struggled to catch up to what he was looking at.

He approached the nearest artifact and examined it—it was a golden ring with small red jewels lining the center. He tried it on. To his surprise, the ring shrank until it was a perfect fit.

"Fascinating," he whispered.

The ring glowed as he examined it. Whatever it was, it wasn't hurting him. He picked up the placard that identified the ring as "The Sapphire Demise."

He read the short paragraph that listed the ring's abilities. According to the description, the ring conserved magical energy, halving the amount of mana required for spells.

"Mana," he mused. "Or the intent and will behind the spell."

He set it down, looking at the rest of the trinkets in the room. All of them had odd names, like "The Hollow Demon" or "Silent Moon" and each one had a notecard with a description of its abilities.

Just what the hell had he stumbled into?

His phone rang, and he looked down at the display, seeing Apsara's number.

"Hey, how's Mike?"

"Good and bad news on that front," Apsara's voice was brusque. She sounded tense.

"What happened?" John asked.

"Mike's back on his feet," she said. "He has already fully recovered thanks to a nifty potion I discovered in *The Omnichron*."

"And?" John asked.

"And we have a major problem. Those three we met back at the library found Mike's daughter. John . . . they took her."

John felt his stomach sink into the ground.

"I'm guessing they want the book in exchange for his daughter." John pressed his fingers against his temples. This was a major problem.

"You got it," she confirmed.

He cursed under his breath. If what they saw back at the library was any indication of what those three were capable of, they needed to keep that book out of their hands at all costs.

"Don't worry," she said. "Mike knows we can't give them *The Omnichron.*"

"Then what?"

"He suggested we meet them back at his house and try to talk them out of taking the book."

"You mean, we use force," John said in disbelief. "No way we survive another encounter."

"Maybe we do," Apsara said. "John, the book has hundreds of spells that can give us an edge over those three. Ellie pointed out that the trio's magic at the library was unrefined and weak compared to what you and I have been able to accomplish."

He chewed the inside of his lip as he thought it over. They might be on to something, but he wasn't convinced.

Apsara's voice remained gentle. "You know we can't go to the police."

He did know that. He resigned himself to the situation. "Text me Mike's address. I'll meet you there soon as I can."

"Will do," she said.

John hung up the cell phone, stunned at this latest development. Mike's daughter was an innocent victim. She didn't deserve to be involved like this.

His phone lit up with a message from Apsara with Mike's address. He took one last look around the billionaire's secret room, unsure what he should take with him.

He cast a stealth spell, the ring surging with power.

He snuck past security in rapid time, hoping he would make it to Mike's house before anything went tragically wrong.

CHAPTER TWENTY-EIGHT

MIKE DIDN'T SAY MUCH while as he rode with Apsara, Ellie, and the professor to his home in Sylmar. Apsara said the professor and the man he'd met in the library would meet them there and help them take on those evil bastards who had taken his daughter.

He glanced back at Ellie, who was sitting on one side of the vehicle, her phone out, still taking photos of the book called *The Omnichron*. He didn't know why these bastards were demanding that in exchange for his daughter, but from what Apsara had told him, it was something that could become dangerous in their hands.

All he cared about was his daughter. There was nothing more important in this world than his little girl. The fact he hadn't been there to protect her was killing him inside.

"I want to know how they found my place," Mike said, anger welling up within him once again. "Professor, they knew everything about us. How could they know things like our names and where I live?"

The professor stroked his white beard and shook his head, his face grave. "There is no telling what they can do. It's possible they have contacts who could track you down. If I've learned anything over the last few years, it's how there is an unbelievable amount of information available on any given person available on the world wide web."

He nodded and looked out the window for a moment, worried sick about his daughter. It was then, while staring at his reflection, he noticed the cartoon ice cream bar on his uniform that his daughter had chosen for him for his business.

"My truck," Mike moaned, slapping himself on the head. "They found my truck back at the library. It matches the logo on my jumpsuit, and they connected the dots."

"That's why they came for you, and not anyone else," Apsara said.

"If that's the case," the professor said, "that puts us at a significant disadvantage. They know more about us than we do about them."

"I might be able to help with that actually," Ellie said from the front seat. "I've been reading the book, trying to get an understanding of all the spells."

"All of them?" Mike asked, an eyebrow raised.

Her face went bright pink, "I used a translator app I found that can help me with the Old English. All I do is take a photo and highlight what I want to translate, and the phone exports it to my notes. Plus, I'm a speed-reader with a decent memory. It's not eidetic or anything, but as far as doctors are concerned, it's as close as they've seen."

"What did you find?" the professor asked, a new respect in his voice for the young woman.

"I found a lot of spells," Ellie said. "Honestly, there are some things in here that make me feel like I'm reading an easy-bake oven recipe for nuclear weapons."

The group became noticeably uncomfortable hearing that. They had already seen the power unleashed by the fireball back at the library. If the book contained other, even more powerful spells, and the trio got ahold of it, the world was in trouble.

"You said you found a spell that could help us get information about them?" Mike said, trying to refocus the conversation.

"Yeah," Ellie said after a moment. "It's a 'knowing' spell that essentially allows the person casting the spell to 'know' everything about that person's life."

"A mind meld," Apsara chuckled. "That could come in handy. Do you think you can perform the spell when we get close?"

Ellie tilted her head and then shrugged. "I don't see why not."

"If that's what Ellie found after a few minutes perhaps we should all get studying," the professor said. He turned to Mike who was still ruminating on the fact his daughter was being held by a trio equipped with black magic. "Are you gonna be okay for this mission, solider?"

He looked up at the professor, studying the man with a newfound respect. "How did you know I served?"

The professor smiled. "Call it intuition. I have seen that look in men's eyes before."

He didn't bother to ask what look the professor was talking about. He'd seen it himself in his friends over the years too.

"Two tours," he said, swallowing. "That's where I met my wife."

"Where is she now?" Ellie asked.

When Mike didn't answer, the car became quiet once again.

"I'm so sorry for your loss," Apsara said, reaching a hand to touch his shoulder. "We'll get your daughter back and make sure she remains safe."

"How can you know that?" he snapped. He looked around at the group of people sitting with him in the SUV and became angry. "How many of you have had any kind of combat experience? How many of you know anything about urban assault tactics and how to deal with an ambush? We have a reporter, a college student, a doctor, and a man eligible for social security about to walk into a buzzsaw."

"Mike!" Ellie exclaimed.

Professor McKaig held out a hand.

"No, Ellie," the professor's voice was solemn. "He's right to be concerned. Our motley crew here isn't exactly the type of posse you round up for a confrontation with people who have already proven to be incredibly dangerous."

The professor turned back to him, keeping his voice even. "But it also appears as if you do not have a lot of choice in the matter. We already know the police and the FBI wouldn't stand a chance against these three. We've all used the same magic they do, and we know what's coming and how to defend against it."

The professor nodded to Apsara. "Dr. Choi has extensive training in healing injuries and is the only person in the world qualified to deal with magical injuries. I'd put my confidence in her a thousand times over any other doctor in the country right now."

Mike felt his temper begin to cool.

"Ellie here is a world class athlete who represented our country in archery, earning a gold medal. I don't think I need to tell you that takes a mental discipline that many people just don't have."

Ellie beamed.

"Our reporter friend may not be here, but he is well known for his clever and shrewd insights into the stories he chooses. And as for myself, I'm about the only man in the world who can translate *The Omnichron*. So, yes, while I understand your doubts, I don't believe you'll find a stronger team in the world who can help you get your daughter back."

Mike felt almost ashamed of himself for losing it with the people around him. He had only met these people a few hours ago, and they were already willing to put their lives on the line for him.

"Truth is"—the professor patted Mike's arm— "you go to war with the army you have."

He looked up at the professor, who shrugged back at him.

"So, what do you say? Care to put some of your training to use?"

Mike considered the professor's speech for a moment and then nodded. "Let me be perfectly clear. My daughter's safety is the only thing that matters."

The professor smiled and clapped his hand on Mike's back. "We're with you. She will be okay."

"Hey, Ellie," Mike said. "You mind if I take a turn with that book?"

She handed it over to him. He opened it and began perusing the spells to find the ones that did the most damage.

He was going to bring those kidnapping bastards a fight they'd never forget.

CHAPTER TWENTY-NINE

Apsara rolled to a stop down the street from Mike's home, eyes searching for any sign of activity. The street was dark and quiet. The houses rested in silence; their occupants unaware of the grave danger threatening their neighborhood.

She opened the door and exited into the cool night air, feeling a fluttering in her stomach as the anxiety of what they were doing caught up with her. She belonged in the hospital, not out here in the middle of the valley trying to rescue some poor girl. With magic.

However, after what she had been able to accomplish at the library, and what she had seen their opponents do, she knew she had no choice. She had to help in any way she could.

She thought back to the words she had spoken that had somehow resulted in a powerful energy barrier capable of protecting them from those three psychopaths. She began mentally rehearsing the spell, as her fingers emitted small sparks every time she thought about casting the spell.

"Hey, careful!" Mike said.

"What?"

"Your fingers are throwing sparks around. I don't want to become the magical equivalent of friendly fire."

"I didn't realize . . ." She looked down and saw he was right—small sparks danced from her fingertips every time she thought about casting the spell. *Interesting.*

She removed the vials of health potion she had created back at the hospital, suddenly extremely glad she brought them along. Someone in their group might need one—or all of them by the time the night was through.

John was waiting for them when they arrived. They joined him, looking down the street where Mike's house was located.

"Ellie, you think you could cast that 'knowing' spell for us?" Apsara asked, directing her attention to the young college student.

She nodded and pushed a lock of hair behind her ear, concentrating on her hand movements. *"Gnarious."*

A black cloud emanated from her fingertips and rocketed toward Mike's home. Ellie drew in a sharp breath. Apsara stepped forward, a worried expression crossing her brow.

John held up a hand and she paused, watching Ellie as the young woman's body fidgeted for a few moments.

Ellie exhaled a deep breath. "They're in there."

"Who *are* they?" Apsara asked. She reached out a hand and Ellie took it gratefully, looking up at the group with terror behind her blue eyes.

"They call themselves the Triumvirate," Ellie began, still breathing heavily. She turned to Mike, a pained expression on her face. "Your daughter is definitely in there."

"Is she okay?" Mike demanded. "Is she hurt?"

Ellie shook her head. "She's scared. But uninjured and healthy from what I can tell."

"What about the Triumvirate?" John asked. "Who are these people?"

"I didn't touch them for long," she said. "The woman, her name is Letty. She's in the front room watching the street from behind the front window."

"What else?" John urged.

"John," Apsara glared at him. "Can't you see that was difficult for her? Give her a moment to catch up."

Ellie nodded. "It was. Not painful, but . . . I feel like I lived three lifetimes over the last five minutes. It's taking me a moment to separate the memories."

John held up his hands. "I'm sorry. Take your time."

"No," Mike said. He turned to Ellie. "Please, you have to concentrate."

Ellie frowned but closed her eyes and nodded. "Of course. I'll try."

The thick black smoke emanated from her fingers again and entered the house.

"The larger man," Ellie said, her voice sounding distant and tinny, as if it were coming from an old-time radio. "That's Cody. He's watching Mike's daughter in her room."

"And the third man?" John urged. Then, seeing Apsara's glance, he tried again in a more concerned tone. "What do you see about the leader who confronted us back at the library?"

Ellie concentrated, a thin line appearing between her brows.

"I don't . . ." Ellie said. "I don't feel him in there."

Apsara's stomach dropped. She turned to John, her eyes wide in alarm. "It's a trap."

"It was always going to be a trap. But we still have to help Mike get his girl back," he said, his voice firm. "We can't leave her behind."

He was right but she'd never felt this tense before.

"Can you set up a shield between us and Mike's home?" he asked

She nodded and muttered the spell. A bright blue energy field snapped into place a yard away from them.

John turned. "Ellie, use that bow of yours and be ready to lay down some cover for us."

Ellie nodded and took the bow off her back, notching an arrow in place.

"Professor, if you cast a cloak over us while we approach, I think we'll be covered from all angles," John said.

The professor nodded and cast the spell as the rest of them prepared for their approach to Mike's home.

Apsara closed her eyes, concentrating on the shield protecting them from harm. When she reopened them, she was surprised to see the world had turned black and white.

But as they approached the curb of the house, Apsara was struck by a bad feeling. "Wait."

The group halted.

She concentrated and extended the shield, hoping to give them room to maneuver. The second the barrier touched the curb to Mike's house, a bright flash of green and orange sparks erupted between them. They held out their hands to shield their eyes from the sparks.

"Stop!" John called out. He glanced at Apsara who was still maintaining the shield. "Thanks for that. We'd have been toast if you hadn't tested the property line."

She nodded, concentrating on holding the shield up between their group and the house. John turned to Ellie.

"Do me a favor. Shoot one of your arrows over the yard and aim for something that won't kill anyone inside."

She nodded and stood, aiming the bow at a nearby tree in Mike's yard. She released the arrow, and it flew toward her target until it ricocheted off a powerful energy barrier where the curb lined the street.

"That's what I was afraid of," he said.

"You five are cleverer than most. I applaud you," a mysterious voice called out to them from the darkness.

Apsara whipped her head around, searching for the source of the voice.

The man in black who had confronted them at the library was casually leaning against a light post, staring at them.

"Who are you?" Apsara called out.

The man held out his hands, his wide smile and bared teeth presenting a terrifying visage. "Your new master."

The man's two friends appeared behind him, and the Triumvirate advanced. Apsara turned, holding her shield in front of them, separating the two groups.

The man in black cocked his head and touched Apsara's energy field, raking his fingernails down it, the sound like a thousand nails grating against a chalkboard. She grimaced in pain, but the barrier remained firm.

"Your magic is stronger than I remember," the man said, grinning. He withdrew his hand and sneered at John. "Then again, you got lucky back at the library."

"That wasn't luck," he said. Apsara watched him prepare the fireball he'd unleashed back at the library, the energy building up around his fists. "Time for you to give up Mike's daughter."

"Or?" the man looked amused.

"Or we'll see what an extra-crispy asshole looks like," John retorted.

The man looked back at his companions and chuckled. He held out his hands as if in surrender. "Well, you've got me. What would you have me do, Mr. Reporter, sir?"

"I don't like this," Apsara told him, but John wasn't listening.

"Drop the curse around this house and leave," John insisted. The energy around his fists grew wilder, sparks flying off his knuckles.

"Hmm." The man in black tapped his finger to his lips and then shrugged. "I don't want to. I guess you'll have to fight us for it."

John looked over at Apsara and then at the rest of his group. Ellie aimed the bow at the bigger man, in the back, the arrow glowing bright orange. The professor had adopted a similar pose as John, sparks falling off his wrists and knuckles. Mike's hands looked very much the same.

"This is your final warning," John said, bracing for what he knew was about to come next.

"Let's dance," the man said and whipped his hand out. A bright, white ball of lightning struck Apsara's shield. She cried out.

John released the fireball he'd been holding, the flames roaring into the street, scattering the Triumvirate.

Letty stepped forward, responding with a spell of her own that countered the fireball with a bright blast of energy. The night sky lit up with a display like the grand finale at a Fourth of July party as the energy unleashed by John, Mike, and the professor's spells came together into an enormous explosion. The street went dark again after the bright flash.

Apsara was nearly knocked to the ground, but managed to keep her feet, barely able to hold the energy barrier that was keeping them safe.

Ellie retreated to get a better bead on their attackers, then rapidly fired arrows from her bow. Her first shot hit Letty in the shoulder, knocking her to the ground.

The woman cried out and the man in black looked at her in concern. He whirled back toward Ellie.

"You'll regret that." He turned his hands in a circle and pushed them forward. Black smoke poured out of his hands and gathered in front of him. Orange and red sparks flew out of the smoke. A short, squat creature emerged from the shadows.

"What in the hell is that?" Mike cried out.

Whatever it was, it was not of this realm. Apsara could only describe it as a hideous monster. The creature's face sloped back into four eyes that swiveled around on its forehead, the long jaw filled with several rows of sharp, jagged teeth. It skittered across the road, the limbs a blur, a scorpion-like tail stabbing at them.

It charged at Ellie, who, after taking a moment to absorb the creature's appearance, unleashed arrows as fast as she could, the bow twanging in a macabre symphony.

Apsara dropped the shield protecting everyone and cast another one between Ellie and the charging monster only seconds before it reached her. The bizarre animal crashed into the barrier and flew back, landing in a snarling heap.

"Apsara, look out!" John launched a ball of energy toward the trio. It slammed into Cody's chest, throwing him back across the street and into a parked vehicle.

The car alarm wailed. Cody tried to get to his feet but was briefly stunned and fell to his knees. Apsara turned her attention to the man in black who was still busy attacking John, Mike, and the professor with a series of energy blasts from his fists.

John, Mike, and the professor threw more magic missiles at the man in black who casually brushed them to either side. The woman lay on the ground, crying out in pain as she struggled with the arrow lodged in her shoulder courtesy of Ellie's marksmanship.

Apsara turned to see the monster chasing Ellie. She watched their young friend jump over a fence and sprint through someone's backyard. The seven-foot monster leapt over the barrier like it didn't exist.

"Do you have this?" she asked them.

John nodded. "Go. Back her up."

The three men fired at the man in black, giving her cover as she raced across the street to catch up with Ellie. It wasn't difficult to see where she'd gone. The monster had made a path while chasing after the young Olympian, leaving behind a clear trail to find them.

After a few moments, she heard a splash and what sounded like screams for help. She redoubled her efforts, running as fast as she could, hoping she could reach her friend in time.

She burst through a fence and saw the monster looming over Ellie in a swimming pool, about to take a bite out of her. She cast a defensive shield. The monster bounced off the energy field, crashing into a pool house.

Apsara lifted the shield and waved. "Come on! Get out! We don't have time."

Ellie swam to the edge of the pool and pulled herself out of the water. Still dripping wet, she turned, aiming the bow at a hole in the pool house, notching an arrow that lit up the night with magic.

The monster poked its head out. Ellie released the arrow. It flew straight into the pool house and exploded. Apsara was barely able to cast a shield in time to protect them from the debris raining down around them.

Once the dust settled, Apsara looked at Ellie in wonder.

Ellie lowered the crossbow, looking satisfied with herself.

"Sorry about that," Ellie said. "I didn't know it would be so messy."

"How'd you do that?" she asked, looking at the now demolished pool house where the monster was dead.

"Something I read in the book," Ellie said. "I cast a spell that imbued my arrows with magical energy. Thought I would need something with an extra kick, ya know?" Ellie looked down at her handiwork and smiled. "I'd say it works."

"Good thinking," she held out her hand, and Ellie lifted her up. "Come on. Let's get back to the group."

They moved back through the park toward Mike's home, hoping they would get there in time to help their friends.

CHAPTER THIRTY

JOHN, MIKE, AND THE professor were doing everything they could to stay alive while fighting with the remaining members of the Triumvirate. All three of them had thrown everything they had learned so far at the man in black and his two companions, but they had absorbed all of it without breaking a sweat and John was beginning to worry his spells weren't working—or worse, the Triumvirate was better with their magic than he originally estimated.

The man in black threw a bright spear of what appeared to be lightning at him. It sizzled past him, straight into the brick wall next to him, the force of the explosion throwing him across Mike's lawn. He landed in the grass, slamming against a sprinkler head.

He rolled over, groaning in pain, and looked up at the night sky, seeing stars.

The professor ran over to him. "Are you okay, son?"

John shook his head. "We need to figure out how to deal with these three or else we're gonna wind up as nothing but a red smear on a street in suburbia."

The professor pulled John to the side as another lightning strike narrowly missed them.

John waved his hand and summoned another fireball to shoot at the man in black. The man grinned as he approached—until the fireball slammed into him and his two companions, sending them tumbling like leaves caught in a particularly strong breeze.

Mike limped over to them and flopped onto the grass, panting. "We've got to get to my baby."

John touched his shoulder. "Don't worry, we're not going anywhere without her."

"Enough of this!" The man in black's booming voice echoed through the neighborhood. John, Mike, and the professor stood, facing the trio as they approached once again. "Give us the book."

"Give me back my daughter," Mike shouted.

"This isn't a negotiation," the woman answered with a sneer.

"We know what that book contains and there is no scenario where we are giving it to you," John shouted back at them.

The man in black considered this for a moment and then waved his hand. As if watching a movie projected in the night sky, they could see Mike's daughter suspended in mid-air inside his living room.

Mike cried out and tried to charge, but John stepped forward to hold him back.

"Her precious little life will be forfeit if you do not turn over the book within the next thirty seconds," the man in black called out to them. "My patience runs out."

Mike looked over at John, a desperate look in his eyes. "Please, John, we tried. We really did, but we can't beat them here. Please, just give him the book."

"We can't," the professor insisted. "You've seen what they're capable of already. If we give them *The Omnichron* there's no telling the chaos they might unleash on the world."

Mike shook his head. "I don't care. This is my daughter. If you don't give it to them, I'll take it from you myself."

Before anyone could protest, Mike turned and ran for the SUV, where the professor had stored the book.

"Mike, no!" John shouted.

But Mike wasn't listening. He was already inside the SUV, rummaging around for *The Omnichron*. After a few moments, Mike emerged from the vehicle, waving the ancient tome over his head.

"Can you stop him?" John turned to the professor. "Cast a protection spell between them?"

The professor tried waving his arms to cast the spell, but he was too late. Mike was already too far away.

"Here it is," Mike shouted at the Triumvirate. "Release her!"

The man in black smiled. "A man who betrays his friends for his family. I respect that."

Mike held the book out in his right hand as the man in black twisted his fingers, summoning the book to him. John reached out a hand to cast another fireball spell, hoping to destroy the book before it reached the Triumvirate, but he wasn't fast enough.

The book flew across the street, landing in the man in black's hands. He snapped his fingers, and there was an audible pop as the barrier surrounding Mike's house disappeared.

The Triumvirate retreated into the night as Mike dashed toward the house, shouting for his daughter.

John could only watch the Triumvirate flee the scene and wondered if they had just unleashed Armageddon on the world.

CHAPTER THIRTY-ONE

EVERY PORCH LIGHT IN the neighborhood lit up after the ruckus they had made fighting the Triumvirate for the only physical copy of *The Omnichron*.

John didn't know what to do but knew they needed to get off the street. The second the curse surrounding the house had disappeared, Mike ran inside to find Shayla and make sure she was safe.

Apsara and Ellie returned from battling their monster and joined Mike and the professor inside. John waited outside for when the police came by to take his statement. He was certain they hadn't been seen, but the authorities had shown up in droves after the Triumvirate fled.

Two uniformed officers came out to speak with him, but he played the friendly, concerned neighbor, telling them that he hadn't seen anything or heard much. They left him with a card with a number he could call in case he thought of anything.

He crumbled it up and threw it away the moment the police left his sight.

He gazed up at the light-polluted skies of Los Angeles and spotted one of the few stars a person could see in the city, his brain attempting to process the events of the last forty-eight hours. As a reporter, chaos was just another part of reporting the news. But the stories he usually reported on followed the logical rules of reality. Now that magic had appeared in the modern world, he was beginning to question everything.

The worst part about tonight was his failure to keep the book away from the three determined individuals who had the capability of using magic with none of the morals or responsibility a normal person might have.

He cringed at the idea of what the Triumvirate would do with the book.

The front door to Mike's house opened and the professor emerged, the man's boots echoing on the deck. He looked over at the older man and flashed a weary smile at him.

The professor sat down next to him. "I hope you're not wallowing in our defeat."

He chuckled, then stood and kicked the side of the porch. "It's hard to say what I'm doing. I feel like we just gave up without a fight."

"That's where you're wrong." The professor's eyes twinkled. "Ellie was able to get a snapshot of every page in the book, so at least we didn't lose the information and spells. Besides, you're forgetting that I'm one of the few people in the world who can translate everything in that book. They have no such resource."

"They still got *The Omnichron*," John grumbled. While he was happy to hear that they had a backup, the knowledge was out there in the world. And that was dangerous.

The professor sighed. "It's a tough loss, that's for sure."

"We've got the spells," John said. "That's something. But what I want to know is what the Triumvirate wanted with that book and how they even knew it existed."

The professor shrugged. "The only reason I knew about it is because it came into our collection at the library after the Knickerbocker estate loaned it to the library in the early eighties. The providence was not particularly strong, but it passed every authenticity test I could think of."

"But how did they know?" John said, beginning to pace up and down the porch. "Magic used to mean smoke and mirrors, Las Vegas lounge acts, and street magicians. Everyone participated in the show because we all knew it was fake and sleight of hand. But this? This is ancient mystical energies that science hasn't just failed to detect, but somehow overlooked entirely for hundreds of years."

The professor stroked his beard. "For magic to return, the rules of our reality had to have been rewritten. That's a power far beyond any of our understanding."

"Did the university have any records about the book besides what was in the catalog?" John asked. "Did anyone ever even check it out?"

"Not until you all came by, asking about it," the professor said. "Of course, any records of who might have checked it out before you would have been lost in the fire."

John felt a flash of shame and hung his head as the professor chuckled. "It's all right, son, you were only trying to protect us."

"Still, it's not a great feeling when you realize you're responsible for destroying a potential lead."

"It's not your fault," the professor patted him on the back. After a moment, the older man said something that he had been ruminating on the last few minutes. "I would have done the same thing, if I were in Mike's shoes."

John grunted. He was still angry with their new friend for giving up their only leverage, but he knew that deep down, he would have made the same choice.

"I feel the same way," John admitted after a moment. "I should have seen the trap coming."

"And now you know better for next time," the professor pointed out. "That's something."

"That's something but is it enough?" he asked. "We don't know what they're going to do with that book and it's not likely to be anything good."

The professor slapped his knee and stood. "Then what sense is it to stand here pissing and moaning about it? This is our chance to regroup and form a better plan for the next time we confront those three."

John looked up in shock at the professor. "The next time?"

"Why yes," the professor stood and made his way to the door to Mike's house. "What did you think was next? Are you coming? We can't do this alone."

The adrenaline from their confrontation with the Triumvirate had worn off and John's nerves were shot. He didn't want the rest of the group to see him like this. He needed a few minutes alone to collect himself.

"I'll be right in. Give me a moment, yeah?"

Professor McKaig regarded him for a moment, then nodded. "We'll be inside. Don't take too long."

John smiled. The professor took one last look at him and then turned to go into the house.

He turned back to the street and looked up into the night sky that still reflected the red and blue lights from the police and fire engines.

It was nearly a new day. And the world was still unaware that everything had changed.

CHAPTER THIRTY-TWO

WHEN JOHN JOINED THE others, the professor, Mike, Apsara, and Ellie were all discussing the battle they had just gone through. Ellie was describing the monster that had attacked them, and how she had managed to destroy the beast. John didn't want to interrupt her story, but he wanted to make sure Mike's daughter was okay. He sidled up to Mike as Ellie and Apsara continued to regale the professor with their tale.

"How's your daughter?" John asked.

"She's sleeping," Mike answered. "Apsara gave her something, and she was out like a light."

"Good," he said, rubbing his face in relief. Mike's daughter was safe. That was all that mattered.

Mike stood and moved closer to him, his eyes darting low. "Listen, John, I know handing over the book wasn't what we had in mind, but—"

"But nothing," John said. "Anyone else would have done the same thing in your position. I know we all feel the same. We tried it my way and failed. You did what you had to do, and I don't blame you for that."

Mike appeared to relax at this, his face releasing the tension that had appeared when John walked in.

"Besides," John added, "thanks to Ellie, we still have access to everything that was in the book. It's not like we're going at this blind."

"What?" Ellie turned to them. "I heard my name, what?"

"We got all the pages, right?" he asked.

She held her phone up and nodded. "I got 'em all."

She picked up a legal pad that was sitting on the table next to her and leafed through the copious notes she'd been taking all night.

"I gotta tell you though, while I was taking photos of the book, I saw some pretty terrifying spells in there—some that make me want to move to Antarctica if they ever get out."

The professor perked up. "How are you able to read it? That's one of the deadest languages on the planet."

She grinned. "At first, I was only able to read the Old English sections thanks to a handy app I downloaded. But then, I found a spell that said it would allow me to read all languages."

"Your Google-Fu is strong, young padawan," John said. "You'll have to teach that spell to the rest of us. We'll need it."

"I ... uh ... took the liberty of casting it on everyone already," she said, her face turning red. When she saw his look of confusion, she shrugged. "I wanted to make sure I had the right spell and wasn't about to turn myself into a newt or something."

"So, we were your guinea pigs?" Mike asked, eyes wide.

"Not you," she said. "John was the closest so . . ."

John grimaced and shook his head. "Well, I guess since I haven't been turned into a frog yet, I may as well see if your spell worked. Did you send the photos to me yet?"

She nodded. "I airdropped everything I have to everyone here."

He opened his phone and navigated to the text she sent him and opened one of the photos of *The Omnichron*. Sure enough, the mess of symbols and incomprehensible scribblings he had seen back at the library had merged into tight, clear, readable text that he understood on an intuitive level. He read the page Ellie had been taking notes on and raised an eyebrow.

He exhaled and glanced over at Ellie, who nodded.

"You better tell them what you found," he said. He moved over to the couch and collapsed on it, throwing a hand up to his face.

"What is it?" the professor asked, sitting down on the couch, next to Apsara. "Don't leave anything out."

Ellie made eye contact with everyone and sighed. "You understand, this is just what I read, right?"

"Of course," Apsara agreed.

Everyone besides John sat forward and gave Ellie their full attention.

"In addition to the spells I found, *The Omnichron* contains a narrative about how magic was used in the world up to about the eleventh century, which is when I'm guessing this book was written."

The professor nodded. "We've dated the book to a similar time period."

Ellie continued. "The book speaks of magic as if it were as common as running water in our time. People with abilities could harness an unseen force contained in every living being and piece of the world."

"I'm sorry," Mike spoke up, his voice derisive. "Are you talking about the Force? As in Skywalkers, droids, and Ewoks?"

The professor shrugged. "It's an idea found in many of the world's religions. The Iroquois called it Orenda. The Melanesians and Polynesians call it Mana. It's been known as having

Mojo, makutu—heck, even Dark Energy could be thought of as science's unknowable force that flows through everything in the universe. But we're getting off track. Call it whatever you want, it sounds like what Ellie is describing is the mechanism through which we're able to summon these powers."

Ellie nodded. "Precisely. The energy Apsara used for her shield, or the fireball John created, had to come from somewhere. *The Omnichron* says there were very few people who could summon that type of power, and most people relied on them for their magical needs. Anyone who demonstrated those abilities kept them secret, lest anyone usurp them for nefarious purposes."

"Tell them about the Agamoth," John said, still covering his face with his hand.

The group looked over at John, who hadn't moved since reading *The Omnichron*.

"I was just getting to that." Ellie shifted. She glanced at her notes, then continued narrating from where she left off, her tone ominous. "The system worked for a time, until one man began culling the souls of everyone who used magic for his own purposes. This warlock, I guess you'd call him, became exponentially powerful with every soul he harvested."

Apsara was stunned. "Sounds like something out of a movie."

"Worse," Ellie said, a grim expression on her face. "At one point, he had gathered enough mana to summon a demon known as the Agamoth in his effort to conquer everything in reach. According to *The Omnichron*, the warlock used the demon to ravage its way across Europe, slaughtering millions. We knew it as the Black Death, or the plague. But according to *The Omnichron*, that was a story implanted in everyone's memories after the fact."

"How were they able to stop it?" Mike asked.

"A group of wizards worked together," Ellie said.

"The Guardians," John said as he glanced at the professor, who didn't seem surprised at this revelation.

Ellie nodded.

"*The Omnichron* says by the time the Guardians reached the warlock, the Agamoth had become far too powerful for them to contain," Ellie said.

"The Guardians went another way," John said.

Ellie nodded. "They cut off the source of the Agamoth's power by removing magic from our reality. The amulet severed the connection between mana used for magical spells and our dimension's ability to access it."

"No magic, no mana for the demon to feed on, poof, no demon," John said. "You gotta give it to them, it's an elegant solution."

The group stared at Ellie for a moment. She shrugged. "You asked. I'm just going off what the book said."

Apsara sucked in air through her teeth. "Well, that explains where magic went for most of history, but it doesn't explain why it's back now."

"I think it does," John said. "I read the inscription at the hospital, giving you and me powers. I read it again at the library and gave the professor, Ellie, and Mike their powers. I'm guessing one of the Triumvirate read it when they killed Knickerbocker."

"Which means we need to figure out a way to get rid of it again," Apsara said, her voice echoing through the room.

"Now hold on," John said, standing. He stood and removed the amulet he had been carrying in his pocket all day. "This isn't something we could just do. We'd be liable to kill ourselves trying."

"He's right," Ellie said. "Even combined, we don't have enough energy to pull off the spell. The book said it took the mana of every Guardian and thousands more to charge the amulet with enough power to sever the connection."

"Chicken and the egg," the professor said from the corner of the room. "You need to imbue enough people with the ability to perform magic before you can harvest their mana to seal magic off from our dimension again."

"And right now, we don't have that kind of firepower or time," John said. "I have a feeling things are going to get a lot worse before they get better."

Mike looked back and forth at the rest of them. "I don't know about the rest of you, but I'm very okay with giving up these stupid powers and staying here to take care of my daughter. I don't need or want this kind of stress in my life. I served my time."

"The stress is coming for you whether you have your magic or not," Ellie said. "They know who you are and what you're capable of. You don't think they'll try and come back to recruit or kill you?"

"Did those three strike you as the type who will be satisfied with a book?" the professor added. "They'll be back."

"The fact is, you're already on board this ride," John said, facing Mike. "I don't know if it's as simple as saying you want to get off."

"Oh yeah?" the Mike asked, fire in his eyes. "Watch me."

He turned on his heel and stormed to the rear of the house where his daughter's bedroom was. John and the rest of the group watched him go. Ellie stood, as if to go after him, but John held up a hand.

"Let him go," he said. "He doesn't have to be a part of this if he doesn't want to."

"But we will need him," the professor protested.

John shook his head. "We're not going to get far with someone who doesn't want to help. What we need to concentrate on is learning some new spells."

"You intend to take them on again." Apsara sounded astonished. "We've only survived so far thanks to luck and their good graces. Do you really think you can beat them?"

"I don't think we can—at least not yet," John said. "But if we don't, we're going to have a lot of scared folks in Southern California, and I don't think they'll stop here."

"What now?" the professor asked.

John picked up his phone and flashed the screen at everyone. "We go back to school and study everything we can in this book. The more information we have, the better prepared we'll be to take on the Triumvirate again."

The professor nodded and stood next to him. "I'm with you."

"Me too," Ellie said. "I haven't felt this alive since Paris."

"I'm in," Apsara added. "If you want to stay alive, you'll need my help."

John nodded in approval. "Then let's get started."

CHAPTER THIRTY-THREE

APSARA INSISTED THEY ALL try to get some rest over the next few hours. It had been a long day and an even longer night. There were minor protests, but they were tired and after the adrenaline rush from the fight wore off, her new friends had tacitly accepted her mandate they all go to bed.

Mike made it clear he had no interest in joining their fight, but he had been gracious enough to allow them to stay at his home while they rested and nursed their wounds. Apsara suspected the real reason he kept them around was in case the Triumvirate returned.

After everyone had taken a shower and retired to where they were sleeping for the night, she snuck off to the kitchen where she wanted to study the pages Ellie had forwarded to their phones.

Because of her experience with the potions section, she decided to start with that portion of *The Omnichron*. After seeing them work for the Knickerbocker boy and Mike, she was fascinated with the potions and spells that claimed to cure all sorts of ailments and boost a person's abilities.

She stepped to the kitchen, eager to try some of the recipes, and helped herself to Mike's pots and pans, along with everything in his cupboards. She didn't think he'd mind.

She had expected 'eye of newt' to appear at least once in the recipes she was looking through, but so far, there was nothing exotic about the ingredients, most of which were common foods and spices and easily found in Mike's well-stocked kitchen.

While the potions were all made from remarkably simple ingredients, they often needed something related to the potion's use. For example, one spell that fortified a front door required dust from the door's hinges. Another spell that guaranteed unlimited hair growth needed a sample hair from the person who wanted the potion.

After an hour of practicing the incantations, she had whipped up another potion she thought would be handy for their upcoming study session. She was so absorbed in her work, she didn't notice John standing at the doorway, watching her as she hovered over the many bubbling pots and pans on the stove.

"Hey," he said, catching her attention. She looked up, startled by his sudden appearance.

"Hey," she rolled her neck around and rubbed her eyes. The clock on the microwave said 3:34. She hadn't realized how late it had gotten.

"I thought you mandated us to all get some sleep." John's voice was friendly, if not a bit accusatorial.

"I got to thinking about the potions," she pointed to her phone, which was next to the stove filled with her newly created experiments. "I wondered if there might be something here we could use for our next encounter."

"Next encounter?" John grunted. "The last two were enough for me."

"This isn't over, and you know it," she said. She held out a vial to John. "Try this."

He accepted the small vial from her, hesitating before he placed it to his lips. "This isn't going to hurt, is it?"

"Where's the trust?" she asked, a slight smile tugging at the edge of her lips. "You're the one who needs this, not me."

"Fine," John said, taking the vial from her. He eyed the blue liquid and then drank it quickly. His face brightened. "What's in this? Red Bull and cocaine?"

"Nothing so dramatic," she said chuckling. "Just a little sugar water, cinnamon, and sage. The magic comes from the incantations."

He frowned. "Strange. It didn't taste anything like that."

She shrugged. "I think that's because of the spell I cast. I think the magic affects the liquid on a molecular level, which changes the flavor profile of the potion as it gains abilities. I wonder if it really matters what I put in the potion so long as it's part of a ritual and I say the magic words."

John shook his head. "Used to be that 'the magic words' meant 'please' and 'thank you.'"

He finished the remaining liquid in the vial and looked at it with an approving look. "That was . . . refreshing."

"*The Omnichron* says this particular potion will restore a person's mana," she said, taking the small vial John handed back to her. "I thought it was a good idea to make a batch before our next encounter with the Triumvirate."

"How much did you make?"

She pointed to the kitchen where an enormous pot simmered on the stove. "Enough to get us through whatever conflict is coming."

John watched her with a new respect in his eyes. She felt her cheeks flush and looked away.

As if sensing she was uncomfortable, John switched topics, looking back down at his phone and the list of spells. "There are hundreds of spells in here. But I can't help but wonder what we're missing."

"A strategy," she said. "We got caught with our pants down because we aren't criminals used to violence. That is an advantage the Triumvirate will always hold over us I'm afraid."

John grunted. "We're just babes in the woods."

"Hardly," Apsara shot him a look. "But we need to start thinking like them and figure out how we can stop them before anyone else gets hurt."

"That's a tall order," he said, thinking of the professor and Ellie, who had fought harder than anyone. "Then again, Ellie didn't blink when she took on that monster. Neither did you."

She blushed. "I keep thinking I'll wake up and all of this will be a bad dream."

John considered that. "We may still wake up yet."

He turned back to scrolling through the pages of *The Omnichron* on his phone.

Apsara did the same. If there was an answer for how to find and stop the Triumvirate, she hoped the four of them could find it in time.

CHAPTER THIRTY-FOUR

DANIEL WAITED IN THEIR stolen vehicle next to an empty lot. Their mysterious employer had directed the Triumvirate to bring *The Omnichron* to an abandoned building in the middle of the San Fernando Valley. Daniel hadn't been to the valley in a long time, and it took some time to find the address.

No sound, no sign of anyone. No indication anyone waited for them.

"Do you sense anyone?" he asked Letty.

She closed her eyes and drew in a breath. "Two people, a man and a woman."

"Then let's not keep our audience waiting," Daniel said.

They opened the door of the car and walked toward the lobby where a flickering light barely illuminated the inside.

"We're here!" Daniel called out.

He heard a loud click, then the buzz of hydrogen lamps coming online. The bright orange light filled the large warehouse. Two people stood next to a computer. The man had a briefcase handcuffed to his wrist.

"Good evening." The woman spoke first as Daniel, Letty, and Cody approached. "My name is Elizabeth Kent. This is Jackson Davis. We are representatives of your employer."

"Where is he?" Daniel demanded. "I asked him to be here."

"Yes." The woman turned to the computer and pressed a button. "Go ahead, sir."

The screen flickered to life and a silhouetted figure appeared.

"They have *The Omnichron*?" The voice was disguised, distorted, the robotic voice disconcerting.

"We have it." Daniel nodded to Cody, who pulled it out of his bag. "We were told there would be a bonus."

Davis stepped forward, unlocked the handcuff, placed the briefcase on the table and opened it. Inside was a USB drive. He pulled it out and offered it to Daniel.

Daniel took it, looking confused. "What's this?"

"That is a cryptowallet worth just shy of one point six billion dollars," the silhouetted figure said. "Depending on market fluctuations of course."

Cody pumped his fist and even Letty's normally stolid face cracked a smile. But Daniel didn't say a word.

"One point six billion," Daniel repeated the number looking at the USB stick in his hand.

"If you wish to verify, Ms. Kent is more than happy to show you how to access your funds on this laptop," the silhouette purred. "But that is of course, contingent on you giving me *The Omnichron*."

"One point six billion," Daniel whispered again. It was more money than he had ever dreamed of having in his life. It was more than he ever expected—even divided three ways.

"Yes. *The Omnichron* now," the silhouette said, the voice beginning to sound impatient.

Cody's eyes lit up. He stepped forward to offer the book, but Daniel raised a finger, stopping his younger brother.

"We have a deal," the silhouette snarled. "There is still a password on that USB key that you will need to access the funds. You won't get that unless I get *The Omnichron*."

Daniel looked at the silhouette on the screen and smiled.

"All right then." He tossed the USB to the confused Davis, who caught it with one hand.

"Don't let them leave!" the silhouette shouted. "That book is mine!"

"Letty, show them what we've learned," Daniel said.

Letty grinned and clenched her fist. Elizabeth screamed as thousands of cuts appeared all over her body.

Davis went to grab a gun from his waistband, but he was too slow. Cody crossed the distance in a split second and threw a glowing orange fist into the man's temple. The man instantly crumpled to the ground; his head caved in.

Elizabeth was bleeding out, still screaming as Daniel approached the silhouette on the computer and leaned down to speak to their mysterious employer.

"We both know that what I have in my possession is worth far more than a few measly billion," Daniel whispered. "I'm going to take a lot more than that. A lot more."

Daniel closed his eyes and projected himself into the computer until he found himself inside the wires. It was a bizarre sensation to be aware of oneself but know his body was made of ones and zeros.

And then, he was in an expansive mansion, standing behind a balding man in a silk bathrobe, who was busy shouting at the camera.

"Ahh, Mr. Mysterious Employer," Daniel said. "How nice it is to meet you."

The man turned and Daniel smiled when he recognized the man in front of him. "Why, Senator, I had no idea you were into the occult."

The man who had represented Kentucky for the last two decades shouted in surprise and anger as he jumped up from his chair. But he was too old and too slow to be any real threat. Daniel waved a finger, casting a spell that froze the man in midair. He closed his fist, feeling the man's body crumple as he intensified the spell. The man screamed until his body popped. Blood and viscera splattered everywhere.

Daniel laughed. The power within him grew even stronger. He closed his eyes and was teleported back to the warehouse where Letty and Cody finished their victims.

"Where the hell did you go?" Letty demanded the second he returned.

"I discovered who our employer was," he said. "And then I killed him."

"Anyone we need to care about?" Letty asked.

A grin spread across his face. "Not anymore."

Letty chuckled and Cody joined in.

"What's next?" Cody asked. "You didn't get the password for the wallet, did you?"

"Crypto is dead," Daniel said. "We have bigger fish to fry, including learning how to read that damn book. That has all the answers we will ever need."

He turned to Letty. "The group who possessed *The Omnichron* had the ability to read it. We must find them and make them translate this for us. There's untapped potential here. And you know how I hate untapped potential."

Letty nodded. "We know their names. I'll contact my sources to see if we can get a ping off their cell phones and find out where they went."

"Good," he said. "After we find them, we'll get this book translated and nothing will stop us."

CHAPTER THIRTY-FIVE

AFTER FINISHING HIS TALK with Apsara, John stumbled his way to Mike's couch where he collapsed into a deep sleep. While it was a far more comfortable place to take a nap than he anticipated, his sleep was anything but peaceful. He tossed and turned the rest of the night with nightmares of hundreds of angry spiders pursuing him through a maze with no escape.

He woke as one of his dreams became all too real and he sat, unsure where he was at first and covered in sweat.

He sat up to see the professor still dozing on the overstuffed recliner, the hair from his lengthy beard laying across his chest as he snoozed.

He smelled coffee brewing, helping to jog his memory. He was at Mike's house in Sylmar alongside a group of ragtag heroes with the ability to cast magic spells.

"Just another Saturday morning." He sat up, slowly rising for the day as he rubbed the sleep from his eyes.

Glancing at the clothes he'd left in the floor, he scooped up the white T-shirt that he had been wearing for the last few days and winced. Unfortunately, the nearest change of clothes he owned was in the go bag in his car back at the hospital.

He put on the sour-smelling shirt and wondered if Mike had any clothes he could borrow. Mike had a similar frame and if he didn't want to smell like a yeti, he could deal with a few tight shirts and pants.

He sighed. What he smelled like was the least of his concerns. His brain was concentrating on small problems in a futile attempt to avoid the big one—namely the Triumvirate and the danger they posed to humanity.

Throughout his entire radio career, John had worked best when he was alone. In school he had loathed group projects and having to count on anyone else for his success. Or worse—someone counting on him being let down because he failed at completing a task. The fact his new friends were turning to him as their de-facto leader made him feel more than a little uncomfortable.

But then again, if not him, who?

He yawned, still feeling exhausted and stretched his limbs, trying to work out the kinks after his night on the sofa. Glancing at the clock, he saw it was only six a.m. and he had only managed to catch a few hours of sleep.

John exited the room and moved into the kitchen where he saw Apsara still pouring over the photos of *The Omnichron* while a cup of coffee steamed next to her.

"Were you able to get any sleep?" he asked, stepping into the kitchen.

She threw him a withering look and rolled her eyes. "Do you have any idea what it's like to work at a hospital and spend 20 hours in the ER? I'm well-acquainted with my friend, Mr. No Sleep."

He raised an eyebrow, tilting his head in concern. "Medice, cura te ipsum."

She grunted and laughed, "Physician, heal thyself. You're not wrong."

"I'm just saying, weren't you the one lecturing the rest of us last night on how important sleep was for our bodies?" he asked.

She waved away his concern. "Do what I say, not what I do. I've dealt with worse."

"Coffee any good?" he asked as he poured himself a cup.

"Better than most," she answered. "Take a look at this."

He approached her, enjoying the scent of the coffee, and leaned over the table where she had spread several photographs of *The Omnichron's* page across the kitchen table.

"You must have used every ounce of Mike's printer ink," he said, picking up one of the photos. "That stuff's expensive."

"Look at this," Apsara said, ignoring him. She pointed to the border of every page that contained an intricate pattern of interlocking swirls and loops.

"I saw that," he said. "I figured they were some kind of decoration."

"I did as well," she said. She re-arranged the photos into sets of four so that the borders lined up.

"When you arrange the pages like this, an illustration appears in the center of each one."

"Huh," he said. "Interesting. So what?"

"Take a closer look."

He leaned down and saw that the intricate swirls and loops were a repeating series of words and phrases.

"What is this? I can't translate it." He looked up. "I thought the spell Ellie cast last night allowed us to translate everything."

"And isn't that interesting?" Apsara's face turned mischievous.

Annoyed, John placed the photo he was holding back on the table. "And?"

"And," she began with relish, "I recognized the pattern."

"What is it?"

"A rune," she said triumphantly as if that explained everything.

"A rune?" he asked. "I don't get it."

"Runes, magical symbols that are believed to contain some seriously powerful magical energy," she said, pointing to one. "Like that ring of yours, the rune allows you to imbue items with a powerful spell that you can use at your discretion. For example, look at this one here."

She pointed at the set of four photographs she had grouped together on the upper right hand of the table. "According to the translation I discovered, this rune will protect the wielder from energy blasts."

"Like what the man in black was using against us last night?" John was beginning to understand that Apsara might have found the edge they would need to defeat the Triumvirate.

"I've already found dozens of these runes hidden throughout *The Omnichron*," she said, pointing to the photos she'd arranged around the kitchen table. "These are just the ones I've found in the last few hours. My gut tells me every single page contains runes just like this."

"This is some truly excellent work, Apsara." He clasped her shoulder, squeezing it in excitement. "I guess you really don't need sleep like us mere mortals."

She blushed and went back to arranging more of the photographs, revealing another rune.

"The question is, how do we use them?" he asked, looking at the scattered pages.

She shrugged. "Traditionally, runes were carved on weapons and places of defense."

He pointed at the rune closest to him. "What's that one do?"

She stood and walked closer to him, and he felt very conscious of how good she smelled and how terrible he must smell. Fortunately, she didn't seem to notice. Or care.

Her lips moved as she silently translated the rune in front of her.

"I think this is good for projectile-type weapons," she said. "It imbues the object with an explosive energy."

John smiled. "I've got an idea."

CHAPTER THIRTY-SIX

JOHN AND APSARA WENT into Mike's backyard holding the bow Ellie had liberated from the library.

"So, all we have to do is draw or carve this rune into the bow and it'll imbue the arrows with an explosive energy?" he asked, looking at the photo they'd taken of the rune Apsara had discovered.

Apsara pursed her lips and shrugged. "That's what this one says. Though, I'm not sure if it needs to be on the arrow or the bow itself."

She took out a Sharpie from her pocket and pointed to the weapon. "Here, try this."

He took the marker and drew the rune on the stock, getting it as close as possible to the image Apsara held in front of him.

When he finished, she inspected his work with a critical eye.

"Looks right to me," she said.

"Great," he said. "Now what?"

She shrugged and handed him the arrow. "Now we see if it works."

He took the arrow, notched it, and pulled it back.

He waved at Apsara, motioning for her to take a step back. "I'm not sure how big this boom might be, so you might want to stand back a bit."

She nodded and stepped back, holding her hands over her ears.

He took aim for a large birch tree growing in Mike's backyard and released the arrow.

The shaft sailed through the air and pierced the bark of the tree with a sharp thud.

He grimaced and lowered the bow. Apsara looked just as confused as he felt.

"I was promised an earth-shattering kaboom," he said, feeling disappointed. "Maybe those runes aren't as magical as we think."

Apsara pursed her lips in concentration. "I don't think that's it. The author wouldn't have hidden them like that if they weren't important."

John turned the bow, examined the symbol on the stock, and compared it to the photo. It was a perfect copy of the rune found in the book—what were they missing?

"What if it's like the potions?" Apsara said after a moment. "Remember, my potion didn't work until I said my incantation over it."

John considered what she was saying, but his gut told him the runes were different somehow.

He examined the rune on the stock of the bow once again.

"Show me the photo again," he said. Apsara obliged, withdrawing the pages, and showing him the rune.

He scrutinized the rune and a broad grin spread across his face. "I think I understand how this magic works."

He notched another arrow.

He traced the rune with his fingertip, focusing his will into the symbol and what he wanted it to do. He muttered the strange words he'd seen in the rune, then took a deep breath and released the arrow.

This time, when the arrow hit the birch tree, it exploded in a fiery shower of sparks, creating an enormous fireball that knocked the tree over, splitting the trunk into a dozen pieces of shrapnel, scattering it across the backyard.

Apsara and John winced. They weren't doing Mike any favors with his neighbors at this time of the morning.

"That was a lot louder than I thought it would be," John shouted, tugging at his ear, trying to clear the ringing the explosion caused.

"How did you do that?" she exclaimed, looking back and forth between him and the now shattered tree. "That was amazing."

Mike burst out into the backyard, holding a gun, searching for the source of the explosion. Ellie was hot on his heels, holding her bow while the professor cautiously observed the scene from behind them.

"What the hell was that?" Mike was dismayed to see the birch tree on fire. "Jesus, what did you do to my tree?"

He ran over to the garden hose and turned it on, spraying the fiery remnants left from the exploding arrow.

"Sorry about that, Mike," John said, stepping forward. "We discovered something in *The Omnichron* and wanted to give it a try."

"My bow did that?" Ellie's eyes were wide as she stepped forward to examine the bow in John's hands.

John turned the bow over to show her the rune he'd drawn on it.

"We got you an upgrade," he handed the weapon to Ellie. "Apsara discovered something in the book that could give us the edge we need against the Triumvirate."

Mike finished dousing the tree with water, white smoke rising from the stump, and turned back to the group, a sour expression on his face. "You couldn't find anything else to explode?"

"You're right." John sheepishly hung his head. "I didn't think about how loud that might get. But on the upside—"

"No, no upside," Mike grumbled. "That was my favorite tree."

The professor approached Mike and patted him on the back. "I wouldn't worry too much, my dear boy. When all this nasty business is through, I'll help plant a new tree. I've got quite the green thumb you know."

The professor turned to John and Apsara. "It does seem important for the rest of us to find an area where we can practice our magic in peace and without drawing too much attention."

John considered what the professor was saying. "You're right, but the Triumvirate has had the book for nearly twelve hours now. I'm worried if we spend too much time studying, we might miss our shot on stopping them before they get too out of hand."

Ellie examined the rune he'd drawn on the stock and grinned. "I like our chances a lot better now that I have a portable cannon at my side."

"That's not the only rune," Apsara said. "There are more."

The professor held up his hand. "Going into a battle un-prepared will certainly mean our deaths. We barely got away from those three last night. I don't like our chances if we don't start using and understanding this magic in a more controlled setting. And"—a smile spread across the professor's face— "as it happens, I have the perfect spot where we can study without attracting too much attention."

John chewed the inside of his lip until deciding the pro-fessor was right. He turned to Mike and held out his hands.

"I know you've got your kid, but is there any chance I can convince you—"

Mike didn't even allow John to finish his sentence. "No."

"You saw what those three could do," John started again. "It's important we stick together."

Mike pointed to the second floor of his house. "That room right there contains the most precious thing I have in my life. I will not risk getting killed, not now, not ever, no matter the threat. I will not leave my baby alone in this world."

John figured that would be his answer, but he had to ask. Mike was a former Marine and knew how to take care of himself.

"I appreciate you putting us up for the night," he said. "We'll do what we can to prevent the Triumvirate from coming back."

Mike extended a hand. "I appreciate that."

John shook his hand and felt the mutual respect contained in it. "I'm sorry we dragged you into this."

Mike chuckled. "Far as I'm concerned, it was my own dumbass fault for going back in the library."

John turned back to the group. "All right, Professor, where are we going?"

"It's a bit remote," the professor began."

"Remote is exactly what we need." John glanced over at the still smoldering remains of the tree. "Because I don't know about the rest of you, but after last night, I'm looking forward to blowing stuff up."

CHAPTER THIRTY-SEVEN

Apsara's SUV was the only vehicle large enough to fit all four of them comfortably. John volunteered to drive, and she accepted his offer for two reasons. For one, she wanted to keep looking through her notes about *The Omnichron* to see if she could find any other secrets hidden within the book's pages. And the second, perhaps more important reason: she wanted time to herself to process everything she had experienced over the last few days.

If what *The Omnichron* said about the runes were true, then they would be a powerful weapon in their fight against the Triumvirate. Destroying Mike's prized tree was proof enough of that.

Many of the runes she had translated so far were turning out to be defensive spells. Traps, confusion spells, and powerful energy shields—all things she knew they could use, but it would take time to catalogue them all.

There were hundreds of runes, but most of them didn't look like they would apply to their situation. One rune she translated claimed to be an effective defense against trolls—which only raised even more questions for her. If *The Omnichron* mentioned trolls as a serious threat, did that mean other types of mythical creatures existed? Were werewolves and vampires something she would eventually encounter?

Her brain instinctively wanted to dismiss the idea, but then again, she had nearly been killed by a literal monster summoned by a warlock last night. There were so many questions about her new powers and the things she had seen over the last few days that the rational side of her brain had all but given up trying to explain things.

"You all right over there?" John asked, interrupting her reverie.

John was driving them down a dirt road the professor had directed them to take, and it was slow-going. The rain had created deep gashes in the road that her SUV was having trouble with.

"Oh, just experiencing a good old-fashioned existential crisis." A slight smile appeared on her face. "You know, questioning the nature of reality and my place in it."

He chuckled. "And the fact we can perform magic?

"I was the perfect student. A skeptic of the highest order. Scoffing at anything that didn't have a rigorous scientific explanation."

"And now?"

She paused, staring out the window at the passing desert scenery. "And now, I feel a bit like the world fell out from beneath my feet and I'm flying without really knowing how I'm doing it."

John grunted and shook his head. "That sounds a lot more pleasant than what's going on in my head."

She turned to him, amused. "And that is?"

John darted his eyes over at her and appeared to internally debate something. After a moment he turned his eyes back to the road and refused to comment further.

"Oh, now you've piqued my interest," she said. "No one hesitates that long without a story."

But before she could cajole John any further, the professor leaned forward from the back seat, positioning himself between them.

"It's just over there." The professor pointed to a gate located on the side of the road about a quarter of a mile ahead of them. "That's the testing range I was talking about."

John slowed the vehicle and pulled onto the dirt shoulder, dust spewing up behind their vehicle. They slowed until the vehicle rolled to a stop in front of the barrier to another longer dirt road that seemed to stretch into the desert for miles.

"Do we have a key?" Apsara asked. "Where are we?"

"My property. I own sixty acres next to the Southern California Aircraft Boneyard." The professor withdrew a ring of keys from his pocket and began pawing through each one. "There isn't another living soul around us for miles."

The professor found the key he was looking for and popped it off the keyring. He handed it to Apsara. "My dear, would you mind?"

She nodded and took the key. Opening the car door, she was about to step out when John reached out and touched her arm.

"I was thinking about what happens in case we fail. Failure . . ." He swallowed. "It's not something I've ever been good at."

She smiled reassuringly at him. "Chaos is a great motivator for change. But putting the weight of the world on your shoulders is too much for one person. That's why we're here together."

She exited the vehicle and quickly unlocked the gate. Waving the SUV through, she closed the gate behind them and hopped back into the vehicle.

After driving for another mile down the dirt road, they made it to the outskirts of the boneyard where dozens of retired B-52 bombers, 737 jets, and other types of passenger planes abandoned to live out their days, rusting in the middle of the Mojave Desert.

"Park over there." The professor pointed. "This will be a good spot for us to practice. The rubbish and planes will block the view of anyone who might be driving along the road."

John obliged and pulled Apsara's SUV into the dirt lot beyond the hull of the craft. He placed the vehicle in PARK, and the group exited the vehicle.

Apsara looked around. The professor was right. This was about as remote a location as one could get from Los Angeles.

She turned, slightly disoriented by the size of the abandoned aircraft that surrounded them. Even after a lifetime of flying all over the world, she sometimes forgot how massive passenger jets really were.

Ellie stepped out, looking around the boneyard. "Where'd all these planes come from?"

"Decommissioned mostly," Professor McKaig said, hopping out of the vehicle behind her. "Some were moved here after the NTSB finished their investigation."

"Investigation?" Ellie asked, looking confused.

"He means after the plane crashed," John answered for the professor.

The professor nodded and pointed down the road where they came from. "The China Air flight that crashed a few years ago in San Francisco is right over there in fact."

"Can we take the tour later?" Apsara interjected. "We don't have a lot of time, and we don't know what the Triumvirate is up to."

"I know what they're up to," John said, looking at his phone.

He showed the screen to his friends, displaying several emails he had received over the last few hours.

"They're using their powers to rob the city blind," John said. "I've been getting emails all morning from my assignment editor about a rash of crimes that occurred last night."

"Like what?" she asked.

"Banks, jewelry stores." John scrolled through his phone and whistled. "One video shows them melting a hole in a bank downtown where they reportedly got away with millions of dollars."

"Magic?" Ellie asked.

"I'm hard-pressed to think of anything else," John said. "For now, the Triumvirate appears to be content robbing the world blind. That's good news for us."

"It is?" Apsara asked.

"I was worried they'd be smart and go to ground. Use that time to learn everything they could from the book before they got started." He waved his phone with a smug smile on his face. "But it seems like greed won out. That gives us time to practice and level up."

"It looks like they're leveling up a bit themselves," Apsara frowned as she looked at the news on her own phone.

He shrugged. "That's why we're out here."

"Something has been bothering me about our confrontation with them last night," Apsara said. "They could have killed us back at Mike's house."

"But they didn't," John finished.

"And I'm left wondering, why?"

"They want our abilities?" Ellie chimed in.

"I don't think that's it," John said, shaking his head. "They have the ability to cast their spells. Perhaps they have a code?"

"You saw what they did to the Knickerbocker boy," she reminded him. "Anyone capable of that kind of curse isn't someone who hesitates to kill."

John frowned, and she turned to the professor.

"It's your show, Professor. Where should we begin?"

The professor ran a hand through his thinning hair and removed the wire-rim glasses from his face. The morning was already growing warm, and the day promised to be a scorcher.

"When teaching someone about a new subject, starting with the fundamentals is always best," the professor said. "I say we pair off and practice the defensive and offensive skills we've learned so far then move onto more advanced spells from there."

"John, you and Ellie pair off and the professor and I will work together," Apsara said, taking charge. "Then we switch?"

They nodded. She turned and walked to a clearing, the professor following close behind. When she felt they were far enough away from John and Ellie, she stopped and concentrated on an energy spell she'd read in *The Omnichron* on the way up. A bright ball of blue energy formed in her hand. She turned to face her friend.

"Well, Professor?" she asked. "Let's see what you got."

She drew back her hand and let the ball of energy go, hurling it toward the professor. He put up a hand and a bright orange energy barrier snapped into place between him and the crackling ball of energy that was coming toward him.

Her spell smashed against his shield, sparks flying everywhere. She grinned.

"Not bad."

He returned her smile with a smirk of his own. "My turn."

CHAPTER THIRTY-EIGHT

ELLIE SANK TO THE ground, exhausted by the effort of trying to summon a shield spell. Despite her best efforts, she had not been able to summon an effective shield, unlike the rest of her companions.

Over the last several hours, she and the rest of her new friends had been practicing their magical abilities in the middle of the Mojave desert. It was hot, with the sun already blazing high above them, bringing temperatures in the mid-nineties.

While she had shown talent with the runes and the more offensive spells, she hadn't been able to master anything more than that.

John approached her, his shadow falling on her face. She looked up, sweat dripping from her brow.

"How are we feeling?" he asked, offering her a water bottle.

"Probably about as good as I look." She took the proffered water and unscrewed the lid, drinking the remaining contents.

"Remember to let go. Allow the magic to appear through your intent," John said. He took a few steps back and motioned for her to get back on her feet.

He lobbed another large fireball at her, and she waited until the very last second to raise a shield and bounce it away.

He nodded. "Nicely done! You should feel proud. It's not exactly chemical engineering."

She grunted. "Honestly, it might be a lot easier to deflect a fireball than it is to describe organic chemistry interactions."

He chuckled. "I have no doubt. How do you feel about your offense? Your archery skills must be coming in handy."

She lowered her head and then looked back up at him. "I'm trying. That's about the best I can say."

John tilted his head and patted her on the shoulder. "Don't sweat it." He waved a hand at her bow and arrow. "I've heard you're pretty good with that thing."

"Better than most." A smile appeared on her face as she thought back to the final shot that had clinched the gold. "Not as good as some. I'm always working on my technique. Speaking of which . . . do you mind?"

John took a step back. "You know, you were impressive as hell out there in Paris. It's a privilege to watch a gold-medal winner in action."

She felt her face flush at the compliment. "Don't get too excited. It's been a few years, and I haven't been to the range as often as I used to."

The professor approached them looking down at Ellie with a triumphant expression.

"How many arrows do you have left?"

"Not enough," she admitted. "I've been working with the few I have left after last night's fight with the Triumvirate. I'll admit, I'm not going to be much good if I run out."

The professor grinned. "Then I think we need to up your offensive capabilities."

Ellie tilted her head in confusion, looking at the professor. He only held up a hand and smiled. He closed his eyes and muttered a few words. As he finished chanting, he pressed his hands together, then pulled them apart.

A bright blue competition bow appeared as he pulled his hands apart, and she looked at the conjured item in shock. He handed her the weapon and smiled.

"I think you can do a little damage with this." He gestured for her to take it.

"I think I can do a *lot* of damage with this," she said with a grin. "How did you do that?"

"I've been delving into conjuring spells," the professor replied. "Just pulled the string back and an arrow will appear. You should be able to conjure however many you need."

"Thanks, Professor," she said, admiring the heft and feel of her new weapon.

"I thought learning how to conjure items might come in handy." the professor said. "In fact, I'd like to show you something if you and Ms. Sarkissian here are through?"

John nodded, then turned his attention back to her. "You gonna be okay?"

"Sure," she said. "I'm going to keep practicing, maybe get some of those runes inscribed on my new bow."

John nodded and then retreated to the shade where the professor was waiting for him. Ellie spotted Apsara working on her form to summon shield spells and approached her.

"Dr. Choi?"

"Please," Apsara turned to her with a gentle smile on her face. "I think you can call me Apsara, Ellie."

"That is a beautiful name, by the way," she said with a smile. "I love it so much."

"Thank you," Apsara said. "Did you wish to join me in doing some shield work?"

Ellie shook her head. "I was hoping you might help me inscribe some of those runes you and John found on my new bow." She showed Apsara what the professor had conjured for her.

"Of course," Apsara said, withdrawing a black permanent marker and her cell phone from her pocket. "Just give me a moment to find the reference photos in my phone. It shouldn't take me long."

Apsara held out her hand and Ellie was flummoxed for a moment.

"The bow," Apsara said. "I'll need it to inscribe the runes."

"Of course," Ellie said, hesitating for a moment before handing it over. She never liked letting other people touch her archery equipment, but this was a special occasion.

Apsara took it from her, a smile on her face. "I promise to be gentle."

Ellie nodded and watched as Apsara set to drawing on the bow. After several moments, she finished, but not before examining her work with a critical eye. Apsara stood, handing the bow back to her.

"These are so cool looking," Ellis said, examining the runes Apsara had drawn on the bow. "What do they do? I recognize this first one as the exploding one, but what about the rest you added?"

Apsara took the bow from her and pointed to the second rune located near the front.

"This one allows you to take control of the arrow and send it wherever you want," Apsara said. She closed her eyes and traced a finger over the rune. It sparked and the bow began glowing.

"Watch."

Apsara nocked an arrow and aimed it at a derelict seaplane located more than three hundred yards away.

"See that seaplane?" Apsara asked. "I'm going to hit the pilot's seat through the window."

"You'll never make that shot," Ellie said. "I sure couldn't. It's too far."

"Not with this rune." Apsara sighted the seaplane, aimed the bow, then released the string.

Ellie wasn't sure what to expect—she turned to watch her new friend use the bow, thinking the arrow would land a few hundred feet away from its target.

Instead, the arrow rocketed out of the weapon and traveled through the air, glowing bright orange as it kept its speed and trajectory until it slammed into the seaplane.

Her eyes went wide, and she grinned.

"You see?" Apsara said, looking satisfied. "The more you focus your will, the farther your arrow will fly."

"Incredible," she said, excited by the possibilities. "What else do you have for me?"

"This one creates a rope of energy that you can use as a grappling hook," Apsara said, pointing to a third rune. She tapped a fourth rune right next to it, with a smile on her face. "This one I thought would be useful."

She raised an eyebrow. "What do you mean?"

"This allows the arrow to ricochet and hit several targets at once."

The doctor inserted another arrow and traced her finger over the fourth rune, activating the magic. She aimed it at a series of discarded airplane panels they had been using as targets.

"Hold the targets in your mind, sight up the primary one, and release . . ."

Apsara released the string. The arrow flew straight and true, hitting the first target with a loud metal *clang*. But instead of the arrow remaining stuck in its target, it ricocheted off onto a second, third, and fourth metal panel, all of which fell to the ground.

Apsara turned, grinning at Ellie who returned the smile.

"You're right, that does look useful," she said taking the crossbow back from her. She pointed to a fifth rune inscribed on the back of the stock.

"What about this one?"

Apsara appraised the rune she carved and hesitated.

"What is it?" Ellie asked.

"It's just that, this one came with a major warning," Apsara said. "I wasn't sure if I should have included it, but it felt like a good idea to have for a 'just in case' scenario."

Ellie tilted her head. "I'm not sure I like the sound of that."

"From what I could translate, this rune disintegrates its target." Apsara's face was grim. "It's a last resort kind of thing."

"You mean like in a fight with the Triumvirate?" she asked.

Apsara shrugged. "As a doctor, I took an oath to do no harm. The world has too many ways to die as it is. But when it comes to dealing with evil . . ."

Apsara trailed off and Ellie could see it had been a difficult choice for her.

"You still carved the rune into the crossbow," Ellie pointed out.

"It's not an easy thing to take a life, Ellie," Apsara said. "I know the stakes are high, but confronting evil with even more evil rarely works out for anyone."

"And yet, sometimes, that's the only thing that works," John said. He approached them both, having finished helping the professor and overhearing the last portion of their conversation.

Apsara sighed. "Perhaps. I'm hoping we find a better way to contain or stop the Triumvirate before we resort to killing them."

"Are you willing to bet your life on it?" John said. "And the lives of everyone else on this planet?"

"If I wasn't, I wouldn't have carved the rune into the bow for her," Apsara replied.

Ellie cleared her throat and interjected before it turned into an argument. That was the last thing they needed right now. "We won't be any good to anyone if all we do is fight. I have the rune and I'm willing to use it."

John raised an eyebrow. "I'm hoping it doesn't come to that. But there may not be any choice."

Apsara shot him an angry look. "I know you feel like you're all gung-ho to kill someone, but have you ever witnessed someone pass away in front of you? Because I have and it is not pleasant."

"I'll take unpleasant over watching the Triumvirate kill either one of you. I guarantee they won't hesitate," John shot back.

He turned on his heel and stomped off.

Ellie watched John walk away, thinking about what he'd said. She didn't think he was crazy or a psychopath who was looking to kill just for the sake of killing. On some level, she knew he was right. It wasn't a pleasant thought to know she might have to take a life.

"All I wanted was to pass my final," she said. "And somehow, I got caught up in a magical conspiracy."

"Pressure creates diamonds," Apsara responded. "At least, that's what my mother used to tell me when I was struggling to get through medical school."

Ellie grunted. "I've heard that before too. That advice always seems to come from someone who's never experienced real pressure."

Apsara laughed and then pointed to the bow. "Until we're faced with a real life-and-death situation, we may as well have some fun blowing stuff up."

She returned Apsara's grin with one of her own and knocked another arrow. Tracing the ricochet and explosive rune on the crossbow, she saw the arrow begin to glow orange.

Taking a deep breath, she aimed at a series of barrels she'd set up as targets and released the bolt. The missile hit the first target, exploding in a glorious cacophony of fire, smoke, and sounds. But the arrow wasn't finished yet—the fireball continued, bouncing between the three other barrels they had set up downrange, each one exploding with a satisfying *clang*.

Apsara cheered and high-fived her.

"Nice shootin' Tex," Apsara said, grinning.

Ellie lowered the bow and watched the barrels burn with a grim satisfaction.

"That . . . was . . . *awesome!*" she said, feeling her face flush. There was something primal about watching stuff blow up—especially when it was you that was making things explode.

Unfortunately, she didn't have much time to enjoy the fireworks. When she turned back to Apsara to see if there were any other runes she could use, she noticed her friend's face had turned from excitement, to confusion, then worry.

"What is it?" Ellie asked.

"Trouble," Apsara said. She pointed to the road where a large plume of dust was being kicked up by a large, dark SUV making their way toward them.

"Who is that?"

"Hopefully some caretaker for the boneyard wondering what the hell we're doing out here," Apsara said, her face growing paler the closer the SUV came to them. "But that truck looks familiar."

Ellie strapped the crossbow to her back and held a hand up over her eyes, squinting to try to get a better look at the approaching vehicle. Her vision was better than most and despite the glare, she recognized the SUV coming toward them.

"It's the Triumvirate," she said, her voice cracking. "They found us."

CHAPTER THIRTY-NINE

JOHN WAS PERFECTING HIS magical skills in a back-and-forth magic missile battle with the professor when he heard Apsara shouting. He looked up and saw her waving her arms, trying to get their attention.

He glanced over to where she was pointing and spotted an approaching SUV trailing a plume of dust.

"Professor?" he patted the older man on the shoulder. "Hey, Professor, how many people know we're out here?"

"No one," the older man said, standing up straight and brushing the dust off his jacket. "You can't get on the property without a key and . . ." The professor trailed off when he saw the approaching vehicle. "Then again . . ."

As the vehicle approached their position, he recognized the driver as the large Triumvirate man who attacked them at Mike's house last night.

"Shall I try to cloak us?" the professor asked.

"Not yet," he replied. "But keep it ready."

The professor nodded. Ellie and Apsara approached and stood next to them as they watched the SUV pull up.

"Is that who I think it is?" Apsara asked, sounding nervous.

Then, as if they had heard her question, the door to the SUV opened and a black boot stepped out.

John felt his stomach drop when he saw the same scarred face that belonged to the man who nearly killed them the other day.

"John!" the man in black stepped out and waved, as if greeting old friends. "So good to see you again. Apsara, Ellie, and Professor McKaig! It's so wonderful having us all together again."

John glanced at the rest of his friends as they gathered around him. Ellie held her bow, an arrow notched and ready to fly at a moment's notice.

The man's two companions exited the vehicle and stood behind their leader.

"I recently realized that we have never been formally introduced," the man in black said, a broad smile on his face. He stepped forward and bowed, holding out his hand as if he were approaching royalty. "My name is Daniel Armstrong."

He stepped aside and waved to his two companions. "This is Letty, my partner in all things, life, love, and of course, crime."

The woman removed her sunglasses and acknowledged them with a slight nod and a grunt.

"And this is my younger brother Cody."

The larger man scowled at their group while Daniel Armstrong grinned, his smile a dark reflection of the man beneath the pleasant facade. The trio were all dressed fashionably, as if they had just finished a shopping spree on Rodeo Drive.

"Can't say it's a pleasure," Apsara replied.

Daniel's face fell, and he clucked his tongue. "Yes. I suppose we have gotten off on the wrong foot, haven't we? That's my fault of course. I had no idea who you were at the time."

"And now you do?" John asked.

The smile returned to Daniel's face, and he nodded. "I do. You are all special. Just like us."

"You really have a way with making normal-sounding conversation ominous, you know that Armstrong?" John said. "We're no more special than anyone else."

"Oh, but you are." The man stepped forward.

John tensed and noticed Apsara shift into a defensive position. He looked over his shoulder to see the rest of the team doing the same and he felt a surge of pride at the people surrounding him. He was also grateful that they had spent the better part of the day practicing their shield spells.

"You are among a very small, select group of people in the world who also have the ability to harness magic," Daniel continued, looking each of them in the eye. "I don't pretend to know how or why we have been blessed with these abilities, but I think it presents a wonderful opportunity."

"Opportunity?" the professor asked. "What do you mean?"

"To team up of course," Armstrong said. "We have the book, but to be perfectly frank, we're having trouble translating it."

"Aww." John's tone was low and mocking. "Do you need someone to do your homework?"

The smile on Daniel's face tightened, but he refused to be baited. "John . . . May I call you John?"

He didn't respond.

"Our shared abilities have taken us beyond the mere mortals who surround us," Daniel said, drawing closer. "Aren't you the slightest bit curious to find out why out of billions of humans on this planet, we are the only ones who can manipulate magic?"

Daniel stepped forward and held up a hand, snapping his finger. A flame erupted and spread up his arm.

"Let us be honest," Armstrong said, taking another step forward. "That is what we're dealing with. No CGI, no tricks, no sleight of hand or mirrors in unexpected places."

John didn't like how close the man in black was getting, but his words made him even more uncomfortable.

"I know you see us as a threat. But I don't see you that way. I simply believe you have the wrong perspective. That has you asking the wrong questions." Daniel snapped his fingers and the flames disappeared. "You should be asking why everyone doesn't have these abilities."

John looked over at his friends, who glared at Daniel and the rest of the Triumvirate. He noticed that Ellie had pulled her bow off her back and notched an arrow.

"There's a lot about this world that's mysterious," John said, trying to sound casual. "I hadn't given it much thought."

"But I have," Armstrong said, stepping back and waving his hand at his companions. "In fact, it's been quite the topic of discussion among my friends here."

"And have you all come to a conclusion?" Apsara asked.

"That we have been mandated by God to correct everything that has gone wrong on this little world of ours," Armstrong said, his eyes flashing. "We are the biblical flood sent to re-balance the scales."

"How?" Apsara snorted. "By robbing banks and jewelry stores?"

Daniel's eyes narrowed. He tutted at her.

"A small diversion to fund our larger plans," he said. "Do you have any idea what we could do with those powers? Imagine the corruption we could expose, the peace we could bring to warring nations."

"That's quite the interpretation," John fired back. "I think you'd find taking power from governments around the world a lot harder than you think."

"Oh, I don't believe that at all," Armstrong said, another cruel smile spreading across his scarred face. "In fact, I believe it will be quite simple once they see this."

He stepped back, held his hands out, palms flat toward the desert floor, and began to chant.

John conjured a shield, and he heard Apsara snap her own shield in place, protecting them all. Ellie and the professor stood behind them as they readied their offensive spells.

Letty and Cody chanted along with the man in black as a fiery circle of energy enveloped them. The hot desert wind kicked up and sprayed them with loose dirt and rocks as the energy vortex swirled and grew larger.

Armstrong opened his eyes and aimed his fist at them. The vortex of energy whirled around his fist and then rocketed toward them. John and the rest of his group ducked, narrowly avoiding the blast of energy.

"You're gonna have to work on that aim of yours," John shouted over the roar of the wind.

"I didn't miss," Armstrong said, the smile even broader now.

John realized the energy summoned by Armstrong hadn't been cast to injure them. Instead, the energy he conjured was swirling around the derelict 737 aircraft next to them, as pieces peeled off the frame and melted into a scrap heap of twisted metal and burning insulation.

"This is the kind of power the world will have to deal with." Armstrong thrust his fist out. Another bolt of energy flew from his fingers and into the burning remains of the plane.

"John!" Apsara shouted, grabbing at his arm. "There are people in there!"

He turned to the burning pile of industrial waste. His jaw dropped. Dozens of figures appeared from the now-flaming pile of airline parts and scraps.

"Oh, what the hell?" John's eyes went wide.

"I think we're gonna get that chance to fight." Apsara projected another shield behind them.

John watched the figures approach their group and swallowed.

He was really beginning to dislike being in charge.

CHAPTER FORTY

THE STEEL GOLEMS EMERGED from the twisted fiery wreck, their metal limbs screeching with effort as they dragged themselves closer to the group. John turned back to the Triumvirate, who had cut off their only avenue of escape.

He saw Ellie notch an arrow and take aim at the approaching figures that were being generated out of the toxic sludge melting off the decaying 737.

"Now do you understand?" Daniel Armstrong shouted over the sound of his amassing army of animated golems. "We can take on the world because the world won't have the slightest idea how to stop our magic."

"What do you want?" John asked through gritted teeth.

"We want the amulet. We want the professor. And we want you all to join us." Daniel shrugged. "Willingly or not, it makes no difference."

The figures grumbled and screeched, drawing closer to the group. The professor, Ellie, and Apsara had tightened up the circle, facing the bizarre golems ambling closer to them.

"Will you comply?" Armstrong demanded over the horrifying sounds being made by the creatures. "Or will you die here today?"

John watched the golems as they clambered over one another, pieces of their bodies falling and reforming as they scrambled to move forward. He could see Armstrong and his crew were enjoying watching them squirm.

"John," Apsara called out to him. "We don't have a choice."

She grabbed his arm, and he looked into her eyes, seeing the steely determination behind them. He allowed a slight smile to touch the edge of his lips and he nodded.

"I know."

John wound up his hands and just like he had been practicing with the professor, channeled the energy through his palms, blasting a path through the golems, ripping them apart like so much tissue paper.

Ellie unleashed her first shot at the approaching golems, the arrow ricocheting around, destroying six with one shot.

John turned to the group and pointed to the path he and Ellie had made for their escape. "Run!"

Armstrong snarled and placed his palm out, sending a large flame shooting toward their group. But Apsara was ready, deflecting the firestorm with a shield she conjured.

The group ran past the burning airframe Armstrong used to conjure the golems—as more of the hideously twisted metal beings dripped out of the sludge. The creatures were fast but couldn't catch them and began throwing red-hot pieces of their metal bodies at the group.

A large piece of burning plastic struck John on his shoulder. He cried out and fell to the ground. One of the creatures was on him in an instant. It grabbed his ankle, the hand burning his skin.

He screamed, which caught Apsara's attention. She took careful aim at the creature holding John down and fired a blast of energy from her right hand, blasting the golem apart.

At the same time, Letty pulled her hands to her chest and the amulet flew out of John's pocket, rocketing toward the Triumvirate woman, who caught it with a grin.

"No!" John cried out. He tried getting up, but his wounded leg made him stumble. Apsara got to his side and helped him to his feet.

"Let's go," she urged, lifting him off the ground.

"The amulet . . ." John said desperately.

"Forget it," she said, pulling him to cover. "We'll get it back, but not if we're dead."

As if to punctuate her point, a large fireball roared over their head, the sound deafening even as it missed them both. John struggled to his feet and limped along to cover with Apsara's help as Ellie covered their retreat. Arrow after arrow flew over their heads and into the crowd of animated steel and plastic zombies which relentlessly pursued them.

"We gotta get out of here," John shouted. He turned to Apsara and tossed her the keys. "Find the car. I'll hold them off while you all make your escape."

"No!" Apsara shouted. "We are not leaving you behind."

"She's right." The professor's face was grim but determined. "We're in this together."

John conjured a fireball and threw it at an approaching golem, knocking it to the ground.

"We need to contain that," he said, pointing to the still burning wreck. "It's the fire. The fire is what's creating those . . . things. Any ideas?"

The professor peered around the corner, looking at the flaming wreckage where more golems appeared. "Project a shield around it and starve the fire of oxygen."

John grunted. "When magic fails, try science. Not bad, Professor."

He turned to Apsara. "You up for it?"

She nodded and shut her eyes, concentrating.

John, Ellie, and the professor did what they could to hold off the oncoming horde of golems while Apsara conjured the shield. But no matter how fast they fired on the creatures, it was becoming clear they wouldn't be able to keep up with the sheer volume of the creeping figures.

"Now would be a good time, Apsara," John called out.

A large blue bubble appeared above the flaming wreckage, but it was too small.

"I . . . can't . . ." she managed after a moment. "It's too much. I need help."

John turned his will to focus on Apsara's blue shield, adding his mana to expand the dome of energy.

"Hold it there," John said, straining with the effort of sending every ounce of energy he could.

Slowly, but surely, the shield extended around the flames, containing them and the golems still animated by Armstrong's spell. John watched with grim satisfaction as the horrid figures melted and reformed but remained trapped behind his and Apsara's shield, screeching and protesting.

The flames on the aircraft's frame subsided as the shield cut off its source of oxygen. For the briefest moment, John allowed himself to feel victorious.

But that moment didn't last long. Behind the remaining legion of golems advancing on their position, the Triumvirate was close behind.

"Professor!" John called out. "They're coming."

Apsara's SUV exploded in a blast of heat and flames as John held up a hand to direct another shield to protect himself and the rest of the group. Letty had destroyed their transportation.

"I just paid that off!" Apsara shouted at the menacing woman. Apsara waved her hands in a wide circle, summoning an intense blast of wind that blew the Triumvirate back on their heels.

"This is our chance," John shouted, grabbing at her arm. "We gotta go."

"Where?" the professor asked, looking at him.

John saw he had a point. The Triumvirate had destroyed their only transportation and cut off any escape. Behind them was the endless expanse of the Mojave Desert.

"Invisibility?" John asked. "If they can't see us, they can't hurt us."

The professor nodded and waved his hand to cast the spell, cloaking them all.

The boneyard fell silent as the conjuring fire around the airplane sputtered and died out, the golems falling silent as their magic faded away. The desert wind picked up, blowing through the alleys formed between the derelict airplanes as the Triumvirate searched for any sign of the five friends.

"Where are they?" Armstrong shouted, his grating voice sounding even harsher. "Find them now. We only need the professor. Kill the rest."

John motioned to his friends to come closer as they huddled under the wing of a discarded 737. Letty approached their position, searching for them as she tossed scrap metal aside, looking for any sign of their hiding place.

He stayed low to the ground, feeling certain the woman would be able to hear his heart hammering in his chest.

Letty's boots scraped the gravel, coming within inches of the group. He shot a glance at Ellie who understood what he was thinking.

She took out another arrow and nocked it into place. Ellie released, and the arrow flew straight toward another plane across the lot, slamming into the landing gear with a solid *clang*.

Letty motioned to the rest of the Triumvirate and pointed in the direction of the noise, moving away from them all.

John exhaled quietly and then motioned to get everyone's attention, pointing toward the boneyard's exit and gesturing for them to get moving.

"Quickly now," the professor whispered, sweat pouring down his brow. "I don't know how much longer I can hold this spell."

John nodded. He knew from experience how much effort the invisibility spell took.

"You and Ellie head for their vehicle," John said pointing to the Triumvirate's empty SUV. "The professor and I will hang back to cover our retreat. Get in and hotwire the car, then pick us up when you can."

"Hotwire their vehicle?" Apsara sounded bewildered by the request. "What the hell do you think they teach us in medical school?"

John grunted in acknowledgement. "It's not rocket science. Pull the wires from the battery, and the ignition and starter wire bundle. Strip them down until you've got both ends exposed. Connect the ignition to the battery wire. Then spark the starter wire. Got it?"

Apsara stared at him blankly for a moment.

"Yeah, I'm gonna go ahead and hope they left their keys in there."

"Don't worry," Ellie said. "I had some not-so-nice uncles who taught me a few things. I can take care of it."

Apsara shrugged and motioned for Ellie to follow her. The pair dashed across the road, the only indication of their presence the footprints they left in the dusty drive.

Armstrong and his companions reappeared from the side of the 737 where Ellie had released her arrow. John knew they were running short on time. If they were going to escape in one piece, they'd have to move fast.

He could hear the professor grunting with the effort of keeping the invisibility spell active on all four of them. They hadn't practiced that spell, so he knew the effort the professor was putting had to be comparable to lifting a two-ton rock all by himself.

"Just a few more seconds, Professor," John whispered. He couldn't take over for him—it was his spell and any interruption in the invisibility would give the Triumvirate an instant bead on their position.

Unfortunately, the effort of maintaining the spell was more than the professor could bear. John watched as his friend's eyes rolled up in the back of his head and he collapsed, their invisibility cloak disappearing at the same time.

"Ellie, fire!" John shouted.

Ellie drew her bow and was about to release, but she was too slow. The Triumvirate spotted Ellie and Apsara standing next to their SUV and shouted, releasing a flurry of spells that froze their friends in place.

The professor had slumped over into his arms. John couldn't shoot off any other spells to help Apsara and Ellie stay invisible. Instead, he watched helplessly as the Triumvirate approached the two women.

John fell back and murmured the incantation to make the professor and himself disappear once again. The weight of the spell was enormous, but he knew if he couldn't hold it, it would be all over for them.

Armstrong and his party approached Ellie and Apsara who were frozen in place and stood in front of them, licking his chops.

"You're not who we came for, but you'll do," Daniel said.

The man nodded to his massive brother who picked up Ellie and Apsara, placing them not-so-gently into the SUV. Armstrong watched his brother load the two women into the vehicle and then turned back to the boneyard.

"Consider my words, Jupiter!" Armstrong's voice boomed across the desolate boneyard. "You've seen the power we possess. It's not too late for you to join us."

John didn't answer, only gritting his teeth as he concentrated to keep the invisibility spell intact over himself and the professor.

Armstrong grinned and twirled a finger in the air, indicating it was time to leave.

"It's been an educational experience, Jupiter," Armstrong shouted again. "I hope you make the right decision."

With that, they loaded into their vehicle. The SUV peeled out and took off.

Only after several minutes passed did John dare drop the invisibility spell. He shook his head and checked on the professor. They were all alive, but they'd lost this round. Badly.

As he watched the dust from the Triumvirate's SUV settle in the morning breeze, he wondered, what kind of chaos would they be responsible for if they lost again?

CHAPTER FORTY-ONE

THE SOUND OF METAL dragging over dirt and gravel was the first sound Professor McKaig became aware of as he regained consciousness. The second thing he became aware of was all the pain. He groaned. His seventy-year-old body complained about the damage it had taken during the fight with the Triumvirate.

He opened his eyes, wincing in pain from the mid-afternoon sun shining directly into his eyes. He tried sitting up but found himself strapped to a makeshift litter made from discarded airplane parts.

John looked back after hearing him try to get loose.

"Easy, Professor," John said over his shoulder. "You took quite the hit back there."

Everything came back to him. The fight with the Triumvirate, the boneyard, those creatures. He shuddered, wondering how he and John had survived.

He tried to speak, but found that thanks to the dry desert air, he was barely able to croak out a gasp. John looked down at him, a smile of relief on his face.

"Thought I lost you back there." John paused, setting the litter down.

"Water?" he managed. His throat felt like sandpaper and from what he could tell, he had stopped sweating—which was never a good sign for a man his age.

"I'm afraid we don't have any water, but I do have something that might help." John removed a small bottle from his pocket, handing it to him. "A special concoction Apsara whipped up for us before the battle."

He eyed the cloudy solution with skepticism.

"Don't worry, it won't hurt you," John said. "In fact, it's meant to help you."

He considered and then shrugged. He uncorked the bottle and drank the potion. It was sweet, with a slight cinnamon taste to it.

The instant the liquid touched his lips, he felt the aches and pains begin to disappear. His headache ebbed, and he felt a surge of energy that made him feel twenty years younger.

John watched his reaction with a grin. "Good stuff, ain't it?"

He nodded and attempted to stand. He was still shaky, and John had to help him to his feet, but he felt a million times better than he had.

"Easy," John cautioned. "I know that stuff works, but I think it takes time for the full effect."

He looked around. "Apsara and Ellie. What happened to them? Where are they?"

John cast his eyes to the ground, his face failing to mask the pain he felt. "The Triumvirate . . . they took them. I was able to hide our position using that stealth spell before they spotted us."

"Smart thinking," he said.

"You started it," John said. "We would've lost everything if you hadn't been able to hang on as long as you did."

He sighed and rubbed his head, feeling about as miserable as he had in his entire life. "But it wasn't enough, was it?"

"No, I guess it wasn't." John said, sounding miserable. "Professor, they got the amulet."

The professor took off his cap and slapped it to his thigh, frustrated at their turn of fortune. But what else could they have done?

"We were outclassed, outgunned, and out-magicked," he said grimly. "How the hell are they able to master their spells so quickly if they needed me to translate *The Omnichron?*"

John sighed. "I've been thinking on that. I believe it goes back to what we've already figured out—that the will and intent is more important than any specific words or movements. I'm thinking *The Omnichron* is more of a guide than a specific set of rules on magic."

He shook his head. "There are still a lot of things listed in there that they don't know about—the runes for instance."

John nodded.

"If they were coming for me, what did they need me for?" He looked at John for the answer, but his friend only shook his head. The professor tapped his fingers to his lips as he often did while in deep though. "They wanted me to translate the book, but not for the spells. What were they looking for?"

"They must have overlooked the Literati spell," John raised an eyebrow. "That's a stroke of luck."

"At this point, I hardly think it matters," he said, waving his hand dismissively. "They have Apsara and Ellie. If they torture them, they might reveal the literati spell and it's all over. I refuse to allow them to get hurt because of me. I'll turn myself over to the Triumvirate. It's the only sensible move left."

"Relax, professor," John said. "For one, I wouldn't count Apsara and Ellie out just yet. Those two are incredibly clever ladies who have shown real talent with magic."

"And two?"

"And two," John looked determined. "I'll be damned before I allow those three to ever beat us again. Those three wanted you for something, I say we find out what that is."

The professor sighed. "They have *The Omnichron* and the amulet."

John took out his phone and waved it at the professor. "And we still have our copy too."

The professor took the phone from John and opened it to the photos section where hundreds of photos from the interior of *The Omnichron* were stored. He stared down at the screen, looking at the tiny font and grunted.

"Why do they make these screens so difficult to read?" he grumbled.

"That's the spirit professor," John said, beaming.

He stood, feeling better after the rejuvenating elixir John had given him. He looked up and down the dusty highway and sighed.

"Onto our next problem, getting ourselves out of the middle of nowhere."

"Time to stick out your thumb professor," John said, throwing his coat over his shoulder. "Hitchhiking is a lost art."

The professor shook his head. "Because of all the murders," he muttered under his breath.

But it wasn't like they had any other options. He caught up to John and stuck his thumb out, hoping that someone would pick them up soon. Without water, they would not last long out in this heat, no matter how many elixirs John might have.

He found himself wishing for the comfort of his couch, a glass of wine in his hand and an episode of his favorite TV show. He swore to himself, if he ever made it out of this, he would never take his 'Me Time' for granted again.

"Come on professor," John called over his shoulder. "We've got some miles to cover."

"Of course, my dear boy," he said wearily. "Of course."

He removed his tweed jacket, tossed it over his shoulder and stuck out a thumb, following John down the highway, hoping that someone . . . anyone, might take pity and pick them up.

CHAPTER FORTY-TWO

THE LAST THING APSARA remembered was a bright flash of light and her body going stiff. Then complete and total darkness.

She awoke to find herself inside the back of an SUV cruising down a freeway next to a still-unconscious Ellie. Whatever spell the Triumvirate had cast on her was beginning to weaken. Her fingers and extremities were starting to tingle as the spell faded.

She wiggled closer to Ellie and nudged her.

"Ellie," she whispered. "Wake up!"

But it was no use. Ellie was out cold. She wondered why she had been able to recover so quickly from the Triumvirate's spell that had knocked them out, but there was no use thinking about that now. She needed to focus on escape.

She was surprised to find the Triumvirate had neglected to tie them up. She wasn't sure if they had been overconfident in their spell that paralyzed them, or if they were simply careless.

She evaluated her range of motion and found the spell they'd used on her was virtually dissipated. While her legs and arms were still stiff, she was again able to move. She took the opportunity to peek over the rear seat of the SUV and look to the front where Daniel, Letty, and the hulking monster known as Cody were seated, having what sounded like an intense argument.

Daniel and Letty were speaking about . . . something. She couldn't quite make it out. It wasn't a pleasant-sounding conversation that's for sure.

The muscular Armstrong leaned over and grabbed Letty's neck, whispering furiously at her. Cody leaned forward, but Daniel waved a hand, smacking his brother in the face, pushing him back, all the while keeping his other hand on the steering wheel.

"Enough!" Daniel shouted. "The powers we have are only as good as the translations we get out of that damned book!"

"You don't need to yell," Letty shot back. "We needed the old man. I was only pointing out the fact that we failed in our mission."

"We have their women." Daniel waved a dismissive hand at her. "They seemed just as able to use magic as the rest of them. I'm betting they can tell us what we need to know. And if they don't, we dispose of them and find the professor like we originally wanted to."

"Why do we even care about that old man and some dusty book?" Letty snarled. "I want to know why we're wasting our time on this inconsequential bullshit when we could be out there robbing the world blind."

"Think about what you're saying," Daniel snapped back at her. "That woman back there was right—looting bank vaults brings us nothing compared to the true power we have in our hands right now. Our sponsor, the late senator, had his own plans with this book that I believe we can usurp and use for our own means now. Robbing bank vaults is a pittance and pales in comparison for what our former employer had in mind."

Letty glanced at *The Omnichron*, which was sitting on the center console between them. "What plans?"

Daniel eyed Letty for a moment and then sighed. "That reporter back there had one thing right—we can create a legion of soldiers out of discarded trash and material but taking on the combined powers of the world will require a weapon far more powerful than anything we've managed to do so far."

"And that weapon is in the book?"

Daniel nodded. "The senator's plans outlined a strategy of world domination by using the book to summon a demon known as the Agamoth. A fearsome creature that is an unstoppable killing machine, capable of destroying anything the world's armies might throw at us."

Cody snorted. "China's got nukes. Russia's got nukes. Pakistan, Israel, India, you think they won't all start throwing down if we start taking over?"

"That's the beauty of the Agamoth," Daniel said. "According to the notes I found in the senator's office, when the creature reaches full maturity, it will be able to use telepathy to influence and control anyone we wish. By the time we are ready, no one will be able to resist us."

"And how long does it take for this . . . Agamoth, to reach full maturity?" Letty asked.

Daniel glared at her. "Information like that is why I needed *The Omnichron* translated. That and for the summoning spell."

Letty sat back in her seat, looking impressed.

"And we do this how exactly?" Letty asked.

"You have so little faith." Daniel jerked his thumb toward the backseat and Apsara ducked, hoping no one had noticed her peeking over the edge of the third seat.

"I counted at least a half-dozen spells they used back there," Armstrong said. "The professor has already translated the book for them. We start by getting those two to tell us how they know how to do so much."

"And if they don't?" Cody asked.

"Then we get persuasive," Daniel replied, his voice sinister. "That spell Letty cast on the boy looked painful enough."

A sly grin spread across Letty's. "I can do even worse now. They won't stand a chance."

Apsara had heard enough. She maneuvered her way to the rear of the SUV and decided she and Ellie were getting out of there.

She whispered a quick spell, raising a shield around the two of them. She positioned her hand and then blasted the rear door off the SUV with a powerful blast of energy.

Apsara gathered Ellie in her arms and jumped out of the vehicle as it sped down the freeway at eighty miles per hour.

They landed, the blue shield she conjured protecting them as they bounced along the freeway, crashing into cars right and left, causing a large pileup on the freeway.

The Triumvirate's SUV's tires squealed as Armstrong slammed on the brakes. Apsara angled their bodies and their momentum shot them off the side of the freeway overpass and down into a canyon that separated the north and south-bound lanes. The shield protected them as they tumbled down the freeway hillside, flattening bushes and bouncing off tree trunks as they rolled down the steep hill.

Eventually, they came to a stop just short of a dry creek bed, about two hundred feet below the highway where the Triumvirate's SUV skidded to a stop.

Dazed, Apsara attempted to stand, but it was too much too soon, and she stumbled, still dizzy from the ordeal. Ellie had been luckier. She had remained unconscious during their escape.

She grasped at her belt, where she'd tucked several vials of the potions she'd brewed back at Mike's house. She opened one, allowing the sweet elixir to pass through her lips.

Instantly she felt her vertigo dissipate, and the wounds she'd suffered at the boneyard heal.

Looking up, she saw the Triumvirate standing at the edge of the road, searching for any sign of them. She dragged Ellie under a large overhang of rocks, hoping it would be enough to hide them from view.

She felt for her phone and when she found it missing, groaned in defeat. Not only was she out of contact with John and the professor, she had also lost her copy of *The Omnichron*.

That left her with the few spells she had memorized. She had spent most of her time studying the potions section, ignoring the practical magic contained in *The Omnichron*.

That lack of study had come back to bite her.

Then, the sound of a heavy weight hitting the ground near them echoed in the narrow canyon where they had hidden themselves. She looked up in shock that they'd been able to track them down so fast. She had hoped they would have more time to make their escape.

Thick rubber soles crunching on the gravel and rocks echoed. She poked her head out to see Cody searching for them.

Apsara knew they were toast unless she could remember the spell the professor had whispered to make them disappear. It was on the tip of her tongue, but she couldn't recall the words.

The man's heavy footfalls approached. She was running out of time.

She shut her eyes and took a deep breath, clearing the negative thoughts from her mind and concentrating on the moment the professor whispered the spell.

She opened her eyes and repeated the sounds.

Cody whipped around the corner where she was holding Ellie's body and looked at the now empty cave.

She held her breath as the hulking man searched for them in the overhang, his eyes darting back and forth. But the stealth spell held.

Finally, the man grunted and gave up. He turned and looked up at the cliff where his two allies were still waiting and scurried up the embankment. It wasn't until the Triumvirate disappeared that she allowed herself to breathe again.

CHAPTER FORTY-THREE

JOHN AND THE PROFESSOR had been walking down the baking southern California highway for several hours, with the hottest part of the day still to come. Even with their magic, he didn't like their chances unless they found a ride. They had already used the revival potions and with no water, they were dehydrating fast—which was dangerous in a desert environment like this.

The professor paused and leaned back, shading his face from the sun overhead. "John, I need a break."

The older man wobbled then plopped down to the ground as John rushed to his side. After a moment, the professor waved him off.

"We need a ride," the professor said. From the sound of the older man's voice, John could tell the professor didn't have much left in him. "I'm not sure how much longer I can do this."

"Hope, Professor. It's a busy highway with lots of traffic," John said even as he waved his hand at the empty freeway. Hundreds of acres of empty scrub brush and desert surrounded them, with nary a soul in sight.

The professor wiped his forehead with a handkerchief. "Hope is a rare resource in this world."

"I used to think like that," John said.

The professor glanced up at him. "And?"

"And I still do," he answered. "But I try to mix in hope anyway."

The professor chuckled and raised a hand. John lifted him up.

"Then hope is what we shall drink instead of water." The professor waved a hand. "Let us continue."

He nodded and turned to follow when they both heard an airhorn as a large semi-truck slowed to a stop a few hundred feet away from them.

John and the professor glanced at each other.

"Like I said, Professor. Hope."

The trucker who had pulled over and picked them up was nice and accommodating—if a little confused as to why they were out in the middle of the desert with no water.

The trucker dropped them off at one of the nicer truck stops in Barstow where they could regroup and plan their next move.

They checked in to take a shower and recover from their ordeal. The professor cautioned John against using his personal cards—there was no telling what kind of resources the Triumvirate had, but thankfully, John had lifted his boss's company credit card for exactly this kind of situation.

Besides, he didn't think his boss would mind—after all, he would get plenty of airline miles.

John emerged from the shower, feeling rejuvenated and ready. He spotted the professor sitting at a table in the corner of the truck stop, having already finished his shower. As he approached the table, he spotted a veritable buffet of snacks and bottled water the professor had purchased.

"Get us anything good, Professor?" he asked.

"Just the four food groups, Doritos, Snickers, potato chips, and Skittles," the professor replied. "They didn't have a lot of healthy options."

"It'll do," John said. "If twelve-year-old me knew my last meal might end up being candy and cookies, he would be pretty satisfied with how his life went."

"We'll need real food if we're going to take on the Triumvirate again," the professor said. "Despite how much I might like the cookies myself."

"What we need is help," John said through a mouth filled with snacks. "We need Mike."

"That's your plan?" The professor shook his head. "You heard him. His fighting days are behind him."

"That was before Ellie and Apsara were kidnapped by the Triumvirate," he said. "It's worth giving him a shout."

"Let's say we convince him to come along," the professor said while munching on his chips. "What then? The Triumvirate is still too powerful."

"Maybe for now," John said. "We were making progress back at the boneyard before we were rudely interrupted. I was able to hold my spells longer and at a higher intensity."

"I was as well," the professor nodded. "It's an interesting phenomenon, but it's possible that has limits. The Triumvirate's spells were as powerful as our own."

"I'm not so sure about that," John said, shaking his head. "When we were fighting them in the boneyard, I didn't think their spells hit any harder than the ones they used back at the library."

"It's an attractive thought," the professor tapped his chin. "But overconfidence is the food of a fool. We'd be betting our lives on a feeling."

"We're already betting our lives on it," John replied thoughtfully as he took another bite out of their carb-laden feast.

CHAPTER FORTY-FOUR

MIKE TRIED TO FOCUS on making a tuna fish sandwich for his daughter. After introducing her to Calvin and Hobbes last year, it had become the only thing she would eat for lunch.

Normally he enjoyed this. He loved seeing her face light up when he reached for the can of tuna.

So why couldn't he stop checking his phone?

He took out his phone when he couldn't resist the compunction any longer. Nothing. No messages or missed phone calls.

What did he expect to see there?

Ellie's smile forced its way into his thoughts, despite his efforts to forget her. He couldn't get involved. His daughter had no one else.

He finished making the sandwich and called out that her lunch was ready.

Shayla burst into the kitchen all smiles and filled with stories about the picture she was drawing in her room. His daughter loved to paint and draw. Mike always did what he could to encourage her—even if her room did get a little messy sometimes.

Besides, the painting had been a good distraction from any trauma brought on by the Triumvirate's visit the other night. He knew there would be nightmares and sleepless nights ahead, and there was no doubt therapy would be needed. But for now, he would do everything within his power to show she was safe and loved.

He handed her the sandwich and listened to her story, clenching his hands into fists to resist the urge to again check his phone.

The guilt ate away at him in the same way it had in the weeks after he'd come home from Afghanistan. He knew his training gave him the abilities and nerves to deal with people like the Triumvirate. But what chance did a reporter, an elderly professor, a student, and a doctor have against a team of professionally trained killers like the Triumvirate?

And why did it have to be him?

Ellie's smiling face reappeared in his thoughts.

Suddenly he realized his daughter was attempting to get his attention.

"What is it, sweetie?" he asked.

"When do you have to go to work?" Shayla asked.

"No work tonight. I'm staying home with you, young lady. Daddy has some sick time and I'm using it to hang out with you."

She sat up and laid a hand on his forehead, just like he did when she wasn't feeling well. He suppressed a smile and grabbed her hand, holding it tighter on his forehead.

"Well, what do you think, Doctor?" he asked. "Am I gonna make it?"

She frowned, looking as serious as an eight-year-old can.

"You're not sick!" she protested. "You always say I have to go to school when I'm not sick."

"Oh? Are you saying you pretend to be sick to get out of school?" he asked, teasing her.

"No," she said, drawing her hand back. "I don't think it's fair you get to have a day off when you're pretending, and I don't."

"I'm not pretending," he protested. "I'm really sick."

She placed her hands on her hips. "Oh yeah? Prove it."

He coughed unconvincingly into his hand. "See?"

She continued glaring at him, and he chuckled. "Lucky for me, I don't have to prove anything because I'm the adult."

"It's not fair," she protested.

"Wow, you're really trying to get rid of me, aren't you?" he teased again. "You just want Nana to come over and babysit tonight 'cause she lets you watch TV late."

A small smile erupted on her face, and he laughed again.

"Well, maybe you're right. Maybe I should be thinking about the example I'm setting around here," he said. "I'll give my guy a call and let him know he's off the hook tonight."

They celebrated with the father-daughter secret handshake they'd come up with.

"Finish your lunch," he said.

Shayla pointed at him. "What's that, Daddy?"

He glanced down to see he had unconsciously balled his hand into a fist, his hand glowing with magic. He glanced back at her, shaking his head. "It was nothing, honey, just a trick of the light."

He took two steps and picked her up over his head, basking in her smiles and laughter.

But instead of happiness enveloping him, anxiety coursed through his body, as he thought about his new friends and what they were up against.

What if he was wrong?

CHAPTER FORTY-FIVE

ELLIE WOKE TO APSARA'S worried face looking down at her. She groaned, feeling dozens of bruises complain as she sat up and tried to get her bearings. She noticed the sun was directly overhead, meaning a few hours had passed since they had confronted the Triumvirate at the airplane boneyard.

Apsara extended a hand, and she took it, standing up. They were in the middle of a field bordered by concrete and cars snaking their way up the nearby mountain pass.

She rubbed her head. "Where are we?"

"We're safe," Apsara said. "At least for now."

"We were . . . taken." Ellie's memories of the fight at the airplane boneyard rushed back to her. "How'd we manage to escape?"

Apsara shrugged. "Their magic isn't as strong as they think it is."

"The professor?" Ellie asked. "What about John?"

Apsara shook her head. "I have no idea. But the Triumvirate didn't seem happy. I'm guessing they got away."

"What else?" she asked.

"The Triumvirate wanted the professor. But after our fight at the boneyard, they took us, intending on interrogating us for a translation of *The Omnichron*. Fortunately for us, their binding spell wore off and I got us out of there."

"You're handy to have around," Ellie said, admiring her friend.

Apsara grinned. "You have no idea."

"What are we waiting for?" she asked, scrambling to her feet. "We need to find John and the professor quick as we can."

"It's not as simple as that," Apsara said. "We may not have time to find them before the Triumvirate translates that book. And if they do . . ."

"What?" Ellie asked.

"Daniel—their leader—isn't satisfied with robbing banks and getting rich," Apsara said. "I overheard him saying he plans on building an army to conquer the world."

Ellie laughed. The idea was absurd. They were talented and magic may give them an edge, but how could three people hope to take on the collected will and might of the entire world?

"How could they possibly . . ." She thought about *The Omnichron* and the spells she had seen in it, including one that allowed the warlock to control peoples' minds.

"Whoever hired them knew about *The Omnichron* and what the amulet could do. When I was in the SUV, I heard them talking about summoning the 'Agamoth' to help them build an army," Apsara said. "But they still need the book translated."

"Wait," Ellie looked at Apsara shocked. "You mean the Agamoth that was about to take control of the world?"

Apsara nodded, a grave expression on her face. "We have to stop them."

"If they find that translation spell," Ellie said, "or someone else to translate the Agamoth's summoning spell, the world will be in for some serious shit."

"You're right," Apsara snapped her fingers. "The professor might've been the easiest person to find, but there must be others out there who could read and translate *The Omnichron*. We need to find anyone else who might be able to read it and protect them."

"I'm betting they'll try to find someone back at the university first," Ellie said. "I can log in to my student account and look up any professors who might be able to translate the book."

"Then we need to find the nearest computer and get on the road," Apsara said.

Ellie pointed across the freeway, where a strip mall and gas station were located. "That's our best bet."

She began moving through the meadow that divided the north and southbound lanes, Apsara following close behind.

The Triumvirate was out there, and someone was going to get hurt. Ellie was determined to do whatever she could to make sure no one else suffered because of their insanity.

CHAPTER FORTY-SIX

JOHN DECIDED IT WAS worth the risk to use his boss's credit card one more time so he could arrange transportation to get them back home to L.A. It didn't take long to rent a car and get on the road. The only problem was, they didn't have a clue where the Triumvirate was located—or what they were doing. Wherever they were, they had gone silent.

He had been skimming Twitter all afternoon, trolling through the trending posts for anyone who might have spotted something out of the ordinary.

"Would you mind keeping your eyes on the road?" the professor asked, gripping the overhead strap, his knuckles white.

Properly chastised, he handed the phone over to the professor.

"I'll make you a deal. Keep scrolling through the feed and look for anyone who mentions something weird."

"Something weird?" the professor asked, wrinkling his nose.

"My guess is, the Triumvirate won't be able to resist using their magic," John said, returning his eyes to the road. "Sooner or later, someone will catch them in the act and then—"

"What?" the professor asked, raising an eyebrow. "It's only you and me at this point."

John grimaced. "I wouldn't count Apsara and Ellie out just yet."

The professor arched an eyebrow. "I admire your faith in them."

"Professor, if you saw Apsara in action while we were working to cure Knickerbocker's grandson, you'd know she's not the type with any quit in her."

John kept his eyes on the road while the professor scrolled through social media searching for any mention of the mysterious Triumvirate. He concentrated on the road while at the same time allowed his subconscious to try to devise a plan for the next time they fought Armstrong—preferably one that wouldn't leave them dead, and the world enslaved.

It was enough to make him wistful for the relatively sane demands of his job as an investigative reporter.

Speaking of which, he should check in with his boss. The station hadn't heard from him for hours, which was out of character for him. Management had to be worried—if not cleaning out his desk for the new guy.

"I should call my boss and let him know I'm still alive," John said. "Hand me the other phone, would ya?"

The professor grunted and leaned forward, removing a second cell phone they had purchased at the truck stop after renting a car.

John fumbled with the small electronic device and dialed the number to his newsroom from memory. He had a good mind for numbers and facts—which had proven useful over the years in his career.

After a few moments, a gruff voice that sounded like it belonged to a man on his last nerve answered the phone.

"Newsroom."

"Clay!" John said. "It's John. Can you connect me with Percy?"

"Back from the dead are we, John?" Clay's brogue turned jovial at the sound of his voice.

"It's a bit of a story—something I've got to explain to Percy," John said.

"He's not here," Clay replied. "He's down at police headquarters reporting you missing. He went to your place this morning and found it wrecked."

John winced. The Triumvirate must have visited his apartment looking for clues. And it didn't sound like they were subtle.

"Uh oh," John said. "I guess I've been out of contact longer than I thought."

"Enough to have our boss demanding a city-wide alert from the LAPD to find you," Clay said. "I can forward you to his cell phone."

"Yeah, can you do that?" John said. "It's important."

"Of course!" Clay said. He paused. "It's good to hear your voice, John. We thought we lost you."

"You can't kill me, Clay," John replied. "Many people have tried and failed over the last forty-eight hours."

"Jesus, I bet you have a story and a half."

"You, me, and a bottle of Balvenie, and I'll tell you all about it," John promised.

"Lemme get Percy on the line for you."

There was a click as Clay put him on hold and transferred the call to Percy's cell phone. The professor grunted as he looked over his notes and began swiping left and right on his phone. John glanced at the professor, who looked panicked.

"What is it?" John asked.

"It's the Triumvirate. I know what they're doing," he said.

The professor held up an illustration that had been in the book. A bright beam of light extended from a massive chasm where a monstrous spider-like figure with eight limbs was being birthed into the world. Above the creature were three ominous looking warlocks, surrounded by a faceless mob.

"Well, that's unsettling," John said.

The professor nodded, then swiped again, showing him a second illustration.

Six figures in a circle surrounded an amulet that glowed bright orange with dozens of runes floating above it. Electricity sparked from the hooded figures' fingers as a bright blue forcefield protected them from another faceless mob.

"The Agamoth," John said, recognizing the photo.

The phone line clicked. John heard his boss pick up line. "Hello?"

John held the receiver for a second, darting his eyes back and forth from the image and the road in front of them. "Are you certain?"

"That man back at the boneyard wanted us to join him to take on the world," the professor said. "After we refused, the Agamoth would be the ultimate weapon to achieve those aims."

"John? Is that you?" Percy's voice sounded from the phone.

John removed his hand. "Percy, yeah, hi, hang on a second—"

"John!" Percy shouted. "Goddamn you. You owe me an explanation!"

But John ignored his boss, entranced by the illustration in the book.

"How many people know what you know?" John asked. "Is there anyone else in Los Angeles who could translate this book and what's inside?"

The professor's face fell, and he nodded. "A student. A brilliant young man named Josh Beckley."

"Who's that?"

Dimly aware of Percy shouting to get his attention, he ignored it. His gut told him what the professor had to say was far more important.

"A graduate student I had a few years back. Promising young man, a polyglot, who was an invaluable resource when I was researching dead languages for one of my papers," the professor tapped his forehead. "Yes, there's no one else quite like him."

"Is there anyone else within a five-hundred-mile radius who might know how to translate that book?" John asked.

The professor shook his head. "No one."

John removed his hand from the receiver and interrupted his boss's rantings about how he was about to fire him.

"Percy, hang on a second," John said, trying to get his boss to calm down. "I'm on to something big—bigger than anything else any outlet has. Bigger than any story in human history if you can believe it. If I can survive the next twelve hours, I swear, I will explain everything."

"If you're in danger, then find the nearest police department and turn yourself in," Percy said, somehow sounding irritated and concerned at the same time. "You can tell me all about your misadventures from the safety of a jail cell. Stealing the company card? What are you thinking?"

"Trust me, Perce, all will all be forgiven once you hear my story," John replied. "But I need your help. Call the cops and tell them to find a man named Josh Beckley. He's—"

"He's on the news now," Percy said, his voice becoming somber. "If you were doing your job, you'd know that."

John stomach sank. "What happened?"

"They found a body in Echo Park earlier this afternoon," Percy said. "Despite the condition of the DB, the police were able to identify him as your Mr. Beckley."

"What happened?"

"Sounds like the same kind of thing that happened to the Knickerbocker kid," Percy said. Then, his boss's voice lowered, sounding concerned. "It's a horror show over here. Bodies are piling up, and the police don't have any answers."

"Bodies? What do you mean, bodies?" John asked, though he wasn't sure he wanted to know the answer to that.

"Fifteen people, just in the last three hours," Percy said. "Like I said, it's a madhouse. I'm at downtown Wilshire and I've never seen the place look like this. The police don't have any suspects. Witnesses describe their minds going blank before and after the murders."

"Any patterns?" John asked. If the Triumvirate were killing people, he didn't think it was random—at least, not yet.

"Most of them are connected to various universities all around Southern California," Percy said. "They've all been history buffs or scientists who have worked on medieval projects."

"Percy, I gotta call you back," John said.

"You do that," Percy said, the ire rising back up in his voice.

John hung up the phone and pressed down hard on the gas. The professor's face became alarmed, and he gripped the armrest.

"By the increase in our speed, I'm guessing that phone call contained unwelcome news for us?" the professor asked, his voice tense.

"They're killing everyone who might know something about the amulet," John said. "They've gone after most of your peers across Southern California, including your former grad student."

The professor swallowed and released his death grip on the armrest to wipe a tear from his eye.

"All of them?" he asked in a small voice. "Then they got what they needed from Josh."

"We don't know that yet." John wanted to be encouraging but knew he was failing miserably. "He might have given them nothing, which is why he was killed."

"Then all the more reason to get us back to L.A.," the professor said.

John agreed and pressed the pedal to the floor, increasing their speed even more. Fortunately, there was little traffic on the road and if they were lucky, they'd make it home before anyone else got killed.

He prayed Ellie and Apsara were not among the dead.

CHAPTER FORTY-SEVEN

AFTER WALKING SEVERAL MILES down the open highway in the blistering sun, Apsara and Ellie finally made it to a gas station where they could make a call. Dehydrated and tired, Apsara stood in place, enjoying the cool breeze as the fan kicked on and the air conditioning flowed over her. Ellie made a beeline for the coolers in the back, opened one fridge, and grabbed a large bottle of water. Without paying, she opened the cap and took a long drink.

She watched Ellie in amusement before realizing the store's clerk watched them both, open-mouthed and in shock.

"We'll pay for that," she said, and felt for her wallet. She realized she didn't have it with her, having lost everything in the fight at the boneyard.

"Err . . ." She shot the clerk her brightest smile and thumbed over at Ellie. "That is, she'll pay for it."

The clerk narrowed his eyes. Apsara excused herself, making her way back to the end of the aisle where Ellie was still drinking the water.

"Hey, you happen to have any money on you?" she asked. "'Cause that clerk over there is getting kinda antsy, and I lost everything when the Triumvirate took us."

Ellie glanced over at the clerk who was still scowling at her. She shrugged and went back to drinking the water. "It's not like we couldn't take him if we just left."

Apsara was disappointed in her new friend's response, even if she knew on some level that Ellie was right.

Apsara grabbed the bottle out of Ellie's hands and twisted the cap back on. "We're paying for that, one way or another. Do you have anything we could use as collateral?"

Ellie held out her empty hands. "Like you, I lost everything during the battle."

"Some heroes we turned out to be," Apsara said. She looked over at the clerk. "If we're lucky, maybe we can convince our friend over there to let us call Mike, and he can bail us out."

She moved back to the front of the store and negotiated their freedom with the clerk. It took a bit of convincing, but Apsara was able to negotiate a five-minute phone call, promising they would return and pay for the drinks Ellie had taken.

The phone rang for a few minutes when a voice answered. "Hello?"

"Mike?" Apsara was hoping he would recognize her voice. "It's Dr. Apsara Choi and Ellie."

"Dr. Choi?" Mike sounded concerned. "Are you all right? What happened?"

"Can you help? Ellie and I are stranded out in Acton without a ride or any money," Apsara said. "We can pay you back."

"Acton? Who goes to Acton? I'll send you a car," Mike said. "Where are the professor and John?"

"We don't know," Apsara said. "The Triumvirate found us, and we got into another fight. They kidnapped us—"

"What?" Mike sounded aghast.

"It's okay, we got away," Apsara said, trying to reassure him. "But we're stranded out here."

"Uber takes care of your transportation problem. I can wire you some cash if that helps."

"We lost our phones, so that won't work," Apsara said. "But we'll take the ride for sure. I know it's expensive, but I'll send you the money as soon as—"

"Forget it. Getting you someplace safe is all that matters," Mike said.

"Thanks for the ride. We can figure out the rest from here."

She hung up the phone and gave a cheery thumbs-up to the clerk, who continued to scowl at her. She made her way back to where Ellie stood munching on some chips and spoke in a faint voice.

"Mike ordered an Uber for us, so we'll get home okay," she said. "But as for money, I'm thinking you may be right. It may be time for a little Chaotic Good."

Ellie grinned and grabbed another bag of potato chips and a bottle of water from the cooler, handing them to Apsara. "I suggest we run."

Apsara took the junk food and water and watched Ellie sprint for the exit, completely baffled. The clerk shouted, which kicked her into action. She made her way to the parking lot where a black Nissan was pulling up.

"Are you Mike?" the driver shouted.

"Close enough," Ellie said, pushing herself into the car.

Apsara dove in after her and the car took off, leaving the angry clerk behind.

CHAPTER FORTY-EIGHT

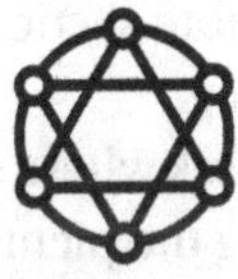

THE PROFESSOR HELD THE armrest tight, as John weaved the car in and out of traffic while driving as fast as he dared. They had been spotted by the highway patrol twice, but each time, the professor used the spell to cloak their vehicle from the police cruisers.

The professor watched for the telltale blue and red flashing lights of the California Highway Patrol. When he spotted them, John would ease off the accelerator while the professor cast the cloaking spell. They'd gotten so good it was almost too easy. There was something funny about watching the CHP race past them in search of an invisible suspect that was disappearing and reappearing along the stretch between Visalia and downtown Los Angeles.

Thanks to their little game of cat and mouse with the police, they made great time in their journey back to Los Angeles.

The professor remained hopeful they could stop the Triumvirate, but there was an unsettling doubt hanging around his head. If Beckley translated the book for those three, then they might have already lost the war.

They had the original *Omnichron* and if they had been able to get Josh to translate even a tenth of what was contained inside, or how to summon the Agamoth, it would bring ruin, pestilence, and disaster to the world.

And it would be his fault.

He wouldn't allow that to happen. He was the reason the book had even made it into public view in the first place. If he had simply kept his mouth shut, they might have avoided all this.

Their first stop was the scene where police had discovered Josh Buckley's body. The professor wanted to see for himself, and John thought the remote section of the park might make for a good place to practice.

They approached the park where couples, college students, families were out enjoying the picturesque Southern California afternoon. The professor idly wondered how they were going to practice their magic in the park. While there weren't a lot of people there now, there were enough to make it awkward if they began throwing fireballs around.

"Park it over there. We might have more space away from prying eyes there," the professor said, pointing at the rear of the parking lot.

John acknowledged the professor and turned the vehicle into the parking lot. To their surprise, they saw a black car sitting there waiting with its engine running.

He exchanged a nervous look with John.

"You think it's the Triumvirate?" he asked.

"I don't know," John said, studying the vehicle on the other side of the parking lot. "Only way to tell is by getting closer."

They inched forward while the other car remained stationary. The passenger side door opened and Apsara stepped out.

The professor raised his hands to his face in relief. "Oh, thank God! Dr. Choi and Ellie!"

Ellie had stepped out of the rear passenger side and stood, grinning as they drew close.

John shut off the rental car and got out, running to reunite with their two friends.

"You made it!" Apsara said. "I was beginning to think we all crashed and burned back at the boneyard."

"We made it all right," John said, staring at them in disbelief. "It's good to see you both. How'd you get out? How did you know to come here?"

Ellie and Apsara glanced at each other. Ellie smiled.

"I cast the knowing spell and found you," she said, looking at John. She blushed. "It wasn't as difficult the first time I cast the spell at Mike's house."

"The Triumvirate also said they needed one of us to translate the book. Once we got away, we figured there might be others who could translate The Omnichron," Apsara said.

"Yeah, bad news there. We think the Triumvirate succeeded in getting the book translated," John said, a grim expression on his face. "One of the professor's former students was found dead here not too long ago."

Apsara and Ellie exchanged a glance. "We were worried about that as well." Apsara said.

"How did you all get away from the Triumvirate?" John asked.

"Apsara has a way with magic," Ellie said. "That control spell they cast on us didn't work as well as they thought it would. She got us out of there."

"I also heard what they were planning," Apsara said, a grim expression on her face. "And it's nothing good."

"Let me guess, they plan on taking over the world and unleashing an evil not seen in five thousand years?" John said.

Apsara raised an eyebrow in surprise. "You really know how to ruin a lady's moment, don't you?"

"Don't blame me. The professor here figured it out," John said.

He felt his face go red at the recognition but decided this was too important for any moments of false modesty.

"That spell they used on you," he said. "We think the Triumvirate intends on using it again—but this time on a much larger crowd."

"They couldn't," Ellie said. "That kind of spell takes a lot of effort and they already failed keeping it on just the two of us."

"They do it one at a time," he said. "It's exponential. They enthrall someone and then use their ability to cast spells to help amplify their own efforts."

"They use people like their own personal battery pack," John added. "Two becomes four, four, sixteen, then thirty-two, and so on and so on until it spreads like an uncontrollable virus."

"Then what?" Ellie looked a bit terrified.

"Then they summon the Agamoth." The professor took out his smartphone and showed them the photo from *The Omnichron*.

"The Agamoth." Apsara went white. "That's what they were talking about."

The professor's stomach dropped. "The Triumvirate?"

"I overheard their conversation. They think they can summon it and use it to influence world leaders to keep them from launching nuclear weapons at them. Or something like that."

John shook his head and sighed.

"Then we better get back to studying and practicing," John said. "The next time we meet the Triumvirate will be our last. For us and for them."

A chill ran down the professor's spine. Looking around the group, he saw the others looked discouraged.

"Life never waits for when you're ready," the professor said. "So, we shall have to make do with the time we have."

They all nodded and shared a moment as they considered the challenge ahead of them.

"Let's get started," the professor said.

CHAPTER FORTY-NINE

THE WHITE-HOT FIREBALL WHIZZED through the park and exploded on the shield John had conjured mere moments before. A second and third fireball followed. He grunted with effort, but the shield held.

His right hand glowed red as he returned fire back at Apsara. She conjured a shield of her own, deflecting his fireball into the ground where it blasted a small crater at her feet.

"Good!" he shouted.

"Not good enough," she called back. She leaned back and sent a volley of sharp ice crystals back at him.

He conjured another shield, hearing the clink and explosion of the deadly missiles she sent his way.

"My turn," Ellie called out. She conjured the bow like the professor showed her back at the boneyard, and traced the runes inscribed on it. The bow glowed with a bright green energy, and she nocked an arrow, releasing at the two of them.

He cast a shield just moments before the arrow reached him. It splintered into dozens of missiles and arced up and over him. He cried out and angled his shield again, deflecting the arrows away from him.

Apsara looked over at Ellie in surprise. "That was a new one."

John raised himself up from the ground. "Let's go again."

The more they practiced, the more they realized John had been onto something the whole time. John found he was able to now summon fireballs with a mere flick of his wrist, without the need for any incantations. Ellie had become proficient as well, though he could still see her lips move every time she threw one of her fireballs at the shields Apsara had mastered over the last few hours.

The runes on the manuscript also helped with their spell-casting. John wondered if they could tattoo one or two of the runes on their wrists and increase the power of their spells. While he figured that would work, they didn't exactly have time to find a tattoo artist. Perhaps a permanent black marker might work?

He walked over to the professor who was meditating on the grass, still holding the illusion spell over their section of the park to keep their activities secret from the unsuspecting public.

"I think we're done for now, Professor, you can take a break," John said.

The professor opened his eyes and the illusion dropped, revealing a few hundred people lounging in the park around the corner from them.

"How do you feel?" John asked.

"Powerful," the professor replied. "You?"

"The same," he admitted. There was something refreshing about using his magic powers. It was like stretching a muscle that liked being used.

"The only thing we need now is to know where the Triumvirate plans to summon the Agamoth," John said.

"I've been thinking that over," the professor said with a thoughtful look. "They'll want someplace where they can blend in, but they'll need as many people as they can to absorb their mana. That narrows it down.

"But still too many places in L.A." John agreed. He considered the professor's words carefully. "I feel like they need somewhere they can establish a home base most places I can think of are far too easy to attack."

The professor got to his feet, brushing his jeans off as he stretched his legs. "Wherever they choose, I believe we are about as ready as we'll ever be."

John didn't answer. He was staring at the line of cars on the road across the street from the park. He glanced up the hill that surrounded the park and squinted into the afternoon sun.

"The game," he whispered. "It's almost too perfect."

"What's that?" Professor McKaig asked.

He turned. "I know—at least, I think I know—where the Triumvirate is going to be tonight."

He waved at Apsara and Ellie who were still practicing takedown moves. He ran over to them, the professor struggling to keep up behind him.

"I know where they're going to summon the Agamoth," he told the group. "They need a huge pool of mana to summon the demon, right?"

"Sure," the professor said.

John pointed to the nearby road, where a line of cars was heading for Chavez Ravine—the location of the largest baseball stadium in the country.

"Are you certain?" Apsara asked, sounding suspicious. "What do you base it on?"

"That . . . makes sense," the professor said. "The Claim Jumpers are in town to play the Thrashers, meaning it'll be a sell-out crowd."

"More than fifty-five thousand people at the game. That's more than enough for the Triumvirate to summon the Agamoth and start their world conquest," John said.

"And that's not even counting those golems they can summon," Ellie said, shuddering.

"Or those," John said, nodding at Ellie. "We've got to get up there and stop that game, or at least prevent any more people from getting to it."

"It's far too late for that. The game is starting in just over an hour from now," Apsara said, checking her watch.

"Then we need to get up there and prevent whatever the hell the Triumvirate has in store," John said. "This is what we prepared for. If anyone thinks they can't continue, then please feel free to leave now."

Ellie, Apsara, and the professor just stared at him. He expected as much but was still grateful for their support.

He nodded. "Let's go save the world then."

CHAPTER FIFTY

Mike woke after a long nap preparing himself for another night of work. He hadn't been at his job since that fateful night in the university library. He was sorry to see that contract go away for now. He knew the college didn't blame him for the explosion or anything—how could they know he had anything to do with it?

But with the library out of commission and the employee cafeteria burnt to a crisp, there wouldn't be much call for his services there for now. Fortunately, the university was only a small slice of his income. He had other small shops set up in various office buildings around Los Angeles and those people needed their snacks too.

After getting Shayla settled with his mother-in-law, he got in his truck and began his rounds early, hitting up the first few stops of the afternoon. The work was easy—all he had to do was drop off packages that had already been packed. He didn't need to do anything but find someone to sign for the food.

It was boring, steady work, but he was grateful for the opportunity to do something boring. After the last few days, he didn't need or want any more excitement in his life.

According to tonight's delivery schedule, his next stop was Stanhope Stadium. He grunted in surprise and saw it was for a specialized dessert his company sold. If he were lucky, he could sneak in a few innings while he was at the stadium. His beloved Claim Jumpers were in town, and he knew the game promised to be a dramatic finish to the season. He took a lot of crap for his Claim Jumpers devotion in a town that loved their local heroes. But as a born-and-bred Bay Area boy, he continued to root for his baseball and football teams even after he moved to Southern California.

He shut the door to his truck and made his way back to the cab thinking about his business strategy. The next few months would be difficult until he could hire additional help, but once he did, he would have much more free time and would be able to concentrate on being the boss. He was looking forward to that.

He felt his hands briefly spark and forced his fists closed. Despite his best efforts to forget about his new powers, his magic kept resurfacing at the most inappropriate times.

He stopped for a moment to breathe and remind himself that he was the one in control of his destiny. He would not risk himself or the life he'd built for his daughter just because he had powers now. Mike had begun hoping they would go away after he ceased using them, atrophying whatever magical muscle that had been awakened.

He opened the door to the cab of his truck and got in. He watched the orange glow around his fists begin to fade as the magic subsided. He released a deep breath that he hadn't realized he had been holding and started the truck.

He forced his thoughts back to baseball and whether he might get to the ballpark before the first pitch. He put the truck in gear and drove off, trying, and failing, to push the thoughts of magic out of his mind.

CHAPTER FIFTY-ONE

APSARA FELT AS IF she were moving on autopilot as their group piled into the SUV John and the professor brought with them and headed for the shining lights over the hill where one of the biggest games of the year was about to take place.

She listened quietly as John and the professor argued about the best routes to take to the stadium. The professor had a shortcut, which John said was useless thanks to the variety of traffic apps pouring traffic into available side streets.

The tension was thick, and she knew they weren't really arguing about the path they were taking. Apsara glanced behind her to see Ellie with her eyes closed, her lips moving as she recited something under her breath.

"Ellie, honey, are you okay?" she asked. Perhaps Ellie was scared about what they were about to walk into. Who wouldn't be frightened of an enemy capable of bringing your worst nightmares to life?

Ellie opened her eyes, and a gentle smile spread across her face. "I'm fine. I'm just meditating ahead of our confrontation with the Triumvirate."

"Sorry," Apsara said, embarrassed she'd interrupted her friend. "I didn't mean—"

"Oh, it's fine, it doesn't take me long," Ellie said, waving Apsara's faux pas away. "When I was competing, I always thought the worst part was the anxiety during the runup to the competition. Once I got there and was in the moment, I never missed a mark."

Apsara saw her friend's face fall for a moment as Ellie bit her bottom lip.

"But during the days before the competition, I would be a complete mess. I would second-guess myself and even found the more I practiced and the closer it got to the day of the tournament, the more shots I would miss. Up to twenty percent. After I discovered meditation, the anxiety faded, and I could hit my targets again."

"I'm not surprised it helps," Apsara said. "I recommend it to many of my patients."

"It helps me release the static. And if what we saw at the boneyard is any indication of what we're about to face in the stadium . . ." She shuddered, then closed her eyes and began moving her lips once again.

Apsara took the hint and turned back to face the front seat, staring into a sea of taillights.

They were close to the stadium, but it was slow going and she could tell the traffic was really bothering John. She reached forward and placed a hand on his arm. He jumped, and she withdrew her hand for a moment, shocked at his reaction.

"Sorry," he said. "It's the coffee."

"And the nerves," she said. "You okay?"

He glanced back at the ruby red glow in front of him and sighed. "When we get into the stadium, I'll start calming down."

"Want to talk about it?"

He didn't answer, appearing to want to concentrate on the road instead. She leaned back into her seat.

The professor glanced back at her and shrugged. "I'll talk to you if no one else will," he said.

She chuckled and felt the tension release. John shot him an annoyed glance, but the professor ignored him.

"I don't mean to bother everyone, but I just feel like we need to confront the fact we're about to take on something no one can ever prepare for," she said. "Shouldn't we plan our approach?"

The professor looked over at John, arching an eyebrow. "She's right you know."

John grunted and slapped the wheel of the SUV in frustration at the traffic in front of them. "It's not like we have anywhere else to go."

"Good," the professor said, drawing himself up and pulling his coat tight. "The first thing any good leader does is evaluate their assets and liabilities. I propose we go over our assets, what we lack, and what we can find at the stadium to further our cause."

Apsara grimaced. She didn't have much in the way of supplies. The pack containing all the potions she'd created had been inside her vehicle when the Triumvirate blew that up back at the boneyard. If she had time, she might be able to whip some up in one of the kitchens at the stadium.

"I don't have much on me," Apsara said, speaking up. "But I do have all the potion recipes memorized. I'm certain if I can get into one of the VIP kitchens, I can create all the health and mana potions we might need."

John shook his head. "You think they'll have what you need at the same place they sell the hot dogs?"

Apsara scoffed at him. "Have you been to a ballpark lately? No, I can sneak into one of the suite's gourmet kitchens and work from there."

"Fair enough. Professor, you stick with her and help her find whatever she needs," John said.

"Why me?" the professor asked.

"Your invisibility spells have proven to be the strongest, which will come in handy if you need to steal something," John said.

He turned and pointed at Ellie. "You'll be our 'eyes in the sky.'"

Ellie looked up at him and smiled, giving him a mock salute. "Aye-aye captain."

"What about you?" Apsara asked.

"I'm going to take my press badge and go to the press suite," John said. "From there I should be able to find the Triumvirate using the stadium's cameras."

This time, it was her turn to grunt. It wasn't the worst idea she'd ever heard. Of course, she didn't want to think about what might happen if they failed.

The light ahead of them turned green and the traffic began moving along the road that would take them into the stadium.

They were moving. But moving closer to the deadliest fight imaginable.

CHAPTER FIFTY-TWO

After a quick scramble to find his wallet, John gave the attendant standing at the gate of Stanhope Stadium his last fifty-dollar bill he had taken out of the ATM the night he learned about Alan Knickerbocker's murder.

John felt as if he had aged a thousand years since then. How often had he complained about the price of parking or ATM fees? Now, knowing what he was about to face, he took a moment to recognize that even life's mundane inconveniences were memorable in their own way.

He parked the vehicle and they got out, each person looking at the other as if this might be the last time they might see one another.

John glanced over at Ellie and pointed. "Get to the highest point of the stadium you can. Use the focus spell to help shift your perspective to any place in the stadium you want."

"Focus?" Ellie's face fell. "I don't know that one."

John opened his smartphone and sent her a text with an image of the spell from *The Omnichron*.

She picked up her phone and read the incantation. She looked up, uncertain. "It doesn't look all that hard."

"Try it out," John said, pointing at a remote area of the stadium. "See if you can see what those people are cooking over there."

Ellie closed her eyes and muttered the incantation. A flash of blue light illuminated her eyes. She opened them, gasping, nearly falling over as she struggled to keep her balance.

Apsara reached out to help steady her friend. "Easy. Take a moment to get used to the feeling."

Ellie steadied herself and then looked at the remote area of the stadium parking lot where John had told her to look. "This is amazing. Three guys, all white, wearing Claim Jumper caps and Rito jerseys standing around drinking beer and cooking . . ." She squinted and then made a gleeful noise. "Brats. That bunch knows how to tailgate."

"Good," John said. "Now shut your eyes and release the spell. You'll go back to normal."

Ellie complied, closing her eyes, and stumbling once again when she removed the spell's effects on her. "I guess I should be sitting down when I cast this one for now," she said, sounding a bit ashamed.

"The cheap seats will come in handy for that," John said. "Get to the highest point you can, somewhere where you can see all the angles."

"How will I keep in touch with you all?" she asked.

John took out his burner cell phone. "Take my phone. Text the professor's number if you see anything." He turned to the professor. "Professor, your first assignment will be to steal some other phones from folks so we can keep in contact with you and Apsara."

The professor sighed and then nodded with a stout expression. "Whatever you need."

"Good." John turned to face the entire group and hesitated a moment before saying what was already spelled out all over his face. "I know what we're doing tonight is insane and not how you thought you'd spend Saturday night. But we've seen what the Triumvirate can do, even with an incomplete translation of the book. If we don't stop them tonight, they'll unleash an evil on this world that humanity can't stop. Not without our help."

He paused and looked out at the crowd around them. "These people have no idea what's about to hit them. They're not ready and they don't deserve to be targets. If we fail and they become enthralled to the Triumvirate, do whatever you can to avoid killing them. We can always bring them back from being enthralled, but we can't bring them back from dead, understood?"

John was relieved to see by the expressions on their faces that he hadn't needed to say it. All the same, he was glad he did just to make it clear the kind of fight they were getting into.

"Our targets are *The Omnichron* and the amulet," John said. "If we get those two things back, they won't be able to give anyone powers."

They murmured an acknowledgement.

He stuck his hand out in the middle of the circle. "I know this looks cheesy, but there's a reason people do it. It's a symbol that we're all in it together. We may not all make it back from this. But what happens here tonight matters because we stood up and did the right thing."

John looked around at his team. "We know our magic works through our intentions and willpower. If we work together tonight with the right intention from the very beginning, nothing can stop us. So, if you're still willing to join me on this quest to stop the Triumvirate from unleashing hell on Earth, then put your hand on top of mine and swear an oath that you intend to roast the Triumvirate until they go home crying."

Apsara grinned and Ellie chuckled. Even the normally stoic professor allowed a grin to touch his lips.

"What the hell else was I going to do tonight?" Ellie asked, resting her hand on top of John's.

He nodded, thanking her for being the first to step up.

"You people have shown me things I never thought possible," Apsara told John. "I'd be lying if I said I wasn't curious to see how it all ends."

She placed her hand on top of Ellie's.

The professor added his. "The only thing that ends tonight is the Triumvirate."

John felt the weight of his friends' hands on his own and nodded in appreciation.

"Let's go kick some ass."

CHAPTER FIFTY-THREE

MIKE'S SATURDAY NIGHT ROUTE was easier than the rest of his Monday through Friday deliveries. And as a bonus, traffic was behaving, allowing him to get through his deliveries faster than he ever had before. He would make the same whether the gig took him eight hours or six, so he was grateful for some off time. He might make it to the game after all.

But despite his happy mood, as he drove toward his last stop at the stadium, he found himself becoming depressed, feeling as if he were losing all hope. He had dealt with depression in the past and recognized the symptoms, but this felt different somehow.

As he was about to get on the 110 freeway that would lead him to the stadium, he felt his vision darken as incomplete images flew in front of his eyes. He cried out and pulled over, putting on his emergency flashers as his head began to swim with scenes of chaos and destruction. When he opened his eyes, he was shocked to see the imposing skyscrapers and various buildings downtown going up in flames, rubble falling out of the sky as the structures crumbled to the ground.

His breathing quickened. He tried to regain control as he gazed at the destruction that surrounded him now. Only moments before, everything had been normal, with impatient drivers, traffic, and pedestrians making their way downtown.

He closed his eyes, and the images overtook his vision. He found himself standing in the middle of a screaming crowd of people fleeing an arena that he recognized as Stanhope stadium. Above him, an enormous creature, tentacles waving in the air, brayed out a blood-curdling scream that sounded like a combination of nails on a chalkboard and what chewing aluminum felt like.

The creature gathered a dozen baseball fans into a tentacle and swept them into its maw, devouring them whole, their screams echoing through the park.

Mike looked around him, aghast at the scene as the people trapped inside attacked one another. Half of the people in the crowd had eyes that glowed bright red as they attacked their fellow fans while everyone else fled for their lives.

Mike noticed a woman floating above the parking lot, controlling the zombies below her. He tried calling out, but his voice failed him. He couldn't say a single word. He could only watch the dreadfulness unfold around him.

The creature climbed its way out of the stadium, as what looked like glowing red lava dripped on top of cars and people, instantly melting them. He paused to look up in horror at the nightmarish monster in front of him and retched when he realized the creature was eating people and growing with each person it absorbed.

Two more tentacles whipped out over the stadium walls, allowing the creature to gain enough traction to pull its now massive body over the top, creeping its way out of the stadium, emerging from the hell behind it.

Mike watched, helpless, as the nightmarish creature spilled out on top of abandoned vehicles and fleeing fans, absorbing their bodies, killing them instantly.

Above the creature, Mike saw a large hulking man watching in satisfaction as the creature devastated everything it touched in the parking lot.

He heard an even louder cry and spotted a human form erupt out of the smoke the creature had left behind.

The figure stepped forward and revealed its face to be that of Daniel Armstrong, the man who nearly killed him back at the library.

So far, he'd gone unnoticed by everyone and everything around him, but Armstrong had spotted him and grinned maniacally.

Mike was struck with a kind of horror and fear he had never felt before—this was nothing like any PTSD episode he'd had before. This vision was *real.* Somewhere deep within, he instinctively knew what he was seeing would come true if he didn't do something to stop it.

He turned and tried to run, but his feet stuck to the ground, as if his boots melted into the pavement by Armstrong's spell.

The figure reached down. Mike closed his eyes, expecting to be crushed by Armstrong's massive grip.

He woke to find himself sweating heavily, the sound of impatient drivers behind him laying on their horns as his hazard lights blinked.

Mike cried out and looked around in a panic, still expecting Daniel Armstrong's massive fist to crush him like a bug.

But it wasn't there. No one was there. Just his empty van with a few scattered cardboard boxes filled with returns and a line of increasingly impatient commuters behind his truck.

He placed his head on the wheel and renewed his breathing exercises to bring his heart rate down. Once he was successful, he opened the mirror on his visor and gazed into his black eyes to reflect on what he'd just seen.

That was no ordinary vision or PTSD episode. No, this was something else. Something influenced by magic.

A thought teased at the back of his mind. He refused to entertain it at first. It was absurd.

But the whisper reminded him about everything he had already seen. Everything he had already accomplished. Mike looked down at his fists to see they were glowing once again, as the magic tried forcing its way through him.

He knew the voice, no matter how small, would never go away. He also knew the voice was right.

He'd had a vision. A vision of the Triumvirate taking over people's minds and summoning a beast straight out of hell's deepest pits.

He also knew that if he wanted to prevent that from happening, he needed to go directly to the stadium to stop the apocalypse.

Because what good was raising a daughter in a world like the one he'd seen in his vision?

He put his van back in gear, turned off the hazard lights, and pulled into traffic. He wasn't far from Stanhope Stadium and knew it wouldn't take long to get there.

He only hoped he wasn't already too late.

CHAPTER FIFTY-FOUR

JOHN AND THE REST of the group approached the gates to the Thrashers and Claim Jumpers game when the professor turned to him.

"How are we getting in? I'm assuming we don't have tickets."

"You'll have to get us in one at a time, Professor," John said. "Apsara, Ellie, you two can go first. You'll have to sneak past the ushers, but once you're inside the ballpark, you should be able to move around freely."

"What if someone asks for a ticket?" Ellie's voice betrayed the nervousness she felt.

"I doubt anyone will even give you a second glance," John said. "But if they do, run."

"Not exactly subtle," she said.

"It's what we have to work with," he said. "If it makes you feel any better, you can go first."

"Put me in, coach," she said, steeling herself for the task ahead.

John nodded to the professor, who turned to Ellie and closed his eyes, murmuring the incantation. A bright veil of orange energy surrounded her, and then, she disappeared.

Apsara gasped and raised a hand to her mouth. She hadn't gotten a good look at what the professor was capable of back at the boneyard and seeing him execute this magic now was shocking in a way she hadn't expected.

"Ellie?" Apsara asked in wonder.

"I'm here," Ellie's disembodied voice echoed through the parking lot. "This is wild! Everything is gray."

"Don't brush up against anyone or say anything when you're trying to be stealthy," John said. "If you can, get up to the gate and get inside as quick as you can. The spell takes a toll on our professor friend here."

"I can manage," the professor said, strain in his voice. His eyes were open, but beads of sweat were forming on his forehead.

"Ellie, get up as high as you can, as quick as you can," John said, urging her to move. "You'll have about thirty seconds of stealth after the professor loses sight of you, so try and find a discrete place to reappear. We don't want you appearing in front of everyone and causing a commotion."

"Don't worry. They won't see me coming," Ellie's disembodied voice said. "I'll text you when I get to my seat."

They heard Ellie's light footsteps as she jogged off in the general direction of the gates where ticket takers were scanning people's tickets.

One ticket taker was busy scanning a family of seven when he appeared to stumble. Alarmed, the ticket taker's head popped up from his duties and scanned the general vicinity. Then, he accused one of the younger members of the family of bumping into him.

"Ellie's in," John said.

The professor released the spell with a visible sigh of relief. "You okay, Professor?" John asked.

The man waved his concerns away and nodded at Apsara. "You're next, Dr. Choi. Are you ready?"

Her face tightened. She took a deep breath and nodded. The professor muttered the incantation and again. A circle of orange energy swirled around her body until she too had disappeared.

"You're good to go," John said to the now empty space where Apsara had been standing only moments ago.

"This is going to work, John," Apsara whispered next to his ear. John nearly jumped out of his skin and yelped.

Apsara's peals of laughter echoed across the parking lot, causing several baseball fans to glance in their direction. However, all they saw was two men standing next to one another in the Stanhope Stadium parking lot, with no woman in sight.

"I've always wanted to do that." Apsara's voice faded as she made her way toward the gate. Unlike Ellie, Apsara didn't appear to have trouble threading her way through the crowd and dodging the usher busy scanning tickets at the entrance.

Their phone lit up with a text message. John read it and nodded. "She's in. My turn."

The professor paused and wiped his brow, breathing heavily. "If you could give me a moment."

John nodded. "Sure. Whatever you need."

He used the time to look around the crowded parking lot at the thousands of baseball fans currently streaming into the stadium. The first pitch was about a half hour away, so there was still time for the fans to get to their seats. Fans were still tailgating, the smell and sounds of people cooking hot dogs and other festive dishes filling the air.

He realized these people had no idea what was coming and that unless they were able to stop the Triumvirate and the

Agamoth, people's sense of what a "normal" world was would quickly end.

"Professor," John said suddenly. "Did you ever see anything in that book about memory wiping?"

Still breathing heavily, the professor removed his glasses and pulled a handkerchief from his pocket. He wiped down the lenses and replaced the glasses. "I'm sorry?"

"In the book—did you see any spells that might help wipe memories?"

The professor narrowed his eyes. "That's some dark magic that could have serious repercussions—"

"But did you see the spell?" John insisted.

The professor didn't answer for a moment. "I saw something like that. But why on earth would you want something like that? That can only be used for destructive purposes."

John pointed at the fans streaming into the stadium. "These people aren't ready for the idea of magic. Think about it. What if we're not the only ones who can tap into this." He snapped his fingers, creating a small fireball that burst out in a flash of red and white.

"What if the military unlocked these abilities for soldiers?" he continued. "But even worse, what if they can't and they decide to come after us and our loved ones so they can figure out how it works?"

"They'll send us to Area 51 and dissect us."

"Well, probably not Area 51 exactly," John said. "But, yeah, they'll take us into custody and stuff us into a hole where we'll never see the light of day again."

"What do you propose?" the professor said.

"We know it's the intent of the spell that matters, right?" The idea was beginning to take shape in his head. "If the Triumvirate reveals themselves or we get caught using magic in front of people, we might need to wipe these people's memories so we can remain safe."

The professor stroked his beard, his ever-present jovial smile gone from his face. "I see your point, and even agree with you, but . . ."

"But?"

"But, even if I wanted to cast that spell, I'm not certain I could. I'm not certain any of us could."

"If I got you the book back, do you think you could cast the spell?"

The professor sighed and rubbed his face. "It's not that. One-on-one, I might be able to wipe their memory. But this stadium can hold fifty-five thousand people. I'm nowhere near powerful enough for that kind of magic. None of us are."

"Are you sure? We've gotten better—"

The professor shook his head. "We'd need to do the same thing the Triumvirate plans to do tonight. We'd need to enthrall all those people, then use their mana to wipe their memories. It's just not possible."

John shook his head. "Perhaps for now, but there has to be a way to mindwipe thousands of people at once."

"My boy, you must come to grips with the fact that the genie is out of the bottle, and the world will forever change if we do not get that amulet back. I do not believe the world is ready to learn magic is no longer a fantasy, but it is far too late for that." The professor watched him with a sad, almost wizened expression.

John examined the older man and sighed. He might be right. Besides, saving humanity from a demon summoned from the underworld had to take priority tonight. He clasped the professor on the shoulder. "You ready?"

The professor nodded.

The pair turned to face the entrance of the stadium and they both began muttering the incantation to cast the invisibility spell. A bright swirl of orange light surrounded both their bodies and they were gone.

CHAPTER FIFTY-FIVE

ELLIE PUSHED HER WAY through the crowded concourse while trying to orient herself using a map of the stadium. The highest point at the ballpark was the center top deck.

The game between the two divisional rivals had attracted fans of both teams from hundreds of miles away. The place was sold out, and as the minutes ticked away to the first pitch, the concourse was becoming increasingly crowded with people trying to order last minute food and drinks.

She ducked under a man carrying four beers filled to the brim and narrowly avoided them spilling on her. The hefty man turned to shout at her, but she was long gone.

A disconcerting thought entered her head as she threaded her way through the crowd. If what Apsara said about the Triumvirate's plan was true, she realized some of these people might be forced to try to kill her in the next few hours. She hadn't thought much about the fact that she may soon face a choice—kill or be killed.

This cold realization brought on a deep sense of guilt. She cast her eyes downward, hoping to avoid looking at people's faces, trying to cut off any emotions she felt to the people around her.

She became so consumed by the thoughts of the possibility of killing someone that she almost missed her section. Ellie shook herself out of her reverie and remembered the description of the Agamoth in *The Omnichron*. If they failed here tonight, the entire world would be lost.

After climbing up the staircase to the very last row of seats, Ellie sat down around a group of rowdy fans, who were too busy drinking beer and regaling each other with stories about the team's past victories to notice her.

Her seat gave her the perfect vantage point to see everything and everyone in the stadium. To her left, the setting sun was painting a vivid sunset filled with pink, red, and blue hues over the downtown Los Angeles district. Some distant clouds added to the horizon. She allowed herself a moment to soak in the beauty surrounding her, knowing that the stadium below was about to turn into a battlefield.

"Hey, you wanna move?" A boisterous voice shouted at her from the end of the row she was standing in. Ellie hadn't realized she'd been holding people up from getting to their seats. She sat down, her face a bright red.

The other fans, dressed head to toe in Claim Jumpers gear, shot her a dirty look and "accidentally" spilled beer on her shirt. She grimaced and reminded herself that she was there to save these people—no matter how ungrateful they may act.

After the Claim Jumpers superfans were able to get past her, Ellie turned her attention back to the ballpark and scanned for anything or anyone who might look out of place. Unfortunately, without her spell, the entire stadium might as well have been filled with ants. The mix of blue and black hats as people ambled through the stadium getting to their seats made it difficult to track anyone for long.

She closed her eyes and murmured the words to the spell John and the professor had shown her back in the parking lot. She felt an overwhelming sense of focus overcome her, and she opened her eyes.

Below her, the players had taken the field and were beginning to warm up. She aimed her focus at them and suddenly, it was as if she were standing next to them on the field. She almost felt as if she could smell their sweat mixing with their aftershave as they warmed up on the field.

She turned her attention to the crowd and began the ultimate game of people watching. With the game about ten minutes away from starting, the stadium was filling up with spectators.

The Triumvirate was coming, and it was up to her to spot them before they could do any damage. She set herself to the task and began scanning the faces of everyone in the stadium, hoping she could make a difference and prevent a lot of needless deaths tonight.

CHAPTER FIFTY-SIX

APSARA MADE HER WAY to the VIP suites where several gourmet kitchens that delivered high-quality food were located. When she arrived, she spotted a young server carrying an armload of dishes and struggling to use her keycard to get back into the kitchen.

"Need any help?" Apsara asked in a friendly tone. "We've all been there."

She rushed up to the woman and a load of plates off her hands.

"For whatever reason, they can't keep the handcarts for our dishes from disappearing," the woman said. "If security did their job, I wouldn't have to keep busing these dishes by hand."

"Those handcarts are popular. Everyone needs one for something," Apsara said, trying to commiserate with the woman. It worked as the young server nodded as she slapped her keycard on a black plastic structure next to the door.

"Here, I'm starting in thirty minutes, so I may as well help you with these," Apsara said. She'd learned long ago that the key to getting into places you didn't belong relied mostly on attitude—sometimes a clipboard as John had recently demonstrated at her hospital.

The server eyed her for a moment and then shrugged. "You're new?"

"Yep," Apsara said. "First game in fact."

The woman grunted. "Hell of a night for your debut."

The server held the door open for her as she made her way into the kitchen. Several cooks were busy grilling and cooking various menu items people in the VIP suites had ordered.

"You can put those over there," the server said, sticking out her hand. "I'm Julie, but you can call me Jules. Everyone does."

"Apsara," she said, shaking the woman's hand. "Maybe I'll see you around."

Jules barked out a laugh and shook her head. "Maybe."

"Is there a spice rack nearby?" Apsara asked. "I'm missing a few ingredients to spice up my recipes for this group I'm cooking for tonight."

"Oh, they brought you in special, huh?" Jules asked with a grin.

"My food truck is famous in Pasadena," Apsara said, thinking fast. "One of the suites hired me special for their event."

Jules nodded. "Always good to see another woman entrepreneur out there making moves."

Apsara nodded, accepting the compliment with a smile. "Hustle or be hustled."

Jules barked out another laugh and grabbed Apsara's arm. "I like you. Stick around after the game, and we'll get a drink."

Apsara thought about the Triumvirate and then nodded, lest she blow her cover.

"Feel free to grab whatever you need. Kitchen's well-stocked. See ya around, Chef," Jules said. Apsara's new friend disappeared in the kitchen.

Apsara turned to the storage bin filled with spices and supplies and opened her phone, looking for the notes she'd taken for the potions they'd need for the night. The kitchen was well-stocked and had everything she would need—even sage, which was a surprise. But there were still some things she would need to send the professor to retrieve.

As if knowing she were thinking of him. the professor suddenly appeared next to her, and she yelped in shock.

The professor shrugged, looking at her with a sheepish grin. "Sorry, John asked me to do that."

She rolled her eyes but had to give him credit. "Turnabout is fair play, I guess."

"Indeed." He pulled out a brand-new iPhone from his pocket and handed it to her. "I lifted this off an unsuspecting grandmother who I don't believe will notice it missing during the game. I programmed the numbers for everyone's phones in there."

"Does Ellie have my number?" Apsara asked, inspecting her newly stolen possession. It was a nice phone—better than the one she owned in fact.

"She does," the professor confirmed. "You'll see in messages that I created a group chat that we can use to stay connected with one another. If you need anything, just send the message and I'll try to find it for you."

"You created a group chat?" Apsara asked, impressed.

"My dear," the professor sounded almost offended, "I've been working with Millennials for more than a decade. If I didn't understand how to create and participate in group chats, I would have been put out to pasture long ago."

She chuckled and turned her attention back to the cabinet of supplies, making notes of everything she would need for tonight. There wasn't much, but the items weren't the type of thing people could just pick up from grocery stores. She handed the professor the list.

He read it, then nodded. "I'll be back, quick as I can."

The professor disappeared in a brilliant flash of orange light.

Apsara turned to her work and began prepping the ingredients for her potion. She didn't know how much time she'd have to put this all together, so she would need to work fast.

She looked up at a TV located in the upper corner of the kitchen and saw they had a little under ten minutes to go until the first pitch.

The pressure was on.

CHAPTER FIFTY-SEVEN

JOHN MADE HIS WAY through the crowds inside the concourse of the stadium, navigating to the press box where all the major networks, newspapers, and reporters were covering the game.

He flashed his credentials to the security guard standing outside the door. The burly man stepped aside and nodded as he entered the press box.

Inside, there was none of that electric energy that coursed through a stadium on game night. The press box was serene, almost sterile, as the dozen or so assorted reporters calmly surfed the web or chatted on their phones quietly while they waited for the game to begin. It was considered blasphemous to cheer or root for your favorite team inside the box—even during the most intense moments of a game. Anyone who got carried away were asked to leave.

The press box afforded the reporters some of the best seats in the house to watch the action, but John never found it to be as much fun as attending a game as a fan in the cheap seats.

He waved to the other reporters in the box he knew, and they nodded back stoically. Some raised their eyebrows in surprise. They knew he'd moved onto the investigative reporting beat long ago, and it had been a few years since he'd stopped by.

One of his old friends from his sports desk days spotted him from across the room and waved him over.

"Johnny boy, what the hell are you doing slumming down here with the rest of us?" Glen Larned was a tall, thin man whose voice immediately took over every room he entered. He was one of the best sports reporters in the country and had earned a number of awards for his critical, but fair, reporting on the league. "You getting back on the beat? Or just here for the cheap seats?"

John took Glen's hand and grinned. "Why on earth would I want to take a pay cut like that?"

"Oh yeah?" Glen pointed at the credentials hanging around John's neck. "Don't tell me you're up here because you couldn't get tickets to the game. Big-time reporter like you?"

John chuckled and then lowered his voice. "Actually, I'm here on a story."

Glen raised an eyebrow at this. "You? I thought you were done with sports reporting."

"You heard about the Knickerbocker murder?" John said.

Glen nodded. "Nasty bit of business. I guess you don't earn billions of dollars without making a few enemies along the way."

"I've got a lead that his killers will be here tonight and they're planning on doing something big," John said.

Glen drew back, a skeptical expression on his face. "Are we in danger?"

John swallowed and looked furtively side-to-side. "It's . . . complicated."

"What are you expecting?" Glen asked.

"Trouble," John said. "Hard to say anything more than that. You know how it goes."

Glen nodded. In fact, the man knew exactly what it was like. Reporting on a story was often two steps forward, one step back.

"Do I need to get my team out of here?" Glen asked, looking alarmed.

"Definitely," John said. "I'm here on a hunch, but I'm about as sure as I've ever been."

"What's your source say? Bomb? Mass shooter? Chemical weapons attack?" Glen ticked off on his fingers each threat that came to mind.

"You wouldn't believe me if I told you," John said. "I'm just here hoping to stop it from happening."

Glen snorted. "When did you turn into James Bond?"

"When I almost lost my life two days ago thanks to this story." He pointed to the bank of monitors that showed every angle of the ballpark as shot by the camera operators around the park. "Before you go, can you hook me into the camera system?"

"Of course," Glen said. He motioned to one of the techs who came over.

"Can you help John get in touch with the camera operators?" Glen asked.

The kid, about twenty-two, gawked at them. "Networks are gonna be pissed if we go off script."

Glen glared at the young man for a moment, until he wilted under his gaze. The tech unclipped a radio from his belt and handed it to John. "Just let them know what they should be looking for, and they'll aim their cameras for you."

"Thanks," he said.

He scanned the monitors, looking for any hint of the Triumvirate. But there were so many people, it was hard to tell one person from another. Whenever he thought he was close to spotting Armstrong or any of the rest of his lot, the person would turn and reveal themselves as being just another baseball fan. He directed the camera operators to scan the crowd row by row. He summoned the focus spell, allowing himself to watch the screen for any sign of the three wizards who'd tried to kill him and his new friends.

His phone buzzed and he pulled it out of his pocket, seeing an update from Apsara that she and the professor had started on their first batch of potions. He allowed himself a moment of relief, knowing his plan was so far going well.

He opened the message and then sent a group text.

JOHN: Anyone spot our friends yet?

Tiny gray bubbles appeared at the bottom of the screen and a reply popped up.

ELLIE: Not yet. The focus spell helps, but there are A LOT of people here tonight.

APSARA: Are we certain they're coming?"

PROFESSOR MCKAIG: This is the only event within five hundred miles that has this many people attending.

APSARA: There's no proof they're coming here.

ELLIE: How long until the game starts?

JOHN: They're about to sing the national anthem. First pitch at 7:07.

A squeal of static and feedback prompted shouts of consternation from the crowd below. John clasped his ear and yanked his headphones off. He had been connected to the stadium's PA system, sending a painful screech directly into his ear canal.

"Good evening, ladies and gentlemen." Daniel Armstrong's booming voice echoed across the stadium's PA. "We regret to inform you that the game tonight has been postponed."

The crowd roared in disapproval as a chorus of boos and disappointment from more than 55,000 fans echoed through the stadium.

ELLIE: JOHN! I see them! The big one we encountered is in the announcer's booth.

APSARA: I'm not ready. The potions need more time.

JOHN: Apsara, keep working on the potions. Ellie, get down to field level and meet me in the main concourse. Professor, you stick with Apsara and protect her from anything coming her way. We NEED those potions.

PROFESSOR MCKAIG: We'll see to the potions. You all do what you can to stall the Triumvirate.

ELLIE: Yep. On my way.

APSARA: Stay safe.

JOHN: Ellie, let me know when you're close. The other two are still out there.

John pocketed his cell phone and shot a look over at Glen who was watching a monitor in alarm. His friend met his gaze, a grim expression on his face.

"I assume this is what you came for," he said.

"That's one of 'em," John confirmed. "There are two others I still need to find. But I'll need your help. Give me your phone."

Glen withdrew his phone and handed it over. John punched in his new number and returned it.

"That's my new number," John said. "I need you to look for two other people. A man, super muscular, looks about seven feet tall, and a woman, Hispanic, curly black hair."

Glen snorted. "That describes about half the women in this stadium."

John shot him a look. "Believe me, you'll know her when you see her."

"How?" Glen demanded.

"It won't be hard," John said, pointing to the monitors. "She'll be casting spells."

Glen looked dumbfounded. "She'll be casting what now?"

John ignored his friend's question. The bank of monitors displaying the game were focused on Daniel Armstrong, who had appeared in the middle of the baseball field near the pitcher's mound. Security guards ran toward him and tried to tackle who they thought was a fan trying to run the bases.

But before they could reach Armstrong, the six guards were greeted with blasts of bright red bolts of energy.

Thrown back, the guards tumbled across the perfectly manicured green grass until they slammed against the inner wall to the stadium with a sickening *crunch*.

The crowd gasped. The fans stood, confused at what they were seeing. Some of the smarter people began moving for the exits, trying to escape the deteriorating situation.

But they didn't get far. Daniel waved a hand. All the doorways to the outside of the stadium bricked off, trapping everyone inside.

The shrieks of panicking people filled the air. Glen looked at John in shock, as the people in the stadium seats trampled over one another as they tried to escape.

"What the hell was that?" Glen asked, his voice cracking.

"What I'm here for," John said, looking back to the monitors. "Glen, it's time to clear everyone out of here."

"You don't have to tell me twice," Glen said. The man turned and began barking instructions to the various other reporters in the room, some of whom were still watching the events unfold as if mesmerized by the bizarre turn of events.

Armstrong closed his eyes and waved his arms, summoning the mana to cast his third spell of the night.

The walls of the stadium shook as the steel and concrete tumbled and broke apart, sizable portions of the walls falling to the ground, crushing dozens of innocents. A bright flash of energy poured out of Armstrong's body and spread across the stadium. The seats came alive and snapped at the people who moments ago sat in them while awaiting the start of the game.

John watched the scene below them unfold as Glen began frantically barking orders to the camera operators still staffing their stations.

"John, I think we found your other friend," Glen shouted, holding a hand to his earpiece. His friend turned to the control board and pushed a button, switching the display away from Armstrong and onto a woman standing on top of the scoreboard.

John recognized her as the woman Armstrong had introduced as Letty back at the airplane boneyard.

"That's her!" John shouted, nodding his thanks to Glen. He sent a text to the group alerting them to the woman's position.

JOHN: Found another Triumvirate. She's on top of the center field board, summoning a spell of some sort. I get the feeling it's meant to amplify whatever the hell Armstrong is doing on the ground.

PROFESSOR: They must be readying the enthralling spell. Everyone, cast your shields now! Protect anyone you can!

John watched the monitor and realized the professor was right. Armstrong had closed his eyes and now two beams of orange and green light streamed down on him, one projected from the top of the scoreboard, and the other from the announcer's booth, opposite the same direction.

Armstrong cried out as the energy flowed through him, even as the fans in the stadium shrieked and screamed for help. Armed security appeared on the field and began firing their weapons on Armstrong, but the bullets bounced harmlessly off a shield.

Armstrong opened his eyes and whispered one word.

"Subjugato."

A brilliant flash of light reverberated through the stadium.

John threw up a shield that encased the press box, protecting himself and his friends.

"Holy hell!" Glen shouted as he dropped to the ground.

John could only imagine the shock his friends experienced, seeing waves of blue energy emanating from his hands.

Armstrong's spell slammed against his shield, and it took everything he had to hold it in place. The force crushed against him like a breaking tsunami, and for a moment, he felt his shield begin to crack.

Finally, Armstrong's spell dissipated. John relaxed, lowering the shield that had protected the reporters in the press room.

Glen stood and stared at him a moment. "You've got some explaining to do."

John lowered his hands, glad to see his friends were still intact.

"Everyone all right?" he asked the room. Small murmurs of acknowledgement came from the other reporters, who were sticking their heads above the wall to see the damage.

John checked the monitors, but they'd been blown out in the surge of Armstrong's spell. It was then he realized how quiet the stadium had become. Before, people had been shrieking and screaming for help.

Now, it was so quiet outside, you could hear a pin drop.

"What is it?" Glen asked. Then he noticed the silence too.

They scrambled to the window where they could see every person still trapped in the stadium standing motionless, facing the field.

"Oh, God." John whispered.

The Triumvirate had done it.

Thousands of men, women, and children, young and old, were all standing, staring straight ahead into the distance. Their eyes glowed bright red, like the burning ends of a thousand lit cigarettes.

John took out his phone and discovered it too had been burned out by the spell Armstrong cast. He had lost communication with the rest of his team, something that he would need to fix. There was no telling what might have happened to them.

He turned to Glen whose face was now a noticeable shade of white.

"I have to find my friends," he said.

"Can they do . . ." Glen made a motion with his hands. "Do that thing you just did?"

"They can," he answered. "Which is why we're here to stop the Triumvirate."

"The Triumvirate?" Glen asked, looking confused. "Are you for real?"

"I think you just saw how real this is." John motioned to the field. He turned and made his way to the door, calling out instructions for everyone who was still standing in the press box.

"Don't allow anyone in here. I think my shield spell may have protected you from the zombification the rest of the fans just went through so you—"

"They're zombies?"

"It's a bad shorthand for what those three did to everyone. They're still alive and still people. We think the Triumvirate will use everyone's energy to summon something a whole lot worse, which I don't have time to explain. Keep yourself locked in here and don't open the door for anyone until the entire stadium is cleared. Got it?"

Glen nodded. "Got it."

John turned and exited the press box, knowing he and his friends were already behind the eight ball. The one and only advantage they held was surprise. Daniel Armstrong and the rest of the Triumvirate had no idea he and the rest of his friends were here. If they could leverage that opportunity, they might end up saving the world yet.

He stepped out into the corridor and began jogging toward the VIP suites, hoping to find Apsara and the professor. Whether they had the potions ready or not, the fight was on.

And they would need all the help they could get.

CHAPTER FIFTY-EIGHT

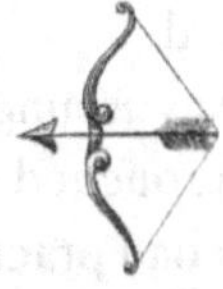

ELLIE LOWERED THE SHIELD she'd cast mere seconds before Daniel Armstrong cast his enthralling spell, saving herself from becoming one of the thousands inside the stadium under the Triumvirate's control.

She looked at the phone in her hand. Burned out and no longer functioning. She grimaced and cast it aside, then looked up where the Triumvirate woman had been standing only moments before.

She pushed her way through the aisle, shoving past all the fans who now stood, staring straight ahead, their faces devoid of any expression. Thousands of red eyes looked down at Armstrong, who was still recovering from the spell he had just cast.

The enthralled stood and left their seats in an organized, efficient manner, making their way down to the field where

Daniel Armstrong still stood. Ellie looked up to see Letty climbing down the ladder. This was her moment.

Quietly, she ascended to a blind spot next to the staircase Letty was descending and crouched down to wait for her. She focused on the spell she wanted to cast and waited.

The woman approached the landing and then paused, just around the corner from Ellie.

"You're not as clever as you believe, little girl," the woman on the other side of the landing sneered. "I could smell your magic from a mile away."

Disappointed the ruse hadn't worked, Ellie still felt like she held the advantage. The woman would have attacked if she believed she could take her on.

"Clever can get you killed," Ellie replied, eyeing the woman, her body tense as her mind raced to recall the powerful offensive spells she had practiced.

The woman edged her way around the corner of the landing and examined Ellie, who crouched and readied herself in an attack position, just as she had practiced.

"I see you still have access to the book," Letty sounded bored. The woman looked her up and down. "You have good form, but I think you lack the will to properly wield these powers."

"What do you know about power?" she shot back. Ellie waved her hand at the enthralled men, women, and children still filing their way out of their seats and down to the field. "Killing and enslaving these people for what?"

"A small sacrifice to bring order to the world," Letty replied. "We are the Triumvirate. We have far bigger plans than you could ever conceive."

"Try me."

"We want to change the world for the better," Letty said, a gleam in her eye. "The Agamoth is a means to that."

"My God, could you be any denser? If you summon a demon and think you can control something like that, you're not just an idiot, you're insane," Ellie rolled her eyes.

Letty raised an eyebrow, a small smile tugging at the edge of her lips, the woman dressed in all black pointed to Armstrong, who was still recovering from casting the spell.

"Not us," Letty said. The woman pointed to the field below. "Him."

Ellie looked down to see Armstrong again muttering a series of chants as the enthralled people in the stadium surrounded him. As she watched, a curious thing happened. The people around Armstrong began to glow a bright orange, their bodies outlined with energy that flowed toward the warlock.

"You're too late," Letty said taking another step toward her. "Once Daniel summons the Agamoth there will be no stopping us. It will be our weapon, impervious to anything the militaries of the world can bring to bear."

An earth-shattering crack resounded, and the ground shuddered once again, the scoreboard structure swaying as a small earthquake rocked the ground beneath them. Ellie looked up in alarm, wondering when she would hear the snap and squeal of failing metal.

"He arrives!" Letty cried out in triumph. "The Agamoth has come."

Ellie turned back to the field to see the earth surrounding Armstrong opened, a large, jagged fault ripping its way from both ends of the stadium. People nearest to the chasm plunged into it wordlessly, without so much as a shriek as their lives were extinguished.

Flames shot out of the ground. A large undulating tentacle emerged. The blistered skin pulsated and looked as if it were made of living lava. The stadium shook harder. The chasm in the ground split wider, allowing the rest of the creature to emerge.

Ellie watched the Agamoth ooze from the netherworld via the portal opened by Armstrong and his enthralled band of zombies. Ellie felt her mind melting at the mere sight of the creature—and fought the urge to retch. At the same time, she found herself hypnotized by the creature as it was birthed into the world, screaming and groaning, its tentacles lashing out wildly, striking and consuming anything that moved.

She watched in horror as one of the creature's tentacles snatched an unsuspecting man and tossed them into its enormous, gaping maw. The man went quietly, without a struggle or indication he even knew he was being eaten alive.

"The Agamoth has risen!" Letty cried out gleefully. "The future has been written. This ends with your death and our triumph."

Ellie turned and cast a powerful fireball spell, inches away from Letty's face, blasting her out of the scoreboard and onto the bleachers below.

"Triumph my ass," Ellie muttered.

Letty screamed, her body bouncing back and forth as she ricocheted down the stairwell. Ellie looked over the railing to see the woman struggling to get to her feet, having cast a shield to cushion her fall.

Ellie took out her phone to text the group when she remembered Armstrong's spell had destroyed it. She cursed and tossed the now useless electronic junk aside. She'd need to figure out another way to contact the rest of the team. Relying on technology had not been their best idea.

She made her way down the staircase, chasing after Letty, when she discovered a group of Armstrong's enthralled blocking her way. She stared at the zombies milling about, reaching for her, and made her decision.

Ellie turned and ran the other way, the enthralled fans in hot pursuit. She cast several spells behind her, hoping they would slow them down, but not wound any of the people chasing her.

John's warning echoed in her head. These people were innocent and didn't deserve to be hurt, even if they were trying to hurt her and her friends.

She ran, nimbly skipping over the seats, taking various routes to avoid confronting the victims of the Triumvirate's spell. She sprinted down the aisles trying to stay out of their way while staying ahead of anyone trying to harm her.

Unfortunately, she was running out of room, and she found herself at the end of the aisle, looking down on the field located several stories below.

To her left, she could see the Agamoth as it continued feasting on innocent people who were lining up to become part of the creature's morbid buffet.

She jumped off the edge of the stairway and cast a shield in front of her, hoping it would absorb the impact and keep her safe.

The ground rushed toward her. She closed her eyes, pouring every ounce of will she had into the shield, hoping it would be powerful enough to absorb the impact of her fall.

She landed on the ground, the shield protecting her, but it was a rough landing, and the wind knocked out of her. She groaned and turned over, laying on her back, staring up at the sky as she tried to catch her breath.

A blast of energy nearly took her head off and Ellie leapt to her feet, conjuring her bow, shooting off a series of arrows at Letty, who was trying to get away. The arrows flew, straight and true, knocking Letty to the ground and pinning her arm to a vendor's display stand. An avalanche of Thrashers merchandise collapsed on Letty, knocking the woman unconscious.

Ellie limped over to Letty and leaned down to check the woman's pulse. Letty was still alive, and she wasn't sure how she felt about that.

She found some rope and tied the woman up, securing her to the cage, making it impossible for the Triumvirate woman to move her hands or cast any spells. She took a step back and checked her work. Letty wasn't going anywhere.

In the distance, she heard the Agamoth feasting and knew there was no time to lay about like this and recover. People needed help, and she would be damned if she didn't try to do everything in her power to help them.

After a moment, she got up and began limping toward the stadium's interior, hoping to reconnect with the rest of her team before it was too late.

CHAPTER FIFTY-NINE

APSARA AND THE PROFESSOR worked as fast as they could in the kitchen. He oversaw assembling the ingredients and she cast the spell and bottled the results. Despite the time crunch, they had managed to create at least two health potions and one mana potion for each member of the team.

After a few moments, she noticed the professor had ceased assembling the potion ingredients for her and was staring at one of the TV monitors inside the kitchen.

"Professor?" she asked. "What is it?"

"They did it," he said, a grim expression on his face.

She followed his gaze up to the monitor and what she saw made her raise a hand up to her mouth in shock.

She had become so caught up in their work, she had missed the Triumvirate summoning the Agamoth.

"Are we too late?" she asked, feeling helpless as she watched the demonic creature consume some of the onlookers on the field, utterly repulsed by the scene.

"We're out of time," the professor replied. "We need to get these potions to the team."

Their cell phones had been sitting on the kitchen counter and she went to retrieve them. However, she was shocked to see the electronics had shorted out and she was unable to get them to turn back on.

"The phones are dead," she announced. "How are we going to find them?"

"Luck most likely," the professor answered. "If they had any sense, they were able to shield themselves from the spell. They'll be the only ones acting normal out there."

They gathered up the bottles, placing them in a Thrashers branded knapsack left behind by one of the workers in the kitchen.

"Will it be enough?" she asked.

The professor sighed. "We go to war with the supplies we have."

In her heart, she knew he was right. If only she had another five minutes. She hated to think that mere moments might mark the difference between life and death for her friends.

"John was in the press box last we heard," he said, hefting the bag onto his shoulder. "Let's start there."

"What about Ellie?" she asked. "She's just as vulnerable without the potions."

The professor stroked his beard and then nodded. "I'm not usually a fan of splitting up, but we have provisions they need."

"You head for the press box, I'll head for the bleachers," Apsara said. "We bring them back to the main entrance and we fight this thing together."

The professor nodded and she grabbed his arm, looking at him warmly. "Thanks for your help, Professor. I wouldn't have been able to get this far without you."

He appeared startled by the sudden gesture. "We'll survive this yet, my dear," he said in his cheery manner.

He turned and jogged down the hall, heading for the press box where John had been. She called out after him.

"Professor, do you have any ideas on how we're supposed to contain that thing?" she asked.

The professor paused, and then looked back and shrugged.

"Together," he answered. He turned and disappeared down the hallway, without looking back.

Apsara swallowed down her fear and then headed for Ellie's last known location, hoping she could get to her friend in time.

CHAPTER SIXTY

MIKE PULLED UP TO Stanhope Stadium and was devastated to see he was already too late. The parking lot was filled with thousands of people fleeing in panic as police and other first responders inside vehicles capped with screaming sirens raced into the parking lot.

Mike followed one of the police cruisers inside the park. He stared out of his front window in awe at the stadium that glowed a bright orange—just as it had appeared in his vision.

He swallowed and eased his work truck up a ramp, very nearly hitting people as they fled for their lives. Mashing the accelerator into the floor of the truck, he crashed through the gates of the stadium, debris scattering across the hood of his car, and skidded to a halt.

He stepped out of his truck, staring at a scene directly out of his vision, including the mass exodus of panicked people fleeing from the exits. He pushed his way through the crowd and found himself confronted with a blocked off entrance. He needed to get inside, but there was no getting in this way.

Mike looked down to see his hands glowing a bright orange. He formed a fist and drove it straight into the metal shutters that isolated the stadium entrance. The shutters exploded, a sizable hole opening an entrance into the stadium.

He looked down at his still-glowing orange fist, amazed at what he had just accomplished. Part of him was relieved it had worked and the other part felt secretly proud at how quickly the shutters had crumbled underneath his strength. He might end up enjoying these powers after all.

He ran into the crowded concourse, where hundreds of people with glowing eyes were standing perfectly still, facing the field and the Agamoth as it continued to consume the fans who had the ill fate of attending the game.

He rushed forward to the first set of stadium seats and looked down at the field where he recognized one of the men who had taken his daughter. The man stood on the pitcher's mound, eyes closed, chanting in front of a chasm the Agamoth was still crawling out of.

Mike raced down the steps, making his way down to the field. He didn't know what he was going to do, only that he needed to do something with the powers he had to protect innocent people.

However, every entrance that led to the ground had been blocked by an energy field of some kind. He kept dashing around the stadium seats, hoping to find anything overlooked by the Triumvirate.

Finally, Mike stopped rushing and squeezed his eyes shut, thinking of the spell John had shown him back at his house.

A powerful blue force exploded from his hands and slammed into the energy field. A bright flash of light preceded what sounded like a gunshot, and the energy field snapped off.

He stood there, shocked at how well it worked, and stepped over the rubble to get to the field. The undulating creature had fully emerged from the crack in the earth and was busy feasting on the people who were willingly sacrificing themselves for the creature's insatiable appetite. Skin prickling, Mike realized the people on the field didn't appear to be aware they were being eaten alive. Somehow, the Triumvirate had turned these people into passive slaves and made them more than willing to become part of the creature's meal.

Mike ran toward the field, blinded by rage at the senseless loss of life, using his powers to push back anyone who came too close to him.

He focused on the leader of the Triumvirate, who was still casting the spell.

But before he could reach his target, a dozen fans enthralled by Armstrong's spell veered into his path. He found himself tossed to one side as a particularly large man tackled him to the ground.

He blasted the offending zombie with a jolt of energy, throwing his attacker clear. He got up and fired at the oncoming horde, hoping to push them back and get room to breathe.

Unfortunately for him, Armstrong noticed what he was doing and directed his army of enthralled baseball fans toward Mike to slow him down and prevent him from getting to the Agamoth.

Mike struggled to keep up, but the sea of bodies overwhelmed him, and the enthralled horde did not appear to have trouble shaking off the spells he was throwing at them. Worse still, his spells were growing weaker as he exhausted his mana and willpower.

He found himself backed into a corner surrounded by hundreds of zombies. He screamed in frustration as he fired energy blasts at the creeping mass, one by one.

Gasping, sweat pouring down his face, he thought of his daughter and hoped she would remember him—assuming anyone survived this apocalypse Armstrong had set in motion.

An enormous explosion threw the group of zombies that were about to kill him across the stadium.

He looked up to see Ellie standing above him on the front row next to home plate, a broad smile on her face.

"Good to see you," he said, relief coursing through his body.

"Nice of you to join us," she replied.

She crouched into a fighting stance and used her bow to continue shooting at the zombies coming after them with single-minded focus. He watched in amazement as the woman who had been moments away from tearing his arm off flew several feet to the side thanks to a blasting spell Ellie had conjured.

She looked over at him and grinned. "We've been practicing."

"I can see that," he said. He charged his fists up again and joined Ellie in the fight as he fired on the oncoming onslaught.

Mike and Ellie stood back-to-back. His training came back to him, as though he'd never left it behind. The fight was always in his blood, and he was good at it.

The Agamoth curled a tentacle around a stadium light and brought it down on the field in a thunderous crash and a bright flash of light. Armstrong turned and raised his arms, calling out a spell. The hunk of metal and debris reformed into a large creature that let out a chilling scream. Mike and Ellie clapped their hands over their ears, the screams from the newly formed golem grating like nails on a chalkboard.

"What the hell is that?" Mike watched, his mouth agape, as the monstrous golem moved around the field, leaving a trail of destruction and death.

"The glowing orange demon crawling out of center field doesn't faze you, but that thing does?" Ellie asked. She closed her eyes and spread her arms out, sending a wave of energy that threw the oncoming surge of creatures back.

"We have to get out of here," he said. "Go, I'll hold them off."

The golem turned toward them and sprinted across the field, screeching, pops of electricity firing from the loose cables hanging from the creature's newly formed body.

"Move!" Ellie shouted at him.

Mike ran for the field level, vaulting his way up and over the rows of seats. He turned back, ready to give Ellie a hand up, but she didn't need his help at all.

They turned, ready to make a run for the exit—and found their way blocked by a large crowd of Armstrong's newly enthralled minions, hissing at them as they approached.

The sound of tearing metal and screeches echoed loudly behind them. Mike refused to look back. They needed to move, or they needed to fight.

That's when the professor appeared, sliding down a wave of energy from the upper levels of the stadium. The blast of energy threw the golem back, giving them a moment of respite as the minions threw their hands up to block the light from the professor's spell.

"Michael, so good to see you again," the professor said, looking relieved to see Mike there.

"I had a vision," Mike said. He turned a hand and indicated the Agamoth, who was still feeding on the assembled minions standing near the center field.

"Foresight," the professor murmured. "Fascinating. What did you see exactly?"

"The end of the world if I didn't join you all here tonight," Mike said. "But, now that I'm here, I'm not sure how much of a difference I'm making."

"What about Shayla?" Ellie asked. "If anything happens to you . . ."

"The vision made it clear that if I didn't come here tonight, my baby girl wouldn't have much of a world to grow up in," Mike replied.

"I admire your courage," the professor said, clasping him on the shoulder.

Mike readied himself as another wave of creatures approached their position.

"Courage is only about half of what we'll need tonight," he said. "The rest is up to how good we are with this magic."

The professor summoned a bolt of energy and threw it into the crowd of oncoming creatures. The bolt nailed three of them, pinning them to the ground.

With the ability to summon endless arrows, Ellie fired at incredible speed, unleashing arrow after arrow, the bowstring playing a tune as she brought down one zombie after another.

Mike's spells weren't as effective as what Ellie and the professor were able to conjure, but he had managed to help, pushing the zombies back by using blasts of wind and stunning bolts of energy that knocked his targets to the ground, usually keeping them there.

But it was, at best, a stalemate. Mike felt himself growing tired and noticed his spells becoming less and less effective. Judging by the cries of pain and effort coming from his two friends, Mike figured they were having trouble keeping up as well.

It was a numbers game. Because Armstrong could continue drawing on everyone's mana around him, he could continue sending creatures and zombies at them all night long. But the professor, Ellie, and he operated with limited mana, and he could feel himself coming to the end of his rope.

The professor waved his arms, causing the golem to float above the field, its strangely assembled legs and arms undulating wildly in air as it struggled to find purchase. The professor then brought his hands down, and the creature followed, falling to the ground, and exploding into a hundred pieces.

Armstrong simply smiled and sent a wave of blue energy back at the pieces. It reassembled itself.

"You have got to be kidding me," Ellie said, exasperated.

"We can't keep this up," the professor said, panting slightly. "With the number of people he can siphon mana from, he could outlast us for decades."

Ellie shouted as she narrowly avoided having her head taken off by a creature made from an advertisement billboard. She stepped back, summoned an arrow for her virtual bow, and released it, destroying the creature before it could try again.

"Whatever it is we do, we'd best do it quick," she said, turning to them.

"I have an idea," the professor said suddenly. "Get behind me and do everything I do."

Mike exchanged a look with Ellie, but he would take any plan at this point.

The professor closed his eyes and concentrated. Purple energy built up along his hands until he shouted, "Intifinititum mirago."

Suddenly, sharp, jagged pieces of mirrors emerged from the earth below them, forming a maze. Mike felt his jaw drop. Just how much had the professor and Ellie been practicing? What else were they capable of?

"Follow me," the professor said, looking over his shoulder.

He charged into the entrance of the maze, which covered the entirety of the left field dugout and disappeared into the hall of mirrors.

Ellie entered just steps behind him. Mike, still unsure of what he was leaping into, decided to trust his team.

He stepped off the deck and into the mysterious vortex.

CHAPTER SIXTY-ONE

APSARA AND JOHN COLLIDED as they rounded the corner of the stadium. John spun to the side and readied himself to cast a spell when he realized who he'd just bowled over.

He reached down to offer her a hand. She took it, shooting him an irritated look.

"Did you finish the potions?" he asked, helping her to her feet.

Apsara picked up the knapsack that had fallen to the side and opened it. He could see about a dozen water bottles filled with either a green, red, or blue watery substance.

"Red is for health," Apsara said, handing him one apiece. "Blue is to help you recover after casting spells."

"And the green?" he asked, eying the strange-colored concoction.

"That's . . ." She hesitated. "That's in case someone dies."

He felt a chill run down his spine, and he was thankful he had someone as smart and capable as Apsara on their team.

"That was good thinking," he said, pocketing the green potion. He'd keep that one safe for now.

"The Agamoth . . ." she began.

He nodded. "I saw."

"Are we too late?"

He glanced to the field below, where he could see the Agamoth scoop up another handful of enthralled fans and toss them into its gaping maw. He decided to ignore her question.

"Come on," he said, his voice gaining strength. "The only way we're going to defeat them is—ooof!"

Picked up and thrown to the side, his body slammed into the wall at an incredible speed. His arm snapped in two. He cried out and crumbled to the ground, barely able to breathe.

Out of one eye, he saw the hulking third member of the Triumvirate approach Apsara. She conjured a shield and slowly backed away, while calling out his name to see if he could answer—or if he were even still alive.

Breathing hurt, and every attempt to draw air into his lungs resulted in a penetrating pain that made him cry out even louder. He had the sudden realization that he was dying and if he didn't get help soon, he would expire right there in the corridors of Stanhope Stadium.

He could feel the world around him growing distant and knew that was because he was going into shock from his injuries. He reached a shaky hand out for the red potion Apsara had given him earlier, inches away from him.

Apsara was up against the wall. She threw energy bolts at Cody, but he brushed them off, conjuring shields, knocking them aside.

John felt his fingertips touch the edge of the health bottle, but he was losing strength. He was running out of time.

Apsara stepped to the side and went on the offensive, engaging directly with Cody. However, the man brushed her initial attack aside, picked her up, and threw her against the wall.

Unlike John, Apsara had the presence of mind to summon a shield that helped to absorb the impact, allowing her to land gracefully.

John saw Apsara staring Cody down—she was there to fight, and she didn't intend to lose.

She launched a series of energy bolts and then conjured a shield behind Cody, sending them ricocheting around until they struck the man from all angles.

Cody yelled and lunged for her, but she was ready this time, using her shield to deflect the large man's attack. She sent him reeling with a well-timed blast to the jaw. Apsara didn't let up and kept firing the magic missiles they'd practiced earlier in the park, blasting the large man back.

One bolt landed on the back of his knee, forcing him to the ground. Apsara jumped and conjured a metal bat, swinging it at his head.

Cody fell to the ground, bleeding from the skull as she stood triumphant over him.

John felt the world around him fade away as his fingers went limp, just as he grasped the health potion.

Then, before the world faded away for good, he felt a trickle of liquid touch his lips. Instantly, he felt better.

He opened his eyes to see Apsara cradling his head, tipping it back as she coaxed more of the healing potion into his mouth. It worked as advertised—not that he ever doubted Apsara's skill as a sorceress.

His bones began knitting back into place, an odd sensation that was both devoid of any pain, yet, extremely uncomfortable. It was like cracking your knuckles after they hadn't been cracked in a long time.

He sat up after feeling his bones go back where they belonged and coughed, spitting out the last remnants of blood and tissue that had filled his mouth. He ran his hands up and down his body, amazed at the change. Only seconds before, he'd been dying a painful death. Now, he felt fine—better than fine in fact.

"I'm happy to report that your potions work as advertised," he managed through coughing fits.

Apsara sighed in relief. "Sorry to say, that's your only one."

"One was enough," John said. He sat forward and Apsara stopped him, cautioning him.

"Easy. He's not going anywhere," she said, nodding to the prone Cody.

"We still have to stop the Agamoth," he managed, and then slumped back against the wall, his knees failing him.

Apsara placed a hand on his chest, trying to keep him on the ground.

"The book said full recovery can take up to ninety seconds," she said. "So don't push it."

"No, no, I'm ready," he said. He tried standing but found he was still light-headed, his body refusing to cooperate with the instructions his brain was sending to his limbs. "Nope, I'm going back down," he said, sinking to the ground.

Apsara caught him and eased him into a sitting position.

"You'll tell me when the ninety seconds is up?" he asked, his head still spinning.

She nodded.

He closed his eyes and concentrated all his willpower on healing his body, hoping that his own magic might somehow help speed things up. Whether it worked or not, he couldn't be sure. But he did know that once Apsara tapped him on the shoulder and let him know time was up, he felt about as good as he ever did.

When he re-opened his eyes, he saw Apsara conjuring bright bands of energy to bind Cody and keep him out of trouble by tying him up.

"That's good thinking," he said. "Leave him here with a note for the authorities."

"Who are you?" she asked. "Batman?"

He chuckled and then nodded to the doorway. "Ready to send the Agamoth back to hell?"

"Let's do it," she said.

They left, running down the corridor toward the Agamoth and the rest of the Triumvirate.

He only hoped they weren't too late.

CHAPTER SIXTY-TWO

ELLIE FOLLOWED THE PROFESSOR into the hall of mirrors and then found herself surrounded by thousands of images of herself, all looking as confused as she felt.

"Keep moving." The professor's voice floated out to her, as if coming in a million different directions from a million different voices. The effect was disorienting and made her stomach queasy as she attempted to keep her perspective straight.

"Where do I go?" she shouted back. Then, she could hear Mike's confused voice yelling out into the void as well, as he entered the hall of mirrors behind her.

"Always move forward," the professor's voice echoed from everywhere around her.

She shrugged and decided to follow his advice—still, it was difficult to tell which direction was forward. The moment she'd stepped into the maze of mirrors, she lost sight of the baseball stadium and the stands they had been fighting in only moments before. All she could see now was an infinite number of reflections of herself standing in a dark room.

Perhaps in a place like the infinite dimension, forward was more a state of mind than it was an actual direction. She decided to take the professor's advice literally and started moving forward.

Her reflections copied her movements. Every image of her leaned forward as she ran faster and faster, moving on as best she could.

She looked up to see one of her reflections running straight toward her as if she were about to collide with it. Still, she kept moving, gritting her teeth as the reflection came closer and closer.

When they were only seconds from colliding, Ellie ran through her doppelganger and entered a brightly lit room where the professor was standing with a wide grin on his face.

"Welcome to the Infinite Dimension," he said with a toothy grin.

She looked around at the interior and was flummoxed by the thousands of scenes playing out on the walls surrounding them. "I'm sorry, where are we? What the hell is the Infinite Dimension?"

Before he could answer, Mike appeared, panting, and leaning over inside the room where she and the professor stood. She rushed to him, but he waved her off as he caught his breath.

"This is some trippy stuff professor," Mike said after catching his breath.

"It should be. We're hiding in between the fabric of reality and unreality." The professor waved his arms around. "They can't find us here."

"And what is here?" Ellie asked.

The professor looked embarrassed. "To be honest, I'm not entirely certain. It was one of the last things I read in *The Omnichron.*"

Ellie felt dizzy looking up and around at the fractal images surrounding them, as if they were viewing the real world from a kaleidoscope. Around them, images from the stadium and the Triumvirate's minions were frozen in place, or at least moving incredibly slowly.

She looked back down at her feet to steady herself. She was becoming nauseous looking out at the field.

"How do we get out?" she asked, still unsteady. "Not that I mind the break from fighting."

"Whenever and wherever we want," the professor said. "It's meant to offer us a last-minute refuge from our enemies."

"That's a great idea," she said. "But what if they followed us in?"

He shook his head. "If I cast the spell correctly, they shouldn't be able to. Anyone who tried to follow us in would eventually become lost among the infinite number of realities being generated by the spell."

There was a roar as one of the Triumvirate's creatures appeared inside the brightly lit room the professor had created. Ellie summoned her bow and drew the string back, an arrow appearing and launching itself at the reanimated creature made from material from the crumbling stadium.

The creature shrieked in pain and tried fighting back against her attack, but there was nowhere for it to flee.

Mike attacked the creature from the rear, using an enormous chain with a spiked ball at the end he'd summoned, and threw it around the creature's legs, pulling it to the ground.

The professor joined the fight by launching a magic spear that entered the creature's eyes, spraying a green viscous substance everywhere.

Ellie wiped the gunk off her face in a huff, spitting and coughing.

"Sorry," the professor said. "I guess my aim still needs some practice."

"Now what?" Mike asked, looking more than a little worried. "We're safe in here, but what about Apsara and John?"

"We can find them," the professor said, his face brightening. He closed his eyes and murmured another few words and a portal appeared in front of them.

Scenes from the ballpark played out across the screen as the professor searched, waving his hands, and changing their perspective.

"Can you see everywhere with that?" Mike asked.

"Anywhere I need to," the professor said, as he scrolled through the various scenes. "The Infinite Dimension allows me to see every probability playing out. According to *The Omnichron*, the spell creates a pocket of time that briefly pauses reality while all possible futures play out. Since that ends up being something on the order of ten to the sixty-fourth power, anything you think could happen, will happen."

"How will we know which universe is the correct one?" Ellie asked, approaching the screen where the professor stood.

"They aren't all being created. Our dimension is still the only one that exists. All I've done is create a pocket reality where time is stopped while all possibilities unfold. Think of it as a snapshot."

"But we could look into the future," she said. "Why don't we just do that to find out how to defeat the Agamoth?"

"Infinite means infinite," the professor shook his head. "There are so many variables to what happens next, the choices other people make in response to your choices, a person could spend a billion years in here trying to find the right way to succeed. Think of the butterfly effect and the chaos you'd introduce. A person would go mad before they discovered what they needed. I don't believe the point of the

Infinite Dimension is to find a way to win, but to take refuge and strategize your next move."

"The Agamoth is about to devour the entire Southland," Mike said. "You don't think this *might* be a useful tool in our upcoming fight?"

The professor stopped what he was doing and looked at Mike gravely. Ellie stood uncomfortably to the side while Mike blushed under the professor's withering stare.

"It's too dangerous to rely on trying to predict the future," the professor said quietly. "How many times would you stop the fight and try to get an edge on your opponent? The very creation of this little dimension is already generating unknown side effects and timeline possibilities. Are you ready to take ownership of all of them?"

Mike raised an eyebrow at the professor, who shrugged.

"I'll take that as a no. Now if you don't mind." The professor continued his search for Apsara and John through time and space.

"It was just an idea," Mike muttered to himself. Ellie pretended not to hear him, lest she start the argument all over again.

"There!" the professor exclaimed. The screen projected the image of John and Apsara on the floor of a hallway. Apsara cradled his head, while tipping a bottle back into his mouth. Ellie felt a range of emotions, one of which, she was surprised to discover, was something akin to jealousy.

"Ready to join our friends?" the professor asked.

"How?"

"That's another advantage of the Infinite Dimension," the professor said, beaming. "Instant travel."

The professor turned and snapped his fingers. A door appeared on the other side of the room. He walked over and opened it, holding an arm out for Ellie.

"After you," he said, bowing low, a smirk on his face.

She hesitated for only a moment and then stepped through the portal into pitch black.

She was suddenly standing inside the corridor somewhere deep inside the stadium. It almost felt like she'd missed a step when she went through, but she recovered fast.

Apsara glanced up to see her appear out of nowhere and gasped in surprise.

"Ellie," Apsara looked shocked to see her friend appear out of thin air. "You made it."

"We all made it," she said, as Mike and the professor stepped into the corridor behind her.

Apsara shrieked in happiness and ran forward to hug the professor, drawing Ellie in the embrace as well. John stood back smiling at their assembled group, but Ellie saw the smile fade once John saw Mike had also appeared. For a moment, the air was tense until John stepped forward, holding out a hand.

Apsara released her and the professor and they watched the reunion between the two men.

"It's damn good to see you, Mike," John said, his face clearly showing he was indeed relieved at the sight of their friend. "It's been a hard fight without ya."

"And it's only going to get harder," Mike shook John's hand and nodded. He turned to the group. "I came back because I had a vision about what will happen if the Agamoth escapes the stadium."

"What did you see, son?" the professor asked, his gravelly voice sounding as alarmed as Ellie had ever heard it.

"That . . . thing swallows up humanity," Mike said after a moment. "Armstrong thinks he has a handle on that creature, but he doesn't. No one does. No one can. The Agamoth is from another plane of existence that doesn't understand morality or that we're even alive. We are just raw material for it to consume."

The group fell silent at Mike's description of the Agamoth. On one level, they'd always known it would be a difficult fight. The creature was already a ten-story-tall living nightmare of tentacles, scales, and claws.

"How do we kill it?" John asked.

"We don't," Mike said. "But if we wound it enough, we might be able to send it back."

Apsara groaned. John put his head in his hands.

Ellie didn't understand why they were so upset. "What is it? Let's just send it back then."

"To do that, I'll need *The Omnichron*," Apsara explained. "Ellie captured the book on her phone, but all our phones were destroyed by Armstrong's spell. The physical copy is the only one left with the spell we need."

"And it's most likely still with Armstrong," John added. "He wouldn't take the chance of allowing Letty to get a look at that book."

"And that other one, Cody, didn't have it when we confronted him," Apsara said.

"Then we face him together and take it back ourselves," Ellie said. "What's so hard about that?"

"With all those people out there giving him their mana, he's far more powerful than us," Apsara pointed out.

"He's faced one or two of us at a time," John said. "If all five of us come at him with everything we've got as a group, we might stand a chance."

"And after we have the book?" Ellie asked.

"We find the spell and send the Agamoth back where it came from," the professor said.

"Then what are we waiting for?" Ellie asked impatiently and stuck her hand out in the center.

John smiled and stepped forward, placing his hand on top of hers.

Mike stepped forward. "I've come this far."

The professor and Apsara joined them, placing their hands in the center. Ellie felt a burst of energy as their hands glowed in unison.

The building shook as the Agamoth screeched again.

"I think that's our cue," John said. "Ladies, gentlemen, if we don't make it out on the other side of this, then I want you all to know, it's been my genuine pleasure going on this journey with you."

"Let's make sure we all come back then," Mike added.

They turned and began heading down the hallway that would take them back to the field.

It was time to end the threat once and for all.

CHAPTER SIXTY-THREE

JOHN HAD TO ADMIT, the plan Mike had thought up wasn't half bad. Of course, he should have expected that from the only person who had any kind of real combat experience.

They had two goals—the amulet and *The Omnichron*. The only thing that mattered was getting those two things away from Armstrong before he was able to direct the Agamoth to attack them. The Agamoth was still feeding on the enthralled baseball fans, but there weren't many of those left. John had a feeling that after the Agamoth exhausted its food supply within the stadium, it would set out for the millions of residents in the city to feed its unending appetite.

The plan was simple. John, Apsara, and Ellie would take on the Agamoth using every offensive spell they knew. They had no illusions that they would be able to defeat the otherworldly monster in one-on-one combat, but if they could distract it and keep it from devouring any more people, which might prevent it from gaining any more strength and killing more innocent fans.

Mike and the professor were tasked to take on Armstrong and get the book and amulet away from the man.

John stood at the top of the bleachers next to Apsara and Ellie. Apsara had dispensed the potions to the rest of their group, instructing everyone on their use. Because he had already used his reviving potion in their fight against Cody, he only had his mana potion left.

He was really hoping he wouldn't need it. But as he watched the Agamoth, he wondered if they were too late. The demon was finishing his meal of baseball fans as the creature's tentacles slithered up the stadium's walls, undulating as they sought to gain purchase.

"John!" Apsara shouted, pointing at the Agamoth.

"Are you ready?" he asked the two women standing next to him. They nodded.

John rubbed his face, trying to think of what to do next. Whatever happened, they could not let that thing into the city.

"Ellie, get as high up as you can and harass that creature with as many arrows as you can sling," he said.

"On it!" She turned to run up the stairs, conjuring the bow and arrow into her hands.

"What about us?" Apsara asked, turning to him.

"We get the fun job of keeping the Agamoth inside the stadium," John said.

He took a breath and concentrated, his fists beginning to glow red with energy while Apsara did the same.

"Ready?" he asked.

"About as I'm ever gonna be," she replied. Her voice, while worried, sounded solid enough. He figured that was the best he could expect given their situation.

"Then let's get firing," he said. He summoned a charged missile and hurled it toward the Agamoth. The creature screeched as his magic missile landed on its upper torso.

The Agamoth's horrifying visage turned to look for the creature that had dared to attack it and shrieked again in protest when it spotted John.

He didn't hesitate and continued firing at the creature as Apsara joined him, blasting away at the Agamoth.

Enraged, the creature climbed back down off the stadium walls and slung one of its tentacles at their position on the upper levels of the stadium.

They ducked, falling to the sticky floor, barely missing the Agamoth's tentacle as it smashed the bleacher seats above them.

"Having fun yet?" he asked, shocked at how fast the massive creature could move.

Apsara didn't answer. Instead, she conjured a shield moments before another tentacle slammed down where they were hiding. The shield absorbed the blow, and he was suddenly very thankful Apsara had spent her practice time on defensive spells.

The tentacle whipped back, allowing them a moment to run—which they didn't waste.

"Move," Apsara shouted.

John scrambled to his feet and charged up his fists once again, firing them both at the tentacle about to slam against them. The powerful bolts of energy vaporized the writhing appendage. The creature screeched in pain.

Several more bolts of energy struck the Agamoth's head as Ellie fired at the creature from her vantage point to distract the creature.

Apsara stood and held her arms to the sky, summoning an energy storm from above. A bolt of lightning ripped through the night and struck another of the Agamoth's tentacles, blasting it to pieces.

The sharp smell of ozone and what smelled like microwaved fish filled the air as they jumped to dodge another tentacle.

"Nicely done!" John shouted. She nodded in acknowledgement, and they continued to fire on the demonic creature.

Unfortunately, John wasn't sure if they were doing anything besides pissing the creature off. They might have been able to take out two of the Agamoth's twelve tentacles, but the creature had begun to learn from its confrontation with them. It held its attacks back, striking only when it had a clear shot.

The Agamoth oozed toward the top of the stadium, ignoring the blasts of energy it was taking from Ellie's bow.

"Where is it going?" he shouted in frustration.

"I think it's hungry," Apsara shouted back.

She was right. The Agamoth paused at the top of the stadium and picked off people who hadn't been enthralled. He could hear them scream as the creature's tentacles pulled them out of the VIP suites where they had been hiding.

Once the Agamoth ate its fill, the demon turned back to John and Apsara with renewed energy and resumed trying to kill them. John noticed that one of the tentacles they'd destroyed was growing back fast after the creature's feast.

"I have an idea!" he shouted at Apsara. "Concentrate your fire on the tentacle to the left." He charged his fists and fired at the one on their right.

If this worked, they could slow the creature down—enough to keep it from escaping the stadium.

Apsara saw what he was doing and nodded.

The creature roared in frustration as their energy bolts dissolved its regrowing limb. He turned and began firing on a second limb until that was destroyed as well. Apsara continued her attack with renewed energy.

With four limbs missing, the creature scuttled toward Apsara and himself in earnest, chasing them through the stands as they continued their onslaught. Between the two of them, they were able to keep up the pressure separating eight of the creature's limbs from its grotesque body.

"It's working," he shouted. "Only four more to go!"

The creature was slowing its attacks. The amount of energy it was expending in the fight needed to be replaced by fresh human beings, and it had already eaten everyone in the stadium. There was no one left for it to consume, and it was fading fast.

John took out Apsara's mana potion and drank it down. Adrenaline surged through his body and charged his fists with every ounce of mana and will he had left. He channeled his focus into one large blast directed at two of the Agamoth's tentacles, shaving them off the creature's body.

The Agamoth roared and fell back into the outfield, slamming to the ground as the entire stadium shook with its weight.

Just as John allowed himself to believe they might win this fight, the Agamoth pulsed, the mottled skin changing colors as orange-red energy covered its body. The tentacles regrew—all twelve of them. John shot a series of magic missiles at the creature, all of which were deflected by a shimmering shield that had appeared in front of it.

He lowered his hands wearily. The Agamoth was generating a force field that he couldn't penetrate, even with his strongest magic.

Apsara sagged next to him, out of breath from the intense firefight.

"The creature is regenerating," she said. "It's up to the professor and Mike to get the amulet and the book now."

He didn't answer, knowing she was right. They'd thrown everything they had at the Agamoth, and it had shrugged off their most formidable attacks.

He only hoped the professor and Mike were having an easier time than they were.

CHAPTER SIXTY-FOUR

THE PROFESSOR RAN WITH Mike through the corridors toward Armstrong's last known location. They'd spotted the leader of the Triumvirate fleeing for the exits after the Agamoth finished feasting on the remaining fans. The professor figured the final member of the Triumvirate wasn't keen on ending up a snack for the very demon he had summoned.

Mike placed a hand over his chest, stopping him before they rounded the corner that would take them into the lobby.

"He's out there," Mike said, his eyes closed.

"Are you sure?" he asked. "How do you know?"

"I had another vision," Mike replied, opening his eyes. He paused for a moment, clearly overcome by what he had seen.

The professor approached him, placing a hand on his shoulder. "Are you okay?"

"Yes," Mike answered after a moment. "The visions are a bit . . . disorienting."

"What was it?"

Mike paused as if unsure how to answer the question and then, ignored it.

"That's not important." The former Marine readied his fists, charging one with an energy bolt and the other with a shield to help protect him from whatever Armstrong could throw at them. "We go in on three. Ready?"

He nodded and Mike counted down from three with his fingers.

They burst into the lobby where they saw Armstrong standing at the entrance to the stadium, his back to them.

"Armstrong, you've lost," he shouted. "Your brother is gone, Letty is neutralized, and your creature defeated. Don't make this any harder on yourself than it has to be."

The professor heard his voice echo through the cavernous hall where thousands of baseball fans had entered expecting a fun night at the ballpark only hours before. But now, there was no one in sight. It was just the three of them. Anyone who hadn't escaped had been consumed by the Agamoth.

Police and other law enforcement personnel stationed at the entrance to the parking lot were assisting with the evacuation. They hadn't shown any interest in confronting the Agamoth or the rest of the Triumvirate yet, but the professor knew they were coming. It was only a matter of time.

"Whatever happens next depends on you, Armstrong." Mike's voice boomed across the field. "You can go quietly, or you can die here today like your friends."

Armstrong turned to face them. The professor could see that all trace of humanity had been erased from the man. He had become a mere vessel for the demonic Agamoth, which had taken control of the man through the amulet hanging around his neck.

"Professor," Mike said, his voice sounding a low warning. "I don't think we're dealing with the same Armstrong anymore."

"I think you're right about that," he said. He took a step forward and extended his hands. "Whom are we addressing?"

The man formerly known as Armstrong did not respond and just stared back at the professor.

"Welcome to our dimension," the professor said, eyeing the transformed Armstrong.

"Your reality is most interesting," Armstrong responded. But much like the man's eyes, the voice was different. Armstrong's voice had shifted to a throaty growl that seemed to echo throughout the stadium.

"You are not welcome," the professor replied, standing tall, holding his palm out in front of him. "You must leave Armstrong's body and return to your dimension. If you do not, we will destroy your form in this realm."

Armstrong cocked his head and then smiled. "You'd be pleased to know your friends have already neutralized it. But their pathetic attempts have done nothing to sap my will. The Agamoth cannot be destroyed on this plane of existence."

"There is nothing here for you," Mike said, his fists still clenched. Bright sparks of energy flew off the ends of his knuckles and fingers.

"Your mewling threats are irrelevant. My physical form is invulnerable while it refreshes itself. Once I absorb enough mana from the rest of you pathetic beings, the Agamoth will become unstoppable."

The professor and Mike exchanged a glance.

"City's closed," Mike said. He summoned a fireball and threw it at Armstrong who deflected it easily, sending the burst of flames into the stands.

The professor waved his arm, firing a blast of energy at the possessed man, who expertly deflected it as before.

Mike followed up his attack with another. The three of them began fighting in earnest, rapidly exchanging, and deflecting each other's energy bolts while each combatant attempted to gain an advantage on the other.

The professor summoned an ice wall to surround Armstrong, but Armstrong's body burst into flames, neutralizing the effects.

Armstrong walked through the thick ice, a wide smile on his face, flames melting the frozen block. However, the smirk on his face didn't last long. Mike threw another magic missile directly at his head. Armstrong's head whipped back. He fell to the ground, his shield barely able to absorb the impact in time.

Mike summoned an energy sword and sliced at the man's head and torso. Armstrong fell back, summoning an energy sword of his own, knocking Mike's weapon out of his hands. He followed it up with a blast of his own, firing it directly into Mike's chest, knocking him down and back across the room.

The professor watched helplessly as Mike's body crumpled against the wall, a dark patch of blood staining the front of his shirt. He turned to see Armstrong flying at him and was barely able to summon a shield in time to deflect the man away.

Armstrong bounced off the professor's shield and fell to the ground. The professor shifted his position attempting to defend his wounded friend and tried to think of a spell that would give him an edge on the man attacking him.

But he was coming up blank. There was nothing except . . .

He waved his hands and muttered the incantation that summoned the Infinite Dimension. Armstrong dove at him just as he summoned the dimension, and they fell into the unreality together.

The professor tumbled to the ground in an undignified heap of limbs. He quickly regained his step and tried to catch his breath as he ignored the thousands of scenes around him. He moved forward until he ran into one of his oncoming reflections. He smashed into himself, appearing in the waiting room of the Infinite Dimension.

Armstrong entered right behind him and stood ready.

McKaig caught his breath.

"You've accessed the Infinite Dimension," Armstrong said, sounding surprised. "You must be a powerful wizard if you're able to cast that spell."

"You have no idea," the professor replied. "You may believe you have an edge on humanity because magic has been missing from our world for so long, but I think you'll find us a quick study."

"Your arrogance will be the death of you," Armstrong snarled.

The man lunged at the professor.

But one of the dimensions opened and the probabilities beginning to swirl all around them at once.

Armstrong looked around him in shock. "No! What are you doing?"

"Collapsing your reality," the professor said through gritted teeth. "Infinitidium!"

The professor and Armstrong were launched into one of the nearest realities. There, they could see Apsara cradling John as he bled to death. First responders covered Ellie's face with a blanket after she died from her wounds. Mike's body was torn in half next to the professor, who was lying prone next to him.

The reality reset, and the scene switched. Now, Ellie was hanging on for dear life at the top of the stadium arena while Mike and the professor fired at the Agamoth. John and Apsara were fighting for their lives in a gritty battle with Cody and Armstrong.

The reality collapsed again. McKaig saw Mike and the professor back at the entrance to the stadium blasting Armstrong with everything they had until he was vaporized.

Over and over reality collapsed and various scenarios played out. They lived through thousands of versions of the battle as Armstrong lost, won, lost again, and won. In some, McKaig's team were killed. In others, the team survived and defeated the Agamoth easily.

They remained stuck in the dimension, living through every scenario until Armstrong screamed, clutching his head in pain as the Agamoth struggled to remain tethered to the reality where it had been summoned.

The professor clutched at Armstrong, hanging on to the man, forcing him through millions of scenarios. He vowed to hang on as long as he possibly could. It was the only way.

Just as the professor felt his strength waning to the point he could no longer casting the spell, the Infinite Dimension collapsed. He found himself on the floor of the stadium, panting next to the unconscious body of the Triumvirate leader.

Barely conscious himself, the professor crawled over to Armstrong and ripped the amulet off his neck. He sat up, coughing, and then sighed, remembering there were two things he needed. He searched Daniel Armstrong's clothes and discovered *The Omnichron* inside a leather satchel slung around the man's neck.

"Like I told you," the professor said wearily. "We're a quick study."

He turned to see Mike still lying on the ground where Armstrong had laid him out with the energy blast, the ugly wound on his chest bleeding profusely. He got up and unsteadily made his way over to Mike, where he uncorked the health potion Apsara had made for him and poured it into the man's mouth.

Mike stirred and sat up, coughing violently. The professor groaned and turned over, hoping it was all over now. He needed a break—but there was no time.

"Did we . . . win?" Mike asked, still sounding dazed.

The professor showed him the amulet and *The Omnichron*. "I've got the Agamoth's return ticket right here."

Mike nodded and held up a hand.

The professor slapped it, celebrating their victory. It was the least he could do.

CHAPTER SIXTY-FIVE

THE FIVE OF THEM gathered at home plate, watching the Agamoth pulsate as it recovered from the beating they had just delivered. Armstrong, Cody, and Letty were also on the field, bound together by energy ties Apsara had conjured to keep them from moving or casting any spells.

"What do we do with them?" Apsara asked, nodding to the three dark wizards on the ground.

"We send them back with the Agamoth," the professor said. "That's the only logical course of action."

John looked over at the professor, confused. "I don't understand."

"But we defeated it, Professor," Ellie said, stepping forward. She gestured toward the Agamoth which was still struggling to move. "We neutralized it."

"You put it into hibernation," the professor pointed to the creature, which still hadn't moved. "That . . . thing feeds on negative energy. And we all know there's more than enough of that in the modern world to bring it back to life."

The professor approached the Triumvirate, who were unable to speak or move thanks to the energy bindings that they had summoned.

"The world saw what happened tonight," the professor continued. "There may be other copies of *The Omnichron*. Before, we were the only ones who understood its power. That is no longer the case."

"What are you saying, Professor?" Mike asked.

The professor looked back at the motley crew that had come together over the last few days, united only by one thing. The older man smiled, and John noticed how old his friend looked in the moment.

"That we have been presented with the same choice our ancestors faced," the professor said. "That in order to protect the world, we must remove magic from the world, just as they did, to prevent this kind of thing from happening again."

"Hold on a second," John said, the anger in his voice making the rest of the group uncomfortable. "Weren't you the one telling me the genie was already out of the bottle?"

"This is our chance to put it back in. Here. Now." The professor's face was pleading with him. "I have seen things that cannot be allowed to come to pass."

John saw his own uncertainty reflected in the others' faces. Apsara even looked angry at the professor's suggestion.

"You can't be serious," she said, her voice filled with a cold fury John hadn't heard before. "The powers we have could help millions of people. The health potions I've created could empty cancer wards in a day!"

"Millions more could be killed, enslaved, or worse," the professor countered. The older man looked to John for support. "I saw it all unfold in the Infinite Dimension."

"Weren't you the one who told us those were only possibilities?" Ellie piped up. "Our world could be very different."

While John didn't agree that getting rid of magic was a good idea, he understood the professor's perspective—after all, they had all nearly died trying to save humanity from a few idiots who had no idea what they were doing.

How many more people would attempt to go down the Triumvirate's path if magic remained in the world?

"John," Apsara said, turning to him. "Think of what we were able to do for that poor Knickerbocker boy. He would have died in agonizing pain if not for our intervention."

"That same magic is what caused the curse in the first place," he reminded her.

Her face screwed up in irritation. "These powers are humanity's birthright. Human beings were always meant to wield magic. It's up to us on how we use it."

"There are always going to be bad actors," Mike said stepping forward. "Apsara is right. I feel much safer with this power in my hands over anyone else."

"Left unchecked, it's possible magic will spread to everyone else in the world," the professor said. "Are we willing to unleash that kind of chaos on the world? Don't we have a responsibility?"

John watched Apsara's face as she ran the scenarios in her head. Magic was dangerous—tonight had proven as much. But was it worth taking away a basic freedom that no one knew they had in the first place?

"I'm not just thinking of me," Apsara said, her voice lowering to a plea. "I'm thinking of the women who cower in their beds from men who would abuse them. I'm thinking of the innocent bystanders who could learn a simple shield spell to help save their lives someday. I'm thinking of the freedom this creates for everyone."

Apsara turned to John who felt increasingly certain she was right.

"I took an oath to 'first do no harm,'" Apsara was looking at him earnestly. "There is nothing I would hate more than to see this magic misused by someone. But I believe magic in the hands of everyone will level the playing field better than anything else in human history. God, the universe, evolution—whatever you want to believe is the source of these powers—we were *meant* to have them."

They were silent for a moment as they considered the precipice on which they stood. They were about to make a decision that would affect billions for the rest of human history.

Did they even have the right to make that decision?

"She's right," John said after a moment. "It's not up to us to take these powers away from everyone just because we have them now. If we did, we may as well anoint ourselves gods of this reality. And I don't think that's the point of these powers."

Professor McKaig frowned. "But think of the—"

He shook his head. "Professor, I can respect your objections, but the world has been in chaos before. It'll sort itself out again. It's not up to us to take away the free will and agency of billions of our fellow human beings. If magic was meant to be a part of humanity, then who are we to take it away from everyone?"

The professor shifted his attention to the rest of the group who all shared his opinion. He sighed, took out the amulet, and handed it to John. "Then one of you should carry this."

To John's surprise, the older man turned his back and walked toward the exit.

"Professor," he called out. "Don't you want to see how it all ends?"

The professor turned, a sad look in his eye. "My boy, I've already seen how it ends."

CHAPTER SIXTY-SIX

THE AGAMOTH HAD FULLY retreated into its larval state and was now no larger than a small dog. Still, Mike approached it cautiously. *The Omnichron* described the Agamoth's hibernation as a defensive measure meant to protect it from anything that would do it harm.

With the battle over, the stadium was filled with the cacophony of a dozen helicopters hovering above them, watching over the four exhausted wizards standing over the Triumvirate.

Mike glanced at Apsara, who was still hanging onto the amulet.

"We're sure about this, right?" John asked, looking at the rest of the group.

"One hundred percent," Apsara said.

"What do we do about them?" Mike asked, pointing to the Triumvirate. "If we're not wiping magic out of the world . . ."

"He's right," Ellie said. "We can't just let them continue casting spells. There's no telling what might happen if they get out again. And it's not like they're coming back to live with me."

Apsara raised an eyebrow at Ellie, who shrugged. "I have roommates."

John ran a hand through his hair, considering their options.

"We kill them now," Mike said abruptly. The group glanced over at him in shock. He shrugged. "We're all thinking it. I'm just the only one saying it out loud."

Mike knew he had spoken the truth when they all severed eye contact with him.

"First do no harm," Apsara said. "I swore an oath, and I don't plan on breaking it tonight."

"She's right," John said. He nodded to *The Omnichron*. "I asked the professor if there was a memory-wiping spell. What if we used something like that?"

Apsara raised an eyebrow. "I read about a potion that can wipe a person's memory. They would become blank slates, entirely new people, with new personalities that develop over time with no memory of what they've done here tonight."

"That sounds better than performing an execution to me," John said.

Apsara nodded. "Without the knowledge they gained from *The Omnichron*, they won't ever be able to cast spells again."

"Then we hand them over to the authorities," Ellie said.

Mike frowned. "I see one problem with that. We would have to go public. We will be known around the world for what we did here tonight."

"Buddy, I don't know if you noticed," John waved at the baseball stadium around them, "but we already went public a long time ago. I guarantee you the world already has an idea of what happened here tonight and who we are. This game was broadcast to the world. At some point, they'll know it was us. It's only a matter of time."

"Not necessarily," Mike said after a moment. "Who saw our faces while we were fighting? We could be another bunch of baseball fans who survived the chaos."

"Security cameras, cell phones, broadcast cameras," John ticked them off, one-by-one on his fingers. "The FBI will spend all the hours they need to figure out a timeline of events here tonight. Believe me, I've seen them on a case before. Someone somewhere will eventually produce photographic evidence of us casting magic spells. And if I know anything after being in the media for twenty years, it's that you only have one chance to control the story. At the beginning."

The rest of the group looked down at the ground, as if wondering what that meant for the rest of their lives.

Ellie was the first to speak up. "To hell with it. I've been in the public eye before. I'm game."

"I suppose if I'm going to take a stand about keeping magic in the world, I may as well make my fight public too," Apsara said.

"Mike?" John asked.

He didn't say anything for a moment. He did not relish the idea of giving up his anonymity.

"Mike?" Apsara asked, touching him on the arm.

"I heard you," he said. "I have the most to lose so I'm hoping you'll allow me a minute to think it through."

"There's nothing to think about," Apsara answered. "Think of your girl."

"I *am* thinking of her," he snapped back.

"No one's asking you to take a step you're not comfortable with," John said. "We just—"

"I know what's at stake," Mike said. His face softened. "You know, you all are the first real friends I've made since I got back. It might not mean a whole lot to you, but for me, I haven't had the opportunity to make too many connections over the years."

"We feel the same way," Apsara said, sounding as if she were trying to smooth over the hurt feelings.

"I have to respect what I'm about to do to my little girl in favor of what the world needs right now. It's not an easy decision and I don't take it lightly, but . . . yes." He nodded at John. "I'm with you all the way."

John sighed in relief, and they looked up at the helicopters still circling around them. He realized they were no longer alone in the stadium. He whispered the focus spell and looked up at the top of the stadium where a team of SWAT members was making their way through the stands toward the field level, weapons drawn as they assessed the situation.

"It looks like we're about out of time for debate anyway," he said, nodding to the bleacher seats. "It's probably a good idea if we ready our shield spells in case they plan on shooting first and asking questions later."

The group formed a semi-circle around the Agamoth's larva and the three captured members of the Triumvirate.

All they had left to do now was wait and see how the authorities would react to tonight's events.

CHAPTER SIXTY-SEVEN

JOHN WATCHED AS THE police threaded their way down the stairs and onto the field. Dozens of red dots from their guns illuminated their chests. He looked around at the rest of the group, happy to see them all standing confident as the officers approached, shouting orders.

But they all refused to move, and John felt a surge of pride in his team. They had come a long way.

"My name is John Jupiter," he shouted at the approaching officers. "We are here in peace and to help. I want to speak with the Special Agent in Charge."

The officers ignored his demands and continued shouting, demanding they get on the ground and surrender immediately. John sighed. This was not going to be easy.

"Shields?" Apsara asked.

"Shields," he agreed. He threw his hands to his sides and powered them up.

The officers stepped back in surprise as the blue-greenish glow slammed down around them, cutting them off from the group. One of the SWAT members fired their weapon, the bullet harmlessly ricocheting off.

John lifted an eyebrow at the point man, who was clad in black. "Like I said. I'd like to speak with the Special Agent in Charge."

The man stepped back, eyeing the shield, then spoke into his mic.

"Now what?" Ellie asked, while they watched the officers regroup around the shield.

"Now we negotiate," John said through gritted teeth. "Just keep that shield up until they're ready to be a bit more friendly."

"How long will that be?" Mike asked.

John looked at the slumbering Agamoth and the three prone members of the Triumvirate and sighed. "I don't know. But we stand firm. As long as it takes."

Fortunately, they didn't have to wait long. John watched the SWAT and other various police officers that now surrounded them on the field, as a tall, Hispanic woman wearing an FBI windbreaker and a badge on her hip stepped through the crowd and approached them.

"My name is Special Agent Maria Cortez," she said in a commanding voice. "You the ones making all the noise around here?"

John shrugged like *gee, I'm sorry* and shook his head. "Not us. You're looking for those three," he said, pointing to the Triumvirate members on the ground.

The woman glanced at the dark wizards and the mythical beast in the corner and sighed. She took off her glasses and rubbed her eyes.

"I saw it all with my own eyes," she said, lowering her glasses and looking at the larval Agamoth. "I guess I didn't really want to believe it until now."

She turned her gaze back to John and surveyed the rest of the group. "And you are?"

"We're the ones who stopped it all," Mike said.

"How?" Agent Cortez demanded.

"Magic," John said.

She examined his face and the rest of their group for a moment, then glanced back at the Agamoth and the Triumvirate on the ground.

"That's a new one," she said after a moment. "But you still haven't answered my first question."

"My name is John," he said. "I'm a reporter with KTLK News. I was covering the Knickerbocker murder when I stumbled on all this."

He pointed to the rest of the group, naming them for the special agent. "That's Ellie, she's our resident archer."

"Gold medal Olympian-level archer," Ellie said, a hint of pride in her voice.

"That's Dr. Apsara Choi. She's an attending physician at Hoover Medical and has been instrumental in keeping us alive."

Apsara nodded at Cortez who tilted her head in acknowledgement.

"Finally, that's Mike Madsen, our secret weapon," John finished.

Mike nodded. The FBI agent eyed him up and down and then turned her attention back to the rest of their group.

"Frankly, Agent Cortez," John said. "I know you aren't going to trust a word out of my mouth right now, but I need you and the rest of your people to understand, we are not the threat. We neutralized the threat for you and the rest of the world."

"Why would you do that?" she asked.

"Because I like living in a peaceful world," he said. "I don't mean to be glib, but the four of us are not interested in going to jail tonight."

He pointed to the three dark wizards tied up on the ground. "That trio there are the reason for all the chaos tonight. It was only through the skin of our teeth that we managed to stop them and that horror-show-inspired monster they summoned from another dimension."

Cortez glanced at the hibernating creature and shuddered. She turned back to the group.

"Using . . . magic?" Cortez asked, her left eyebrow arched.

"Exactly that," Apsara responded.

John watched as the Special Agent absorbed the scene and figured she was going through the same kind of shock they had all experienced after discovering that magic had returned.

He wasn't sure she trusted them yet, but he was beginning to feel optimistic that she no longer considered their group a threat.

She motioned to the officers behind her. They lowered their weapons.

"How do I know you weren't the ones who started it all?" Cortez asked.

"I know the FBI and your procedures," John said. "I know you're going to find every piece of available footage within one hundred miles of this location and go over it with a fine-tooth comb. I know you're going to build a timeline based on all the evidence you collect, and I know exactly what that timeline is going to show you. But you'll only know after you've spent hundreds of man hours on this case. Eventually, you'll have to admit we are telling the truth, and hell, we may even get an award for what we did here tonight. But for now, please trust that we're the good guys. We intend no harm to you or the rest of humanity."

She chewed on the bottom of her lip for a moment. Eventually, she spoke. "The public saw everything tonight. Most of the action was captured by news helicopters and TV stations that had a feed into the stadium. I already know you're the reason this whole thing is over. But until I can guarantee to my bosses that you all are safe to let loose, my hands are tied. You're all under arrest."

John's face fell. They'd failed.

Apsara stepped forward, touching John on the shoulder. "They don't know us yet." She turned to the FBI agent. "You can take us into custody. I swear none of us will resist in any way or use any magic to deter you."

Agent Cortez's eyebrows rose in surprise.

Apsara held up a hand. "In return for giving ourselves up, I have three conditions."

"All right," Cortez looked at her, suspicious. "What are they?"

"One, the Agamoth is in a larval state. It will remain like this until it manages to collect enough negative energy that it can move again."

"What do you want me to do about it?" Cortez asked.

"Put it somewhere safe, where no one can reach it," Apsara said. "Find a spot far away from any human civilization. Do you know Point Nemo? Put it there. Or the Mariana Trench."

Cortez grunted. "Point Nemo?"

"It's a place on Earth located in the ocean farthest away from any land," Mike spoke up. "It won't find much negative energy there."

"He's right. It doesn't matter where that thing is so long as it's far, far away from people," John said. "We need to starve it until we can figure out what to do with it."

"Treat that thing like nuclear waste," Ellie added. "Except a lot more dangerous."

Cortez regarded them for a moment and then nodded. "We might be able to arrange something like that. What's your second demand?"

Apsara nodded to the Triumvirate. "Those three dark wizards can never be allowed to cast any spells or access any magic ever again."

"And what can I do about that?" Cortez asked. "Treat them like nuclear waste too?"

Apsara shook her head. "Nothing so dramatic. But I will need to create a potion that will wipe their memories. They'll have no knowledge of magic or the spells they were once able to cast."

Cortez raised an eyebrow at Apsara and then glanced over at John who refused to say anything. He had failed with his attempt at negotiations. As far as he was concerned, this was Apsara's show now.

"Agent?" Apsara asked. "Are we agreed on my second demand?"

Cortez turned her head back to her and angled her head.

"It's possible, but you'll have to be strictly supervised," Cortez said.

Apsara shook her head. "I can't risk the recipe getting out or being leaked by one of your people."

Cortez sighed. "You're not making this easy you know."

"What if you cleared out a room with no cameras, microphones, or anything else?" Ellie asked after a moment of awkward silence. "You all can even station a bunch of guards outside to make sure nothing bad happens."

Cortez glanced over at the college student and looked mollified. "I might be able to agree to something like that. So long as you can trust we won't have any hidden cameras in there."

"Believe me," Apsara said, chuckling. "If you attempt to hide a camera, I'll find it."

Cortez huffed and shifted her weight. "And your third demand?"

Apsara glanced around at the rest of the group. "It's more of a request, I suppose. I request that once you gather all your evidence and our statements you allow us all to go home and live our lives."

Cortez looked uncomfortable. "That I can't guarantee. For all I know, you committed various felonies while using your magic. I'm betting the ATF would be extremely interested in people who can shoot fireballs out of their fists."

"In defense of the free world," Mike snapped at the FBI agent.

"How many people out of the fifty-five thousand here tonight do you see left?" Cortez asked, shooting him a look.

"We did what we could," John said.

"Which may not be enough for the general public," Cortez said. She sighed and then rubbed the grass in center field with her toe. "It doesn't matter what the government does or doesn't do to you. You'll never live a normal life again, but you knew that already, didn't you?"

"That's why we came to you face-to-face instead of slinking off into the night," John said. "We're good people. We're only asking for a chance to prove that."

Cortez watched them for a moment, then nodded. "Lower the barrier."

Apsara shot a look at John who nodded. The team concentrated for a moment, breaking the energy barrier that surrounded them. SWAT members moved forward in a rush to take them into custody. They offered no resistance.

John felt the cuffs clamp around his wrists and wondered what his boss would think after seeing him on the front page of the news instead of reporting it.

CHAPTER SIXTY-EIGHT

As John predicted, the FBI's investigation process was slow. It took their agents the better part of a month to piece together the timeline of what happened that night at Stanhope Stadium and in the days before. Through it all, the media was buzzing about the reports of magic seen at the park and the incredible death toll.

For her part, Apsara remained quarantined away from her friends. Her days in prison had become routine over the last week where they had isolated from society. She'd used the focus spell to listen to one of the guard's radios one cellblock over to get updates on the news and what the world was saying about them that night. If there was one thing she was thankful for, it was the fact that AM radio never died.

Breakfast came to her through a slot in the door. She approached the tray, looking down at it with disinterest. The food here hadn't been terrible, just the blandest, cheapest stuff a government contract could buy.

Leaving the stadium in handcuffs meant they were all processed like common criminals. Despite Agent Cortez's promises, agents had stripped, searched, and fingerprinted her. Through it all, she did her best to keep her dignity, knowing that at any moment she could escape custody using any number of spells.

But she'd made a promise to Cortez and subjugated herself to the process entirely, offering no resistance. She had no intention of letting them think she might turn on them like the Triumvirate.

Apsara wondered how the other members of the team were holding up. John was probably fine. His background as a reporter meant he had been through riots, war, and all the other vulgarities offered by the world. Ellie might be going stir-crazy, but the young woman had so far proven to be just as resolved and impressive as she looked.

She was far more concerned about Mike—Mike had to be going crazy over not seeing his daughter.

As for herself? Apsara thought she was holding up better than she believed she would. They were high-value prisoners, so they didn't have to go through the same grungy conditions most inmates experienced. In fact, due to the condition of the room she was in, she wondered if the FBI had stashed them all in a hotel or safehouse. She never saw anyone other than her guards—something she believed they did on purpose.

They had interrogated her several times, and her story had remained the same through each one. They'd tried to shake her, make her say things that would make her go back on her story or reveal something she might not have otherwise. But because she was telling the truth, it was easy for her to keep up.

She had decided that if things got terribly bad, she would use her magic to escape. Of course, that would mean a total disconnect from her previous life, but she had no intention of dying inside a brightly lit, fifteen by fifteen cell.

A knock at the door alerted her to visitors. Two guards stood outside, looking ready for anything when they stepped aside, allowing Agent Cortez to step inside.

"Agent," Apsara said cordially. She'd met with Cortez twice since the night in the ballpark—both times in an interrogation room.

"Dr. Choi, how are we feeling this morning?" Agent Cortez greeted her. Apsara realized this was the first time Cortez had used her title when addressing her.

"Optimistic," she was pleasantly surprised at their interaction. "You seem happy."

"You should be too," Cortez replied. "I'm here to let you know my bosses have given me permission to grant all three of your requests. You're going home."

Apsara closed her eyes, feeling a rush of excitement flow through her until she realized she had inadvertently summoned some mana, which surrounded her body, causing it to glow.

She opened her eyes to see the guards watching her, alarmed.

"Sorry. That happens sometimes when I'm excited." She turned to the agent, who was smiling at the show Apsara had just put on for them. "What about the rest of the team?"

"Your story checked out," Cortez said. "John was right. There will be a battle over which politician gets to meet you and shake your hand first. Everyone wants to give you the key to the city, the state, hell, even the nation it sounds like with the way they're talking about you on TV."

"That so?" Apsara felt amused by her sudden fame. "That's encouraging."

"It's a new age of magic," Cortez said. "I think you'll find the world a hugely different place once we get you out of here. You're a popular woman from the looks of the tabloid magazines."

"Popularity ain't what it's cracked up to be," Apsara replied after a moment. She looked over at the FBI agent and smiled. "Thank you, Agent Cortez."

"No, thank you," Cortez replied, looking at her gratefully. "Humanity dodged a major bullet last week because of you all, and the world knows it now. Let's get you out of here, yeah?"

They handed Apsara a fresh pair of jeans and a white T-shirt that fit snugly around her torso. It wasn't much, but at least it wasn't the faded scrubs she'd had to wear over the last few days. If there was anything left of her closet by the time she got home, she figured this outfit would become one of her favorites.

A person never appreciates their freedom until they lose it, she thought.

The guards escorted her through the prison where she spotted John, Mike, and Ellie all milling around in the lobby waiting for her. She rushed to them, and they grabbed each other in a group hug, crying, laughing, and celebrating the fact they were still alive and free.

And in that moment, Apsara knew what true magic felt like.

CHAPTER SIXTY-NINE

THE NEXT FEW DAYS were a blitz of media appearances, calls, interviews, and meetings with various politicians and their underlings. Everyone wanted to know about that night at the stadium and the type of magical threats countries around the world might expect in the next few years.

After the FBI released John from jail, all he wanted to do was take a nap that lasted for six months, but because he was the one with the most media experience under his belt, the group had elected him to be their spokesperson.

Still, it wasn't all bad. Fan mail poured in for all of them, thanking them for saving the world or begging them for help. More than a few included marriage proposals from both sexes. At one point, the messages and mail became so overwhelming, they hired a public relations firm to manage the avalanche of well-wishers and hate mail alike.

The group had split up for now and had all returned to their lives as best they could.

Mike disappeared back into his family life. He had asked for privacy, and John respected his request. He knew that if the time ever came when they needed his help, they could count on him. Until then, Mike deserved to live the life he wanted and watch his daughter grow up.

Ellie tried to return to her studies, but her newfound celebrity made it all but impossible for her to attend class. She finished the remainder of her semester online and stayed on track to graduate. She and John texted multiple times a week to talk about life and anything else that came up. He made sure that she knew she could come to him if she ever needed anything.

He and Apsara spoke on the phone at least once a week. She too had found the celebrity life overwhelming and had resigned from the hospital. She had opened a private practice in Taos, New Mexico, where she was helping patients who came to her with impossible cases. She went by word of mouth and only saw those who truly needed her services. She was happy, and John didn't want to intrude on that any more than he already did.

Besides, he had his own career to deal with. Thanks to his experience in the media, he had become the official spokesperson for their group and the go-to expert on magic. He often made nightly appearances on the cable news shows and earned a decent living to go along with it. The networks wanted him to explain how magic worked, but he never told his secrets.

It's not like he could explain much anyway.

John spent the rest of his free time searching for the professor. Their friend had disappeared after the incident at the stadium. The man's office was empty, with little trace he had even been there. His house stood empty with a 'For Sale' sign hanging outside.

Wherever the professor had gone, it had become clear it would be difficult to find him. John had called in a few favors to some well-placed friends to assist with his search, but so far, his sources had come up empty.

His phone beeped, reminding him that he had an appearance scheduled for CNN in ten minutes. He reached back for his jacket and put it on. He stood and went over to the home studio he had set up in his apartment (complete with a green screen) and turned on the TV lights.

The phone chirped again indicated that the network had connected to his receiver and was ready to begin taking his transmission. He fum

bled for the earpiece and heard the producer on the other line talking to him through the IFB.

"Hey, John! Good to have you on again," the producer's voice sounded tinny through the connection. "Just a quick one tonight debating the merits of the legislation on magic."

"You got it," he answered.

Congress had introduced new legislation to attempt to regulate magic, but he didn't believe it would get far, something he intended to tell the millions of Americans watching tonight.

"Great, seven minutes to air," the producer said over the line.

John began mentally preparing himself for the appearance going over his notes. "Showtime," he said quietly to himself.

There was a knock at the door, and he checked his watch. He had no idea who that was. He had moved to a high-security building after his fame exploded, so no one was even supposed to know he lived here.

Still, he thought it might be a neighbor popping by to introduce themselves. Scuttlebutt about him and his heroics at Stanhope stadium had spread through the building and it felt like everyone in the neighborhood wanted to say hello.

He took out the earpiece and removed the microphone from his lapel and walked to the door. Before opening it, he put on his best smile, lest he make the person on the other side nervous.

When he checked the peephole, there was no one there. Confused, he opened the door and stepped into the hallway, looking for whoever had ding-dong ditched his apartment.

Seeing no one, he turned to go back into the apartment when he noticed a large black envelope taped to the doorway.

Re-entering the apartment, he scanned the envelope using the focus spell to see if it held anything that might hurt him. Finding nothing out of the ordinary, he returned to the kitchen, where he used a knife to open the envelope.

He removed the letter inside and was surprised to see it was from the professor.

John,

I know you've been searching for me over the last few weeks, but I can assure you, you're wasting your time. You'll never find me until I want to be.

I understand the group's decision. I've often thought about the moment I walked away and why I believe we're making a mistake allowing magic to remain on this world.

I'm an old man, John. You're no spring chicken either, but by the time you get to be my age, you get to see patterns in how humans treat one another. Our species has accomplished a great deal of technological progress since our ancestors banished magic all those years ago, but I don't believe humanity has evolved much socially—or at least, not as much as we need to be to manage this level of power.

The next few years are going to be filled with pain and trauma. I've seen it all. I don't want you all to think I blame you for what happens next. That's just people being people. Like the fable of the scorpion and the frog, people just can't help themselves.

I do know it's on you—it's on all of us—to prevent another disaster like what happened at Stanhope Stadium where we can, when we can.

You chose to wear this mantle, and I feel like it's my duty to tell you it's not always going to be about your appearances on cable news shows. As a White Wizard, you are bound to protect humanity from the worst of themselves, both from this dimension and outside it.

I think you're up to the challenge. But I still don't think it was a wise idea.

If you ever truly need me, I will be there.

Professor Desmond McKaig.

John gazed at the note in his hand, which was shaking. He'd believed himself ready to face anything the world threw at him, but so far, it had only been softball interviews. The professor was right.

He picked up the IFB and clicked.

"Hey, anyone there?"

"Yeah?" the producer sounded distracted.

"Something's come up," John said, still eyeing the letter in his hand. "I'll have to cancel my appearance tonight."

He could hear the producer's frustrated groan and muffled curses on the other side of the line, hanging up the phone.

He looked down at the letter in his hand and made his decision.

It was time to show the world exactly what he could do.

Afterword

Thank you so much for reading! Look for more adventures with our magical friends coming soon! In the meantime, check out some of my other novels, including my Jim Meade, Martian P.I. series that I'm incredibly proud of. If you enjoyed the book, please take a moment to go to Amazon or Goodreads and leave a review! Independent authors like myself live and die by the number of four- and five-star reviews we get, so every little bit helps!!

You can also sign up for my newsletter at www.rickerthewriter.com (and get a free book!) to find out when I'm releasing more adventures with the crew.

Keep making magic,

RJ Johnson

May 17th, 2022

About the Author

RJ Johnson is an award winning author living in Los Angeles, California. He was inspired to become an author after his second grade teacher bound together a short story he had written for class into a small book. His passion for writing ignited, Johnson spent the next twenty years learning everything he could about writing while pursuing a career in broadcast radio.

His greatest hope is to write something worth reading. The results of his efforts so far, are available anywhere books are sold.

Follow RJ Johnson on Facebook, Instagram, and Twitter: @rickerthewriter

ALSO BY

The Jim Meade: Martian P.I. Series

Change in Management

Rosetta

A Wilderness of Mirrors

The Dreamslinger Series

Dreamslinger: Book One